APR 12

P9-CFE-720

His eyes darkened as he stared at her . . .

She didn't look away, even though her heart pounded in her ears.

He lifted a hand, then stopped with his fingers a mere inch from her cheek. "You have no idea what I want."

The intensity of his gaze made her arms pebble with gooseflesh.

He stepped back, lowering his hand. "I'll return for you in thirty minutes." His form wavered, then vanished.

She dragged in a deep breath to calm her racing heart, then reached up to press her fingertips against the cheek he'd come so close to touching.

Oh God, what had she gotten herself into? She'd let her emotions dictate her actions. Always a dumb thing to do. Now she would be going back to Wyoming.

By Kerrelyn Sparks

KERRELYN
SPARKS

WANTED:
UNDEAD or ALIVE

AVON

An Imprint of HarperCollinsPublishers

AVON BOOKS
An Imprint of HarperCollins*Publishers*
10 East 53rd Street
New York, New York 10022-5299

Copyright © 2012 by Kerrelyn Sparks
ISBN 978-0-06-195806-9
www.avonromance.com

First Avon Books mass market printing: April 2012

Printed in the U.S.A.

10 9 8 7 6 5 4 3 2 1

For my father, Les.
You are greatly loved
in this world and the next.
Stay strong.

Acknowledgments

$\mathcal{D}$oesn't this book have a beautiful cover? If you agree, you can join me in thanking Tom Egner and the art department at Avon Books/HarperCollins. I also want to thank Erika Tsang and Amanda Bergeron and the editorial department; Pam and Jessie and the publicity department; and all the others at HarperCollins who work tirelessly to make each book a success. My thanks also to my agent, Michelle Grajkowski.

Here on the home front, I have another support team I wish to thank: my critique group/best friends, MJ, Sandy, and Vicky, who miraculously never get tired of patting me on the back or kicking me in the rear; my children, who miraculously think I'm cool; and my husband, who miraculously believed in me from the beginning.

And then there are you, all of you readers who have embraced the Love at Stake series and kept it going for twelve books now. I thank you for keeping me happily employed. My characters thank you for keeping them alive. May they continue to bring you hope and joy.

Chapter One

*G*et real, Phineas! You can't expect me to believe this crap!"

Phineas McKinney frowned at his younger brother, who was clutching the steering wheel with white-knuckled desperation. Obviously, last night's confession had not gone as well as he had thought. "Freemont, you gotta know I would never lie to you—"

"I know that!" Freemont shot him a frantic look, then turned the windshield wipers up to a higher speed to combat the rain that pelted his thirteen-year-old, dented Chevy Impala. "But that doesn't leave me with a lot of options, you know? First I thought you'd gone crazy. Then I thought you must be doing drugs. Then when I tried to talk to you this afternoon, I thought you were dead! I mean, seriously, start-the-damned-funeral *dead*!"

"I'm not crazy," Phineas muttered. "And I don't do drugs."

The atmosphere in the car sizzled with tension, interrupted only by the noise of the wipers swishing back and forth. A wet, slushy sound, followed by a high-pitched, prolonged screech reminiscent of fingernails on a blackboard.

Phineas winced. There were times when having supersensitive hearing was not an advantage.

Freemont gave him a wary look. "What—what about that last part? The . . . dead part?"

Slush-screech. Slush-screech.

Freemont gulped audibly. "You weren't really *dead*, were you?"

Slush-screech. Slush-screech.

"I'm alive now," Phineas said quietly, then gave his brother a reassuring smile. "Don't I look alive to you?"

Freemont didn't look reassured. His eyes had grown so wide, the whites gleamed as his gaze darted back and forth from his brother to the busy street in the Bronx. "You're alive *now*? What the hell does that mean?"

"It means my heart is beating. I'm breathing—"

"You weren't breathing this afternoon! You scared the shit out of me! I almost called Aunt Ruth—"

"I told you not to." Phineas didn't want his aunt and sister to know the truth. Aunt Ruth would probably drag him into church and insist the Reverend Washington perform an exorcism on him. Luckily, the female members of his family were out of town this weekend, singing with the choir at some event in Buffalo.

"I didn't know what to do! I thought about calling an ambulance, but—" Freemont stomped on the brakes, tires spinning on the wet cement before the Impala halted with a lurch. He slammed a fist on the horn, and the blaring noise made Phineas grit his teeth.

"What the hell are you stopping for, asshole?" Freemont hollered at the car in front of them.

"People usually stop for red lights. You should try it sometime." Phineas's attempt at a joke fell flat. His brother was still looking at him like he'd grown a second head. "I have excellent night vision, you know. You want me to drive?"

"*No!*" Freemont leaned forward, a possessive glint in his eyes as he squeezed the steering wheel with fisted hands. "I need to drive. It keeps me calm."

This was calm? Phineas hadn't expected a full-fledged panic attack this evening. Last night his brother had remained quiet during the confession, just nodding his head as if he accepted it all. But Phineas had to admit now that it was highly unusual for his brother to remain quiet for more than sixty seconds. Freemont had been stunned speechless.

"I did warn you," Phineas reminded his brother. "I told you not to go down into the basement."

"I thought you were quoting a line from a bad movie."

"Why would I do that?"

"How the hell would I know?" Freemont yelled. "I told you, I thought you'd gone crazy!"

"I explained it all last night, how I ended up a vampire, and how I needed to do my death-sleep all day in the basement with the window boarded up."

"Yeah, well, I didn't really catch that last part, you

know what I'm saying? The minute you said 'vampire,' I thought you'd gone bat-shit on me. I didn't hear nothin' after that. I was too busy trying to figure out how we could afford to send you to a nut hut so you could get your head screwed back on."

"I'm perfectly fine, Freemont. I was just . . . dead for a few hours."

"That's not normal, bro!"

"It is for a vampire."

Freemont flinched, then turned to glare at the stoplight.

Slush-screech. Slush-screech.

The light turned green, and Freemont accelerated slowly. "You really believe this stuff, don't you?"

"I'm not shittin' you, Freemont. Didn't you see me drink a bottle of blood?"

"You said it was blood, but what the hell, you could have had a V8. If you were really a vampire, wouldn't you be chomping down on people's necks? Not that I'm offering mine, you understand—"

"I hang with the good Vamps. We don't bite people." Phineas sighed. He'd explained all this last night, how some bad vampires had transformed him and held him prisoner until he'd been able to join the good Vamps and help them fight the bad vampires they called Malcontents. He'd even shown Freemont his fangs, although he hadn't extended them. He'd tried his best not to freak his brother out. "You saw my fangs, remember?"

Freemont waved a hand in dismissal. "You could have had them filed into points. It's totally wack, but there are crazy people who do weird shit to themselves. Hell, I saw a guy on TV who had his tongue split so he'd look like a snake."

"I'm not crazy."

"You think you're a vampire. If that's not seriously crazy, I don't know what is." Freemont took a deep breath. "We'll get you better, Phin. I'll get a full-time job, drop out of school—"

"No! You just finished your freshman year, and you're doing great. I'm not letting you drop out."

Freemont stiffened with an indignant look. "You can't tell me what to do. You've been taking care of us, paying all the bills, for eight years. It's my turn now. I can do this."

"You're finishing college," Phineas said sharply, then noticed the stubborn clench of Freemont's jaw. Sheesh. His little brother was becoming a man.

Five years ago, when Phineas had been transformed at the age of twenty-three, his brother had been a skinny fourteen-year-old, all bony elbows and knobby knees. The aging process had screeched to a halt for Phineas, so he tended to forget that his younger brother and sister kept growing. He and Freemont looked close to the same age now.

Phineas softened his voice. "I need your help, bro."

"Anything, man. Whatever medical attention you need. I'll get it for you. You can count on me."

Phineas's chest expanded with warmth. His brother had grown into a good man. Now if he could just convince him of the truth. "Turn right at this next street."

"Why? I thought you wanted to go to Brooklyn."

"I do, but we need to make a stop first."

"Okay." Freemont turned onto a street lined with narrow wooden-framed houses with sagging front porches.

"Pull in there." Phineas pointed at an empty space between two parked cars.

"I'll be blocking a driveway."

"We won't be here long." While his brother stopped and shifted into park, Phineas surveyed the neighborhood. Because of the rain, the sidewalks were empty. The house was dark, no lights glowing in the windows.

Slush-screech. Slush-screech.

"I don't think anyone's home," Freemont said.

"That's for the best."

"Huh? Then why are we here?"

"A demonstration." Phineas unlatched his seat belt. "Don't go anywhere. Keep your eyes on the porch."

"There's nothin' on the porch."

"There will be."

"What are you—" Freemont's words cut off when Phineas teleported to the dark porch. He waved at the car, then teleported back to the front seat.

Freemont was a few shades paler, and his mouth was hanging open.

Slush-screech. Slush-screech.

Phineas couldn't help but smirk. "Now do you believe me?"

Freemont gulped, then his jaw dropped open again.

Slush-screech. Slush-screech.

Phineas snapped his seat belt on. "Told you I wasn't crazy."

"Then *I* must be crazy," Freemont whispered. "I'm trippin'."

"You're not crazy."

Freemont shook himself. "I didn't see you get out of the car. You're not even wet, bro. How did you get to the porch?"

"Teleportation."

"Tele-what? Isn't that some sort of spaceman shit?" Freemont stiffened. "Were you abducted by aliens? Did they stick a probe up your ass?"

"No! Freemont, I'm a vampire!" Phineas grabbed the rearview mirror and twisted it toward himself. "Can you see me?"

Freemont leaned over to peer into the mirror. He gasped, looked at Phineas, then back at the mirror. "What the hell?"

Phineas shoved the mirror back in place. "Do you believe me now?"

"You—you're really a *vampire*?" Freemont whispered.

"Yes."

"Damn, Phineas." Freemont sat back with a horrified look. "Are you sure? I mean, this is some weird-assed, spooky shit."

"I know, but it's true, bro. I'm a vampire."

"That sucks!"

"I don't suck. I drink from bottles." Phineas motioned toward the gearshift. "Let's get going."

Freemont continued to stare at him. "How did it happen?"

Phineas waved a dismissive hand. "I was attacked by some bad vampires. Can we go now?"

"Attacked?" Freemont grimaced. "What did they do to you, man?"

"I don't want to talk about it. It was scary as hell and really nasty."

Freemont's eyes widened. "They stuck a probe up your ass?"

"No! They ripped my fuckin' throat out, okay? So now that you know how grisly it was, will you shut up and take me to Brooklyn?"

"Okay, okay." Freemont shifted into drive and pulled out into the street. "Sheesh. You act like you got a bug up your—"

"Don't say it!"

While Freemont drove, he shook his head and muttered to himself, "A vampire? *Damn.* I thought he was a security guard for some old white dude."

"The old white dude is a five-hundred-year-old vampire named Angus MacKay. He and his wife, Emma, run MacKay Security and Investigation."

"Five hundred years old? Sheesh! Can he still get it up?"

"I would assume so, since they seem happily married, but I've never asked." Phineas looked out the window at the rain pouring in sheets off storefront awnings and splattering on broken sidewalks. It was thanks to Angus and Emma that he'd discovered the good Vamps. He'd found more than employment with them. He'd found a new extended family, mostly guys. He'd laughed with them, fought with them, mourned with them. The guys had become his brothers.

It had started off like one big bachelor party, but in the last few years, the men had fallen like flies. Even Gregori, the famous playboy of the vampire world. He'd hooked up with the president's daughter.

Phineas enjoyed teasing them that all their new-found marital bliss was due to his expertise as the Love Doctor, but the joke was on him. He was like the painter who owned the only house in the neighborhood that needed painting. Everybody could find love but the Love Doctor.

And it wasn't for lack of trying. He'd dated some Vamp women he'd met at the vampire clubs. He'd thoroughly enjoyed playing the role of a popular ladies' man until he realized they saw him as nothing more than a novelty act, something to try out of curiosity before they flitted away to the next distraction.

He wanted to be more than that. He wanted someone who would look past his outward appearance to connect with his soul. Someone who would see him as special. Worthy of a lifetime, not a single night.

He'd tried over and over with the mortal LaToya, believing his perseverance would eventually pay off. It never did. She'd taunted him that the Love Doctor didn't know what love was.

Bullshit.

Meanwhile, the other guys were all snagging some

luscious babes. Shoot, Connor had even scored a real live angel. Carlos had found a girl willing to risk death in order to become a were-panther like him. The ladies who'd married Vamps were all willing to give up mortality to stay with their husbands. Angus's wife, Emma, was a Vamp, and just recently, Roman's wife, Shanna, had changed over. And they all did it for love.

Where was the love for the Love Doctor? Who would ever see him as worthy? Certainly not *her* . . .

"You look bummed out," Freemont said, dragging Phineas away from his depressing thoughts. "Is it hard being a . . . you know . . ."

"Vampire?" Phineas gave him a wry look. "You can say the word without getting bitten. And yeah, sometimes it's kinda hard." He'd gained a life that could last for centuries, but it could only happen in darkness.

Freemont grimaced. "If I was a vampire, I'd miss fried chicken. And waffles."

"I miss . . . blue. I can never see a blue sky again." His brain was instantly flooded with a memory of her pretty blue eyes. *Her* again. He quickly shoved her from his mind.

Brynley Jones was beautiful, brave, and clever—the perfect female human, except for one problem. She wasn't always human. And her hatred of vampires was as big as the snout on her face when she shifted. She was the worst possible woman to obsess over. But that didn't stop him.

His brother took a deep breath. "Okay. I'm with you, bro. What kind of help do you need?"

"You're already doing it. I needed a place to stay. Some wheels. I quit my job last night."

Freemont's eyes widened. "What happened? Did you get pissed off with the old dude?"

Phineas shrugged. "It doesn't matter. I already have another career lined up. We're going to the Digital Vampire Network in Brooklyn. It's a TV network just for Vamps."

"You're shittin' me."

"No. I made a commercial there about two weeks ago for a drink called Blardonnay—half synthetic blood, half Chardonnay."

"I'm being punked, right?"

"No, it's true." First Phineas had made a commercial with the president's daughter just as a joke, but he'd performed so well, the director had asked him to do it for real with a vampire costar named Tiffany. The commercial had enjoyed an instant success, making Phineas McKinney an overnight sensation in the vampire world. "They call me the Blardonnay Guy now. I'm really popular."

"From a commercial?" Freemont pulled to a stop at another red light. "How come I haven't seen it?"

"It's a DVN commercial. Only Vamps see it. And now they want me to star in one of their TV shows."

Freemont blinked. "Hot damn, Phineas! Are you famous?"

"I . . . guess. But only around other vampires."

"That's awesome, man." Freemont's eyes gleamed with pride. "I always knew you'd be famous someday, although I thought it would be with boxing. Never could figure out what happened with that."

Phineas quickly changed the subject. "We're going to DVN, 'cause I'm doing a special interview at the end of the *Nightly News*."

"You're going on television tonight?" When Phineas nodded, Freemont looked him over, frowning. "Oh no. Hell no. Not like that."

Phineas looked down at his jeans and bright orange, number seven Knicks T-shirt. "What's wrong with—" He stopped when his brother stomped on the gas, swinging the car into a U-turn. "Where are you going?"

"It's simple, dude. If you want to be a celebrity, you gotta look like one. Right now, you look like a giant Cheez-It. You just leave it to me. I know what to do."

Phineas smiled. "What are you, my agent?"

"Can I be?" Freemont's eyes lit up. "I'll take care of everything, bro. You can count on me."

Ten minutes later, Phineas was slipping on a black tuxedo jacket in a dressing room at Leroy's House of Class.

"I don't know about this." The white shirt had ruffles on the cuffs. He'd look like a gigolo, or a Scotsman, he thought with a snort. He'd seen Angus and some of the other guys wear frilly shirts like this with their fancy kilts. "You don't think this is overdoing it?"

"You're looking fine, bro." Freemont clenched a fist. "Solid. Like James Bond, going to a casino. You want to take a look in the mirror?"

Phineas gave him a wry look.

Freemont grimaced. "Sorry, I forgot. Sheesh. How do you shave in the morning?"

"Once the sun comes up, I don't do anything."

"Damn." Freemont handed him a black silk tie. "You gonna be able to put this on?"

"I think so."

"You want some new shoes?"

"No, the boots need to stay." Phineas knotted the tie around his neck. "How much is this gonna set me back?"

"It's free, bro. Leroy is Lamont's dad. You know, Lamont?"

With a smile, Phineas nodded. Lamont was Freemont's best friend from high school. When the two were together, the other kids called them the Full Monty. "I didn't know his dad ran a tuxedo rental place."

"Oh, this is a lot more than tuxedos. Leroy's House of Class has everything! Wedding dresses and fancy gowns. Costumes for everything from Renaissance fairs to pimp-and-ho parties. He's even got hula skirts and tiki torches if you want to do a luau. He's got canopies and tables and chairs and fancy tablecloths." Freemont yanked his T-shirt over his head, then put on a gold silk shirt. "Lamont works here full-time, but they let me work part-time as much as I can."

"What do you do?"

Freemont shucked his jeans and pulled on some black leather pants. "I do deliveries, help set up tables and chairs. I usually drive one of their limos on Saturday night, but there's nothing happening tonight, so they didn't need me. Which is good news, 'cause Leroy is letting us borrow a limo."

"That's great. Thanks." Phineas paused a moment while his brother put on some shiny black dress shoes. "I appreciate you working to help pay your tuition, but don't overdo it. You need to keep your grades up."

Freemont rolled his eyes like he usually did when Phineas acted more like a father than a brother. But with nine years' difference in their ages, it was something Phineas had trouble avoiding. He was the one who had run off their father, so he felt responsible for his younger siblings.

Freemont shrugged on a purple velvet jacket trimmed with faux leopard fur, then plopped a leopard-skin fedora on his head. "Now I'll look like your agent."

Phineas winced. "You look like a pimp."

"Pimp? Agent? What's the difference?" Freemont flipped up his collar. "Show me the money!"

"Freemont—"

"I know what I'm doing, bro." He grabbed a wooden walking stick with a gold knob on the end and twirled it through his fingers. "Should I ask Leroy to loan us a few party girls for the evening? You'll look more like a celebrity with some pretty ladies on your arm."

"Party girls?" Phineas frowned, wondering if Leroy had a little business going on the side.

"It's legit, man. Sometimes people want a few pretty girls to tend bar and wait tables at their parties. The girls are under strict orders not to fraternize. Believe me, I've tried."

Phineas snorted. "Don't worry about women. There'll be plenty at DVN, hoping to get on TV. And my costar will be there. Tiffany."

"What does she look like?"

"Blond and booty-licious."

"Hot damn!" Freemont gave him a knuckle pound. "You da man!" He led Phineas down a hall toward the back door of Leroy's establishment. "As your new agent, I'm gonna need a name that's tight. You need one, too, bro."

"I'm Dr. Phang in the vampire world. Also known as the Love Doctor."

Freemont's eyes narrowed as he nodded. "That's buck. I bet you get laid all the time."

Phineas winced inwardly. The silly names had worked well enough for one-night stands, but eventually, he'd grown tired of feeling like a joke that was funny only one time.

Freemont grabbed a set of keys off a peg by the back door. "Will you introduce me to the Tiffany babe?"

"Yes, but remember she's a Vamp. She might see you as a snack more than a stud."

Freemont gulped and eased a finger around the collar of his gold silk shirt. "You've got a weird life, bro."

"Don't worry. I won't let anyone hurt you." Phineas patted him on the back. "And I appreciate your help." Thanks to his brother, he now looked a lot more convincing in his new role as a television star.

Freemont opened the back door and strode into the parking lot. "So if you're Dr. Phang . . ."

Phineas followed him, grateful that the rain had finally stopped. He stepped around puddles to keep his boots as dry as possible.

Freemont halted with a jerk. "I know! I'll be Da Freeze. Kinda like Freemont, but better. Da Freeze, the Ice Man. What do you think?"

Phineas bit his lip to keep from grinning. His brother reminded him of himself five years ago. "It's . . . cool."

"It's more than cool, man. I'm an icy cold blast of refreshment!" Freemont opened the door to a purple limousine. "Only the best for my famous brother."

"What a bunch of hot babes," Freemont whispered as they entered the lobby of the Digital Vampire Network. "Are you sure they're all . . . ?"

"Yes, they are," Phineas whispered back. "And they all have super hearing, so be careful what you say."

Freemont nodded, his wide-eyed gaze darting around the crowded lobby. "Your life is seriously weird."

"You ain't seen nothin' yet," Phineas muttered, then headed toward the reception desk.

"Oh my God, it's the Blardonnay Guy!" a pretty brunette squealed.

More gasps and squeals emanated from the scantily clad young ladies who frequented the lobby every night, hoping to be discovered. They rushed toward Phineas, all talking at once.

"I just love your commercial!"

"You're even more handsome than Denzel!"

"Can I have an autograph please?"

Phineas held up his hands to ward off the full-court press, but before he could say anything, Freemont blocked the girls with his walking stick.

"Ladies!" He flashed a wide grin. "We appreciate your enthusiasm, but Dr. Phang has to do an interview right now. If you can wait till he's finished, he might be able to spare you a few minutes."

"We'll be here!" A blonde held up a Blardonnay bottle. "Will you sign my bottle, Dr. Phang?"

A brunette in a cheerleader costume winked at Phineas. "I want you to sign my thigh."

"I'll let you sign my breast!" Another posed, show-ing off her most talented assets, barely contained in a tight spandex halter.

"That's all good." Freemont used his walking stick to herd them back. "But I will need to thoroughly inspect all writing surfaces before I can allow my client to sign. Security protocol, you understand."

Phineas snorted as he approached the receptionist's desk. "Hey, what's up? It's Susie, right?"

She blushed, almost as red as the dyed streaks in her black hair. "You remembered. I just love your commer-cial, Dr. Phang."

"I'm his agent." Freemont slid his pinched thumb and forefinger along the brim of his fedora. "You can call me Da Freeze."

"Nice to meet you. For security reasons, we ask all our visitors to wear name tags." Susie smiled shyly at Phineas. "Of course, you don't need a name tag, Dr. Phang. Everyone knows who you are." She wrote Freemont's new name on a name tag. "Here you go, Mr. DeVries."

"No, Da Freeze. The Ice Man."

"Oh." A confused look flitted over Susie's face, then she scribbled another name. "Mr. Theismann." She passed him the name tag, then scurried toward the double doors behind her.

Frowning at his name tag, Freemont whispered, "Doesn't she understand English?"

"We really should hurry now." Susie held open the door. "They were expecting Dr. Phang in makeup five minutes ago."

After a few minutes in the makeup chair, Phineas was escorted to Recording Studio #3 where he greeted Gordon, the director.

"Hey, Phineas." Gordon shook hands with him, then gave Freemont and his name tag a curious look.

"I'm Dr. Phang's agent," Freemont boasted.

"And my brother," Phineas added with a grin.

Gordon nodded, his eyes twinkling with excitement. He and Stone Cauffyn were the only ones at DVN who knew what Phineas was really up to tonight. "Stone and Tiffany are ready for you. Good luck."

As Phineas approached the set, which consisted of three chairs on a carpeted dais, Tiffany jumped to her feet, her breasts jiggling and dangerously close to falling out of the sexy red dress she was wearing.

"Dr. Phang!" With a big grin, she threw her arms

around his neck. "Don't you just love it? We're famous! I want to kiss you, but I don't dare mess up my makeup."

"I understand."

"I'm getting fan mail, can you believe it? And all the girls want to know if I've slept with you. You don't mind if I say yes, do you?" She pressed closer, rubbing her breasts against him as she slid her hands down his chest. "It wouldn't have to be a lie, you know."

"Well, I—" Phineas grabbed her hands to keep them from venturing too far south. How could he put this? He didn't want to have sex with her just to give her something to talk about with her fans.

"Places!" Gordon shouted. "We go live in three minutes."

"We'll talk later," Phineas told Tiffany, then he took a seat, sandwiched between her and Stone Cauffyn, the newscaster who had just finished doing the *Nightly News* in Studio #2.

The sound guy clipped tiny microphones onto the guys' lapels, then struggled to find a place to attach Tiffany's mike.

She giggled. "Oooh, that tickles!"

"Does my hair look all right?" Stone asked the makeup girl.

"You look perfect," she replied, then winked at Phineas. "So do you."

"Two minutes," Gordon announced.

"Testing, testing," Stone said, and the sound guy gave him a thumbs-up. "Take a taxi, tally-ho."

Phineas gave him a questioning look, then realized the newscaster was warming up.

"The voluptuous vampire ventured into the velvet night," Stone announced in a serious tone. "Peter Potter from Poughkeepsie packs a pretty pickle in his pants."

Phineas glanced at his brother who was being herded toward the back of the room. Freemont grinned at him and punched the air with his fist.

"Billy Baker bumped into a barmaid and barfed his Blissky on her bosom," Stone continued, then lowered his voice to a soft whisper. "I hope this works."

"It will." Phineas shifted in his chair and unbuttoned his tuxedo jacket. He took a deep breath, then let it out slowly. *You can do this.*

"Ten seconds," Gordon announced, then held up his hand to show them five seconds, four, three, two, then he pointed his index finger at them.

They were live on the air.

Chapter Two

"*G*ood evening." Stone focused on the camera with the red glowing light. "Tonight, the Digital Vampire Network is proud to bring you the moment you've been waiting for—our special bonus feature."

The red light blinked to a second camera, and Stone shifted his gaze. "As the threat of global Vampire Apocalypse fades into the sunset, the Undead have turned their attention to . . . something completely different. I'm referring to the latest sensation on DVN—not a show, but an advertisement for the most recent addition to Vampire Fusion Cuisine, a mixture of synthetic blood and Chardonnay called Blardonnay, which is, of course, manufactured by one of our sponsors, Romatech Industries."

Stone motioned to his guests as the camera backed up for a wider shot. "It is my pleasure to introduce the actors from that commercial: Dr. Phang and Tiffany, otherwise known as the Blardonnay Guy and Girl."

Tiffany giggled and waved at the camera, while Phineas smiled.

"Now that your acting careers have skyrocketed," Stone continued, "can you tell us how your lives have changed?"

"Oh, I'm so happy now!" Tiffany clasped her hands together. "I've always known I was destined to be a star. I mean, when you look like this"—she twisted in her chair to strike a provocative pose—"it's obvious you belong in front of a camera."

"Indeed." Stone's face remained expressionless as he regarded her. "There is a theory that those who are extremely good-looking could also be considered more attractive."

Phineas's mouth twitched. "A bold theory, Stone."

"Yes, I have been incredibly blessed, but"—Tiffany heaved a forlorn sigh that carried the added bonus of causing her breasts to heave—"unfortunately, beauty such as mine tends to be overwhelming. Some might even call it . . . a curse." With a sniffle, she wiped away an imaginary tear.

Phineas struggled to keep a straight face as he patted Tiffany's hand. "Buck up, sweetness. It'll all be good."

She leaned to the side to give him a hug, which mashed her breasts together. "You're so wonderful, Dr. Phang. And I have to say that I'm ever so grateful to DVN for giving me this opportunity to show the vampire world how truly talented I am. Now everyone will know that I have much more to offer than an exquisitely beautiful face."

Stone's gaze flitted to her breasts. "Yes, I can tell you are truly gifted."

"Why, thank you." She giggled. "I'm just thrilled everyone is taking me seriously now."

"You can say that again." Phineas winked at her. As far as he knew, half the men at DVN had already taken Tiffany quite seriously. No way was he getting in line.

"And how about you, Dr. Phang?" Stone asked. "Has your life changed for the better?"

"Yes, it has. I was finally able to quit my old job."

Stone nodded. "There's a rumor going around DVN that you've agreed to play a role on one of our popular soap operas."

"It's not a rumor." Phineas aimed a dashing grin at the camera. "I'm in contract negotiations to star on *As the Vampire Turns.*"

Tiffany squealed and latched on to his arm, leaning toward him for another hug. "Oh, Dr. Phang! I'm so happy for you." She grinned at Stone. "I have good news, too. I was just hired to do a commercial for Vampos, the after-dinner mint that gets rid of blood breath."

"And I plan to make more Blardonnay commercials," Phineas added, then touched Tiffany's hand. "With you, of course."

"Oh yes, Dr. Phang! I just love working with you." She squeezed his arm and gave the camera a dramatic look. "We've become very close."

"Tell me, Dr. Phang," Stone continued. "How did you acquire such an interesting name? Are you really a doctor?"

"I took on the name five years ago when I was transformed," Phineas explained. "The title of doctor is honorary and refers to my high level of expertise in all manners of love."

Stone's face remained blank. "Indeed?"

"Yes. They call me the Love Doctor." It was a load of crap that Phineas felt like he'd outgrown, but it probably fit his new persona of an up-and-coming, supersexy star. "I don't like to brag, you understand, but I'm naturally attuned to universal love vibrations, and that gives me an uncanny ability to sense a woman's needs and fulfill her every desire."

"Oh yes!" Tiffany pressed against his arm. "Nobody fulfills me like Dr. Phang."

"You don't say," Stone continued. "Well, I can certainly attest to Dr. Phang's newfound popularity. DVN has been flooded with calls and e-mails. The women love the way you look in a bath towel, and the men want to know if you have a special workout regimen."

"He has a gorgeous chest," Tiffany purred while she rubbed a hand over his tuxedo jacket.

Phineas grabbed her hand before she could get carried away. "I was already in good shape when I was transformed. I used to be a boxer." And a drug dealer on the side, but he didn't want his family to know about that. Hell, he didn't want anyone to know.

"A boxer? How fascinating," Stone continued in his bland voice. "You mentioned quitting a job. Weren't you employed by MacKay Security and Investigation?"

Phineas nodded. Finally, Stone was getting to the

point of the interview. "Yeah, I worked for Angus MacKay. For five lousy years."

"Lousy?" Stone asked.

"You wouldn't believe how lousy. Seven nights a week, no time off, no vacation. And no hazard pay! They ordered me to risk my life, over and over again, and for what? Minimum wage?"

For the first time, Stone's face showed an expression. He frowned. "I didn't realize Angus MacKay was a bad employer."

"Bad?" Phineas snorted. "He's the worst. And you know what really pisses me off? That he has the gall to pretend that he's the good guy!"

Stone sat back with a stunned look. "You don't believe Angus MacKay is a good guy?"

"Hell no! I tell you, the whole time I worked for him, I never saw any of his employees get killed. But boy did they slaughter a bunch of other vampires."

"You're referring to the Malcontents they killed in battle?" Stone asked.

Phineas waved a hand. "Angus calls them Malcontents, but I like to call them by their real name: the True Ones. I mean, since when is it a crime to stick to old traditions? The True Ones just want to be left alone so they can eat the old-fashioned way."

"You mean feeding off mortals till they die," Stone muttered.

Phineas shrugged. "It's not like we have a shortage of mortals in the world. Besides, this is about basic vampire liberties. We should be able to feed however we like. Angus and his sanctimonious friends—who the hell are they to decide what's the right way for the rest of us to live our lives?"

"So you don't see anything wrong with the so-called Malcontents?" Stone asked.

"No, of course not. They're the ones who transformed me and gave me eternal life. I'm grateful for that."

"But you worked for MacKay S and I for several years," Stone reminded him. "They're the number one enemy of the Malcontents."

"I needed a paycheck, you know. I'm a young vampire, so I haven't had centuries to acquire wealth like those rich old farts who ordered me around like a servant. But now that I have a new career, I can finally do what I've wanted to do for a long time." Phineas glared at the camera. "Angus MacKay, you old turd, go to hell!"

Stone winced. "Those are strong words."

"I mean it," Phineas insisted. "All those Vamps make me sick. Acting so morally superior because they drink out of bottles while they go around murdering other vampires. They're a bunch of hypocrites! Do you know they executed Casimir without even giving him a chance to surrender? What kind of shit is that?"

Stone shifted in his chair. "Well, I—"

"And you want to hear something really funny?" Phineas continued. "For the last couple of years, Angus thought one of the Malcontents, Stanislav Serpukhov, was betraying the Russian coven in Brooklyn and reporting to me. But the truth was, I was reporting to him."

A series of gasps reverberated around the studio. Tiffany tilted her head with confusion, while Stone stared at him with his mouth open.

Phineas narrowed his eyes on the camera. "So you guys out there who've been trying to assassinate Stanislav, you need to stop. Cut it out. He's not a traitor."

Stone cleared his throat. "Are you saying you were a double agent?"

"Sure. No harm in letting out the big secret now that I've changed careers." Phineas winked at the camera. "I like to live dangerously, you know."

"I see." Stone took a deep breath. "Well, that's all the time we have for tonight. I'd like to thank our guests for coming and congratulate them once again for their phenomenal rise to stardom."

"Yes!" Tiffany blew a kiss at the camera. "I'd like to thank all the little people for admiring me so much."

"Thank you for watching DVN, the world's leading vampire network," Stone added with a bland smile.

"Cut!" Gordon announced. "Good work." He gave Phineas a thumbs-up.

"You *are* living dangerously." Stone stood as he unclipped his mike.

"It'll be worth it." Phineas handed his mike to the sound guy, then strode toward his brother, who was studying him with a puzzled frown.

"Wait for me!" Tiffany latched on to his arm.

"What the hell was that?" Freemont asked.

"I can explain." Phineas motioned to Tiffany, who clung to his arm. "You wanted to meet my lovely costar? Tiffany, this is my brother and my agent, Da Freeze."

"Hi!" She grinned at Freemont. "Aren't you adorable! You look like Phineas, except younger and more . . . alive." Her gaze drifted to his neck.

Freemont stepped back. "I just ate a bunch of garlic."

She giggled.

"We need to go somewhere private," Phineas said.

Tiffany's eyes widened. "You want a threesome?"

"No, I need to talk to my brother."

Freemont scowled at him. "Yeah, you do."

"You—you don't want me?" Tiffany's shoulders slumped.

Phineas sighed. "All right. You can come, too."

She perked up and grinned. "I know the perfect place. Come with me."

She ushered them out of the studio and down the hall to an unmarked door. "This is a storage room for old costumes. I have secret rendezvous here all the time."

Phineas followed her inside, flipped on the lights, and shut the door. "It's not exactly a secret if you meet all the guys here."

Freemont snorted, then strode down an aisle lined with crowded clothes racks on each side. He was pissed, Phineas could tell, but Phineas would deal with him later.

"Okay, Tiffany." He grabbed her by the shoulders. "Listen to me good."

She wrapped her arms around his neck. "Yes, Dr. Phang?"

He dragged her hands off his shoulders. "You're not having sex with me."

"I'm not? Then . . . ?" Her gaze flitted toward Freemont, who turned left at the end of the aisle and disappeared behind a rack of clothes.

"No, not with him, either," Phineas said. "Tiffany, look at me. You have a contract for three more Blardonnay commercials and a Vampos commercial. You don't need to sleep around anymore."

She stared at him blankly. "But it's worked well—"

"Tiffany, you made it. Put your old life behind you, and let you talent shine through. You're a success now, and you deserve it."

She blinked and whispered, "I . . . deserve it?"

"Yes, you do."

Her eyes glistened with tears. "That's the nicest thing anyone's ever told me."

Phineas gave her a wry smile. "I learned the hard way how easy it is to screw up your life when you don't respect yourself."

She nodded slowly. "Thank you, Dr. Phang."

"Now off you go. I need to talk to my brother."

"Okay." With a shy smile, she headed toward the door.

Phineas turned and couldn't spot his brother. "Freemont, where are you?"

A hand waved in the back corner, so Phineas tunneled between some dresses on a rack and found himself in a second aisle. He dove through another rack of clothes and discovered a wall lined with shelves. Shoes, handbags, and hats decorated the shelves, and toward the back wall, Freemont was examining a pair of cowboy boots.

Phineas heard the click of the door, signaling Tiffany's departure. "Okay, we can talk now."

Freemont grimaced as he stuffed the boots back on the shelf. "You told me you were a good vampire."

"I am."

"Then what was all that—"

"I'm working undercover."

"Yeah, I heard what you said! You're a stinkin' double agent, working for the nasty vampires that kill people!"

"No, I'm a good guy," Phineas insisted, then lowered his voice. "Freemont, you gotta trust me. I still work for MacKay S and I. The interview was a setup."

"Huh?"

"Did you see a video on the Internet a few weeks ago that claimed vampires were true? It showed a sword-fight, and a guy in a kilt decapitated another guy who turned to dust."

"Yeah." Freemont nodded. "I thought it was a movie trailer. Lamont and I wanted to see the movie, but we could never find the name of it. It just disappeared."

"The government removed it. Because it was real."

"Huh?"

"It was a real battle. I was there."

Freemont's eyes widened. "You fought in a real battle? With a sword?"

"Yes. I've been in several battles, and I've killed a few Malcontents. The guy whose head was cut off was Casimir, the leader of the Malcontents."

"So the bad guys were defeated?"

"Yes, but there are still a few Malcontents out there. Casimir had a girlfriend, Corky Courrant, who does a TV show called *Live with the Undead*."

"Huh?"

"She recorded the video of Casimir's execution, then posted it on YouTube. That means she broke the secret of vampire existence. That's about the biggest crime you can commit in our world."

"Her name is *Corky*?"

"Yes! Stay with me, Freemont. After she posted the video, she came back here to DVN and continued doing her show as if she'd done nothing wrong. She claims she's heir to the Malcontent throne and vampires all over the world should follow her and call her Queen Corky."

"Oh God, I hate her!" Tiffany hissed from across the room.

Phineas jerked around, but couldn't see her. "Tiffany! You were supposed to leave the room."

"It's okay." She emerged through a rack of hanging clothes. "I won't breathe a word. I hate Corky as much as anybody."

"So this Corky is really bad?" Freemont asked.

"She's evil," Tiffany hissed.

"Evil queen bitch," Phineas clarified. "She's been badmouthing us good Vamps on her show, calling us a bunch of thugs and murderers. She even bragged about how she started the Vampire Apocalypse. Roman summoned her to Coven Court three times, but she ignored him."

"Roman?" Freemont asked.

"Roman Draganesti, Coven Master for the East Coast," Phineas explained. "And he's owner of Roma-tech Industries where they make synthetic blood and where I'm head of security."

"Okay." Freemont nodded.

"Corky's been mocking Roman and the good Vamps, claiming she's above our system of law and justice," Phineas continued. "Roman had no choice but to issue a warrant for her arrest, but then she went into hiding and now she records her show somewhere in secret. We haven't been able to locate her."

"Oh my gosh," Tiffany whispered. "That's why you acted like a Malcontent sympathizer during the interview. You want to convince Corky you're on her side, so you can flush her out."

Phineas regarded Tiffany with surprise. She wasn't as stupid as she pretended to be. "You're right."

She grinned. "This is awesome! You really are working undercover."

Freemont's eyes lit up. "Hot damn! We're undercover brothers!"

"Don't get too excited." Phineas gave his brother a stern look. "I want you to stay out of trouble."

"No way! I've got your back, bro."

"I appreciate that, but I don't want you—"

"Don't tell me to stay out of this," Freemont interrupted with a scowl. "You involved me when you invited me here."

Phineas sighed. "I needed to convince everyone that I'd left MacKay S and I, and that I'm hanging with a new crowd. I suggested going to you, and Angus agreed. We always have a shortage of day guards, since not many mortals know about us, so Angus is interested in hiring you. He said they could work around your college schedule."

"Really?" Freemont's eyes widened. "I could work with you?"

"Yeah. I told him you might be interested." Phineas winced inwardly. He had jumped at the chance to include his brother, but now he wondered if his decision had been selfish.

For the past few years, he'd felt like there was a ticking bomb over his head. Sooner or later, and probably sooner, it would explode the instant that his family realized he wasn't aging. When that happened, he would be left with only two options. One: Tell his family the truth and deal with the consequences. Two: Disappear. He could fake his death, leave them to mourn, and never see them again. Or he could spare their grief by erasing himself from their memories. As if he had never existed.

Angus recommended the last option. A swift surgical strike, he called it, somewhat like amputating a limb. A part of you would be forever lost, but you would survive.

For Phineas, the thought of losing his family felt more like having his heart ripped out. Too painful to consider, so he'd settled on telling them the truth, starting with his brother. When Angus offered to hire Freemont, it had seemed like the perfect solution. Guarding Vamps in their death-sleep during the day was usually a safe job since the Malcontents were in their death-sleep, too.

But now that his current mission was under way, Phineas worried that his decision would expose his brother to some real danger. Had he selfishly saved himself pain, only to foist it onto his family? "Freemont, listen to me. It's already dangerous enough for you to be here, pretending to be my agent. I don't expect anything more from you. I have backup, so when things get dicey, I'll be covered. I want you to lay low and—"

"I can handle the spy stuff." Freemont lifted his chin. "This is my mission if I decide to accept it. As usual, if I am captured, the government will disavow any knowledge of my actions. See? I know how it works!"

Tiffany nodded. "I want to help, too!"

Phineas groaned. He had a bad feeling about this. "All right. But this is what you do. You continue to play the roles you're doing now. And if anything dangerous comes up, you stay clear of it, understood?" When they nodded, he continued, "We'll hang out in the lobby, sign autographs, and see if Corky sends any of her minions for me."

"You'll have to be quick to take her prisoner, or she'll teleport away," Tiffany warned him.

"I know," Phineas conceded. That was always a major problem when it came to catching bad vampires. Casimir had eluded them for years by simply teleporting away whenever they got close. "Go on to the lobby. We'll be there soon."

"Okay." Tiffany strode toward the door, and this time, Phineas watched to make sure she left.

He turned to his brother. "Are we good now?"

Freemont nodded with a sheepish look. "I shouldn't have doubted you, man."

"It's okay." Phineas clapped him on the back. "You've had a lot of weird shit thrown at you tonight."

"That's for sure." Freemont followed him to the door. "One thing I don't understand, though. Why didn't you take Tiffany up on her offer? She's beautiful and willing—"

"I like her. As a friend."

"Yeah, but she's willing, dude. And you're the Love Doctor. You gotta spread the cure."

Phineas smiled. His brother kept reminding him of himself about five years back. "I admit there was a time when I would have jumped her." He cracked the door and peered outside. The coast was clear.

"What happened to you, bro? You seem different these days."

Phineas shrugged. "I grew up." And he'd seen some bad shit. Ravaged, dead bodies left behind by Malcontents. .Whole families, even children, murdered because the Malcontents enjoyed terrorizing the innocent. He'd been thrust into life and death situations, and he'd killed in battle. He could no longer pretend life was one big party.

"Just because you're older doesn't mean you have to be boring," Freemont muttered.

Phineas led him down a hall lined with dressing rooms and offices. "When I first discovered I was Undead and I could possibly live forever, it sorta went to my head, you know, like I was invincible and super-macho and could do whatever the hell I pleased with as many Vamp ladies as I pleased. But then I realized they were all doing whatever they pleased, too."

"What's wrong with that if you're having fun?"

Phineas slowed his steps and lowered his voice. "They didn't see me as a person. You think we're a minority in the real world, you should try the vampire one. I was a curiosity that all the ladies wanted to experience, and once it was over, they moved on to the next form of entertainment."

"So you got tired of one-night stands?" Freemont wrinkled his nose. "Is that even possible?"

"Yes, it is. Eventually, I realized that being wanted as an oddity is an insult. I want to be appreciated for being myself."

Freemont nodded his head slowly. "You want . . . respect. And that's why you told Tiffany that stuff."

"You got it, bro." Phineas continued down the hall toward the lobby. Yes, he wanted respect. He wanted love. He wanted the brass ring, the whole shebang, the happily-ever-after that the other guys were getting. But he was having trouble finding the dream girl. LaToya had slipped through his fingers like mist, a dream that never became reality.

A different vision invaded his mind. Sky-blue eyes and a long mane of hair that glimmered with shades of brown, red, and gold. Beautiful, impossible Brynley. She wasn't a dream, but a nightmare. Dressed in a fur coat.

He gestured to a door they passed by. "That's Corky Courrant's office. I snuck in there two weeks ago when we were shooting the Blardonnay commercial. I was searching for a clue as to where she could be hiding, but she'd already cleaned it out."

"Bummer."

Phineas nodded. "If she takes the bait tonight, we'll find her." He pushed open the doors to the lobby, and they were greeted with a chorus of high-pitched squeals.

He joined Tiffany, signing autographs, while Freemont protected him from any ominous-looking legs, arms, and breasts he was asked to sign. The fun lasted about ten minutes, and then it happened.

Three armed men crashed through the front doors, shouting and waving their weapons. The crowd, mostly women, screamed and scrambled toward the back doors.

"Everyone down on the floor and shut the hell up!" one of the intruders yelled. In case anyone had trouble understanding his thick Russian accent, he punctuated his demands by shooting a few bullets into the ceiling.

As the blare of gunfire echoed about the lobby, the screams quickly hushed. Sheetrock particles rained down, leaving traces of white powder on the intruders' black coats. The crowd dropped to the floor, women huddled together, quivering with a few frightened whimpers.

Phineas remained standing and motioned to his brother to stay put. Freemont had crouched behind the receptionist's desk with Susie and Tiffany.

The Russian guy was the leader, Phineas figured. A Malcontent, no doubt, sent by Corky. He was armed with an automatic pistol and an AK–47. The guys flanking him were mortal, judging from the bite marks on their necks. They either served Corky voluntarily, or she had them under vampire mind control. One was tall and skinny, with a narrow face and long nose. Rat Face, Phineas dubbed him. And the other guy, short and square, was Blockhead. The three thugs scanned the room before focusing on him.

"You." The Russian Malcontent smirked. "You are the one called Dr. Phang."

"What do you want?" Phineas asked.

"You will come with us. The queen wants you."

Phineas paused as if considering the invitation, then shrugged. "No thanks. I don't know any queens."

The Russian pointed his automatic at the nearest girl, the cheerleader with Phineas's autograph on her thigh. "You will come, or this one will die. Her Majesty, Queen Corky, must be obeyed."

"Oh, that queen!" Phineas raised his hands. "Sure. Why not?"

With a sneer, the Russian motioned to his minions. "Prepare him for the journey."

Rat Face and Blockhead approached him slowly, slipping their pistols into the shoulder holsters beneath their black coats.

"Take off your jacket," the Russian ordered, keeping his pistol and AK–47 trained on nearby girls.

After Phineas removed his tuxedo jacket, Blockhead grabbed it and rifled through the pockets. He stuffed Phineas's wallet and cell phone into his own coat pockets. Phineas kept his face blank, careful not to show how relieved he was that he'd deleted all contacts and messages from his phone.

"Roll up your sleeves," the Russian demanded. "We have heard MacKay embeds tracking chips in all his vampires."

"I no longer work for them." Phineas shoved his shirtsleeves up to his elbows. "Angus cut the chip out last night."

The Russian gave him a dubious look. "You have no wound on your arm."

"It healed during my death-sleep."

The Russian jerked his head toward Rat Face. "Check him."

Rat Face took a small electronic device from his pocket and skimmed it up and down Phineas's arms. "He's clean, Dimitri."

"Check him for weapons," the Russian ordered.

Blockhead skimmed his hands over Phineas. "He's clean."

"Very well." Dimitri inclined his head. "We will now escort you to the queen, where you will appear on her show."

"Sounds good to me." Phineas put his jacket back on. "It'll be good publicity."

Freemont straightened and adjusted his hat. "My client will expect reimbursement, you understand. He doesn't do appearances for free."

Phineas shook his head, glaring at his brother.

Dimitri narrowed his eyes on Freemont. "Who the hell are you?"

"Nobody," Phineas said at the same time Freemont said, "I'm Dr. Phang's agent."

"Freemont," Phineas gritted out through clenched teeth. "Stay out of this."

Dimitri's sharp eyes darted back and forth between Phineas and his brother, then he smiled. "You have a mortal friend, Dr. Phang?"

"No, he's a pain in the ass," Phineas growled.

Dimitri chuckled. "Cuff them both. Having the mortal with us will ensure Dr. Phang's good behavior."

"Dammit," Phineas muttered, glowering at his brother while Rat Face and Blockhead snapped silver handcuffs around their wrists.

"The cuffs are just a precaution," Dimitri said. "We can't have Dr. Phang teleporting away and taking his mortal friend with him."

Rat Face and Blockhead seized Phineas and Freemont by the napes of their necks and steered them toward the front door. Outside in the parking lot, Phineas and his brother were shoved into the back of a delivery van. It was empty, except for stained carpet on the floor. The back doors slammed shut, and they were locked inside. No windows, Phineas noted, so he wouldn't know where they were going.

But just seconds earlier, he had spotted a black SUV across the parking lot. Robby and Jack were prepared to follow.

Phineas heard more doors on the van bang shut. That was probably Dimitri and his buddies climbing into the front seat. Corky had to be located fairly close by if they were driving to her.

"What do we do now?" Freemont whispered.

Phineas scowled at him. "You have a lousy way of following directions. You were supposed to stay out of danger."

"I wasn't going to leave you alone with them." Freemont glared back. "I'm not a coward."

The van lurched into motion.

Freemont gulped. "Do we have a plan?"

"Shh." Phineas motioned with his head toward the front seat of the van, then mouthed the words, *Super hearing.*

Freemont nodded.

Phineas slid the heel of his right boot to the side, revealing a hidden red button. He punched the button, activating the new soundless tracking beam Roman and

Laszlo had perfected in the lab at Romatech. He slid the heel back in place.

Freemont's eyes twinkled with excitement.

Phineas smiled. *Oh yeah, Queen Bitch. We've got you now.*

Chapter Three

*H*ow kind of you to appear on my show," Corky Courrant said, smiling for the camera.

"My pleasure." Phineas returned her smile. As far as he could tell, Corky's makeshift studio was in the basement of a duplex somewhere in Brooklyn or Queens. They hadn't driven far, and he'd been able to catch a glimpse of the residence after Corky's minions had hauled him and Freemont from the back of the van.

He sat on a tufted footstool, low to the ground to emphasize his inferior status, while next to him, Corky posed in a high-backed, ornately carved, red velvet upholstered chair. He had to crane his neck to avoid peering straight at her massive bosom, which threatened to escape her low-cut, shimmering gold gown. Her jeweled tiara and numerous rings glittered under the bright overhead lights.

They had started the show with a recording of a trumpet fanfare befitting a queen. Corky had confided in him that she'd first heard the piece at the court of Henry VIII where she'd been one of the king's favorites. Phineas figured she had a long history of using powerful men to get ahead.

The wall behind them was draped in purple silk. In front of them, Rat Face worked the camera, and Blockhead held the boom suspended over Corky's head. Across the room, Freemont perched stiffly on a metal folding chair while Dimitri aimed his automatic pistol at him. Another armed Malcontent stood by the door, and Phineas had counted three more upstairs on the ground floor. A total of seven men, but that shouldn't be a problem. Angus was planning to hit with a dozen guys from MacKay S&I.

Even though the mission was simple—capture Corky—a nagging fear pricked at Phineas. His orders were to stick close to Corky and to not let her get away, but he hadn't counted on his brother being here.

He swallowed hard, then pasted a smile back on his face. "Thank you for inviting me, Corky—"

She kicked him in the shin.

"Miss Corky." Another kick. "Queen Corky." His smile barely wavered. "Your most glorious Majesty. I've always been a big fan of your show."

"Well, of course you are." She waved her hand in a regal fashion. "My show has always enjoyed the highest ratings of any show on DVN. Everyone adores my show. Naturally, since everyone adores *me*. But enough about me."

She gave a throaty laugh. "Let's talk a moment about those despicable, hateful bastards who've been persecuting me, forcing me to take my spectacular show into hiding. I'm talking, of course, about those bottle-drinking cowards who refuse to behave like true vampires."

"Yes—"

"And I'm especially referring to their ringleaders," Corky continued. "Roman Draganesti, who invented that nasty swill he calls synthetic blood, and then he contaminated it even further with his disgusting Vampire Fusion Cuisine." She paused, looking down her nose at Phineas. "You don't actually enjoy that Blardonnay, do you?"

"Shit, no." Phineas made a face. "I can barely stomach it. But a man's got to make a living, you know."

"I understand." She patted the top of his head like he was her new pet. "Sadly, there are times when we must suffer for our art. But back to those vicious ringleaders—the worst one, without a doubt, is that wretched Angus MacKay, the head of MacKay Security and Investigation. Of course, we all know that organization is nothing more than a notorious gang of armed thugs."

Phineas nodded. "I'm so glad I finally got away from them. They treated me like a dog."

Corky gasped with indignation. "You poor man. Do tell us more." Her smile turned vicious. "Every vile and disgusting detail."

"Of course. First of all, I think they're mentally unstable."

Her eyes gleamed. "I've always suspected as much."

Phineas shrugged. "Well, it's just a personal opinion, you understand, but I think they carry those huge swords around 'cause they're compensating. When a guy runs around in a skirt for five hundred years, you gotta wonder about him, you know."

Corky snorted. "So true. The bastard who murdered my poor, beloved Casimir was wearing one of those stupid kilts. Those Scottish barbarians will never—" She gasped when the door crashed open and a horde of kilted barbarians rushed in at vampire speed.

On second look only Angus, Robby, Ian, and Dougal were wearing kilts. The others wore pants, but would probably enjoy being called barbarians.

Swords clashed upstairs, and Phineas realized some of Angus's team had engaged the guards on the ground floor.

He leaped on Corky and wrapped his arms around her. If she tried to teleport away, she'd have to take him with her, along with his boot that still emitted a tracking beam.

Corky struggled against his hold. "Let me go, you traitor!" She froze, stunned by the sight of Robby zooming toward her with a silver chain stretched taut between his gloved hands. Not only would the silver burn if it came into contact with her skin, but it would prevent her from teleporting.

She shrieked.

"Release her!" Dimitri yanked Freemont to his feet and jabbed a pistol against his temple. "Or I'll kill him!"

Phineas's heart lurched. His brother would never be

able to overpower a vampire. He shoved Corky toward Robby, then teleported behind Dimitri and wrenched the gun from his hand. He pulled back his arm to punch Dimitri, but the Russian vanished. *Shit*. The damned Malcontents were always running away.

But to his surprise, Dimitri didn't bail on his queen. He rematerialized behind Robby, who had looped the silver chain around Corky. A knife flashed in the bright studio lights.

"Robby, behind you!" Phineas shouted.

Robby spun to face his attacker and grabbed Dimitri's arm. Angus zoomed toward them and clunked the Russian on the head with the hilt of his claymore. Dimitri collapsed on the floor unconscious.

Meanwhile, Corky wiggled free from the silver chain, and just as Robby made a grab for her, she teleported away.

"Nay!" Robby and Angus shouted in unison.

A pall of disappointment fell with a whoosh over the room. They had taken everyone prisoner except the target.

"She got away?" Freemont asked. "Can you follow her?"

With a curse, Phineas kicked the metal folding chair. "We don't know where she went."

"Hot damn," Freemont whispered. "I've never seen so many booty-licious babes in one room."

"They can hear you." Phineas cast an apologetic look at Caitlyn, Toni, and Lara, then leaned close to his brother. "Watch what you say once their husbands arrive. They have super hearing and super strength."

"Right." Freemont stopped ogling the women and gazed forlornly at the leopard-skin fedora he'd placed in front of him on the long wooden table.

They were sitting in a conference room at Roma-tech, waiting for the strategy meeting to begin. After the fiasco at Corky's hideout, Phineas had offered to teleport his brother back to DVN, so he could return the limo to Leroy's House of Class, but Freemont had insisted on sticking by his side.

"A friend of yours is a friend of mine," Freemont had told him. "And an enemy of yours is an enemy of mine. I've got your back, bro, you know what I'm saying?"

Phineas had pulled him into a hug, his heart swelling with love and pride. Then he'd teleported Freemont to Romatech and introduced him to his friends.

The two mortals, Rat Face and Blockhead, had been teleported to Romatech, along with an unconscious Dimitri. The prisoners were downstairs in the base-ment, the mortals in an interrogation room, and Dimitri in the silver room to keep him from teleporting away.

"I screwed up, didn't I?" Freemont mumbled. "The old dude will never hire me now."

Phineas shifted in his chair. "You never know. Angus is pretty cool—"

"But the bitch got away 'cause you had to save me. I should have stayed out of it, I guess."

"You guess?" Phineas gave him an annoyed look. "Didn't I tell you to lay low?"

Freemont winced and slumped lower in his chair. "I totally blew it."

Most of the MacKay S&I employees were busy elsewhere, but a few of the ladies had gathered early in the conference room. Across the table, a very pregnant Caitlyn Panterra was discussing baby things with Toni MacPhie.

"Are all the women here knocked up?" Freemont whispered.

"Toni and Caitlyn are," Phineas mumbled. These days, he was surrounded with happily married couples.

Lara di Venezia grinned at them. "Scary, isn't it? Olivia's expecting, too. I feel all alone these days."

Freemont sat up, smiling at the pretty redhead. "I'd be happy to keep you company."

Phineas nudged him with an elbow. "Lara is married to Jack, one of the best swordsmen in the vampire world."

Freemont huffed with disappointment. "Are all the babes here married?"

"Very happily married," Phineas grumbled.

"Have you seen LaToya lately?" Lara asked him.

He groaned inwardly. "No."

"Oh." Lara's smile faded. "I thought you might have gone to New Orleans for her birthday. I sent her a card last week, but I haven't heard back from her."

Phineas sighed. LaToya had never told him her birth date. Probably because she didn't want a present from him. Hell, who was he kidding? She'd never wanted *anything* from him.

"Who are you talking about?" Freemont asked.

"LaToya Lafayette," Lara replied. "We were room-mates when we both worked for the NYPD. More than roommates, actually. Best friends. But she's never been able to accept the fact that I married a Vamp."

"Bummer," Freemont mumbled.

"Yes." Lara heaved a big sigh. "I miss her. She moved back to New Orleans, and joined the police force there. You went to see her at Christmastime, didn't you, Phineas?"

He nodded.

Freemont eyed him curiously. "You have a girl-friend?"

"No." Not unless there was a new tradition for mistle-toe that involved a girlfriend threatening to shoot off her boyfriend's head. "We don't get along very well."

"I'm sorry it hasn't worked out for you," Lara said, then shook her head sadly. "I tried so many times to tell her what a nice guy you are, but—"

"It's okay," Phineas interrupted her. "She just doesn't like Vamps."

"Exactly," Lara agreed. "So you shouldn't take it per-sonally. She would have rejected any—"

"I know." Phineas gritted his teeth. "It's no big deal."

Lara gave him a dubious look, then thankfully turned her attention to Freemont. "I don't mean to pry, but I heard you talking about MacKay S and I. Are you going to work with us?"

"I'd like to." Freemont glanced at Phineas. "It would be buck."

"Don't forget you need to finish college," Phineas murmured.

Freemont rolled his eyes. "I can do both. I'm free for the rest of this summer. And I could take night classes from now on." He made a face. "I'm just afraid I blew my chance. The old dude's not going to want me now. I screwed up his last mission."

"It wasn't your fault," Lara insisted. "Vampires and shifters are stronger than us—"

"Shifters?" Freemont's eyes widened. "What the hell is a shifter?"

"Oops," Lara whispered.

Phineas winced. "I didn't quite tell you everything."

Freemont sat back. "What do you mean? There's more spooky shit?"

"Yeah. Some of the people you'll meet tonight aren't vampires. They're not exactly human, either."

"They're *aliens*?"

"No, they're from Earth."

"Oh, good." Freemont exhaled with relief. "Those aliens really freak me out. I mean, why do they travel a jillion light-years just to stick a probe up someone's ass?"

"They're not aliens," Phineas muttered, aware that the ladies in the room were snickering. "They're shifters."

"So how do they shift? Do they phase from one alternate reality to another?"

Phineas scoffed. "What kind of crap have you been watching? There is no alternate reality."

"So you say." Freemont's gaze darted suspiciously around the room. "But how can you be sure?"

"Because this is it! Has anyone in the entire history of our planet ever found a portal to another dimension?"

Freemont lifted a finger to make a point. "If they stepped through, then they're not here to tell us about it."

Lara chuckled. "That's a good point."

"Don't encourage him," Phineas muttered.

"So how does the shifting thing work?" Freemont's eyes lit up. "I know! They ascend into a more advanced, spiritual form, one that goes beyond the restraints of a physical body, so they exist as pure transcendent energy—"

"They're animals."

"Huh?"

"They shift into animals," Phineas repeated. "Like wolves."

"You mean *werewolves*?" Freemont stiffened, his expression tinged with panic. "You're messing with me, right? I mean, vampires are bad enough, but I figure they like to pick on the pretty ladies, so I'm safe. But werewolves! They'll chew on anything. They're big! And bad!"

"And they'll blow your house down." Phineas's smile quickly faded as the same old vision flitted through his mind. Pale blue eyes the color of a summer sky. Why did the most beautiful woman on Earth have to belong to the canine family? *Stop thinking about her!* Brynley was all wrong. And she hated Vamps even more than LaToya.

Why couldn't he do like most of the Vamp guys and fall for a nice mortal girl? A mortal girl would be safe. And logical.

Maybe Freemont was right, and he needed to go to a psychiatric hospital. He had to be crazy to have a female shifter constantly invading his thoughts. And not just any hairy old shifter, but a rich princess wolf who enjoyed snarling and growling at him. And that was when she was in human form.

"You're not punkin' me?" Freemont asked.

"No," Phineas said. "You'll meet Phil. He's a were-wolf." And twin brother to Big Bad Wolfie-Girl. *Don't think about her!* If she knew how much he obsessed over her, she'd probably bite off one of his ears. While she was still in human form. God knows what she'd do to him as a wolf.

"There are other kinds of shifters, too," Lara added. "Howard is a were-bear, and Rajiv's a were-tiger. Caitlyn here is a were-panther."

Caitlyn raised a hand in greeting. "Meow!"

Freemont gasped. "You're a cat?"

"Not at the moment." Caitlyn grinned. "The lack of fur is a major clue."

Freemont's gaze drifted down and then back up. "But you're pregnant."

Still smiling, she patted her big belly. "Twins."

He gulped and shifted his gaze to Toni. "What are you?"

"The most awesome creature on the planet," she replied with a wry look. "A human female."

"You go, girl." Lara gave her a high five.

Freemont gave Phineas an incredulous look. "Your life just gets weirder and weirder."

The door swung open, and a group of MacKay employees filed in. Ian MacPhie and Jack di Venezia pulled up chairs to squeeze in next to their wives.

"Another cat?" Freemont whispered when Carlos Panterra sat next to Caitlyn.

Phineas nodded. "And that's the werewolf taking the chair beside you."

Freemont glanced warily at Phil, who gave him a wolfish grin.

At the foot of the table, Emma MacKay set Phineas's wallet and cell phone on the table and slid them down to him. "One of the mortal prisoners had them."

He pocketed them. "Thanks."

Emma took a seat. "Angus will be here shortly to begin the meeting. Howard and J.L. are still at Corky's place, scouring it for clues. Robby and Olivia are handling the mortals. Rajiv's in the security office, keeping an eye on things, and we left Mikhail and Austin in the silver room to guard the Malcontent."

Jack chuckled. "They piss him off the most. Dimitri hates Mikhail for being a Russian on our side, and he hates Austin because he's immune to vampire mind control."

"I wish you let me talk to him." A newcomer strode into the room, talking with a thick Russian accent. "I would make him really mad."

"Hey, Stan." Phineas gave him a knuckle pound as the former Malcontent passed by.

"I'm sorry, Stanislav," Emma said. "But we can't let any Malcontents know you're here, not with the bounty they've put on your head."

Stan nodded, then sat next to Phineas. "That was good what you said in the interview. Maybe now my old friends not be so eager to kill me."

"I liked yer interview." Ian's mouth twitched. "Especially the part about Angus being a rich old fart."

Everyone chuckled, including Emma.

"And then, ye told him to go to hell," Ian continued. "What was it ye called him?"

"An old turd."

The laughter ended abruptly at the sound of Angus's stern voice. He stood in the doorway, his arms crossed over his chest as he glowered at Phineas.

Freemont gulped and gave Phineas a worried look.

"I was trying to sound convincing," Phineas said.

Angus continued to stare at him.

"It was all an act, you know," Phineas added.

Angus strode toward him, then grinned and slapped him on the back. "I was just playing with you, lad. Ye did verra well. Ye led us straight to our target."

Phineas winced. "But she still got away."

Freemont jumped to his feet. "It was my fault, sir. I apologize."

Angus turned to regard him curiously. "Ye're Phineas's brother? Freemont, is it?"

"Yes, sir." He squared his shoulders. "It was my fault Corky escaped."

"No—" Phineas began.

"Why do ye say that?" Angus interrupted, focused on Freemont.

"My brother told me to lay low, and I didn't—"

"Why?" Angus asked.

Freemont glanced at Phineas. "I couldn't let him go into danger alone."

"Och, so ye're verra loyal to yer brother?" Angus narrowed his eyes. "Can ye be that loyal to his friends?"

Freemont nodded. "Yes, sir."

Angus rested a hand on his shoulder. "Doona blame yerself for what happened. 'Tis no easy task to capture a vampire. It took us years to catch up with Casimir. We'll get Corky, too."

"Yes, sir." Freemont looked relieved as he sat back down.

"Now, let's get on with the briefing." Angus strode to the head of the table and gripped the back of the chair. "So far, Dimitri has told us nothing."

Jack shrugged. "He will once he gets hungry enough."

"Aye," Angus agreed. "But we willna know if he's telling us the truth. Olivia's lie-detecting skills only work on mortals. She's verified our two mortal prisoners are telling the truth. They know nothing, other than the nonsense they were programmed to believe. They love Queen Corky and want to die for her."

"What will we do with them, then?" Toni asked.

"Robby will erase their memories, and we'll take them back to their homes," Angus replied. "Hopefully, they can go back to their normal lives."

"So we have no idea where Corky may have teleported to?" Phineas asked.

Angus drummed his fingers on the back of the chair. "We can make a good guess. The Malcontents we encountered on the ground floor teleported away when they realized they were outnumbered. But we heard them talk to each other, and it sounded like Hungarian. And of course, Dimitri is Russian."

Ian leaned back in his chair. "Most Malcontents are Eastern European or Russian."

"Aye." Angus nodded. "As for Corky's whereabouts, since Roman issued a warrant for her arrest here in the States, I doona think she'll remain here. She's declared herself the Malcontent queen, so I believe she'll seek refuge with them. She's originally from England, so she probably teleported there, and then plans to move on to Eastern Europe or Russia whenever it grows dark there."

Everyone murmured their agreement.

"We'll have three search teams working out of three different bases," Angus continued. "One in Moscow at Mikhail's house, one in Budapest at Zoltan's house, and the last one at Stanislav's house in Minsk. Emma and I will be in charge in Moscow, Robby and Stan in Minsk, and Jack and Lara will assist Zoltan in Budapest. We doona expect any trouble at the school, so Ian and Carlos, I apologize for separating you from yer wives when they're expecting, but we need every available man to help with the search."

Carlos touched his wife's shoulder. "Caitlyn is due in about two weeks."

"We'll bring you back in a week, or sooner, if need be," Emma assured him.

Angus went on to assign everyone, making sure each team had at least two day guards. Olivia, Toni, and Caitlyn, the three pregnant women, would remain behind to protect the Dragon Nest Academy, a fairly easy job since no Malcontents knew the school even existed.

"Phineas, ye'll remain here at Romatech, in charge of security," Angus announced.

"But I thought you needed every available—"

"I have to leave someone here in charge, and I trust you," Angus said.

Phineas sighed. He would have liked to see some faraway places, but he knew the other guys were better suited for the search. Jack could speak Czech and Italian. Austin knew several Slavic languages. Robby and Angus knew French and Russian. "Okay, I'll stay here."

"It's an important job," Emma reminded him. "Our attempt to capture Corky will have angered the few remaining Malcontents here in the States, and you know that Romatech is one of their favorite places to attack. We also need you to keep Roman safe."

Phineas nodded. "I understand."

Angus smiled. "And since ye'll be here, ye can start yer brother's training. That is, if he's interested in working for us."

"Yes, sir!" Freemont sat up. "Phineas will train me real good. I'll be solid. Hard-core."

Angus nodded, his smile widening. "I'm sure ye will. Welcome to MacKay S and I."

Everyone at the table congratulated Freemont.

With a grin, Phineas gave his brother a knuckle pound. "Way to go, bro."

"Phineas can get you the forms to fill out," Angus said, then strode toward the door. "As for everyone else, gather the weapons and supplies ye need. We start teleporting to the London office in ten minutes."

Chapter Four

A week passed by at Romatech with Phineas and Freemont manning the MacKay security office at night. Eventually, Freemont would guard Vamps during the day, but with most of the Vamps overseas hunting for Corky, there weren't many left behind, just the night shift at Romatech. Phineas and his brother were responsible for their safety—Vamps like Roman, Laszlo, and Gregori, and a few mortals like Gregori's fiancée, Abigail.

There was a mortal security team that worked out of a separate office during the day, and they guarded Romatech's mortal employees. Most of the day shift was blissfully unaware of what happened at Romatech after sunset. That was when the night shift came in to make Vampire Fusion Cuisine.

For right now, Freemont needed to work the same hours as his brother so Phineas could train him. They began with lessons in fencing and martial arts, and they practiced marksmanship in the shooting range in the basement. Freemont also learned how to make the rounds and file reports.

With so many MacKay employees out of the country, it was quiet at Romatech. Roman's usual day guard, Howard Barr, was in Budapest, so whenever Roman wasn't working at Romatech, he teleported to the Dragon Nest Academy, where his wife, children, and mother-in-law were now living.

Angus and his Vamp employees e-mailed their reports to Phineas since they were awake while he was in his death-sleep. The shifters, Howard, Carlos, and Phil, called to give him updates. So far, no luck in tracking down Corky. To help out, Phineas made an old-fashioned wanted poster with Corky's picture on it and faxed it to every vampire Coven Master and shifter contact on Angus's list.

The Malcontent prisoner, Dimitri, had been released after a tracking device had been embedded in the back of his neck while he was in his death-sleep. They couldn't be sure how long the device would remain on Dimitri, but it was worth a shot in case he tried to reunite with his queen. According to the device, he was still in the Brooklyn area, hanging out with the few Russian Malcontents who remained there. Roman's father-in-law, Sean Whelan, had his CIA Stake-Out team watching the Russian Coven House. No sign of Corky there.

After a few nights, Phineas decided his brother could handle a few hours on his own, so he agreed to do another Blardonnay commercial. The next night, he teleported to DVN, where his costar, Tiffany, was waiting, along with Gordon, the director, and Maggie, the producer.

This time, the set was made to look like a tropical island. The backdrop showed a lush green rainforest to his right and a tropical blue lagoon to his left. Lighting had been set up to look like there was a full moon overhead.

He stood ankle-deep in white sand with a brightly striped beach towel tied around his hips. Tiffany wore a red bikini that emphasized her considerable talents. After a few takes, Gordon and Maggie declared the commercial a great success and broke open a few bottles of Bubbly Blood to celebrate.

Maggie poured some of the synthetic blood and champagne concoction into a flute glass and handed it to Phineas. "You really have a flair for this. Any of the soap operas would snatch you up in a minute."

He took a sip of Bubbly Blood. "It's a lot of fun, but I don't want to quit my job at MacKay."

Maggie gave him a sly smile. "So you like working for that rich old fart?"

He winced. "That was acting."

"I know. That's my point. You're good at it, Phineas. If you ever need another job, you can find one here. They're getting a lot of disappointed e-mails that you're not going to appear on the soap."

"Sorry about that." He had announced a possible acting gig during his interview with Stone, but it had been a sham. Since then, Stone had reported on the *Nightly News* that contract negotiations had fallen through. "I like working for MacKay. When I was a mortal, I totally screwed up, but now that I have a second chance, I want my life to count for something. I want to be one of the good guys."

Maggie's eyes softened. "You are a good guy, Phineas. We're all very proud of you."

He shrugged. Only the married women seemed to think that way.

"I have some good news." Maggie refilled their flute glasses with more Bubbly Blood. "Since Corky's show is off the air, and there's a gap in the schedule, Darcy Erickson and I pitched an idea for a new show, and they bought it!"

Phineas clinked his glass against hers. "That's great! Congratulations!"

She grinned. "Darcy and I are so excited! I was getting kind of tired of working on the ranch, and Darcy's been wanting to quit MacKay S and I now that she has two kids. So now we're coproducers of DVN's new celebrity talk show, *Real Housewives of the Vampire World*!"

"Hot damn, woman! That's gonna be a hit!"

Maggie laughed. "I hope so! We're going to travel to different locations to interview wives of famous vampires. We'll tour their houses or castles or wherever they're living, and what's really cool is that Darcy can record what their homes look like during the day."

"Right." Darcy was the only Vamp Phineas knew of

who had managed to become mortal once again. The procedure couldn't work on him, though, because he didn't have a sample of his blood from when he was mortal.

"Can you imagine actually seeing things in daylight?" Maggie asked. "It'll just be an image on television, of course, but I think it will be very exciting for Vamps."

Phineas's chest tightened. He would love to see a blue sky again. His world was now black with shades of gray, and it would remain that way for centuries. A pair of sky-blue eyes invaded his thoughts, but he quickly chased the image away. Brynley was impossible. As impossible as his chances to ever see the sky again.

He swallowed hard. "You're right, Maggie. Vamps are going to love it."

"Heather Echarpe has agreed to be our first victim, so we're off to Texas tomorrow to start filming."

"Good luck." Phineas said his good-byes to everyone, then teleported back to Romatech.

Still no luck in finding Corky. According to the latest reports, Angus, Mikhail, and Phil were following a lead in Siberia. Zoltan, Jack, and Carlos were investigating another lead in Bulgaria, while Stan, Robby, and Austin were checking out a nest of Malcontents in Lithuania. The rest of the MacKay employees remained at the bases comparing reports and searching for new leads.

Sean Whelan and his Stake-Out team were still watching the Russian vampires in Brooklyn. The tracking device on Corky's minion, Dimitri, was still working, and he had remained at the Russian Coven House.

At the end of the week, Phineas received a call from the police chief in Wolf Ridge, Maine. Wolf Ridge was a werewolf community near the compound Angus had confiscated from the Malcontent Apollo. The compound was now used as a summer camp for the werewolf boys who attended Dragon Nest Academy.

"We got your wanted poster regarding the female vampire," Chief explained. "And we may have a possible lead for you."

"Someone has seen her?" Phineas couldn't imagine Corky hiding out in the northern wilderness of Maine.

"Not here," Chief replied. "But my sons are on all the Lycan loops and chat rooms, and they heard something interesting. Some werewolf guys were hunting in Wyoming and came across an unconscious mortal. When they took him to the local emergency room, they discovered he'd lost a lot of blood and had two puncture wounds in his neck."

"So there's a vampire in Wyoming," Phineas concluded, not terribly impressed. There were thousands of vampires around the world.

"It's not a normal place for a vampire," Chief continued. "The area is too sparsely populated. Anyway, after the mortal gained consciousness, he said the last thing he remembered was a beautiful blonde with huge breasts who approached his campfire at night and asked for help. He thought it was his lucky day."

Phineas snorted. "He's lucky to be alive. The description sounds sorta like Corky, so I'll check into it. Thanks, Chief." He hung up.

"What's up?" Freemont was sitting in front of the desk, munching on a hamburger from the Romatech cafeteria.

"A possible lead on Corky." Phineas paced across the security office. "Or more like impossible. Wyoming is the last place we would expect her to go."

"In other words"—Freemont popped a French fry into his mouth—"it's the perfect place for her to hide."

Phineas halted. Could it be true? Could Angus have ninety-nine percent of his employees on a wild-goose chase halfway around the world while Corky was hiding in their backyard?

"I need to call Angus." Although he was probably in his death-sleep right now. Phineas grabbed the phone off the desk and dialed Angus's number.

"Hey, Dr. Phang," Phil answered. "What's up?"

"Got some news, Wolf-Bro." Phineas repeated what Chief had told him.

"Interesting," Phil murmured. "I'll pass it on to Angus as soon as he wakes up. But you can guess what he'll say. He'll expect you to check it out."

"You should be the one checking it out," Phineas insisted. "You've got that place in Wyoming, and you know the territory." Phil Jones's father was Supreme Pack Master of Wyoming, Montana, and Idaho, so Phil had grown up there. He owned a bunch of land and a cabin in Wyoming, a gift he'd received on his eighteenth birthday.

In the werewolf world, Phil had the status of a prince, which meant his sister, Big Bad Wolfie-Girl, was a princess. *Don't think about her.* Phil had been banished shortly after acquiring the cabin, and over the following years, his sister had used the site to hide other young werewolf boys who were banished. Now the Lost Boys lived at Dragon Nest Academy.

"I'm stuck here in middle of Siberia," Phil grumbled. "I can't leave Angus and Mikhail unguarded, and I doubt they'll want to teleport me back when we're following a legitimate lead here. Why don't you go? You've teleported to my cabin before, so you know the way."

"I can't leave Romatech unguarded. My brother's here, but he's a rookie."

"Hey." Freemont gave him an indignant look.

"Look," Phil continued, "Roman and Gregori aren't helpless. They know how to fight. They'll be fine with your brother. And if Roman thinks it's too dangerous, then he can close Romatech for a few nights and take a vacation. He won't mind. He wants Corky captured as much as anyone. She's making a mockery of his position as Coven Master."

Phineas took a deep breath. Phil was making a lot of sense. He would discuss the matter with Roman, but it was a safe bet that Roman would urge him to check out this latest lead. As Coven Master of East Coast Vampires, Roman couldn't afford to have his authority questioned and his court decisions blatantly ignored.

"All right," Phineas conceded. "I'll go." But he still

didn't know his way around Wyoming. "Do you think any of your werewolf boys from school could go with me?"

"That's a good idea, but I'm not sure if Toni will let them go right now. You'll have to check with her."

"All right. Let Angus know what's happening. I'll e-mail a report when I have more details." Phineas hung up.

Now he'd have to teleport to the Dragon Nest Academy. And *she* was there. Phil's twin sister, Big Bad Wolfie-Girl. If he was lucky, he'd get in and out without having to see her. And her beautiful sky-blue eyes.

"So I'll be in charge here? And you're going to Wyoming?" Freemont stuffed the last bite of hamburger into his mouth.

"Yeah. Think you can handle it?"

Freemont nodded with his mouth full.

Phineas took a deep breath. "Looks like I'll be headed out West with a couple of werewolf boys."

Freemont snickered. "Yee haw! Git along, little doggies."

"I'm afraid it's not possible," Toni MacPhie said, seated behind the administrator's desk in the main office of the Dragon Nest Academy. "We start finals in a few days, so we need all the students to remain here."

Phineas groaned inwardly. It was dangerous for a Vamp to go into strange territory alone. Without a day guard, he would be too vulnerable while in his death-sleep.

He glanced at Phil's wife, Vanda, who perched on the corner of Toni's desk. She was a Vamp, so she couldn't guard him during the day, but it was better than being alone. "How about you? Want to come hunt for Corky?"

Vanda snorted. "I'd love to see that bitch in chains. She tried to sue me for a fortune."

"Well, you did assault her," Toni murmured. "You practically squeezed her head off on live television."

"She deserved it!" Vanda protested. "She was rude to Ian."

Toni grinned. "I know. I was cheering for you."

"So do you want to come, Vanda?" Phineas asked.

She made a face. "I wouldn't be much help. I'm as useless as you are during the day. And I've never ventured very far from the cabin, so I don't know the area at all."

"Do you really think Corky could be there?" Toni asked with a dubious look. "She doesn't seem like the Wild Wild West type to me."

"Our husbands call us every day, and they're not finding her," Vanda said. "Maybe Corky's doing the unexpected."

"We won't know for sure until I check it out," Phineas said. "Are you sure you can't spare one wolfie-boy?"

Vanda ran a hand through her spiky purple hair. "Normally, one of the seniors could help you, but not now. They can't graduate if they don't take their final exams."

"Can one of them postpone his tests for a week?" Phineas asked.

Toni shook her head. "Their final in Werewolf Studies requires them to shift, and the moon will be full three nights from now. I'd send Davy with you—he graduated last year—but with Phil gone, we need him here to administer the test."

"Oh my gosh!" Vanda jumped to her feet. "Why didn't I think of this before? There's a perfect solution." She gave Toni a pointed look. "Right down the hall in the teachers' lounge."

Toni sucked in a deep breath. "Of course!" She and Vanda smiled slowly and turned toward Phineas.

He stepped back. The glint in their eyes looked downright suspicious. Surely, they weren't thinking—

"No one knows the territory better," Toni said. "She grew up there."

With a gulp, he stepped back again. *Oh no. Hell no.*

"And she could guard you during the day," Vanda added.

"She'd probably kill me," he grumbled.

Vanda exchanged another sly smile with Toni, then gave Phineas a wide-eyed innocent look. "You know of whom we speak?"

"You're not setting me up with her," he growled.

"It's a job, not a date." Vanda's eyes twinkled with humor. "Unless you would like a date?"

"I'm not taking Big Bad Wolfie-Girl with me, and that's final!"

Toni's mouth twitched. "Big Bad Wolfie-Girl?"

"Sounds like a term of affection to me," Vanda murmured.

"Are you crazy?" Phineas shouted. "Why would I have any affection for her when she hates me?" Why, indeed? He had to be crazy.

Toni stood. "We'll just ask her about it."

Phineas's breath caught. "You don't have to ask her. I know why she hates me. I'm a Vamp. She hates all Vamps—"

"Whoa, Phineas," Toni interrupted him. "We're just going to ask her if she'll go to Wyoming with you." She strode toward the door.

"But I told you I'm not taking her," he insisted.

"Don't be such a wuss," Vanda fussed at him. "You'll be fine with Brynley." Her mouth twitched. "As long as you follow her Three-Step rule."

He frowned. "What's that?"

Toni snickered. "You'll have to ask her. We'll get her. She's just down the hall."

"We'll be right back." Vanda accompanied Toni into the hallway, and he heard their poorly concealed laughter.

His hands curled into fists. This was bad. He couldn't share a cabin with Brynley Jones. It would be sheer torture. In many ways. She would torment and tease him. He would waffle between wanting to jab at her or jump her.

He couldn't jump her. She was the daughter of the most powerful werewolf Pack Master in North America, a rancher with huge amounts of land, money, and influence. She was a freaking princess.

And he was a poor Vamp from the Bronx. If he laid

a finger on her, she'd probably bite it off. Hell, she'd chew all ten of his digits down to mere stubs, and then her father would sic a pack of werewolves on him to rip apart the rest of this body.

Her dad was already pissed that his eldest son, Phil, had married vampire Vanda. Pissed enough that he'd disowned Phil and declared his second son the heir to his empire.

So as much as Phineas was tempted by Brynley, he didn't dare pursue her. For her sake, as well as his own. She could end up disowned and rejected by her own people. She could lose her status as princess.

Jumping her was out of the question, so all that was left was jabbing at her to keep her at a distance. And since she always poked back, that had to mean she didn't want anything to do with him. Why would she? She could have her pick of any werewolf in the world. Someday her prince would come. And he'd be a rich and hairy Alpha dude who howled at the moon and pissed on fire hydrants.

Phineas hated him already. He hated this whole situation. Tension coiled inside him, threatening to spring into full panic. He couldn't allow Brynley to accompany him. He had to find someone else. Fast.

LaToya. She knew about Vamps and could guard him during the day. If he could explain how much he needed her help, she might agree to come with him. As a police officer, she understood the importance of catching bad guys.

Anger seethed inside him that he was forced to beg

a favor from a woman who had rejected him. *Damn.* What a desperate fool he was. He'd do anything to avoid being with Brynley.

He pulled out his cell phone, then recalled LaToya's threat to never answer a call from him. He grabbed the phone off Toni's desk, so the call would come from the Dragon Nest Academy.

"Hello?"

"Hey, LaToya." There was a pause, so he quickly told her what was going on before she could hang up. "So what do you say? You could have an all-expense-paid vacation in Wyoming while we hunt down a nasty vampire villain."

"Phineas—"

"She has to be stopped, LaToya. She betrayed vampires in the worst way, and she's killed mortals. The world would be a safer place if you help me bring her in."

There was a pause, then LaToya finally spoke. "Can't you find someone else? Why don't Lara and her husband go with you?"

"Lara's in Budapest. I told you, all the MacKay employees are across the world. There's no one else available. I wouldn't have called you if I wasn't desperate."

LaToya sighed. "I can't take a week off work on such short notice. And frankly, I'm too busy chasing down live criminals to worry about the Undead ones."

"She's really bad—"

"I'm sure she is, but you need to find someone else to help you. Good luck."

"Wait!" He stopped her from hanging up. "Look, I know you don't like vampires, but—"

"It's not that," she interrupted. "I know Lara is happy with Jack, and I know she'll eventually become a Vamp, too. It's her life and her decision, so I'm trying to be understanding."

"You mean you're starting to accept Vamps?"

"I don't want to lose Lara, so I've decided to accept Jack for her sake."

Phineas bit back a sharp reply. Three years it had taken her to come this far? If she hadn't been so damned slow, he might have had a chance with her.

"But I don't want you to get the wrong idea," LaToya continued. "Just because I'm making an exception for Jack, it doesn't mean I'm accepting the rest of you guys."

"Of course not," he gritted out.

"I'm morally opposed to the whole vampire thing."

"You don't have to explain. I know why you rejected me."

"I don't think you understand," she said quietly. "Even if you were mortal, I wouldn't go out with you."

"What?" All this time he'd thought it was his Undeadness that turned her off. It wasn't personal, he'd told himself.

LaToya huffed. "The problem is you, Phineas. I just don't like you."

Chapter Five

So who do you think is the father?" Sarah asked.

Brynley shrugged and stuffed a handful of popcorn into her mouth. She was in the teachers' lounge at the Dragon Nest Academy with Sarah, a mortal who taught preschool and elementary grades; Teddy, another mortal who served as headmaster and taught math and science; and Marta, Vanda's vampire sister who worked in the office.

The vampire sisters. Brynley couldn't see either of them without being reminded of the sister she'd had to leave behind. She missed Glynis something awful, and that just added fuel to the anger that simmered inside her. She couldn't even call Glynis. Her father might trace the call and find her.

They were watching the soap opera *All My Vampires* on the Digital Vampire Network. One of the Vamps, rich and debonair Rodrigo, had a gold-digging mortal wife named Lola, and he'd just discovered she was pregnant. Since all his sperm was dead, she'd obviously cheated on him.

"Could be the pool boy," Marta suggested.

"I hope not." Teddy wrinkled his nose. "He's only sixteen years old."

Brynley shook her head as she gathered another handful of popcorn. That wasn't too young for the Three-Step rule.

Marta used the remote control to mute a commercial for custom-made coffins. Room for two, lined with red silk, and equipped with a built-in ice chest for stashing a few bottles of Bubbly Blood.

The vampire version of a love nest, Brynley thought with a snort. She crammed more popcorn into her mouth.

"Maybe it's the gardener," Marta continued.

"Or the mailman." Sarah reached for the popcorn.

Brynley passed her the bowl. "I'm not surprised she cheated on Rodrigo. Who would want to be married to a vampire? The guy is literally dead all day."

Sarah aimed a flirtatious smile at Teddy, who sat beside her on the couch. "I definitely prefer a live boyfriend."

He smiled back, regarding her with a look akin to worship.

True love. With an inward groan, Brynley sank deeper into her comfy chair.

Marta sipped from her bottle of Chocolood. "Not all of us asked to be vampires, you know."

Brynley leaned her head back, frowning at the ceiling. She knew Marta and her sister, Vanda, had both been attacked and turned by a Malcontent. Same thing with Phineas. It wasn't his fault he was a Vamp, but it still stuck in her craw.

She hated vampires. She hated the way they'd existed for centuries by seducing the innocent so they could feed off them. They were naturally seductive, damn them. Gorgeous, mysterious, powerful, charming—it was all part of their vampire allure. And these Vamp men who took on the role of superheroes, battling the forces of evil, they were even more seductive because they appeared to be good. But if she looked past the façade, she could see their true nature. They were still vampires. Parasites. Users.

And she hated users more than anything. She'd grown up surrounded by them. Werewolves who catered to her powerful father in hopes of using him, while he encouraged it so he could use them in return. It was a constant, never-ending game of deceit and manipulation, and she'd spent most of her life as an unwitting pawn, forced to exist in an atmosphere that made her feel like a helpless, trapped bargaining chip. Used.

She was alone now, alone with her anger and resentment. She'd escaped the Lycan world, but had landed in the Undead world with another group of users. They'd used her brother for years, keeping him away from his pack and his family. Keeping him away from her when she'd needed him the most. Sure, it had been Phil's choice to remain far away from the pack. But he'd abandoned his own twin sister. He'd chosen vampires over her.

She hated them. And she hated how damned susceptible she was to vampire allure.

Especially from Phineas.

She sat up to reach for the popcorn bowl, then halted with a jerk, her gaze riveted on the television screen.

"Oh my God!" Marta set down her bottle of Chocolood. "It's the new Blardonnay commercial! Look at Dr. Phang!"

Oh yeah, she was looking. Brynley bit her bottom lip to keep the drool from escaping. Phineas was gorgeous. Broad shoulders, bulging biceps, and corded muscles that deliciously defined his bare chest and abs. He was standing on a beach with a striped towel tied around his hips. The beach was obviously fake, but who gave a damn when Phineas was standing there, proud and defiant liked a bronze god.

"Wow," Sarah breathed. "What a chest."

Teddy rolled his eyes.

"Quick! Unmute it!" Brynley snatched the remote away from Marta and punched the mute button. She couldn't miss hearing his voice.

"Hello, ladies." Phineas's deep voice filled the room.

An electric thrill sizzled through Brynley. Oh God, his voice could melt chocolate. It certainly left her feeling all warm and gooey.

"He's so handsome!" Marta exclaimed.

"Shh," Brynley hushed her so she wouldn't miss anything he said.

"Would you care to join me on the beach?" Phineas focused his dark chocolate eyes on the camera with an intensity that made Brynley forget to breathe.

"Look at the man beside you," Phineas continued.

"Now look at me. Him? Or me?" The camera zoomed in on his chest. "Yes, ladies. You made the right choice."

"Wow," Sarah breathed.

"Hey." Teddy gave her an injured look.

"He's so hot," Marta whispered.

"Shh," Brynley hushed them again.

The camera pulled back to show a beautiful blonde jogging toward Phineas, her breasts jiggling in her skimpy red bikini. "Oh yes, Dr. Phang! I want you!"

He gave her a seductive look. "Of course you do. Now look at my hand. Yes, I have the family jewels."

The blonde gasped, then the camera jumped to Phineas's hand. In his palm was a stash of loose diamonds and rubies.

"Oh, Dr. Phang! What lovely stones you have."

"All for you, baby." In a flash, the jewels were gone, and Phineas was regarding her sternly, his fists planted on his narrow hips. "What do you have for me?"

The camera shifted to a bottle clutched in her hand. "I brought your favorite drink—Blardonnay!"

Phineas smiled. "A moonlit beach, you, and Blardonnay—what more could a man want?"

"I could think of something." The blonde leaned into him and caressed his muscular chest.

Brynley's hands curled into fists.

"Later, baby. First, we'll enjoy our Blardonnay, and then—" He whipped off his towel.

Marta and Sarah squealed. Brynley's heart lurched up her throat.

He wasn't naked, but the little swimsuit he had on left

no doubt that the Love Doctor was truly gifted in his field of expertise.

"Oh, Dr. Phang." The blonde's hand drifted down his washboard abs. "Let me pop your cork."

Phineas took the bottle from her and gazed into the camera. "Remember, ladies. If you want me, you'll want my Blardonnay."

Brynley dragged in a shaky breath as the commercial ended. Another one started, one for Vampos, the vampire after-dinner mint guaranteed to get rid of blood breath, and she muted it.

"I just love the Blardonnay commercials!" Marta exclaimed. "Phineas is so hot!"

Brynley clenched her jaw shut. *Stay cool. Don't let anyone know how strongly he affects you.*

"He's a nice guy, too," Sarah added. "He helped rescue Lara and me at Apollo's compound."

"He sounds wonderful. And so *hot*!" Marta gave Brynley a sly look. "Don't you think he's hot?"

She squeezed the remote in her fist. Did they suspect her true feelings? "He's a Vamp. He's not my type."

Marta scoffed. "Handsome, muscular hunks aren't your type?"

She shrugged. "I'm used to werewolf guys. They're all well built. Phineas is nothing special."

Toni chuckled as she strode into the room. "Then you won't mind seeing him. He's waiting for you in the main office."

The remote control tumbled from her hand.

Vanda grabbed it off the floor. "I'll take care of this while you go talk to him."

"What?" Brynley whispered in a faint voice.

"You need to talk to him." Vanda's mouth twitched. "You remember how to talk?"

Her mouth dropped open. Phineas was here? He wanted to see her?

"Dr. Phang is here?" Marta pressed a hand to her chest. "Oh my gosh, do you think he would give me an autograph?"

Sarah lifted a hand. "I'd like one, too."

"He's here for *me*," Brynley snapped, then winced at the fierceness of her tone. Dammit. She was too much on edge. Her inner wolf had wakened and jumped to her defense.

She softened her voice. "I'll ask him about the autographs."

"Great! Thanks!" Marta exchanged an amused look with her sister, Vanda.

Anger sparked inside Brynley. They were finding her situation humorous. She sprawled in her chair as if she had no intention of getting up for a week. "On second thought, I have no interest in seeing him at all."

"He's not too keen about seeing you, either," Vanda said wryly.

Her fingers dug into the chair's upholstery. "Then why is he here?"

"He needs help." Toni quickly explained his mission to Wyoming and why she'd had to refuse his request for assistance from the werewolf boys. "But then we realized you were the perfect solution."

"Absolutely," Vanda agreed. "You know the territory, and you can guard him during the day."

Brynley's heart raced. Her inner wolf trembled, ecstatic at the thought of returning home. But how could she live alone with Phineas in a tiny hunting cabin? Guard him? "I'd be more tempted to kill him."

Toni snickered. "That's exactly what he said."

Ouch. Somehow that hurt, coming from him. He didn't trust her. Hell, he didn't even like her. He was always calling her ugly names like Snout-Face. She couldn't do this.

She needed a legitimate excuse, and unfortunately, she had a doozy. "There's no way I can go back to Wyoming. My father would hunt me down and force me into a marriage against my will."

"If you find yourself in a bad situation," Vanda said, "then Phineas can simply teleport you back here."

Only at nighttime. During the day, he was useless. He couldn't protect her against the numerous minions that her father controlled. She crossed her arms. "I'm not going."

Everyone regarded her with disapproving frowns. Even her inner wolf snarled at her.

"Corky must be brought to justice," Teddy said.

"Not my problem," Brynley muttered. "It's a vampire thing."

Toni helped herself to some popcorn. "Well, if that's how you feel, you'll have to tell him no."

"Right." Vanda sat next to her sister, Marta. "You can tell him."

Brynley remained seated, her anger spiking. One more game of manipulation. They thought it was amusing to force her to talk to Phineas. She jumped to her feet. "Fine! I'll tell him to buzz off. And I'll enjoy it."

She marched down the hall, then halted in the office doorway, ready to berate him from afar before making a quick exit.

He was on the phone, his back to her, and her extra-sharp hearing could pick up the voice that was talking to him.

"The problem is you, Phineas. I just don't like you."

Brynley's breath caught. Who was this woman?

Phineas stiffened. "You should have told me that before I wasted two and a half years pursuing you."

The voice on the phone heaved an exasperated sigh. "Sheesh, I was trying to chase you away from the beginning. It's not my fault if you were too stupid to get the message."

Brynley's eyes narrowed. This lady was a real bitch.

"I was being persistent," Phineas muttered. "I thought I could win you over with time."

"I don't want to be won over," the bitch insisted. "Not by a former drug dealer."

Brynley's jaw dropped. What the hell? Phineas had a dark past?

"I told you I could explain that," he said.

"I don't want to hear it! I'm subjected to stories all day long from the criminals I bring in. It's never their fault. They're always innocent. They're just victims. Blah, blah, blah. It's all a bunch of bullshit."

"I'm not a criminal, LaToya."

"Yes, you are. There's an outstanding warrant for your arrest. And if drug dealing isn't bad enough, you have this whole Love Doctor thing that really turns me off."

"That was a joke," he gritted out. "I thought it would make you laugh."

"So you're a clown?"

Brynley shook her head. This LaToya bitch was a judgmental shrew. She didn't deserve Phineas.

"I never trusted you!" LaToya's voice rose. "I know you're a sleazebag. You're always coming on to women with your slimy Dr. Phang routine. 'I'm the Love Doctor and I've got the cure.'"

Brynley's hands balled into fists. Now the bitch was mocking him. She affected a sweet, but loud voice that LaToya would be sure to hear. "Oh, Phineas, darling! When are you coming back to bed?"

He jumped. The receiver popped from his hand and clattered onto the desk as he whirled around.

She smirked at the flabbergasted look on his face. "Oh, please, Phineas! Make love to me one more time! No one makes me scream like you."

A shriek erupted from the phone. "You see? I knew you were a womanizing asshole! If you ever call me again—"

Phineas snatched up the receiver. "Not a problem. You'll never hear from me again." He slammed the receiver down, then glared at Brynley. "What the hell are you doing? You have no right to interfere in my personal life."

She lifted her chin. "I didn't want to listen to her anymore. She's a bitch."

He glowered at her. "Takes one to know one."

Ouch. "Instead of insulting me, you should be thanking me. I helped you get rid of her."

"I don't need your help."

"I believe you do. I heard you need someone to guard your dead carcass during the day."

"My dead carcass is none of your business."

She scoffed. "Then who's going to keep the field mice from nibbling on your toes?"

"I'll keep my boots on."

She took a step toward him. "It's not safe for you to be alone during the day."

"Since when would I be safe with you?"

Ouch. He really didn't trust her at all. She planted her hands on her hips. "I can show you around Wyoming and help you with your mission."

His eyes narrowed. "Are you volunteering?"

"Are you hard of hearing?"

"What about your father? I thought you ran away from him. You're not afraid—"

"You calling me a coward?" she snapped.

Phineas studied her a moment, his dark eyes searching her own.

She stared back, determined not to back down. But dammit, he could probably hear her heart racing.

"You're the bravest woman I've ever met," he said softly.

Her chest tightened. She didn't know what to say, so responded by crossing her arms. She had to be crazy, agreeing to go to Wyoming with him. But she hated the way that bitch LaToya had treated him. He deserved better than that.

And there was another reason. Ever since she'd run away from home, her inner wolf had grown increasingly pervasive. She could feel it inside her now, snarling and demanding to go home. It didn't care about Phineas or Corky. It just wanted to go home.

Phineas cleared his throat, drawing her attention. "Vanda said you would want me to follow a Three-Step rule?"

Her mouth fell open. Holy cow, she'd been set up. She might have to kill Vanda for this. And that would really upset her brother.

"What are your rules?" Phineas asked.

"Don't worry about it. I don't think they apply to you."

He stiffened. "Why not? Because I'm a Vamp?"

Because you don't like me. She quickly changed the subject. "Before I forget, Marta and Sarah want your autograph."

"Why?"

Brynley snorted. "Because Marta wants to steal your identity and become the next Blardonnay guy. She'll look great, topless with a towel around her hips. I don't think anyone will notice the difference."

Phineas frowned at her. "I don't have breasts."

"Man-boobs." Brynley motioned toward his chest. "They do stick out a little."

"That's muscle!"

She waved her hand dismissively. "The autographs, please. Your rabid fans are waiting."

He grabbed a pen and pad of paper off the desk. "One to Marta?"

"Yes, and one to Sarah."

He scrawled their names and his signature on two pieces of paper, then handed them to her. "I don't suppose you want one?"

She scoffed. "I know who you are."

"Fine." He tossed the pen and pad of paper on the desk. "Can you be ready to leave in thirty minutes?"

"Sure." She stuffed the autographs in her jeans pocket. "I suggest you pack more than a beach towel and your skimpy little swimsuit. You'll need boots, a hat, and a jacket. You're only alive at night, and it can get chilly then. And make sure you bring plenty of bottled blood."

His brow arched. "Afraid I'll bite?"

"Afraid I will?"

He stepped toward her. "Why are you doing this?"

It was obvious he didn't trust her. She lifted her chin in defiance. "Are you worried, Phineas? You should be. Who knows what I'll do to you when you're completely helpless and totally at my mercy. I painted Connor's fingernails pink, you know."

His mouth twisted with a wry look. "Do you enjoy playing with dead bodies, Brynley?"

"Maybe I just enjoy seeing you dead, bloodsucker."

"Snout-Face." He stepped closer. "I know you hate Vamps, so why are you doing this?"

She shrugged. "I heard you were desperate. Must be your charming personality. It's left you all alone with no one to help you."

"I'm charming enough that you agreed."

"I was your last choice."

His jaw clenched. "You think so?"

"You wanted some of the boys to go with you, but they can't leave school. I'm the last one you wanted."

His eyes darkened as he stared at her.

She didn't look away, even though her heart pounded in her ears.

He lifted a hand, then stopped with his fingers a mere inch from her cheek. "You have no idea what I want."

The intensity of his gaze made her arms pebble with gooseflesh.

He stepped back, lowering his hand. "I'll return for you in thirty minutes." His form wavered, then vanished.

She dragged in a deep breath to calm her racing heart, then reached up to press her fingertips against the cheek he'd come so close to touching.

Oh God, what had she gotten herself into? She'd let her emotions dictate her actions. And her inner wolf. It was thrilled to be going home. Excited that in a few nights, it would be running through the forest, feeling completely free.

As a teenager, she'd been trained to pay attention

to the desires of the inner wolf. Its instincts were raw and simple. Animalistic, but blatantly honest. *Trust the wolf*, the elders had always told her. *The wolf knows best.*

But this time, she feared the wolf was wrong. Going to Wyoming was dangerous. If her father found her, he'd drag her back home. She would end up losing her freedom.

And she couldn't let Phineas know she was hopelessly attracted to him. She'd have to be strong. And ruthless. Or she might end up losing her heart.

Chapter Six

*W*hat the hell are you wearing?" Brynley demanded.

"Polite, as always," Phineas muttered. Thirty minutes had passed, and he'd returned to the main office at the Dragon Nest Academy to pick up Brynley.

He glanced down at his stylish new clothes. Maybe a little too stylish, but Leroy of Leroy's House of Class had personally selected his new Western wardrobe with assurances that he looked one hundred percent authentic.

He hooked his thumbs into the snakeskin belt that sported a huge buffalo-shaped brass buckle. "I'm dressed like a cowboy now. I thought it would be best to fit in—"

"Where? On stage at the Grand Ole Opry?" Brynley moved closer and skimmed her fingertips across his white silk shirt. "Fringe?"

His chest expanded in response to her touch, so he stepped back, out of her reach.

Her gaze lifted to his head. "Oh, God help us. Your hat is . . . sparkly."

He removed the black Stetson. All the cowboy hats at Leroy's House of Class had sparkled. Some had sparkled all over. He'd thought he'd done well, selecting a plain black hat with a narrow band of red sequins. "I went with the understated look. It seemed more buck."

Her eyes widened. "Are you kidding me?"

"No. The black hat matches the black fringe on my shirt, and the red sequins go with the embroidered red roses. But Leroy wanted me to pick the red hat, because it had lots of sequins and some feathers—"

"Enough!" She snatched the Stetson out of his hands, ripped the red sequined band off, then tossed the hat onto the desk, where it landed next to her plain leather handbag and duffel bag. "Maybe I can find some scissors to cut off the fringe." She rummaged in a drawer.

Phineas frowned. "Is it that bad?"

"Do you want to live through the night? If we go into a bar with you looking like—"

"Why would we go into a bar?"

"To ask questions. We're hunting for Corky, right? You go around looking like that, and I'll have to break some arms."

He stiffened. "I can take care of myself."

"Not during the day. You'll be totally helpless."

"I'll be sleeping in the basement during the day. And my clothes won't be a problem." He gave her a pointed look. "I won't be wearing any."

She gulped.

Damn but he enjoyed shocking her.

"Well." Her cheeks blushed a pretty pink as she

slammed the desk drawer shut. "You'll still have to wear clothes when you're awake, so I'll run up to my brother's room and see if he has anything you can borrow." Her gaze drifted over him once again. "You look about the same size. Actually, those . . . jeans you're wearing will do just fine."

Was it his imagination or did her eyes linger on his groin area a little too long? "Are you sure? I didn't know if I should go with a zipper or a button fly. I've got a zipper here—"

"You're *fine*!" Her blush deepened. "I'll be right back." She rushed from the office.

He took a seat, smiling to himself. There was something about Big Bad Wolfie-Girl. He was always tense with excitement around her. Part of him longed to touch her. The other part urged him to run. Fast. No doubt, that was the part controlled by his brain. Unfortunately, his brain never worked well around her.

She was part animal, that was the problem. It gave her a wild, aggressive nature, and that appealed to a primitive need inside him. An ancient and raw caveman need to possess her.

But the civilized part of him knew Brynley was not the kind of woman who should ever be possessed. She was a free spirit. A wolf. A princess.

She would always be beyond his reach.

He drew in a deep breath and let it out slowly. In the last thirty minutes, he'd zipped through a bunch of tasks as quickly as possible. He'd stocked an ice chest full of bottled blood, then he'd teleported it to the cabin.

It had been a few years since he'd been to Phil's cabin in Wyoming, and a quick inspection had left him pleasantly surprised. Phil had modernized the place into a vacation home for himself and Vanda, and it now had electricity and running water. A bathroom and utility room had been added onto the back of the cabin.

It was still basically one room—combination den and kitchen with a table and chairs, and some furniture arranged around a large stone fireplace. A trapdoor led to the basement, which was now furnished with a king-sized bed. A second bed was in the loft above the kitchen, which could be reached by climbing a ladder.

He made several trips to the cabin, teleporting back and forth from Romatech. He brought a laptop and Internet card, plus a stash of weapons and ammo from the security office. Then he raided the cafeteria for food to stock the refrigerator and pantry. Brynley was doing him a big favor, agreeing to go with him, so he wanted to make sure she was comfortable.

With the cabin ready, he turned his attention to himself. The MacKay uniform of khaki pants and navy polo shirt wasn't going to blend in. He needed to remain as inconspicuous as possible. Freemont told him there was Western wear at Leroy's House of Class, so he made a quick trip there.

Freemont also remembered there was a great pair of cowboy boots in the wardrobe closet at DVN, so Phineas teleported there to grab them. Back at Romatech, Laszlo had embedded a tracking device into one of the boots while he packed a duffel bag with underwear, socks, T-shirts, jeans, toiletries, and his fancy new shirts from Leroy's House of Class.

He teleported the duffel bag to the cabin, then back at Romatech, he went over all the job details with Freemont one more time.

"It's all right, dude," Freemont assured him. "I got it covered. Besides, you're just a phone call away."

"I can't be sure I'll always get a connection," Phineas warned him. "I'll be out in the middle of werewolf country."

"With Big Bad Wolfie-Girl." Freemont snickered.

Phineas winced. He shouldn't have shared that name with his little brother. "This is a business trip."

"Yeah, but I know what kind of business the Love Doctor's into." Freemont slapped him on the back. "Just don't let her bite you."

Phineas groaned inwardly as he waited in the school office. He had to be crazy, taking Brynley with him. He glanced at his watch. She'd been gone ten minutes. Maybe she'd changed her mind about going. To his surprise, that thought didn't bring him relief, but a twinge of sadness.

He enjoyed being with her, looking at her beautiful sky-blue eyes, creamy skin, and mane of wild hair. He even enjoyed the way she prodded and poked at him. It was a challenge to keep up with her. And fun.

A smile tugged at his mouth when he recalled how she'd given LaToya a shock. She'd been outrageous, calling him back to bed, claiming he made her scream. He'd known, of course, that she was joking, but his groin had still responded. Now he had to wonder—why had she come to his defense? Had she felt angry on his behalf?

No, he pushed that thought aside. She hated vampires. She'd made that clear many times in the past. Still, he couldn't help but wonder. Had she objected to his clothes because she enjoyed picking on him, or was she trying to protect him? And if she was concerned about protecting him, was she doing it out of a sense of duty or because she actually liked him?

He sighed. He needed to stop looking for emotions that didn't exist. He'd wasted two and a half years imagining that LaToya actually liked him. How pathetic it would be to make the same mistake twice.

He heard footsteps approaching and rose to his feet.

Brynley entered with a few shirts draped over her arm. Behind her, a group of women hurried into the room. Toni, Caitlyn, Olivia, Marta, Vanda, and Sarah. They greeted him as Brynley dropped the shirts on the desk.

He nodded at them. "Hello, ladies."

They exchanged looks and giggled.

"I told you he'd say it," Sarah whispered.

"He sounded just like he does on TV," Marta added.

Olivia smiled at him. "We really enjoy your commercials, Phineas."

"Okay." Brynley shook out a plaid shirt and gave the women an annoyed look. "You heard his sexy voice. You can go now."

Sexy voice? Phineas studied her, not sure what to

think. One time she'd told Connor and Marielle that he had a tight ass, but he could never figure out if she was complimenting him or insulting him.

"Try this on." She handed him the shirt.

He glanced at the blue plaid shirt, then at the other women. They showed no sign of leaving.

"Come on, guys." Brynley waved her hands to shoo them away. "You're embarrassing him."

"How could he be embarrassed?" Vanda asked. "He has a great chest."

"And he has to know it," Marta added. "Why else would he show it off on television?"

He frowned. Did people think he was an exhibition-ist? "I'm sure the clothes will fit. Brynley and I need to get going."

The women all moaned with disappointment.

"Please, Dr. Phang," Sarah whined. "We're your big-gest fans."

"Oh, get a grip," Brynley fussed at them. "It's just a chest. If you've seen one, you've seen them all."

Oh really? Phineas had a sudden desire to prove her wrong. He dropped the blue plaid shirt on the chair, then unbuttoned his fringed shirt with vampire speed and tossed it on the floor.

The ladies squealed and clapped, but he ignored them, focusing only on Brynley to see how she reacted. Her gaze darted over him, then quickly looked away as if she wasn't interested.

With so many people in the room, he found it diffi-cult to focus on her heartbeat alone, but he could swear that hers was the one that was pounding the fastest. And her cheeks were blushing again. She *was* affected, dammit. He could feel it.

His own heartbeat sped up as he put on Phil's blue plaid shirt. Instead of buttons, there were snaps. A vision flitted through his mind of Brynley popping all the snaps open as she ripped off his shirt. And then they would get naked and it would be—

"A perfect fit!" Vanda announced.

He jumped. Oh, she meant the shirt. He pushed aside the vision.

"That's wonderful!" Marta clapped her hands. "Now we can send you off to Wyoming looking your best."

Toni stepped forward to shake his hand. "Best of luck to you and Brynley."

"Thank you." He was going to need luck. And a lot of cold showers.

All the women shook his hand and hugged Brynley. Vanda stuffed her husband's shirts into a Dragon Nest Academy tote bag and handed it to him.

Brynley swung her handbag over her shoulder and grabbed hold of her duffel bag. "I'm ready." She approached him hesitantly.

He slipped a hand around her waist to draw her closer. "You'll have to hold on to me when we teleport."

"I know how it works," she muttered, then placed her hands on his shoulders while staring at a white button on his shirt.

"I'm up here," he whispered.

Her gaze lifted.

"That's better."

"That's debatable. Can we go now?"

He pulled her closer. "You need to hold me tighter."

She made a face but slipped her hands around his neck. "Are we there yet?"

He glanced over at the ladies, who were still watching with smiles on their faces. "Good-bye, ladies."

They waved as everything went black.

Brynley hung her shirts and jeans in the armoire in the loft. She'd packed light for this trip, knowing the cabin now boasted a washer and dryer and a fully stocked bathroom.

She had to admit she was impressed by how much Phineas had managed to do in thirty minutes. The pantry and refrigerator had food, and the kitchen table was covered with pistols, knives, two rifles, and ammo. She'd figured their first task would be a trip to the grocery store and gun shop, but it was all taken care of.

She climbed down the ladder to the ground floor, then peered through the open trapdoor. He'd gone down into the basement a few minutes earlier to settle in.

Since Phil and Vanda came here often on vacation, the basement had been made cozier for Vanda's death-sleep. It now sported a real bed and bedroom furniture, two recliners, and a flat-screen television. Obviously, Phil spent a lot of time down there with Vanda.

"Need any help?" she asked.

"No, I'm almost done," he called up.

"You took down the ladder." She spotted it on the cellar floor.

"I don't need it. I can levitate in or out."

But she couldn't. "You don't want me coming down there to check on you?"

"No need. Once I fall into my death-sleep, I'm not going anywhere."

"You're just afraid of what I'll do." She straightened with a smile. "I think I'll draw a rainbow and unicorn on your chest with permanent markers. It'll be so—"

"Don't you dare," he growled, suddenly behind her.

She squealed, jumped away from him, and teetered on the edge of the open trapdoor, her arms flailing.

He grabbed her and pulled her back against his chest. "It's okay. I've got you."

"*No!*" She spun away from him and shoved him hard in the chest. "Don't ever attack me from behind!"

"I didn't attack you. I rescued you."

She glared at him, her heart pounding, her whole body trembling. Tears blurred her vision, and she blinked them away. Her inner wolf hissed. *Dammit.* She hated to show any weakness. "You teleported behind me. Don't ever do it again."

His eyes narrowed. "Okay."

Damn. He was wondering why she'd freaked. She strode toward the kitchen area. *Get a grip.* "I think we should eat while we wait."

He closed the trapdoor. "Wait for what?"

She exhaled with relief. He wasn't going to ask why she'd freaked. "Transportation."

She opened the refrigerator and took out a bottle of blood for him and a cola for herself. "While you were busy bringing supplies here, I was busy, too. I called a few female friends who live close by, and they agreed to help us. They both have sons at Dragon Nest." She unscrewed the top off her cola. "I have to warn you, though. If we run into any werewolf guys, you have to act like you never met these women. If their husbands find out—"

"They'd get in trouble for helping you?" Phineas stuck his bottle of blood into the microwave. "Why? Because you left home?"

"No, because of the Lost Boys at school. They were all banished." Brynley took a sip of cola. "That means they're dead to the pack, and their families can't have anything to do with them."

"That's terrible."

She shrugged. "It's the way it's always been. The dads go along with it 'cause it's the law, and they don't want to get kicked out, too. The pack is everything to them. But the moms—well, they tend to see things differently. No pack can tell them to stop caring for their children."

Phineas nodded. "Good for them."

Lights flashed outside.

"That could be one of them now." Brynley rushed to the front window and peered through a narrow gap between the window frame and the curtains. She needed to make sure it was Sherry or Trudy before stepping outside. "If it's one of my father's men, I'll hide in the laundry room while you go outside to meet him."

She glanced back at Phineas. "Tell him you're one of Phil's friends, and he's letting you stay here a few days. Don't let him inside the cabin. He might pick up my scent."

"Got it." Phineas strode to the kitchen table and loaded a clip into an automatic pistol.

A pickup truck pulling a horse trailer came to a stop in the gravel driveway.

Brynley exhaled in relief as she saw a woman emerging from the truck. "It's Trudy. Corey's mom." She rushed over to her handbag she'd left on the sofa, pulled out two envelopes, then hurried out the front door.

"Trudy!" She met her in front of the truck.

"Brynley!" Trudy hugged her, then stepped back to look her over. "You're looking good."

"Thanks. And thank you so much for helping us out."

"It's the least I can do. How is Corey?"

"He's great. I saw him about thirty minutes ago and told him I'd be seeing you, so . . ." Brynley waved an envelope in the air.

"He wrote to me?" Trudy snatched the letter from Brynley's hand and pressed it to her chest. "Thank you! I thank God every day that you were able to find a home and a school for my boy. Is he eating all right?"

"Of course. The food is great at Dragon Nest. I swear I've gained five pounds—"

With a gasp, Trudy stiffened.

"What?" Brynley turned to see what Trudy was staring at with such an alarmed look.

"There's a man on the porch," Trudy whispered.

"That's Phineas. Remember, I said there would be two of us?"

"But he's . . ." Trudy stepped closer. "Honey, he's not one of us."

"He's a good guy, a friend of my brother's." Brynley glanced back at Phineas, who was staring into the woods, frowning. No doubt he could hear everything with his supersensitive vampire ears.

"But you're alone here with him?" Trudy asked. "If your father finds out—"

"He won't." Brynley gave her a pointed look. "You never saw him. Or me. Just like we never saw you."

Trudy took a deep breath. "Right."

Brynley glanced at the horse trailer. "Your husband isn't going to wonder why two of your horses are missing?"

"He was invited to your dad's ranch in Montana for the monthly hunt, and you know he can't refuse that. So he'll be gone for a full week."

Brynley nodded. Her father held a huge hunt every month at the full moon. No werewolf would dare refuse an invitation from the Supreme Pack Master. It was considered a great honor. "Have you seen my sister lately?"

"A few weeks ago." Trudy gave her a sad smile. "You miss her?"

"Yeah." Brynley looked away, determined not to get emotional.

"Well, let me get these horses into the barn for you." Trudy strode to the back of the horse trailer. "And I brought some hay in case you didn't have any."

"That's perfect. Thank you." Brynley followed her, then noticed Phineas had come down the front steps to stand on the grass.

"Horses?" he asked.

"Sure." She walked toward him. "In case we need to go off-road."

"Isn't that what four-wheelers are for?" He grimaced at the first horse being led out of the trailer.

Brynley smiled slowly. "You've never ridden a horse before, have you?"

"Never wanted to," Phineas muttered.

The horse pranced about, clearly upset.

"I don't think he's too happy about it, either," Phineas added.

"She," Brynley corrected him. "That's a mare. And she's probably nervous because she's picking up your scent. It would be different from ours."

"Right," he grumbled. "Because I'm not one of *you*."

She winced. So he had heard Trudy's remark. "I'm afraid werewolves tend to be a bit clannish."

"A bit?" he asked wryly.

She shrugged as she watched Trudy lead the mare and a gelding toward the barn. "We've learned over the centuries that it's best to stick together. It's basic self-preservation."

"Why would a horse get upset over *my* scent?" Phineas asked. "Don't you guys smell like a pack of wolves? How do you even keep horses and cows? It's like a fox guarding the chicken coop. Seems like they'd get one sniff of you and run away."

Brynley grinned. "My father's been ranching for over a hundred years. The animals are used to our scent. Come on, help me get the hay into the barn."

With Phineas's superior vampire strength, he had no trouble transporting whole bales of hay to the barn. Brynley introduced him to Trudy, then brought her up-to-date on her son's progress at school while Phineas finished moving the hay.

A Honda Civic pulled up next to the pickup truck, and Brynley and Trudy strode from the barn to greet the driver.

"Sherry!" Brynley hugged her. "Thank you for coming."

"No problem." Sherry handed her the car keys. "It's all yours for a week. And the tank is full. How is Gavin doing?"

"He's great." Brynley retrieved the second envelope from her jacket pocket. "He wrote a letter for you."

"Oh thank you!" Sherry grabbed the envelope. "I can't thank you enough!"

"That goes for both of us," Trudy said.

Sherry's gaze shifted to Phineas as he emerged from the barn. "Is that young man staying here with you?"

"Young is right," Trudy murmured. "I think he's only about twenty-three."

"Well." Sherry's mouth twitched as she regarded Brynley. "Are you a wolf or a cougar, girl?"

She gritted her teeth. As far as she was concerned, she didn't look any older than Phineas. Sure, she was thirty, but as soon as werewolves reached maturity, their aging process slowed to a near halt. That was how they managed to live for five centuries.

And although Phineas had been transformed at a young age, that was a few years ago. They had to be fairly close to each other's age now.

With a start, she realized she was mentally defending herself and Phineas as a couple. And they weren't. They couldn't be.

Sherry's eyes widened as she caught Phineas's scent. "He's not one of us."

"I know," Brynley ground out.

"A shame," Trudy said. "He's incredibly strong. You should have seen him tossing around those bales of hay."

"Hmm." Sherry gave Brynley a pointed look. "Great stamina, too?"

"I wouldn't know about that," she muttered.

"*Yet*," Sherry added, then she and Trudy snickered.

Brynley sighed. They thought Phineas was her mortal boy toy. A logical mistake, since werewolves tended to be highly sexual creatures. "This is a business trip."

"Right," Trudy murmured. "Because there's so much business going on around here."

Brynley glanced over at Phineas. He was standing by the barn, pretending not to listen, but there was a definite glint of amusement in his eyes.

She turned back to the women. "Thank you for helping us. And remember, you didn't see us here."

Sherry nodded. "I understand."

"Ready to go?" Trudy asked her.

"Yep." Sherry climbed into the passenger seat of the pickup, then Trudy drove off, pulling the empty horse trailer behind her.

"All right." Brynley waved the car keys in her hand as Phineas approached. "We've got wheels."

"And horse power." Phineas glanced back at the barn, frowning.

"So what's our first move?" Brynley asked.

"We track down the guy who was bitten."

"I thought he didn't remember much."

Phineas shrugged. "I can use vampire mind control to take a look inside his head."

Brynley grimaced. She hated the way vampires could manipulate people's minds. "Bloodsucker."

The corner of his mouth curled up. "Snout-Face."

Chapter Seven

*P*hineas frowned as he slipped a knife into the sheath he'd attached around his calf so that it nestled just inside his cowboy boot. He'd made one simple decision, that they would teleport to the medical clinic, and Brynley had gone ballistic.

He recalled the way she'd reacted when he'd teleported behind her. She'd yelled at him then, and now she was shouting again. Were all werewolves this high-strung? She was behaving like one of those over-bred, expensive little dogs that yapped all the time. He couldn't recall Phil ever acting like this. Apparently, the little princess was used to always getting her way.

"I can't believe this!" She glared at him, her hands on her hips. "I go to all this trouble to make sure you have a car, and you don't even want to use it?"

He tugged his pants leg down and straightened. "I explained why—"

"You don't appreciate what I've done. Or the trouble those ladies went to."

"I do—"

"Then let's drive the damned car!"

Yap, yap, yap. Would he have to put a muzzle on her? "Brynley—"

"Don't you understand? I want to be more than just a babysitter for you when you're dead. I want to help you when you're awake."

That gave him pause. It didn't sound like something a spoiled princess would say. He dragged a hand over his short hair, wishing he could figure her out. "You are helping. I'm really glad we have the car. At some point, we'll need it." He wasn't so sure about the damned horses, though. "I thought it was very clever, the way you arranged it all."

She scowled at him. "Now you're just being condescending."

Damn, she was touchy. "I mean it. I think you're very clever. And brave. You and your friends have got this whole underground female liberation thing going on. And you're the leader. It's radical. Rebellious. Totally cool."

Her cheeks turned pink. "It's . . . no big deal."

"It *is* big. And it's gutsy. I like it."

She looked away and waved a dismissive hand. "Someone had to help the Lost Boys."

Phineas blinked when it finally clicked. She had trouble accepting a compliment. And that seemed really strange. A princess should be used to flattery, but obviously, Brynley wasn't.

What if he'd misinterpreted other things about her? He'd always thought her anger stemmed from being a spoiled princess who would throw a temper tantrum if she wasn't getting her way. But what if she was angry because she never got her way? What if her prickly nature was due to a lifetime of criticism rather than compliments?

It was a bizarre theory, so he needed to put it to the test one more time. "You know, your brother's really proud of you. Brags about you all the time."

Her blush deepened. She opened her mouth to speak, then closed it and looked away.

Amazing. She didn't know what to do with a compliment. And even more amazing—he'd found a guaranteed way to shut her up. It was sad, though, if she'd grown up never receiving any kind words. He knew she'd run away from home because her dad had tried to force her into an unwanted marriage. Maybe the dad had a long history of being an overbearing jerk.

He slipped on a shoulder holster. "You know what I really like about your underground rebellion? The way you're sticking it to your dad."

She flinched. "I . . . he . . . this has nothing to do with him. And I still think we should take the car."

Man, did she change the subject in a hurry. Some major denial going on. He strongly suspected dear old dad *was* the source of her problems. Which meant, he thought with a wry smile, that he and Brynley had something in common after all.

And she wasn't the spoiled princess he had thought. She'd risked everything to help the Lost Boys, and she'd given up her cushy life when she ran away from home.

Damn. The more he got to know her, the more he liked her. And admired her. *Don't think about it. Stick to business.*

He checked his automatic pistol to make sure it was loaded, then slipped it into the shoulder holster. "The hospital is in Buffalo. It could take over an hour to drive there, and we can teleport there in just a second."

"It's a twenty-four-hour emergency room," she argued. "There'll be people there. We can't just pop in and scare everybody."

"Don't worry about that." He slipped a large sheepskin jacket on to conceal his weapon. "I can erase people's memories if I need to."

She made a face at him. "You seem awfully eager to use your vampire mind control."

"You seem awfully sensitive about it."

"I'm just saying you'd better not try it on me. Mess with me and I'll mess with you while you're in your death-sleep. I could do something terrible like . . . donate one of your kidneys."

He grinned. "Don't worry. I have no desire to invade your brain." Her body, yes, but not her brain. "Some places are just too scary to visit."

She scoffed. "That's right. I'm so complicated you'd get lost and never find your way out."

That was the problem. He wouldn't want to find his way out.

He checked the information he'd written about the emergency room. "I'm going to call now and teleport. Are you coming with me?"

She hesitated. "I can't let any werewolves see me."

"I understand." He extended a hand toward her. "I can protect you."

She took a small step in his direction. "Can you avoid using my name in public? My dad's a powerful land-owner, so even mortals could recognize my name. And if the news gets back to him—"

"I got it." He slipped his hand around her waist and urged her closer. "We have to keep you secret."

She placed her hands on his chest. "I don't mean to sound paranoid about it. I just don't want to be forced to marry against my will."

"I'd never let that happen."

She glanced up at him. "You don't know how ruth-less my father can be."

He gripped her tightly around the waist. "You don't know how determined I can be."

Her eyes widened, and her heartbeat accelerated. "Why are you willing to protect me?"

Because no matter how much she fussed and snarled, it was music to his ears. When he breathed in her scent, he was in heaven. And when he gazed into her sky-blue eyes, an eternity wasn't long enough.

But he couldn't tell her that, so he shrugged. "I don't like people to be unhappy."

She snorted. "You don't even consider me 'people.' You call me Snout-Face."

He smiled and tapped the end of her nose. "But it's such a beautiful snout."

Her mouth fell open, drawing his gaze there. Soft,

luscious lips, ripe for kissing and sweet to taste. He pulled her close, and his groin hardened as her lips turned a rosy pink.

She inhaled sharply. "What the—?"

He stiffened with the sudden realization that the whole cabin was now tinted pink. And that could mean only one thing. His eyes had turned red.

"Excuse me." He looked away, squeezing his eyes shut. *Shit.* He'd gotten hot from just touching her nose?

"Are you all right? You look like you're in pain."

He gritted his teeth. "It's nothing. Just a vampire thing. It'll pass." Although it was difficult to ignore her sweet body pressed up against his.

"Excuse me a minute." He zoomed at vampire speed into the bathroom and splashed cold water on his face. *Shit.* He hadn't made it through one night without his eyes betraying him. His attraction to her was stronger than he'd thought.

He took a deep breath and closed his eyes. What he needed was self-control. He pictured a snowy blizzard in his mind, then a pack of growling wolves. Bared teeth. Snapping jaws. They hated him. They wanted to rip him to shreds. And Brynley was leader of the pack.

He opened his eyes. His image didn't show up in the bathroom mirror, but the room was no longer pink, so his vision must have returned to normal.

He dashed back to the table and grabbed his cell phone. "Let's get going." He dialed the number of the emergency room and wrapped an arm around Brynley without looking at her.

When a woman answered, he teleported, taking Brynley with him.

Nothing? Ha! Brynley glanced quickly around the emergency room's waiting area. It was empty, except for the mortal receptionist. No werewolves in sight. She was safe. Safe enough to freak out over what had just happened. If it was nothing, why had Phineas run off so fast to the bathroom?

A vampire thing? That was a huge understatement. She knew good and well what red glowing eyes meant. Vanda had explained it to her and the angel, Marielle. A vampire's eyes turned red when he wanted sex.

And that meant Phineas was attracted to her! Her heart lurched up her throat. Why hadn't she realized this before? Well, how could she when the rascal was always tormenting her and calling her Snout-Face? That was not the way to win a woman's affections.

Her heart plummeted. The conclusion was obvious. Phineas was rude because he didn't want to win her affections. That was why he'd shot off to the bathroom like the hounds from hell were after him. He didn't want to get involved with a werewolf.

Well. She squared her shoulders. She didn't want to get involved with a vampire, so there. They were even.

And alone.

It was a bloody shame. While all the Lycan males would want her for her werewolf status, Phineas rejected her for it.

Her heart sank even further. His red glowing eyes

were probably nothing more than an indication that he was susceptible to the Three-Step rule. It was a theory she'd come up with years ago that at any given time, a man's thoughts were only three steps away from sex. She should have known it would apply to Phineas. He was about the sexiest man she'd ever met. He was probably attracted to every woman he met, and his eyes were constantly turning red.

After all, he called himself the Love Doctor. And he was the Blardonnay Guy, too. Every woman who watched DVN wanted him. She had a sudden urge to slap his handsome face. And then kiss it to make it better. She groaned inwardly. The man had no right being so sexy. It had to be that damned vampire allure.

She glanced at him. He'd been quiet since they arrived, but she figured his brain was busy zapping the receptionist with vampire mind control. He approached the receptionist's desk, staring intently at the woman sitting there. The nurse had gasped when they'd teleported into the waiting room, but now she was simply gazing at Phineas with a blank look.

He smiled at her. "I believe you had a patient here a few days ago with bite marks on his neck?"

Brynley joined him at the counter. "Can you tell us his name?"

The nurse looked at her, then shook her head slightly as if she were dispelling cobwebs from her mind. "Are you from the newspaper? We figured you guys would show up eventually with a bunch of questions, but I'm afraid I can't discuss the case with you."

Phineas leaned close to Brynley and whispered, "You messed up my control. Let me handle this."

She shot him an irritated look, but he ignored her and refocused on the nurse, who soon regained her glassy-eyed blank expression.

"We're from the Centers for Disease Control." He whipped out his wallet and flashed a credit card at her.

"I see." The nurse nodded. "How can I help you?"

"I'm Inspector Mc—" Phineas halted, obviously having second thoughts about using his real name.

"Man-boob," Brynley finished for him.

He stiffened.

"What can I do for you, Inspector McMan-boob?" the nurse asked.

He gritted his teeth. "It's muscle."

"Inspector Muscle?" the nurse asked.

"Yes. Exactly." He gave Brynley a triumphant look. "And this is my assistant, Nurse—"

"Doctor," Brynley corrected him.

"Doctor . . ." He glanced down at her chest. "A-cup."

"B-cup!"

He arched a brow. "You'll have to prove it."

She lifted her chin. "Maybe I will."

With a smirk, he turned back to the nurse. "We need to see the file on the patient who came in with bite marks."

She stood. "That would be Jason Pritchard. One moment, please." She wandered into the adjoining office that housed the file cabinets.

Brynley leaned close to him and whispered, "I know

why a Vamp's eyes turn red. Vanda told us." She stifled a grin when he visibly gulped. Let him worry about that for a while.

He glanced at her with a stern look. "We'll discuss it later." Again his gaze dropped. "Doctor B-cup."

"Inspector McMan-bo—"

"It's muscle," he interrupted her.

"You'll have to prove it."

"Maybe I will." He turned back to the nurse as she came forward with the file. "Thank you." He opened it on the counter.

Brynley sidled up closer so she could see what was in the file. The top page listed all the vital information about Jason Pritchard.

Phineas handed that page to the nurse. "Will you make a copy of this for us, please?"

"Of course, Inspector Muscle." She took the paper and strode into the adjoining office.

Phineas pointed at the bottom of another page. "He was released this morning."

"Yes." Brynley glanced over her shoulder when she heard the emergency room door opening, then quickly turned her back as a man entered and his scent wafted toward her.

Werewolf.

Beside her, Phineas stiffened. He opened his jacket, the side without the shoulder holster, then abruptly pulled her against his chest and covered her halfway with his jacket.

Brynley let out a surprised and muffled moan, her

face pressed against his chest. A very hard chest. He'd been right about the muscle.

She listened to the werewolf's steps as he approached the receptionist's desk and came to a stop behind her. She winced. He would smell werewolf, too. Hopefully, he would think the scent was coming from Phineas.

"Where's the damned nurse?" the werewolf growled. "I think I cracked a rib."

"That's gotta hurt," Phineas said with a sympathetic tone.

Obviously, this werewolf wasn't an Alpha, Brynley thought. Or he would have simply shifted to wolf form and back to heal himself.

"Yeah, I fell off a damned ladder," the werewolf grumbled. "What are you here for?"

"Oh, it's not me. It's my girlfriend here. Betsy. She's in a lot of pain."

Brynley let out a miserable-sounding moan.

"There, there, darlin'." Phineas patted her on the back. "We'll get your medication. Don't go psycho on me again, okay?"

Psycho? She pinched him underneath his jacket and heard him wince.

"She's got leprosy, you know," Phineas continued. "Goes a little crazy when a body part falls off."

"*What?*" the werewolf squeaked.

Brynley smiled as she heard him scurrying to the other side of the room.

"Here's your paper, Inspector Muscle," the nurse said.

"Thank you," Phineas answered. "Let's go, Betsy." He steered her toward the door with her face still hidden beneath his jacket.

She exhaled with relief as they stepped onto the sidewalk.

Phineas paused. "Okay, I released the nurse from my control, and she won't remember us. Let's go."

Brynley ran around to the back of the building with him. "*Leprosy?* You made me a leper?"

"It worked. It kept the wolf dude away from you." He stuffed the paper from the clinic into a jacket pocket as he scanned their surroundings. "Coast is clear. Let's teleport back."

With a smile, she slipped her hands around his neck. "Thank you for protecting me, Inspector Muscle."

"Anytime, Betsy B-cup." His dark chocolate eyes twinkled as he flashed his perfect smile at her, and a flood of desire almost knocked her off her feet.

She tightened her grip around his neck. She'd felt twinges before around Phineas, pleasant little bursts of lust that passed quickly, but this—this was a strong surge that swept over her entire body and clung to her, refusing to let go. This was a desire that went past the physical. It was seeping into her soul.

"Are you all right?" he whispered.

He knows. She shook her head. "I'm in trouble."

"We both are." His eyes glinted with a hint of red, then everything went black.

Chapter Eight

*M*uch to Brynley's disappointment, Phineas simply let go of her when they arrived at the cabin. He didn't even look at her, just retrieved the paper about Jason Pritchard from his jacket pocket and studied it.

She folded her arms over her chest. "Aren't we going to discuss this?"

"Okay. This Jason dude lives in Sheridan. I think we should call his number and—"

"That's not what I'm talking about."

He gave her an irritated look. "It's what I'm talking about. I'm gonna drink some blood, then I'll teleport to Jason's house. You can come with me if you want."

She glared at him as he strode toward the refrigerator. "I saw your eyes turn red twice now. Are you going to deny that you're attracted to me?"

"No." He stuffed a bottle of blood into the microwave.

Not the most romantic of confessions, but it still made her heartbeat speed up. "So you like me?"

He glanced at her. "Don't get excited. Nothing's going to happen."

Ouch. "No need to be rude."

"I'm just being realistic."

"Well, good. That's all I'm asking, that we both face reality. And the truth is we're . . . mildly attracted to each other."

He scoffed. "You call that the truth?"

"Yes." She grabbed a bottle of water from the fridge. "You already admitted you're attracted to me. You can't take it back."

"I *am* attracted." He retrieved his bottle of blood from the microwave. "But there's nothing mild about it."

The bottled water slipped from her hand and tumbled onto the wooden floor. She snatched it up quickly. "Damned thing is slippery."

He took a sip of blood. "It's simple. We're here to do a job. We do it as quickly as possible, then go back to our normal lives and put this all behind us."

She groaned inwardly. He thought that was simple? About as simple as torture. "What about our attraction?"

"What about it?" He strode toward the couch, then sat and stared at the empty fireplace. "It would be wrong for us to get involved. You know as well as I do that it could never work. And never last."

She winced. Part of her acknowledged that he was right, but another part wanted to curl up on the floor and cry. It hurt. Hurt enough that she wanted to hurt him back.

He took a long swig from his bottle, then glanced at her. "How can you be attracted to me? Did you stop hating vampires all of a sudden?"

"No. I think you're a disgusting bunch of parasites and users." She gave him a wry look as she wrenched the top off her bottle. "But don't take it personally."

With a frown, he plunked his booted feet onto the coffee table. "Then it's good you haven't forgotten I'm a vampire."

"No, I haven't. That's why I ignored my feelings for so long. You have to admit we're horribly, dreadfully mismatched."

He grimaced. "I wouldn't say it's that bad."

"Oh, it is. A real disaster waiting to happen."

His eyes narrowed. "I guess your father would find me totally unsuitable."

"That goes without saying." Though to be honest, she couldn't care less what her father thought.

Phineas gritted his teeth. "He'd never accept a poor guy from the Bronx for his princess."

She winced. She hated being called that. "I was never a princess. I was more like a pawn."

When he gave her a curious look, she waved a dismissive hand. "It doesn't matter anymore. I refuse to let my father dictate my life."

He leaned back against the sofa cushions, studying her. "Is that why you're attracted to me? Is it part of the rebellion against your father? So you can piss him off?"

"Don't be ridiculous," she snapped. But could he be

right? No, she didn't want to think that. Her feelings had always felt genuine, not like some sort of twisted, sordid quest for revenge. "I've always thought you were gorgeous. And courageous. And—" What was she doing, complimenting him when he'd rejected her? "But like you said, there's no future for us. I'm sure I can manage to resist you for the few nights that we're here."

His jaw shifted. "Fine. I'm sure I can resist you, too."

"Fine." She put the bottle back into the fridge. "Then let's get back to business, shall we?"

"Fine by me." He strode back to the kitchen table, set down his empty bottle, and picked up his cell phone. "Are you coming?"

"Yes." She strode toward him, then jerked to a stop a few inches away. This was awkward.

He punched in the number. "You'll have to hold on to me, but don't let it bother you. I'm sure you can resist fondling my manly body."

"Exactly." She slipped her hands around his neck. "This is business."

With an abrupt move, he pulled her close. "Exactly." He gave her a fierce look, then everything went black.

Phineas was relieved when Jason Pritchard didn't answer the phone. It was so much easier to teleport to an answering machine that talked for a minute without asking any questions.

They landed in a dark foyer, and his eyes quickly adjusted. Most of the house was dark, not surprising since it was after midnight. It was also Saturday night, so a young guy like Jason might be out on the town, but Phineas suspected he was asleep in his bedroom. After all, he'd just been released from the hospital that morning.

He placed a finger against his lips to remind Brynley to be quiet, and she nodded, giving him an annoyed look that probably meant she didn't need reminding. Prickly, as always.

He moved quietly through the small house, relieved they couldn't talk right now. Their last chat had ripped his ego to shreds. She thought he was a disgusting parasite? They were horribly, dreadfully mismatched? A disaster waiting to happen? Sheesh, she acted like the polar ice caps would melt if they got together. Half of Wyoming would blow up like a giant geyser. The sun would go supernova, and a freakin' black hole would swallow the universe.

Thank God she found him so easy to resist. The universe would remain safe for one more night.

What was really frustrating was he knew this situation was his fault. The truth had come out because his eyes had turned red. He'd known it was dangerous to spend time alone with her. He'd known he needed to keep his attraction to her a secret, but damn, his feelings for her were too strong. He hadn't survived one night without blowing it.

Now she knew. And what was even more shocking, she appeared to be attracted to him, too.

Not too attracted, he thought wryly. Not if she considered him easy to resist. After all, they were horribly, dreadfully mismatched. A disaster waiting to happen.

The den and kitchen were empty. He stalked down a hallway and peeked inside the first door. An empty bedroom. He was tempted to drag Brynley inside to prove they weren't so horribly, dreadfully mismatched after all. But making love to her might knock the Earth off its axis, so he'd have to resist.

He checked the second door. Bingo. Jason Pritchard was sound asleep in bed.

He eased the door open as he slipped inside Jason's mind. *Keep on sleeping. This is just a dream.*

He motioned for Brynley to follow him inside, and she tiptoed after him.

You are under my control. You will sleep and answer my questions.

Jason rolled onto his back, but his eyes remained shut and his breathing normal.

"Do you remember who attacked you?" Phineas asked softly.

"A woman," Jason mumbled.

"What did she look like? What did she do to you?"

"Blonde. Pretty." Jason frowned. "I don't know what she did to me."

Phineas delved through Jason's memories and spotted blank spaces, a sure sign that the man's mind had been tampered with. Still, he persisted, digging deep in search of a memory that would show him the attacker's face.

Jason moaned and shook his head.

"He can't remember her face," Phineas told Brynley, then tried another tactic. "Did you hear her voice, Jason? Did she say anything to you?"

"She . . . she said she was my queen."

Phineas's breath caught.

"Oh my gosh," Brynley whispered. "That sounds like Corky."

Phineas leaned over the sleeping man. "Where were you when she attacked you?"

"Cloud Peak Glacier."

"I know where that is," Brynley said quietly.

"Good." Phineas touched Jason's forehead. *This was all a dream. Sleep and forget about me.*

Jason let out a loud snore and rolled onto his side.

Phineas reached a hand out to Brynley. "Let's go."

She stood stiffly in his arms as he teleported back to the cabin. As soon as they arrived, she jumped away and strode into the kitchen.

He scowled. How noble of her. She was so determined to keep the polar ice caps from melting. "So where is the Cloud Peak Glacier?"

She pulled a map out of a drawer and unfolded it on the kitchen island counter. "See this area here?" She jabbed a finger at a northern area of Wyoming. "This is where we are."

He joined her at the island and studied the map. The sweet scent of her hair filled his nostrils. Peaches. And vanilla. It reminded him of the homemade peach cobbler his aunt Ruth made. He used to love it hot and topped with vanilla ice cream. Come to think of it, he wouldn't mind a taste of Brynley topped with some va-nilla ice cream. Or was he lactose intolerant now?

"And this," Brynley continued, "is the Bighorn Na-tional Forest. It lies east of Phil's land. Inside the forest, you'll find the Cloud Peak Wilderness Area. The gla-cier is located about here."

"Okay, let's go."

She gave him a wry look. "Are you going to call the glacier? They don't generally come equipped with a telephone."

"Then we'll take the car." He smiled. "See? I knew it would come in handy."

"It's a wilderness area. That means no motorized ve-hicles are allowed off the main roads."

His smile faded. "Then how do you get around?"

"You walk." Her mouth twitched. "Or you ride a horse."

He stepped back. "I don't think so."

"Aw, come on, Phineas. It'll be fun!"

"Those horses don't like me."

"They don't know you." She gave him a sly grin. "To know you is to like you."

He frowned at her. Was she flirting with him? Didn't she know that was torture? "I tried getting to know them. When you and Trudy left the barn to greet the other lady, I stayed behind for a little while. I tried mentally communicating with the horses to let them know I would never hurt them."

"Ah, that was sweet."

"Not too sweet. One of them tried to bite me."

She laughed. "Which one?"

"I don't know. They all look alike."

"Horses look alike?" She shook her head. "You're such a city boy."

His brow arched. "Country girl."

"And proud of it. I can bring down an elk in sixty seconds."

"I didn't think your breath was that bad."

She huffed and punched him in the shoulder.

"Ah, foreplay." He rubbed his shoulder. "And here I thought you were going to resist me."

She scoffed. "That's not my idea of foreplay."

"Then what is?"

Her eyes widened, then she looked away.

"Sorry," he mumbled.

She shrugged and turned back to the map. "No big deal. And actually, I don't think we should ride in at night. Our best bet is for me to go in the late afternoon. Trudy can bring her trailer and drop me and the horses off. I'll ride one and lead the other, then set up a base camp below the glacier. As soon as the sun sets, I'll call you and you can teleport." She winced. "Although the cell phone probably won't work."

"I can zip back to Romatech and pick us up some satellite phones," Phineas suggested.

"That would work." She wrinkled her nose. "The problem with this plan is it'll leave you alone here for a few hours."

He glanced at the basement trapdoor. Did he dare risk it? "How often do people come around here?"

"Never. And I would lock up. But still . . ."

"You would worry about me?"

She shrugged in an unconcerned manner. "It's my job to guard you."

He gritted his teeth. "I'll be fine. We can move the couch to conceal the trapdoor. I'll teleport in and out of the basement."

"Are you sure?"

She was worried about him, he knew it. She just didn't want to show it. "If I wasn't sure, I'd spend the day at Romatech."

She nodded. "Okay. Then we have a plan."

"All right." He sat at the kitchen table and booted up the laptop. "I'll find a map of the wilderness area."

"Cloud Peak, and the Bighorn National Forest." She rummaged inside the fridge and pulled out some sliced roast beef. "I'm going to make a sandwich. You want anything?"

"I'm fine." He pulled up a search engine. "There are camping areas in the forest, right?"

"Yes. Over thirty of them."

"We'll need to check those. Corky may have commandeered one of them." He glanced at Brynley. "Don't check anything without me. It could be dangerous."

She opened a loaf of bread. "Seems to me that it would be safer to look for her during the daytime when she's dead."

"She wouldn't dare sleep unprotected. She'll have a few mortals under her control, and they'll be brainwashed to kill anyone who comes close to her. Don't do any investigating without me."

Brynley glowered at him. "Okay."

He found a good map that detailed all the camping areas. "I'll zip over to Romatech and print this out and grab our sat phones."

"Okay." She slathered some mustard on her bread.

"I'll probably stay there for a few hours. See how my brother's doing. File a report and catch up on what the other guys are doing." It would be a lot easier to resist her if he put over a thousand miles between them.

"Okay." She slapped her sandwich together.

"You'll be all right here?"

She shot him an irritated look. "I'll be fine."

"You have a lot to do tomorrow. You should get some sleep."

"Go ahead and teleport. I know you don't want to hang around me for the rest of the night."

"It's not that I don't like you. Quite the opposite—"

"Just go!"

"Fine!" With a sick feeling in his stomach, he vanished.

"Who's afraid of the big bad wolf?" Brynley sang to herself in the shower. She'd finished her snack, then checked on the horses in the barn. Phineas had not returned.

She turned off his computer, then gathered up some supplies for the trip to Cloud Peak Glacier. Some beef jerky, a few granola bars, some bottles of water, a roll of toilet paper, and a sleeping bag. Phineas might be able to teleport in and out, but she'd be with the horses, so she'd have to do things the old-fashioned way. She made a note to herself to bring some weed-seed-free feed for the horses.

By one o'clock in the morning, he still wasn't back. She took a shower and sang the Big Bad Wolf song at the top of her lungs, hoping he'd come back and hear it.

He didn't.

She left the light on in the bathroom with the door partially closed, so the cabin wouldn't be totally dark, then climbed the ladder to the loft and crawled into bed.

With a groan, she punched a pillow. It was her fault he was uncomfortable around her. She shouldn't have told him that she knew what the red eyes meant. She'd wanted to tease him, but to be honest, she was flattered. More than flattered. Amazed. Astounded. He'd admitted he was attracted to *her*. The real Brynley.

All the guys in the past who had pursued her had never bothered to find out who she really was. They'd simply seen her as the Supreme Pack Master's daughter, the ticket to win more power and prestige in the werewolf world.

Phineas had nothing to gain from a relationship with her. Unless you counted gaining a bunch of enemies. Her father and his countless followers would want to kill him.

She sighed and nestled under the covers. It was for the best that he was staying away from her. They couldn't be together. He knew it. She knew it. Her inner wolf knew it. They were from two different worlds.

How much did she actually know about him? Had he really been a drug dealer? Was it true there was an outstanding warrant for his arrest? It didn't seem to fit the Phineas she knew. She'd always felt safe around him. She knew her brother and the Vamp guys liked and respected him. Angus MacKay had promoted him to head of security at Romatech. He wouldn't have done that if he didn't believe Phineas was absolutely trustworthy.

But how well could she trust him? He was the Love Doctor, the Blardonnay Guy. Hundreds of Vamp women would gladly throw themselves at him. She rolled over and punched a pillow. Lucky Phineas. He could see his brother whenever he wanted. She didn't dare even contact her sister.

She must have dozed off, for when she next looked at the bedside clock, it was almost four. The cabin was totally dark. The bathroom door had been shut. And the water was running.

Phineas was back. And taking a shower. She pictured him the way he looked in the commercials with a towel wrapped low around his hips. And his chest, his glorious chest would glisten with droplets of water. A tiny rivulet would sluice down his chest, right between his man-boobs—

Her breath caught. The water had turned off. She slipped out of bed and tiptoed to the edge of the loft.

The moon, now low in the sky, shone through the

windows, softly illuminating the room below. He'd moved the couch back a few feet to cover up the trap-door to the basement. And he'd moved the chairs back, too, so the whole arrangement would look normal.

The bathroom door opened, and the light switched off.

Her heart pounded, and she took a deep breath to try to stay calm. She didn't want him to hear her racing heartbeat.

He moved into view, and her heart stuttered. He was wearing a towel, just like in the commercials. Oh God, his shoulders really were broad. And his back . . . so strong and muscular. She bit her lip. If only he would turn around so she could see his chest.

Suddenly, he yanked the towel off and rubbed it over his head. She gasped. His rear end was showing!

He stiffened and turned his head slightly.

She slapped a hand over her mouth. He must have heard her gasp. But oh my God, when he had stiffened, it had caused the muscles in his buttocks to flex. It was about the most beautiful sight she'd ever seen.

"Brynley?" He turned toward her with the towel lowered to cover his groin.

She scrambled back onto the bed and held her breath. Her heart was beating too damned fast. He was going to hear it.

"Good night, Brynley," he said softly.

The cabin was quiet. She strained her ears, but heard only crickets chirping outside. And an owl hooting.

She eased back to the railing and peeked over. The

room was empty. He must have teleported into the basement.

She crawled back into bed and lay there, staring at the ceiling. If she had the nerve, she'd shove the couch aside, open the trapdoor, and jump down into the basement. Straight into his arms.

But she couldn't. She squeezed her eyes shut, and the vision of his naked back and buttocks filled her mind.

With a moan, she pulled the covers over her head. Easy to resist, she'd told him. What a big fat liar.

She'd never wanted anyone as badly as she did Phineas.

Chapter Nine

The next evening, Brynley sat on her sleeping bag at the camp she'd established at the base of Cloud Peak and watched the sun slip over the horizon. Any second now, Phineas would be waking from his death-sleep. She'd give him a few minutes to dress and drink some blood before calling him.

She breathed deeply of air scented with spruce and lodgepole pine. The two horses munched on the green grass of the meadow where she'd camped. Far up the side of the mountain, nestled in a beautiful cirque, the glacier gleamed white in the moonlight. Patches of snow still dotted the mountainside. Tiny bits of ice sparkled as if a divine hand had tossed a stash of diamonds across the side of the mountain.

Beautiful. She closed her eyes and enjoyed the crisp night breeze that nipped at her cheeks. *Home.* Her inner wolf trembled with joy. It knew instinctively that she'd returned, and it was eager for the full moon that would come in two nights. Eager to burst free from her human skin and run wild through the forests, chasing deer and elk.

She would have to explain to Phineas that she needed the night off. It wasn't a choice for her. On the first night of a full moon, she shifted, no matter where she was.

The teaching job at Dragon Nest Academy was perfect for her since she was able to live in the same building with her brother and the banished werewolf boys. She shifted with them every month and roamed the extensive grounds around the school. It was fun being with her brother, but she missed her sister. And the Adirondacks were not the same as the mountains out West. Her inner wolf knew the difference and had longed for her to return home.

While the wolf celebrated, her human half tensed. She was taking a terrible risk. If she stayed here, her father might find her. And if he captured her, he'd make it extremely hard for her to escape a second time. He knew not to trust her now.

A twinge of paranoia skittered through her. She stood and surveyed the woods that encircled her camp, her extra-keen eyesight adjusting to the darkness. She listened with her extra-sharp hearing. A rustling in the grass as a field mouse scurried to its home, the beating of the air as an owl took wing.

"Hurry, little mouse," she whispered. She knew the feeling of being stalked, the terror of being hunted. *Princess, my ass.* Phineas had no idea. In her father's world, she was prey.

She felt a sudden need to have Phineas there with her. He'd said he would never allow her to be forced into a marriage against her will. He would protect her.

Because he wants you for himself. And why should she object? A spark of rebelliousness ignited inside her, inciting an urge to tell the world to buzz off. She wanted Phineas.

But since when did she ever get what she wanted?

She grabbed the sat phone off the sleeping bag and called him.

"Hello, Brynley."

His voice did the usual warm, fluttery things to her stomach. "You're all right! I was so worried about leaving you all alone in the cabin. I'm glad you're okay. Are you ready to come here?"

"I already have."

Her heart lurched and the phone tumbled from her hand as she whirled around and found him standing behind her. "Don't do that! I told you to never sneak up behind me!"

"It wasn't on purpose." He pocketed his sat phone. "I'm never exactly sure where I'll end up when I teleport."

"Oh." She pressed a hand to her chest as she willed her heart to stop pounding. *Great.* She'd freaked out again.

"Are you all right?" He was regarding her curiously, so she quickly changed the subject.

"It's beautiful around here, don't you think?"

"Yeah." He glanced around quickly, then focused again on her. "Are you sure—"

"There's the glacier over there," she interrupted, motioning to the cirque. "I'm not sure where Jason was attacked. The mountain still has a lot of snow on it. I can't imagine anyone trying to hike up there in the dark, so I'm figuring Jason was attacked somewhere down here. I'm glad you wore that heavy coat. It's pretty chilly."

He studied her silently for a while, and she felt her cheeks grow warm. She was babbling, and he knew it.

"I'll look around," he said quietly.

"All right. But don't take too long. We have a lot of campgrounds to check out. I'll get the horses ready."

He gave the horses a wary look, then zipped around the meadow and nearby woods at vampire speed.

With a sigh, she rolled up her sleeping bag. She needed to stop freaking out whenever he was behind her. The attack had happened five years ago. Time to get over it. She attached her sleeping bag behind the saddle on the gelding. Phineas was an inexperienced rider, so she'd let him ride the gentler mare.

He zoomed toward her in a blur of movement, and she gripped the reins of the horses as they shied away. "Cut it out!" she fussed at him. "You're scaring them."

"Sorry." He stopped abruptly, casting a worried look at the horses. "I found the spot where the attack happened." He gestured toward a giant spruce. "The grass is crushed, and I found a few drops of human blood on the ground."

Impressive. She hadn't detected any blood, and her sense of smell was excellent, although not nearly as good as when she was in wolf form. "Can you tell if it's Jason's blood?"

Phineas winced. "The older Vamps probably could, but I'm not as experienced as them. I can't tell if Corky was here, either."

She nodded. He seemed embarrassed, but that only made him more attractive to her. Werewolf men, especially the Alphas, tended to be overconfident to the point of arrogance, and that had always annoyed her.

He retrieved a piece of paper from his jacket pocket and unfolded it. "I printed out a map that shows the location of campgrounds. Vampires would need a cabin or a cave to stay protected from sunlight."

She patted the sheath attached to her belt. "I brought a good hunting knife. I'm ready for them."

He lifted his hands. "Wait a minute, Wolfie-Girl. If there's any fighting, you have to stay out of it."

"I'm not going to leave you alone."

"Your brother would kill me if I let anything happen to you."

She scoffed. "So it's just my brother you're worried about?"

"What do you need to hear, Brynley? That I couldn't bear it if anything happened to you? That if I failed to protect you, the shame would kill me?"

Her eyes widened. "Is that true?"

"Yes! So stay the hell out of trouble, okay?"

"Okay." She smiled, her cheeks flushing with heat. "Let's go, bloodsucker."

"After you, Snout-Face." He handed her the map.

She pointed at a spot on the map. "We'll head to this one first. It's not too far." She folded the map, stuffed it into her jacket pocket, then mounted her horse.

He stood still, eyeing the mare with an anxious look.

"Come on, city boy." She bit her lip to keep from grinning. "Mount up."

"I think that's the one that tried to bite me."

"That's Molly. She's as gentle as can be."

"Until she sinks her teeth into you."

Brynley snorted. "A vampire afraid of biting?"

"Hell yeah, if I'm on the wrong side of the bite." He inched closer to the horse. "Do you just sort of jump on their back?"

"Put your foot in the stirrup. No, the other foot." Brynley chuckled. "Unless you want to ride backwards."

He put his left foot in, then hopped on his right foot as the horse shied away. "Whoa, Nelly!"

"It's Molly." Brynley gasped when Phineas suddenly teleported right onto the horse's back.

With a frightened whinny, Molly reared up and dumped him on the ground.

"Ow. Damn." He hefted himself to his feet and glared at the horse. "What did it do that for?"

"You frightened her." Brynley dismounted and grabbed Molly's reins. "Here. I'll hold her still while you mount."

He rubbed his rear, scowling at the horse. "She doesn't like me."

Brynley smiled as she patted Molly's neck. "Poor

Phineas. Must be hard, mounting a female who doesn't like you."

He glowered at her. "I wouldn't know. They've always been willing."

Her smile faded. How many women had been seduced by the Love Doctor's sexy voice and handsome face? "I suppose you've had a whole herd of willing females? And you rode them like a cowboy?"

"If I did, would you be jealous?"

"No, more like nauseated."

He snorted, then slipped his foot into the stirrup and mounted neatly. "How's that?"

Gorgeous. She was sorely tempted to pull him to the ground and give him the ride of a lifetime. Make him forget about the herd of willing females he might have had in the past. Instead, she handed him the reins. "Hold them lightly. Molly won't need a lot of direction."

"She knows what she wants?" His hands brushed slightly against hers as he took the reins.

She swallowed hard. "We don't always get what we want." She hurried back to the gelding and mounted up.

This wasn't so bad once you got used to it, Phineas thought. The trail was wide and smooth, and well lit with a nearly full moon and a million stars.

His horse was happy to follow Brynley's gelding. And he was happy to watch her from behind. Her back was graceful and curved into a slim waist. Her long ponytail swayed from side to side.

The stars shone more brightly here than at home, and the sky seemed bigger. Even the Earth seemed bigger, more expansive without the cramped and crowded feel he was used to in the city. Here, he could easily believe that he and Brynley were the only two people on the planet.

It was a tempting fantasy—he and Brynley all alone with a moral obligation to repopulate the Earth. And no angry werewolf father to object. But in reality, his sperm was dead, and Brynley hated vampires. He was ninety-nine percent positive that she had spied on him when he'd gotten out of the shower, but of course, she'd found him easy to resist.

He took a deep breath. The air was definitely fresher here. No smoky scent of meat grilling at the local street vendor or stench of trash overflowing from a Dumpster.

At first, it seemed deathly quiet. No horns honking, no sirens, no throbbing bass from passing cars. But slowly, he became aware of different sounds. More subtle. A breeze ruffling the leaves, a twig snapping beneath a paw. The scenery appeared peaceful on the surface, but danger lurked in the dark depths of the forest. A different set of predators existed here—wolves, bears, mountain lions. But the predator that had attacked Jason Pritchard was one he knew well—a vampire.

Just like other predators, a vampire always left a trail. It was their need for blood, and their options were limited. They could order blood from Romatech, raid a blood bank, or drain animals dry. Or if they were Malcontents, they left human victims in their wake.

As Phineas relaxed into the swaying movement of the horse, he congratulated himself. This cowboy stuff wasn't so hard after all. Brynley would have to stop calling him a city boy. Unfortunately, at that moment his horse decided to leave the path and turn right into the forest.

"What the hell?" He sat up. "Horse! What are you doing?"

Brynley glanced back over her shoulder. "Where are you going?"

"I don't know."

Brynley pulled to a stop. "Steer her back onto the path."

"There's no steering wheel!" He looked frantically about as his horse continued to walk into the forest. "How do I put this thing into reverse?"

Brynley's laughter drifted toward him. Dammit, he couldn't even see her now.

"She's not a thing. She's a mare," Brynley yelled. "You have to let her know you're in charge!"

"I thought I was!" Typical female. The mare had only let him *think* he was in charge.

"Pull on the reins," Brynley called. She sounded closer, thank God.

He pulled hard, and the horse reared up, dumping him onto the ground. "Umph." He fell back, hitting his head. Stars danced around the sky. "Damn."

"Are you okay?"

"I think so," he mumbled as she walked past him.

"I was talking to Molly." She smirked as she grabbed Molly's reins. She rubbed the horse's neck. "Poor girl."

With a grunt, he hefted himself to his feet. The muscles in his rump and legs twinged with pain. "Damn."

"Come on." Brynley led his horse back to the path, her mouth twitching as she passed him by. "Don't forget your hat, city boy."

He spotted his hat on the ground, but when he leaned over to pick it up, his muscles objected. "Ouch. Damn." He walked slowly and stiffly back to the path.

Meanwhile, Brynley had tied a rope from Molly to her gelding. "I'll have to lead your horse since you don't know how to control her."

"It's not my fault the horse is weird."

She chuckled. "Do you need help mounting?"

"No. I can mount just fine." He ignored her dubious look, and swung his leg over the horse. His muscles groaned as he settled into the saddle. "See?" He grimaced, hoping it looked like a smile. "Piece of cake."

"Okay." With a grin, she headed back to her horse, then mounted up.

After about half an hour, they arrived at the first campsite. It was bare. No cabins. No pitched tents. No heartbeats. They dismounted, and he wobbled on legs that now felt like rubber. He gritted his teeth, determined not to show any weakness.

Brynley chuckled. "City boy."

Dammit, she knew he was in pain. "Country girl." He tipped his cowboy hat as she gathered the reins from both horses. "Mighty obliged, ma'am. I heard that in a movie."

She gave him a wry look. "Why, land sakes! You're practically a cowboy."

He reached inside his coat to remove his pistol from his shoulder holster and winked at her. "Pardon me while I whip this out."

She rolled her eyes. "I've seen bigger."

"Darlin', you ain't seen what I'm packing."

Her mouth twitched. "I've heard all you Vamps shoot blanks."

He arched a brow. "You want some cowpoke with a quick trigger finger, or a man like me who can go all night long?"

"I wasn't referring to your finger."

"Neither was I."

Her cheeks blushed a pretty pink. "Fancy talk coming from the Love Doctor." She turned to tether the horses to a hitching post.

He was tempted to tell her the whole Love Doctor act was just that, an act. It had started out as a joke, a way to make ladies laugh. But it seemed to have backfired on him, because no one wanted to take him seriously.

He paced along the camp's perimeter as he surveyed their surroundings. "I'll check the boulders over there. Maybe there's a cave."

"If you find one, make sure there aren't any bears inside," Brynley called after him. "Or cougars."

Sheesh. What a friendly place. He trod carefully

with his pistol ready. The wilderness was beautiful, but primitive. He couldn't imagine Queen Corky hiding here. If she was in the area, she'd use vampire mind control to land herself some better accommodations. A fancy ski lodge, maybe, or a ranch house.

He holstered his sidearm and returned to Brynley. "There's no one here. And I can't tell if anyone has been here recently."

She nodded. "It's part of the 'leave no trace' program. You're not supposed to—" She stopped suddenly with a gasp.

"What?" He reached for his gun once again.

"Look," she whispered, her voice hushed with awe. She pointed at the far side of the meadow. "Do you see him?"

Relief rushed through him and he released the weapon. "Yeah, it's a horse."

"That's not just any horse. It's the wild white stallion. Isn't he beautiful?"

"He looks like a horse." When Brynley gave him an exasperated look, he continued, "You've seen him before?"

"I've only seen him a few times in my life. He just seems to appear out of nowhere like magic. He's totally wild. No one has ever been able to catch him, and believe me, they've tried."

"He sounds cool."

She smiled at him, her face radiant in the almost full moon. "He *is* cool. The coolest horse in the entire world. Even my father couldn't catch him."

Behind them, Molly whinnied and tugged at the reins Brynley had looped over the hitching post.

"I think Molly likes him, too," Phineas added with a wry smile.

Brynley patted the mare to calm her down. "She has excellent taste."

"Is that why she veered off the path? Did she catch his scent?"

"Maybe."

Phineas watched as the stallion reared up, then galloped off into the woods. "There he goes."

Brynley nodded, still smiling. "He roams a wide area. I've spotted him in Montana a hundred miles from here. He goes wherever he wants."

"Completely free," Phineas murmured.

"Yes." Brynley's smile faded as she untethered the horses. "I've always had this feeling that if the wild white stallion remained free, then all was right in the world." She shrugged and looked embarrassed. "That probably sounds silly to you."

"No, not at all." He moved closer to her. "You figure that as long as he's free, you have a chance to be free, too."

Her eyes widened. "You do understand." She glanced away, her cheeks blushing. "Not bad for a city boy."

He brushed back a wavy tendril of hair that had come loose from her ponytail and tucked it behind her ear. "I could understand a lot more if we talked to each other instead of sparring."

"I suppose." She shifted her weight. "Maybe we

could be . . . friends. There wouldn't be any harm in that, right?"

It would be sheer torture. "I'd like that."

"Well, good. We can talk while we ride." She mounted the gelding.

"Okay." He mounted Molly, wincing inwardly at the pain. *Thank you for giving me a ride*, he attempted to communicate mentally.

Molly snorted and shook her head, and he felt an air of resignation about her as if she'd accepted long ago that she must do as she was told. He wondered briefly if she wanted to be free like the white stallion. Or when the snow piled up in winter, was she grateful to have a warm stable?

Freedom versus security. It was the choice Brynley had been forced to make when she'd left home.

They rode side by side, but neither of them spoke. Now that they'd called a truce, he didn't know what to say. It had been easier to communicate with her when he had picked on her and pretended not to like her.

The awkward silence stretched out, broken only by the thudding of horse hooves and the occasional bird-call.

Say something, he slapped himself mentally. "I like your eyes." He slapped himself again. That was not something a mere friend would say.

She tilted her head toward him. "My eyes?"

"Yeah. They're . . . blue." Sheesh, now he sounded like a preschooler who had just learned his colors.

"I like your eyes, too," she said softly.

"Mine? They're the color of mud."

"Dark chocolate," she corrected him, then smiled. "I love dark chocolate."

"Yours are like the sky on a bright sunny day. I . . . I can't see the sky anymore. Unless I look at you." He cast a nervous glance at her.

She was staring at him like he'd grown a second head.

"I shouldn't have said—"

"No," she interrupted him softly. "It's the most beautiful thing anyone has ever told me."

He shrugged. "I know you don't like compliments."

"But I do. I'm just not used to receiving them." She smiled sadly. "But I think I could adjust."

"Good. 'Cause I have a lot more where that last one came from."

"You're a sweet man, Phineas."

Sweet? Was that why she wanted him for a *friend?* Next, she'd be asking him to go to the mall with her to get a manicure. "I'm not always sweet," he grumbled.

She gave him a curious look. "Is it true what that woman said on the phone? You were a drug dealer, and there's a warrant for your arrest?"

He winced. He should have stuck with the sweet perception. The more Brynley found out about him, the more she would want to avoid him. The truth would only convince her that she was right.

They were horribly, dreadfully mismatched.

Chapter Ten

Boy, did he clam up fast. Brynley slanted a glance at Phineas. She must have pushed a button. Well, she could hardly blame him. She had things in her past she refused to talk about, too.

A sudden notion pricked at her. Maybe they had something in common after all. Maybe they were both . . . survivors. Their wounded souls recognized each other and were being pulled together by a magnetic force they couldn't stop or control.

She shook her head. What romantic nonsense. She'd been slapped around by reality too much to believe that souls could be destined for each other. Phineas was like any man, and they were all governed by the Three-Step rule. He couldn't help but think about sex, and since she happened to be the only female in the vicinity, she automatically became the subject of his sexual thoughts.

She waved aside a mosquito that buzzed past her ear. "Damned bloodsucker."

"Talking to me?" Phineas gave her a wry look.

"Should I? I thought you'd stopped talking to me."

He sighed. "There are things in my past I'm not proud of. I'd rather be judged for the real me and not for my mistakes."

"You think I'll judge you?"

He scoffed. "Haven't you already? I'm a disgusting parasite. A user. Your words."

"What about *your* words? You call me Snout-Face."

"You do have a snout when the moon is full. Would you rather I talk about your hairy legs?"

She stiffened, and her inner wolf bristled. "There's nothing wrong with my fur. If you weren't so ignorant about wolves, you'd know that I have a very nice pelt."

"You're extremely argumentative—"

"I am not!"

"And touchy. I've never met anyone so prickly."

"You bastard!"

His mouth twitched as he gave her a pointed look.

Her face grew warm as a sheepish smile tugged at her mouth. "All right. I might be a little touchy. But I have good reason."

"Then tell me about it."

She swallowed hard. No way was she talking about her past. She needed to change the subject fast. "Hairy legs? If that's how you flatter a woman, then you've got a lot to learn, Mr. Love Doctor."

He flashed his perfect smile at her. "I was getting to it. My point is that even with your pretty snout and gorgeous legs and cheerful personality, I would never hold it against you. I like you exactly the way you are."

She tightened her grip on her horse's reins as her heart started to race. *He likes me. For myself.*

Last night, he'd admitted he was attracted to her. She'd figured that was simply lust. A common result of the Three-Step rule. But now, with this latest confession, she could no longer pretend the attraction was purely physical.

And she wasn't sure she liked that. Lust was easy to handle. If it itched too much, you simply scratched it. But once the heart was dragged into a relationship, it always ended in heartache. Abandonment, betrayal, abuse. She'd endured them all and couldn't bear to go through it again.

She gave him a wary look. "I suppose a Love Doctor like you has enjoyed a lot of conquests."

He snorted. "What conquests? You heard how LaToya talks to me. She judges me on my past mistakes."

"And you think I will?"

"Don't you hold it against me that I'm a vampire? A disgusting parasite?"

She grimaced. "It's not personal. I just don't like users."

"Have I ever used you?"

She rode in silence for a moment. She could accuse him of using his vampire allure on her, but she was beginning to question that idea. She'd lived at Dragon Nest Academy for a few months now, and she'd never felt any kind of allure from the other male Vamps she came in contact with. They were handsome guys, but they never affected her like Phineas.

She needed to face the truth. It was only Phineas who attracted her. She liked him exactly the way he was.

Did she dare tell him?

"You didn't answer my question," he said softly. "Do you think I've used you?"

"No." She shook her head. "I think you're a . . . a good guy."

The corner of his mouth tilted up. "Well, I guess we found something we can agree on."

She smiled, her cheeks growing warm. "I guess so."

His gaze met hers and their eyes locked for a few seconds. Her heart squeezed in her chest, and she looked away.

Oh God, who was she kidding? Her heart was already involved.

A silence stretched out between them, but she could sense an undercurrent that sizzled with electric energy. This was dangerous. Feelings this intense had a way of filtering through to her inner wolf. It was becoming aware of the desires of her heart, sharply attuned to the lustful needs of her body. And once the animal inside her latched on to the scent of her chosen prey, it didn't give up.

Phineas wouldn't stand a chance.

Phineas stiffened as they approached the next campsite. This one was definitely inhabited. The stench of unwashed human was strong enough to knock over a moose.

Brynley wrinkled her nose as she stopped the horses.

"I think whoever is camping here had a run-in with a skunk."

He winced inwardly as he dismounted. "I'll check it out. Stay here with the horses."

"No way." She dismounted quickly and tethered the horses to a nearby aspen tree. "I'm supposed to be helping you."

"You are helping me, but I don't want you in any danger."

"I'm not a wuss, Phineas. I can handle myself."

"Are you two gonna fuss at each other all night?" a gruff voice rumbled from behind a large lodgepole pine.

Phineas whipped out his automatic as he spun toward the voice.

"You call that little stick a weapon?" A huge man stepped from behind the tree, chuckling. He carried a double-barreled shotgun with the breech open. A fly buzzed around his head, and he waved it aside.

His smell wafted toward Phineas, making his eyes water. Still, he focused on the shotgun to make sure the safety catch was visible. "We don't want any trouble, dude."

"But we can defend ourselves if we need to." Brynley drew her shotgun out of its leather case attached to her saddle.

The huge man tilted his head back and laughed. "Will you look at that? The little lady's got the big weapon. I reckon we can tell who's the boss here."

Phineas gritted his teeth. Before he could reply, Brynley butted in.

"Who are you, and what's your business here?" she demanded.

With a chuckle, the huge man removed his battered, sweat-stained hat and held it to his chest. "Pleased to meet you, ma'am. I'm Digger. Spent so many years digging for gold and silver that the name stuck. And you are?"

"I'm Bryn—" She stopped herself from saying her full name. "And this is Phineas."

Phineas nodded at him. "What's up?"

Digger looked up, then shrugged. "Not much. It's been pretty quiet till you two showed up." He regarded them as he scratched his scraggly long beard. "Are you two running from the law?"

"No," Phineas replied. "We're cool."

"We just like riding at night," Brynley added.

In the middle of nowhere, Phineas thought with a snort. They probably did look suspicious.

But Digger nodded as if it were normal. "Put away your weapons. I ain't gonna hurt you. Mine ain't loaded right now. And come on to my campsite. I've got some beans cooking." He turned and lumbered through the woods.

Phineas holstered his sidearm.

"Should I keep my shotgun ready?" Brynley whispered.

Phineas shook his head. "He's mortal and harmless, as far as I can tell."

"If his smell doesn't kill us."

Phineas smiled. "If we get into any danger, I'll just teleport you out."

"Okay." She slid her shotgun back into its case, then took the reins of the horses. "He reminds me of the old mountain men. I thought they were all gone."

They walked the horses into the camp. While Brynley tethered them to a hitching post, Phineas surveyed the area. Three small cabins, no heartbeats inside. Digger appeared to be here alone. He was squatting and stirring the contents of a black cast-iron pot that sat on a rock near the fire. His shotgun was resting against a tree.

"So you're camping here alone?" Phineas asked as he approached.

"Not exactly." Digger straightened with a grunt. "I got my boy, Jake, with me. You want some beans?"

"No, thank you. I just ate." Although this camp had cabins, Phineas couldn't imagine Corky staying anywhere near this smelly mortal. Or trying to feed off him. Beneath Digger's battered hat, hanks of greasy gray hair fell to his shoulders. His tattered jeans were held up with suspenders, and his undershirt had once been white, but was now stained and gray with age.

Digger nodded at Brynley as she approached. "Would you care for some beans, ma'am?"

"No, thank you." When Digger slumped with disappointment, she added, "But they sure do smell good."

He brightened with a smile that showed a few crooked teeth and a few more gaps where teeth were missing.

"It's my own special recipe. You gotta add some bacon fat and squirrel meat."

She nodded. "I'll try that sometime. Thank you."

"Have you noticed anything odd around here?" *Other than you?* Phineas added in his thoughts.

Digger's eyes lit up and he slapped his thigh, which caused a cloud of dust to puff around him. "Dagnabbit, I knew it! I knew that was why you're gallivantin' around at night. You're hunting *them*, ain't you?"

"Them?" Brynley asked.

"Yep. They're new to these parts, but I'm on to them." Digger scratched at his shirt. "I'm hunting them, too."

"Them?" Phineas asked.

"You know the Carson ranch south of here?" Digger asked. "Two cows mutilated last week. That's what they do, you know. They drain all the blood, then cut up the carcasses so no one will figure out what they're doing." He pointed to his head. "But some of us are too smart for them. We got 'em figured out."

Phineas exchanged a look with Brynley. Had Corky become so desperately hungry that she'd fed off cows?

"I think they're hiding in these here woods." Digger turned his head and spit on the ground. "They're some sneaky devils, that's for sure. You only see them at night." He nodded with a knowing look. "That's why you're riding around in the dark. You're hunting them, too."

"Well," Brynley drawled. "I reckon you got us all figured out."

He chuckled and slapped his leg. "That's right! You

can't put one past old Digger." His eyes gleamed as he looked Brynley over. "You're a pretty little thing. Are you taken?"

Her eyes widened. "Excuse me?"

"It's been a while since I had me a woman—"

"She's taken," Phineas interrupted, and moved quickly to Brynley's side. "We're married." He wrapped an arm around her shoulders and pulled her close.

She stiffened, then gave him a hesitant smile. "Yes, we're . . . newlyweds."

Frowning, Digger motioned to her hand. "You ain't wearing no ring."

Her eyes widened, then she blurted out, "It's a secret. We . . . we haven't told anyone yet."

"Her father doesn't approve of me," Phineas added.

Digger gave him a sad look. "Now ain't that a shame? Is it because you're black?"

Brynley flinched. "No!"

"Yes," Phineas answered at the same time.

"Phin," she whispered and touched his cheek. "No."

"You know it's true," he whispered back. "Your father will never accept me." If his race didn't upset the old werewolf, the fact that he was a vampire certainly would.

The pained look in Brynley's eyes made his heart swell with tenderness. He slipped his hand around the back of her neck to pull her closer and kissed her brow.

"Yep, you two are newlyweds, all right." Digger chuckled. "I ain't never seen two people so in love."

Brynley's gaze lifted to his with an alarmed look,

and he swallowed hard. In love? Was he? *Damn*. If he couldn't fool Digger, why was he trying to fool himself?

"Dammit!" Digger bellowed.

With a start, Phineas turned toward him, making sure he kept a safe grip on Brynley. "What?"

"It just makes me so damned mad! A nice couple like you, having to keep your marriage a secret. I mean, can you help who you fall in love with?"

"No." Phineas glanced at Brynley. "I can't." Time seemed to halt for a second as their gazes locked and sizzled. Would she think he'd just confessed to loving her? Or would she think this was all an act?

"Of course you can't help it," Digger growled. "Why, my own Jake fell in love with a squirrel."

Brynley blinked, and they screeched back to reality.

"Say what?" Phineas asked.

"You heard me. He's in love with a damned squirrel." Digger leaned toward them and lowered his voice. "Don't tell him about the squirrel meat in the beans. It'll upset him."

"We won't say a word," Brynley assured him.

Digger grunted, then turned toward some bushes that were trembling. "I know you're back there, Jake. Stop spying on us and come on out."

There were *two* crazy guys? Phineas held on to Brynley in case he needed to teleport her away.

The bushes parted and a dog padded into the clearing. He was big, yellow, and dirty, but his most striking feature was the hat strapped to his head. It looked like an old leather football helmet, crowned with a layer of aluminum foil that gleamed in the light of the campfire.

"Oh, the poor thing," Brynley murmured. "He's had a head injury?"

"Nope." Digger regarded the dog fondly. "My Jake is sharp as a tack. He's what you call a receiver."

"For a football team?" Phineas asked.

Digger broke into laughter, slapped his thigh hard, then coughed when the cloud of dust reached his face. "That's the craziest thing I've ever heard! Dogs don't play football!"

Phineas exchanged a look with Brynley as Digger started to laugh once again.

"He's got to wear that hat to keep them from talking to him," Digger explained. "First, they tried talking to me, but I was too wily for them."

"Them?" Phineas asked.

"Them aliens, boy! The ones mutilating all the cattle around here. They've been using my Jake as a receiver."

"What do they say to him?" Brynley asked.

"How the hell would I know? You think I can talk to a dog?" Digger snickered. "I ain't crazy, you know."

"Right," Phineas murmured.

"So I've been hunting those little devils, so they'll leave my Jake alone."

"That's very thoughtful of you," Brynley said.

"We should be going now." Phineas retreated, taking Brynley with him. "So you can get back to your hunting."

"You don't want to hunt together?" Digger asked with a hurt expression.

"Sorry, but we prefer to be alone," Phineas explained. "Newlyweds, you know."

Digger chuckled. "I got you. You two are making more hay than hunting. Well, I'll see you around."

"Nice to meet you." Brynley mounted her horse. Phineas mounted, too, ignoring the painful twinges in his rump and thighs. He waved at the old man.

"Be careful," Digger called after them. "Them nasty aliens are close by. I can feel 'em."

Phineas rode down the path alongside Brynley. Neither said a word until they were sure Digger wouldn't hear.

She pulled her shirt up to her nose and sniffed. "I may need to change clothes. And shower."

"I could teleport you to Phil's place. I'll come back to watch the horses while you clean up."

She smiled. "That's very sweet of you. Thanks."

Sweet. He was starting to hate that word. Why didn't she see him as sexy and desirable? Why couldn't she ache for him the way he did for her? Was it because she considered them horribly, dreadfully mismatched?

It was true what he'd said earlier. Her father would never accept him. A poor guy from the Bronx. A vampire.

Brynley could have any man she wanted. A rich rancher. An Alpha wolf. She could have wealth, land, and security. Why would she give all that up for him?

"Thank you for coming to the rescue," she said quietly.

"Huh?" The pain in his rear was rapidly becoming

unbearable. Maybe he should walk the rest of the way. "What rescue?"

"You rescued me from Digger's advances."

"Oh. No big deal."

"You're a sweet—"

"Don't say it!"

Her eyes widened. "Are you angry?"

Yes! Digger could tell I'm in love with you, and you can't! "It's nothing. I . . . I need to get off this damned horse."

"Okay." She pulled the horses to a stop. When he dismounted, she gave him a sympathetic look. "It's normal to feel sore the first few times."

"I'm fine." He gritted his teeth and walked stiffly beside her. "I'm just annoyed that we're not finding anything about Corky. I don't think she would hide out here. It's too primitive. She'd use her vampire mind control to take over a ranch or ski lodge."

"You may be right," Brynley murmured.

"And I'm wondering about those dead cows. Digger said they were drained of blood. We should check that out."

"You think Corky would feed off cows?"

"If she was desperate enough, yeah."

"But why mutilate them?"

"To hide what she did. When Malcontents feed off humans, they slit the throats to conceal the teeth marks."

Brynley nodded slowly. "Okay. I'll have Trudy help me bring the horses back to the cabin during the day, and then tomorrow night, we can go to the Carson ranch and ask Nate about the cows."

He glanced up at her. "Nate?"

"Nathan Carson." She smiled. "He's an old friend. And a mortal. A really sweet guy."

Phineas ground his teeth. Sweet Nate was probably rich. "Did he want you, too? Like Digger?"

"No." She gave him an exasperated look. "Not every man who sees me wants me."

"Some men are fools."

She shook her head. "Nate is plenty smart. His brother's a problem though. If we're lucky we won't run into Kyle."

"What's wrong with Kyle?"

She was silent a moment. "He did want me."

"Shit," Phineas muttered. She could have her pick of a million men. Why would she ever choose him?

Chapter Eleven

*W*ho's afraid of the big bad wolf?" Brynley sang to herself as she rolled out her sleeping bag.

He'd run away again.

Over an hour had passed since they'd arrived at the trailhead campsite where Trudy would meet her in the morning. After helping Brynley take care of the horses, Phineas had teleported her to her brother's cabin so she could shower and change. He'd returned to the camp to babysit the horses, and then, thirty minutes later, he'd teleported to the cabin to bring her back here.

He didn't stay. He claimed he needed to shower, too, and he needed to drop by Romatech for some bottled blood and to see how his brother was faring. He also wanted to see if Angus was sending anyone back to the States to help them with their search. She suspected he didn't want to continue the mission alone with her.

I ain't never seen two people so in love. Digger's words had haunted Brynley ever since they'd left his campsite.

The old man was crazy as a loon, so maybe she

shouldn't read too much into it. Still, she wondered how strong Phineas's feelings were for her. He'd been quick to pretend they were married when Digger had shown interest in her. He'd held on to her and kissed her brow. Last night he'd admitted he was physically attracted to her. And tonight he'd said that he liked her.

But love? Could he ever love her? She didn't know.

And she sure didn't know how she felt about him. Yeah, she wanted to jump his bones, but that wasn't love. That wasn't something you based a long-term commitment on. And yet, when Phineas had claimed they were married, her heart had nearly leaped out her throat. Shock. Then a tingly spark of excitement. And then . . . an odd sense of contentment.

Dammit, she wanted to be loved. She wanted to be cherished and treasured. For herself. Not for being a werewolf, or for being her father's daughter.

Her dad had been trying to marry her off for years, but she'd never felt a need to rush into anything. As a werewolf, she could live another five hundred years. Why saddle herself with a husband now?

But if a husband truly loved her, wouldn't it be wonderful? Why couldn't she be as happy as Vanda? Or Toni or Caitlyn? Any day now, Caitlyn would be giving birth to twins. Why couldn't she do that? Why couldn't she make her own family that was based on love instead of power and manipulation?

She stretched out on her sleeping bag in the bare cabin. She was wearing a clean pair of sweatpants and a sweatshirt to sleep in, and she had a flashlight and her shotgun on the floor beside her. It was a quiet and peaceful place, and she was exhausted, but still she couldn't sleep.

I ain't never seen two people so in love. Could Phineas fall in love with her? Did she want him to? What did she really know about him?

You're just scared, she told herself. *You've been burned and abused too many times before.* Phineas was sweet, smart, and respectful. He made her laugh. He made her horny. He made her want to jump—

She jumped when a man's form materialized in the dark cabin. "Phineas?"

"You're still awake?" He wandered over to her with a plastic bag in one hand and a Styrofoam cup in the other.

A delicious smell wafted toward her. "You brought food?"

"Yes." He handed her the cup topped with a plastic lid and straw. "A chocolate shake."

"Oh, I love chocolate!" She took a long sip, then moaned. "That's good. I was really getting tired of water and beef jerky."

He pulled a Styrofoam box out of the bag. "This is a hamburger and French fries from the Romatech cafeteria."

"You're so *sweet*." She grabbed the box and wondered why he suddenly looked pissed. "Is something wrong? Is your brother all right?"

"He's good." Phineas dug a ketchup packet out of the bag and handed it to her. "Angus is sending some guys to help us out. Since Jason said the lady who attacked him insisted on being called his queen, it's one of the best leads we've had. So as soon as it gets dark over there, Zoltan, Jack, and Lara will start teleporting our way."

"Who's Zoltan?" Brynley asked as she squeezed ketchup over the French fries.

"He's Coven Master for Eastern Europe. He doesn't work for Angus, but he's always helpful when it comes to fighting Malcontents."

Brynley nodded and took a bite out of her hamburger.

"Is there anything else I can bring you?" Phineas asked. "Some pillows or blankets?"

She gave him a wry look. "In a hurry to run off again?"

"I just want to make sure you're comfortable. Since you're stuck here with the horses."

"I'm good. More than good." She stuffed a French fry into her mouth. "Nothing like home delivery."

"Well. If you don't need anything else . . ."

He was going to run off again, dammit. "Why don't you stay for a while? I'm tired of being alone." Boy, was that an understatement. She'd felt alone for twelve years, ever since her mom died and Phil ran off. "We could talk. Until I fall asleep."

He gave a wary look. "What do you want to talk about?"

"Anything. Why don't you tell me your life story?" She smirked. "That would probably put me to sleep."

"Very funny."

"Come on. Talk. I want to know more about you." Her wolfish instincts told her she could trust him, but the human part of her wanted to make sure.

He eased slowly into a sitting position beside her. Even though he kept his face blank, it was obvious he was sore.

"You'll feel better after your death-sleep, right?"

"I'm okay." He scooted back to lean against the wall.

"So?" She turned toward him, sitting cross-legged. "Tell me about yourself."

"There's not much to tell."

"I doubt that. You don't get a warrant for your arrest doing nothing."

He winced. "I've done a few things I'm not proud of."

"Haven't we all?" She ate a few fries, and when he remained quiet, she prompted him. "You were born in the Bronx?"

"Yes. I grew up in my grandmother's house with her, my great-aunt, and my mom."

"No dad?"

"He went to jail when I was a baby. Armed robbery."

"Oh wow. I'm sorry."

"Don't be. I had a great childhood." He smiled with a faraway look in his eyes. "I had my gran, my aunt Ruth, and my mom, all taking care of me, making sure I always felt loved and cared for."

"That sounds wonderful." She ate another fry. "Three women spoiling you rotten. No wonder you became a ladies' man."

"I did learn how to sweet-talk them." His smile faded.

"It didn't last. Gran passed away when I was eight, and soon after that, my dad got out of prison."

"Oh." She had a bad feeling his dad was as domineering as her own father.

"He moved in with us, and about a year later, my mom had a baby. My little brother. She wanted to name him Lamont, but my dad wanted to name him Freedom to commemorate his getting out of jail. They ended up naming him Freemont."

"And he's working at Romatech now?" Brynley took another bite of hamburger.

"Yeah. He's nineteen years old now. Going to college. He's real smart."

She smiled at the obvious pride in Phineas's voice when he talked about his brother.

"Two years after Freemont, my little sister, Felicia, was born. I was about eleven then, and I started to notice things. Like my mom would walk with a limp sometimes, or her arms would be bruised."

Brynley winced. "Your dad was abusing her?"

Phineas nodded. "I could hear him yelling at her late at night, but I kept telling myself that was all he was doing. I couldn't admit what was really happening."

"You were just a kid," Brynley murmured. "Denial can be the safest way to go." She knew that all too well.

"One morning when I was twelve, my mom had a black eye, and my aunt Ruth started fussing at my dad, and he threatened to shut her up for good. That's when it finally hit me. Something snapped in me that day, and I told him if he ever hurt my mother or Aunt Ruth again, I'd kill him."

"Oh my gosh, Phineas." She set the box of food down and moved closer to him. "What happened?"

"He beat the crap out of me."

She gasped and touched his shoulder. "I'm so sorry."

"Don't be. It changed my life. I'd been a little kid before that with no purpose or direction. I was a lousy student and a lazy athlete, but that day, I woke up. I realized I needed to man up. I started working hard in school, so I could get a good job to support the family. And I started going to a gym every afternoon to learn how to box."

Man up? Brynley's heart ached for the twelve-year-old boy who'd tried to become a man overnight so he could provide for his family and protect them.

"By the time I was fourteen, I was a pretty good boxer. I won a few local bouts. And I was as tall as my dad, so he started being more careful."

"That's good."

He shook his head. "It didn't last. He came home drunk one night and started in on my mom. That time, I beat the crap out of him."

"Wow," Brynley breathed. He'd stood up to his dad. Something she'd never had the nerve to do with her own dad.

"Then I told him to leave and never come back."

"Did he?"

"Yeah." Phineas shrugged. "Turned out he had another woman on the side, so he just moved in with her."

"What a pig."

"He got what he deserved. His girlfriend had cheated on him and passed the AIDS virus to him." Phineas sighed. "He'd passed it on to my mom."

"Oh no."

Phineas was silent for a moment with his eyes closed. When he opened his eyes, they glinted with unshed tears. "She died of AIDS when I was nineteen."

"Oh, Phineas." Brynley leaned her head against his shoulder and rested a hand against his chest. "I'm so sorry. I know how it feels."

"Do you?" He placed his hand on top of hers.

"Yes." Tears filled her eyes. "I lost my mom when I was eighteen."

"Really?" He squeezed her hand. "I thought werewolves could live for centuries."

"Not with lung cancer." Or a broken spirit. She'd always suspected her mother hadn't fought to survive.

"I'm sorry." He laced his fingers with hers.

"Do you still have your aunt?" she asked.

"Yes." He leaned his head back against the wall. "She worked hard to support us. And I won some money in boxing matches, so we managed all right. But toward the end when Mom was really sick, we ran up some bad medical bills. And then there was the cost of the funeral." He grimaced. "I did something really stupid."

"What?"

"I agreed to throw a fight for a lot of money. I thought it would solve all our problems. It did pay everything off, but . . ."

"It screwed up your career?"

He nodded.

"Oh, Phineas." Tears crowded her eyes once again. He'd destroyed his boxing career in order to bury his mother.

"I couldn't get a decent fight after that. Or when I did, they expected me to throw it, and I refused. They didn't want me around anymore."

"I'm so sorry."

"I tried getting a regular job, but it wasn't enough to support everyone, especially when Aunt Ruth had to retire. She has diabetes really bad. I felt responsible for my younger brother and sister. I was the one who'd chased off their father. So I . . . I made another stupid mistake."

"That's when you sold drugs?"

"Please don't ever tell my family. It would kill them. It . . . well, it did kill me. The Malcontents attacked and transformed me so they would have a drug connection." He heaved a long sigh. "So now you know what a screwed-up, miserable excuse for a mortal I was. And why I didn't want to tell you. You'll probably hate me now."

She blinked away the tears in her eyes. She could never hate him. "Why did you tell me, then?"

"Remember how I said I like you just the way you are? I guess . . . I want you to like me the way I am. And so—"

"You told me everything," she finished his sentence. She'd been right. He was a survivor. Like her.

He'd lost his mother like her. He'd tried to take care of his younger siblings like she had. All this time she'd thought they had nothing in common, when in truth they were very much alike. Their wounded souls were reaching out to each other.

And she was falling for him. A tear rolled down her cheek. God, no. She didn't want to feel this strongly for him. Not when there was no future for them.

"I know you hate vampires, Brynley, but it's really the best thing that ever happened to me. It gave me a second chance. I have a good job now, and I provide for my family. And I'm doing something important, helping to keep the world safe from Malcontents."

She wiped her cheek. "You're able to be a hero now?"

"I try to be. Angus and the other guys have given me some good examples to follow. I want to be . . . honorable like them."

"Phineas." She touched his cheek. "How can you be so dense?"

He blinked. "What?"

"You were always honorable."

He scoffed. "I was a damned drug dealer."

"You were a young man, desperate to take care of his family. You threw away a promising career to get the money to bury your mother. You were brave and selfless." Another tear fell down her cheek. "You were always a hero."

He regarded her with a stunned look. "You don't think badly of me then?"

"I think you're wonderful." Desire swelled up inside

her. She wanted him so bad. But she didn't want to love him. It would hurt something awful if she lost him. And she would definitely lose him if her father and his minions found out about him.

Then don't love him, her inner wolf whispered. *Just screw him.*

She drew in a sharp breath, and her inner wolf latched on to Phineas's scent. Animal lust flooded her, overwhelming her womanly desire. *Take him. You know you want him.*

Her heart raced. She couldn't do this. She was just distraught, and that always made her wolf aggressive. *Give in to me. Trust the wolf. The wolf knows best.*

Moisture seeped between her legs, and she stifled a groan. It would kill her if she got close to Phineas, only to lose him. *Don't think about the future. Take him now!*

Phineas stiffened when she suddenly straddled his lap. "Brynley? What are you doing?"

Her hands trembled as they skimmed over his shoulders. "I have a sudden, insatiable hunger—"

"I brought you a hamburger—" He inhaled sharply when she popped the snaps open on his shirt. "What—"

"Oh my gosh." She smoothed her hands under his shirt. "You were right. Your chest is pure, hard muscle."

He gave her a dubious look. "What happened to last night's 'you're so easy to resist' strategy?"

"Why fight it? You want me. I want you." She brushed her hand over his jaw, and the prickle of his whiskers made her all fluttery inside. Just like his voice did. "Say it for me."

"Say what?"

"You know. The line you say in the commercial. 'Hello, ladies.' I love it when you say that."

He frowned. "I don't know why women like that."

"Don't you know how sexy your voice is?" She skimmed her hand down his neck to his chest. "You're sexy all over." She leaned closer, pressing her hands against his chest. "Say it. Say the words."

"Hello, ladies?"

"Yes!" More moisture pooled between her legs. Her inner wolf caught the scent of her arousal and clawed its way to the surface. *Take him!* She ripped open the rest of his shirt, then attacked the huge buffalo-shaped buckle on his belt. "Let's do it!"

"But . . . we haven't even kissed."

"Oh." She let go of his buckle. "Okay, then." She lunged forward, planting her mouth on his.

"Wait," he grumbled as she ground her mouth against his. He grabbed her shoulders and pushed her back. "What's gotten into you all of a sudden?"

"What do you mean? You said you were attracted to me. And that you liked me. I saw your eyes turn red. That means you want sex."

"Are they red now?"

"No, but they will be." She nipped at his ear.

"Wait!" He pushed her back again. "Look, I sorta figured we'd take this slowly. You know, kiss a few times, and then make out before we . . . and I sure the hell thought I would be the one initiating it all."

"Fine!" She glared at him. "Then go ahead. Initiate."

"Are you ordering me to initiate?"

"I want sex, Phineas! Is that a crime? I want you, and my inner wolf wants you—"

"Your *what*?"

"My inner wolf."

"Damn. Is that why you're so aggressive?"

She huffed. "I can't believe this. Are you going to analyze this to death? Let's just have sex and get it over with!"

His eyes narrowed. "Get it over with?"

"Yes! That's why we're bickering all the time. 'Cause we're hot for each other. So let's get it out of our system—"

"So we can go back to our normal lives?"

"Why not?" She jabbed a finger at his chest. "Are you man enough to handle it?"

He grabbed her hand. "Stop and think about this. If your father finds out about us, he'll disown you forever—"

"I don't give a damn what my father thinks. He's always treated me like shit!"

Phineas flinched. "That's what's going on, isn't it? This is your way to get back at him. Screw the man he would most hate for you to screw."

"Don't make it so complicated! It's simply lust."

His jaw clenched. "*Lust?*"

"Don't say it like it's a dirty word. If you weren't lusting for me, your eyes wouldn't have turned red. I'm just saying there's nothing wrong with having a little bit of fun. No one would ever know—"

"You would keep our relationship secret?"

"I would keep it private." She planted her hands on her hips. "You said yourself there's no future for us. So screw the future. Let's just do what we want."

"Have a secret affair."

"Yes." She brushed her hair over her shoulder. "I guess you don't understand. Werewolves are by nature lusty creatures. We never deny ourselves the pleasure whenever—"

"I'll deny it."

She blinked. "Excuse me?"

"You heard me. You're not gettin' any."

Her mouth fell open. He was rejecting her? "Are you crazy? What man turns down sex?"

He moved her off his legs and onto the sleeping bag, then stood. "I'll see you tomorrow night, Brynley. Get some sleep."

"What?" She scrambled to her feet. "You can't just leave."

"Watch me." He vanished.

Chapter Twelve

*D*ammit! Dammit to hell!" Phineas strode across the grounds at Romatech where he'd materialized just seconds earlier. He was not in the mood to see anyone, so instead of going inside, he'd headed for the nearby woods.

"Shit!" He punched a tree trunk. The rough bark ripped at his knuckles, but he punched again. And again. "Let's get it over with? Let's keep it secret? It's simply *lust*?" With one last bellow of outrage, he slammed his fist into the tree.

Damn, that hurt. He clenched his bloodied hands, relieved to have the pain torment him. Anything to keep him from feeling desire. Anything to keep him from teleporting back to Brynley. God, he was crazy. Brynley wanted him, and he'd refused her? *You fool! Go back and make love to her.*

"No!" It wasn't love for her. It was lust. And a desperate, pathetic way to get back at her father. She'd admitted in a fit of anger that he'd treated her like shit. She thought dear old dad had used her like a pawn? She was doing the same damned thing to him.

"Shit!" He paced toward the basketball court. His hands throbbed so much he no longer felt the pain in his legs.

Dammit. Had he made a terrible mistake? What if rejecting her destroyed what little affection she had for him? What if he'd lost her for good?

"Phineas!" Freemont ran toward him. "What's going on, bro?"

"Nothing." He kept walking.

"Bullshit. I saw you on a monitor, beating the crap out of a tree." Freemont caught up with him. "What happened?"

"Nothing. Go back to work."

"What have you got against the tree? Did it look at you funny?"

Phineas ground his teeth. His brother's attempt to cheer him up wasn't working. "Go back inside."

"You were here less than an hour ago," Freemont continued. "Everything was cool. And now it's not? Did you take the food to the wolfie-girl?"

"Yes."

"I thought you were worried about her camping alone. You were going to hang out with her to protect her."

"She'll be fine," Phineas gritted out. She had a shotgun and an inner wolf that was scary as hell.

"Oooh." Freemont halted. "I sense some lady trouble."

"You're a real sensitive guy, aren't you?"

"Don't snarl at me. Is that what happened? The wolfie-girl snarled at you?"

"I'm not talking about it."

"Your shirt's open. Did you make a pass at her?"

Phineas snorted. He pressed a few snaps together to close his shirt and left the plaid material stained with blood.

"Your hands are bleeding, bro," Freemont said quietly. "You should come inside and get cleaned up."

"They'll heal during my death-sleep." But his heart might never be the same. Phineas retrieved a basketball from the large Rubbermaid bin, then dashed onto the court and levitated to do a slam dunk.

"Cool!" Freemont retrieved the ball and started some fancy dribbling around his legs.

Phineas grabbed for the ball, but his brother neatly passed it between his legs and out of his reach.

"Give me the ball," Phineas growled.

Freemont dribbled down the court, heading for the other basket.

"Give me the damned ball!" Phineas zoomed past him at vampire speed and blocked him.

Freemont screeched to a halt. "Hey! No fair pulling your vampire tricks when I don't have any." He twisted when Phineas made a grab for the ball. "Is that what happened? You tried some vampire tricks on her, and she rejected you?"

"She didn't reject me!" He lurched for the ball, but Freemont surprised him, throwing it at him hard.

It hit him in the stomach, knocking him back a few steps. "What the hell was that for?"

"You tell me!" Freemont scowled at him. "Why are you so pissed? Why are you attacking trees?"

"Because she wanted sex!" Phineas threw the ball all the way down court and it plopped neatly through the hoop.

Freemont's mouth fell open. "Wow, you scored."

"No, I didn't. I turned her down."

"You—you turned down *sex*?"

"Yes." Phineas trudged down the court to retrieve the ball.

"How could you do that?" Freemont followed him. "You're the Love Doctor."

He shook his head. "Not anymore. I can't do it anymore."

Freemont gasped. "You can't get it up?"

Phineas shot him an incredulous look.

"Don't worry about it, bro." Freemont smiled encouragingly. "There are doctors for that sort of thing. And drugs. We'll get help for you."

"I'm not impotent, dammit! I'm falling in love!"

Freemont's eyes widened. "You are?" He grimaced. "With a wolf?"

"Werewolf. And I'm falling for the human part of her."

"What about the wolf?"

"What about it?" Phineas yelled. "I love her just the way she is."

"Okay, okay." Freemont held up his hands. "So I guess she doesn't return your feelings?"

"No, she doesn't." Phineas picked up the ball and tossed it back into the plastic bin.

"But she wanted to have sex?"

"Yes." He slammed the lid down.

"Then why are you here?"

He glared at his bloody hands. "She wants to keep our relationship a secret. I want to shout it to the world. She wants to jump right into it. I want to take it slow and savor every moment. She wants to get it over with, and I want it to never end."

Freemont was silent a moment, then said, "You've got it bad."

Phineas sighed. "I've had one-night stands with women I can hardly remember. I'm not doing that with Brynley. It would be an insult to her and to the feelings I have for her."

"Damn, you're tough, bro. I don't think I could have turned her down."

He smiled sadly. "Believe me, I want to make love to her more than anything. But I want it to be *love*."

Freemont nodded. "Let's get your hands cleaned up." He motioned toward the side entrance. "Don't give up, bro. She could still fall in love with you."

Phineas groaned inwardly. Even if his wish came true, and she somehow magically fell for him, there were still major obstacles in the way. She would never be happy if she were forced to live in the vampire world. And he would never be accepted in the Lycan world. Hell, her father would probably send his minions to kill him.

* * *

The next evening, Brynley paced nervously about her brother's cabin. The sun was setting. Phineas would be waking soon. And when he teleported to the cabin, her mortification would be complete.

If he teleported to the cabin. She wasn't sure he'd come. He might never want to see her again.

Early that morning, Trudy had arrived at the trailhead campsite with her trailer, and they'd transported the horses back to the stable at her brother's cabin. After Trudy left, Brynley had dashed into the cabin to see if Phineas was all right. She shoved the sofa away from the trapdoor, then moved the ladder from the loft to climb down into the basement.

No Phineas. He hadn't returned to the cabin.

After lunch, she fell asleep on the sofa, exhausted from a sleepless night at the campsite. She hadn't been able to relax after Phineas had left. She'd felt too insulted. Too angry. Too frustrated. And eventually, too embarrassed. *Mortified.*

She'd practically forced herself on him! What had come over her? She'd never behaved like that before. Sure, the inner wolf was a lusty creature, but she'd always had control over it. Until last night.

Her inner wolf had never been so strong before. And she'd allowed it to overwhelm her. Hell, she'd welcomed it. The wolf had given her the wild boldness she'd craved. It had matched her desperate passion with its fierce power. Together, she'd never felt stronger. She'd felt invincible. Her prey was targeted, and he couldn't escape.

But he had. He'd abandoned her without explanation. And it had hurt. It hurt so bad, she knew she could no longer deny what was happening. She was falling in love. And she'd chased him away!

What if he never came back?

What if he did? How could she ever face him? *Mortified.*

She strode outside to the porch and watched the last rays of the sun disappear over the horizon. If Phineas had spent the night at Romatech in New York, he was already awake.

The nearly full moon tugged at the wolf inside her, and it tensed in anticipation. Tomorrow night, it would be free. A surge of power shot through her, and she gasped. Why was the wolf so strong? Was it because she'd come home? Or because she'd fallen prey to such strong emotions?

A sound in the cabin made her heart lurch. She whirled around to peer in the window. Phineas was back! And he was loading bottled blood into the refrigerator. That meant he intended to stay. *Yes!*

Her sense of relief was short-lived. She still had to face him.

She opened the door and stepped inside.

He glanced at her and smiled. "You made it back."

"Yes." She inched forward. At least he was smiling. "So did you."

"I brought some more blood from Romatech." He shut the refrigerator door and motioned to a box on the island. "And I brought you a dessert from the cafeteria."

"Really?" She eased toward the island. He didn't seem to be angry about last night.

"Yeah. Chocolate cake. You like chocolate, right?"

"Yes." She peeked inside the box and nearly drooled at the sight of a seven-layer double chocolate piece of heaven.

"We have a lot to cover tonight." He retrieved a folded piece of paper from his jacket pocket. "I hope you got some rest."

"Yes. I slept most of the afternoon." She shifted her weight. "Maybe we should talk . . ."

"Sure." He unfolded the paper. "I got an e-mail from Angus. After reading my report, he thought we should check all the local clinics and hospitals to see if any other people were admitted with a severe loss of blood. So I made a list here, and we'll hit as many as possible tonight."

"I thought we were going to the Carson ranch? To check out the cow mutilations?"

"We will, if we can fit it in. But Angus thinks, and I agree with him, that Corky will stick to human victims if at all possible."

"Okay." Brynley retrieved a fork from the cutlery drawer and tried a bite of the cake. It looked like Phineas didn't want to talk about last night's fiasco. Maybe he was as mortified as she was. The chocolate melted in her mouth, a warm, gooey comfort.

"Good?" He smiled, his eyes softening and looking as sweet as chocolate.

"Mmm." She swallowed. "Yes, thank you. So, did you want to teleport?"

"Actually, I mapped the trip for us." He handed her the paper. "If you don't mind driving me around."

"Oh." Her heart swelled, grateful that she could help him. "Sure. Let me get my purse and a bottle of water, and we'll hit the road."

They were halfway to the town of Shell when Brynley finally worked up the nerve to talk.

She glanced at Phineas, who was sitting calmly beside her, sipping from a bottle of blood and looking out the window. "I owe you an apology."

"I don't think so."

"Oh, I do. I . . . I practically attacked you last night."

He shrugged. "No big deal."

"But it is! I scared you away."

His head turned slowly toward her. "Scared?"

"Yeah. I chased you away."

"Bullshit." He glowered at her. "I wasn't scared. And I wasn't chased. I chose to leave."

"Because I attacked you. I'm really sorry. I don't know what got into me."

"You knew last night. You called it lust."

She winced. "Yes. But I don't usually lose control like that. My inner wolf seems to be unnaturally strong all of a sudden."

"You can feel the wolf inside you? I always thought

you were either human or wolf, not both at the same time."

"The wolf is always with me." She pressed a hand to her chest. "But I've never felt it so strongly before. It—it's very strange."

He regarded her silently for a while. "Maybe it's because the moon is almost full."

"I . . . I suppose." Though she'd never experienced this before when the moon was waxing. "I thought it might also be because I've returned home. The wolf is very excited about that."

"I guess you'll have to turn tomorrow night?"

"Yes. I won't have any choice. For ordinary werewolves like me, we have to turn on the first night of the full moon. The two nights after that, we can choose to shift or remain human. Alphas like my father or Phil can shift or even partially shift whenever they like." She gave him an apologetic look. "I won't be able to help you tomorrow. Sorry."

He waved that aside. "Don't apologize for what you are."

She recalled the words he'd said the night before. He liked her just the way she was.

He took another sip from his bottle. "And don't apologize for last night. I was . . . flattered."

She glanced at him, then back at the road. "You were?"

"Of course. I hope someday we will make love."

Her heart jumped up her throat. He did want her! She

clenched the steering wheel as her heart pounded. *Calm yourself.* He could probably hear her heart racing.

A question popped into her mind. If he wanted to make love, why did he turn her down last night?

"Okay, here's the town." He motioned to the lights up ahead.

She parked in front of the emergency clinic and accompanied him inside. In a matter of seconds, he had the receptionist's mind under his control and she gave them the news. No one had been admitted in the past two weeks with bite marks or a low level of blood. No unexplained deaths.

They went on to Greybull, Manderson, and Worland. No victims there. Brynley headed east to Ten Sleep.

Bingo.

The receptionist nodded, glassy-eyed. "Yes, we had a patient last night. Dead on arrival."

"What can you tell me about it?" Phineas pressed.

The receptionist tilted her head. "It was very strange. No sign of trauma, but somehow he had bled out."

"May we see his file?" Phineas asked.

Brynley leaned close to read the page detailing the victim's personal information. Earl Giddons had worked as a cowhand on a nearby ranch. "See this?" She pointed at Nate Carson's address.

Phineas nodded and closed the folder. "Looks like we'll be visiting your old friend after all."

Chapter Thirteen

*W*hat can you tell me about Nate?" Phineas asked as Brynley drove toward the Carson ranch house.

"He's a really nice guy. A mortal. Served in the army. He would never get involved with the Malcontents."

She was quick to defend him, Phineas noted. "If Corky's taken over his mind and his ranch, then it doesn't matter how nice a guy he is."

Brynley winced. "I hope he's all right. He's been through so much already, poor guy."

Another twinge of jealousy pricked at Phineas. "If he's a mortal, how did you meet him? At college?"

She shook her head. "Rodeo circuit. I used to do barrel racing."

"You raced barrels?"

"No, my horse and I raced around them." She gave him an incredulous look. "You've never been to a rodeo?"

"They're not big in the Bronx."

She snorted. "Well, they're a lot of fun. You should see one sometime."

"I'm surprised your dad let you hang out with a bunch of mortals."

"Well, he wasn't very happy about it. When I first started, I thought I was being so clever, that I'd found a way to get away from him and make some money of my own. But I soon realized that the rodeo had plenty of werewolves, and they were reporting everything I did to my dad. He could have ordered them to bring me home whenever he wanted. My freedom was only an illusion." She made a face. "Still, it was a lot better than being at home. It was one of the happier times in my life."

"And this guy Nate was in the rodeo, too?"

"Yep. He and his brother were into team roping. Kyle was the header, and Nate was the heeler."

"What—"

"Kyle would lasso the head of the calf, and then Nate would manage to lasso the hind legs. It's really amazing to watch."

Phineas frowned, picturing her gazing at Nate in amazement. "So it takes two guys to tie up a little cow?"

"The calf is moving at the time." Brynley shot him an annoyed look. "And they're on horseback. It takes a lot of skill, and they manage to do it in a matter of seconds."

"Okay. So what was the problem with Kyle?"

Brynley waved a dismissive hand. "It was no big deal. He kept pestering me for a date and wouldn't take no for an answer. Nate told him to leave me alone."

Phineas strongly suspected that was the sanitized version of what had happened. He recalled her fear of being attacked from behind. "Did this Kyle hurt you?"

"No. It wasn't that bad." She glanced at him. "Really. It was never bad enough to make me quit the rodeo circuit."

"Then why did you quit?"

Her hands gripped the steering wheel, and he heard her heartbeat speed up. He'd touched on something, but he wasn't sure what.

They rounded a hill, and some bright lights came into view in the distance.

"Nate's house." She motioned ahead. "Do you really think Corky could be there?"

Phineas winced. The house looked more like a mansion. Nate had to be rich. And he probably had a thing for Brynley. "Corky would definitely prefer this to a cabin in the woods. And she would have some handsome cowboys here to nibble on."

Brynley snorted. "Not all cowboys are handsome."

"I'm glad to hear it." He checked the knives he had hidden in each of his boots and the automatic in his shoulder holster. "You have the silver chains I gave you?"

"Yes." She patted her jacket pockets.

"If we see her, I'll grab her. You get the silver around her as fast as possible."

"Got it." Brynley turned into the long driveway. "I'm glad you included me in the plan."

"I'm grateful for your help as long as it's safe. But if we come under attack, I'm teleporting you out."

She rolled her eyes. "I'm not helpless, you know. I've fought in a few of your vampire battles."

"Yes, but you were in wolf form." He gave her a wry look. "Which makes you even scarier than usual."

She scoffed. "You'd better believe it, bloodsucker."

"Snout-Face." He spotted a surveillance camera by the front door. "We're being watched. Stop in front and wait in the car till I come around to your door."

She braked and turned off the engine. "I don't see any guards. It looks peaceful."

"Appearances can be deceiving." He climbed out of the car, and scanned the area. Listened. Nothing but the rustle of the wind blowing through trees.

He skirted the front of the car and opened Brynley's door. "Stick close to me, so I can teleport you out if I need to."

She groaned with frustration, then climbed out of the car and dropped the keys into her handbag. "Stop worrying so much about me, Phin."

"Impossible, Bryn."

Her eyes met his for a second, and a wave of desire ripped through him. He clenched his fist to keep from caressing her face and looked away. This was not the time. Nate's house could be infiltrated with Malcontents.

"Come on." He escorted her to the front door.

She glanced warily at the camera and pressed the doorbell. "It's almost midnight. They may not answer."

Phineas slipped his hand inside his jacket, ready to pull his weapon. When the last jangle of the door chimes faded away, he could hear footsteps echoing in what sounded like a large foyer. "Someone's coming. Maybe it's Nate."

"No, it couldn't—" She stopped when the door swung open and a well-dressed elderly man glared at them.

"It is a bit late to be calling, don't you think?" he asked with a British accent.

A butler? Phineas removed his hand from his jacket. As far as he could tell, the man was mortal and not suffering from any vampire mind control. "We'd like a word with Nate Carson, if you don't mind."

The butler looked down his nose. "And you are?"

"Phineas McKinney, and this is Brynley Jones."

"Nathan and I are old friends," Brynley added.

The butler glanced at her. "Quite old, obviously, since you've never darkened this doorstep in the three years of my employment."

"John," a voice called from across the foyer. "Let them in."

An annoyed look flitted over the butler's face, and he lowered his voice. "Very well. You may come in, but do not overly tire Mr. Carson." He stepped back and motioned for them to enter.

"Nate!" Brynley ran into the foyer.

Phineas followed and stopped short. Nate was hurrying toward Brynley. As fast as he could in his wheelchair.

"You seem surprised," John murmured as he shut the door. "You didn't know?"

Phineas shook his head. "I heard he was in the rodeo."

"That was before his unit was called up and he was sent to Iraq," John explained. "He jumped on some fellow soldiers to protect them from an explosion. Took some shrapnel in his back. Saved his buddies, but injured his spinal cord."

Phineas watched Brynley hug her heroic friend and felt lousy that he'd ever entertained bad thoughts about the guy. "So he's paralyzed?"

"From the waist down, yes. But he manages the ranch. By the way, I'm John Brighton, his personal valet and physical therapist."

"Oh." Phineas shook hands with him. "I thought you were a butler."

John smiled. "My father was a butler. I'll take that as a compliment. Good evening." He inclined his head and strode away.

"Come on, Phineas." Brynley waved him over. "This is Nate."

"Hey, dude." He shook Nate's hand. "It's an honor to meet you."

"You too." With a grin, Nate turned to Brynley. "It's great to see you again. You're looking good!"

"Thank you." Her smile faded. "I should have come sooner. I'm sorry."

"Don't worry about it." Nate waved a dismissive hand. "I heard that you'd flown the coop, and I was relieved you'd managed to escape."

She winced. "You heard about that?"

"Everybody around here gossips about the mighty Jones family. According to the rumor I heard, your dad threw a big birthday party for you when you turned thirty, then announced you were engaged to be married. In three days. When everyone woke up the next morning, you were gone."

She made a face. "That's pretty much what happened."

"Are you kidding?" Phineas asked. She was thirty years old?

"It's true," Brynley muttered. "My father arranged a wedding with a groom and a twenty-piece orchestra, but forgot to tell me."

"Because he knew you would refuse," Nate added. "Who was the groom? Some rancher from around here?"

She shrugged. "Some dude from Alaska. I never met him. He was supposed to arrive the day I left."

"Your father has some gall," Nate grumbled.

"Yeah, speaking of which—" Brynley lowered her voice. "I don't want him to know that I'm back. I'll only be here a few nights, and I really need to avoid him and his minions."

"I understand. I won't say a word." Nate motioned toward an open door. "Let's go into my office, so we can talk." He started wheeling his chair in that direction.

Brynley held back, then whispered to Phineas, "Well? What do you think?"

"You're thirty years old?"

She swatted his shoulder. "About Nate. Is he under vampire mind control? Do you think there are any Malcontents around here?"

"It looks safe so far. And your friend is fine." Phineas rubbed his shoulder. "You don't look like you're thirty."

"Of course not," she hissed. "I'll look this young for hundreds of years."

"So will I." He arched a brow. "We have more in common than you might think."

Her face flushed a pretty pink. "You're still a blood-sucker, and I'm a—"

"Snout-Face?"

"Shh." She motioned with her head toward Nate. "He doesn't know."

"Okay." Phineas accompanied her into Nate's office.

"Can I get you two anything to drink?" Nate asked as he pulled open the door to a small fridge.

"I'll take a diet cola." Brynley took the bottle he handed her.

"Nothing for me, thanks," Phineas said.

Nate dropped a water bottle in his lap, then wheeled behind his desk. "So what brings you out here so late at night?" He unscrewed the bottle and took a sip.

Phineas sat in the chair next to Brynley. "You had a ranch hand named Earl Giddons who passed away."

"Yeah." Nate frowned. "I heard he died last night. Terrible news."

"Do you know what happened?" Brynley asked.

"Not really," Nate replied. "Kyle found him and rushed him to the clinic in Ten Sleep. He's supposed to report back to me, but I haven't heard anything yet. When I called the clinic, all they could tell me was that Earl was dead on arrival."

As far as Phineas could tell, the rancher was telling the truth. His heartbeat had remained steady. "Have there been any other strange occurrences lately?"

Nate gave him a curious look. "Are you with the sheriff's department?"

"MacKay Security and Investigation." Phineas pulled his ID from his wallet and showed it to the rancher.

"Interesting." Nate examined his ID. "Never heard of them. It's international?"

"Yes. We provide security for select clientele around the world." They also conducted investigations related to the vampire world, but Phineas needed a safe way to explain his interest in Earl Giddons's death. "We specialize in investigating odd, unexplainable events."

"Like the X-Files?" Nate handed the ID back.

"Yes." Phineas pocketed his wallet. "For instance, according to his medical file, Earl Giddons suffered no visible trauma, but he was completely drained of blood."

Nate flinched.

"That surprises you?" Phineas asked.

"Well, yes." Nate ran a hand through his thick sandy hair. "We had two cows mutilated the night before last, and they were drained dry, too."

Phineas exchanged a glance with Brynley.

"I figured it was wolves that attacked the cows." Nate grimaced. "We've had a lot more wolves than usual this year. I told Kyle to shoot them, but he—"

"I've never heard of wolves draining all the blood from their prey," Brynley said quietly.

"That's true," Nate conceded. "But I don't know how else to explain the mutilations."

"We don't believe Earl Giddons was attacked by an animal," Phineas said.

Nate's eyes widened. "You think a person is behind all this? Some crazy person is out there collecting blood?"

"It's very possible," Phineas murmured.

Nate's fists clenched. "Whoever he is, he's graduated from cattle to humans. He's a murderer."

"We agree," Phineas said. "We have reason to believe the murderer is female."

Nate blinked. "Really?"

"Do you know of any new women in the area?" Brynley asked. "She could be living at one of the nearby ranches."

Nate tilted his head, considering. "A few of the ranch hands have mentioned a beautiful blonde they've seen recently at the old Haggerty ranch. Some wealthy guy from out of state bought the place about six months ago, but I haven't met him. Don't get out much. I have to rely on Kyle a lot these days."

Brynley smiled. "You two were always close."

A pained look crossed Nate's face. "It's . . . not the same. Don't get me wrong. Kyle has been great. He was always insisting that I'd walk again and he'd take care of things while I recovered. But after a few years, he . . . well, I think he's tired of doing so much work on a ranch that's not his. I don't blame him. I pay him as well as I can afford, and he does a great job, but . . ." Nate drifted off with a sad look.

"I'm sorry," Brynley whispered.

Nate shrugged. "It's not his fault. He . . . fell into a bad crowd—the rich guy who bought the Haggerty ranch. Kyle was talking about him all the time, and then, four months ago, he changed."

"For the better!" a voice declared from the doorway.

Phineas spun around to see a younger and more muscular version of Nate standing in the doorway.

Brynley rose to her feet. "Kyle!" She stepped back with a gasp.

Phineas understood her reaction the instant Kyle's scent wafted toward him. Nate had been right about his brother changing.

He'd become a werewolf.

Kyle smirked as he approached Brynley. "Oh yeah, princess. How do you like the new me?" His mouth twisted into a snarl. "Maybe you won't turn me down now."

Brynley lifted her chin. "It wasn't your species I objected to. It was your personality."

He lurched forward with a growl.

Phineas jumped to his feet and pulled Brynley close. "Back off, furball."

Kyle glared at him. "Who the hell are you? You have no right to her. You're not one of us."

"Cut it out, Kyle." Nate wheeled his chair around the desk. "These are my guests."

Kyle laughed. "You never figured it out, Nate? Your sweet little friend Brynley is a werewolf."

Nate halted, his eyes wide.

Brynley turned toward him. "Nathan—"

"Is it true?"

"Yes." She glanced at Kyle, then back at Nate. "I didn't ask to be changed. I was born this way."

Nate nodded slowly. "I was shocked when my brother first told me about Lycans, but then I realized I should have figured it out earlier. I always knew there was something strange going on with some of the ranchers. Their followers show a loyalty that goes far beyond what you'd expect of a hired ranch hand."

"We're loyal to our Pack Masters," Kyle boasted as he regarded Brynley with a gleam in his eyes. "And this is our princess, daughter of the Supreme Pack Master."

Phineas tightened his arm around Brynley when he felt her shudder. It was obvious Kyle would run straight to her father to tell him she was back.

He aimed a strong surge of vampire mind control at the werewolf. Kyle was caught by surprise and stumbled back a few feet. His face went blank.

You will forget you saw Brynley here. You will not speak of her to anyone. Now go!

Kyle turned and wandered from the room.

Brynley took a deep breath and squeezed Phineas's arm. "Please tell me you erased his memory."

"I think I did." But he wasn't sure if it would last.

"What's going on?" Nate studied them warily. "You erased my brother's memory? How?"

"I didn't harm him. I'm only trying to protect Brynley."

She hunched down beside the wheelchair. "Please,

Nate. Don't tell anyone I was here. My father would capture me and force me into a marriage I don't want."

"With another werewolf?" Nate asked.

"Yes."

"So Caddoc Jones is the Supreme Pack Master?" When Brynley nodded, Nate regarded her sadly. "You should have told me everything years ago. I thought you trusted me."

"I did," she insisted. "But you didn't know Lycans existed, and I was afraid if you knew the truth, you'd . . . no longer be my friend."

Nate patted her shoulder. "I would have understood. Your father is so damned powerful, and the way so many people kowtow to him makes me sick."

"Those aren't people," Phineas muttered. "They're werewolves."

Nate looked him over. "You're not one of them?"

"No."

"Then what are you?" Nate asked. "Some kind of psychic?"

"Something like that." Phineas removed a MacKay business card from his wallet and set it on the desk. "If you see or hear anything out of the ordinary, please let us know. There could be something . . . evil in this area, and it must be defeated."

Nate's eyes widened. "Evil?"

"And please, Nathan," Brynley whispered. "Don't let my father know I'm here."

"You have my word." He wheeled closer to his desk and wrote on a slip of paper. "This is my number if you need any help." He handed it to her with a wry look. "Not that I'm much help to anyone these days."

"Oh, you are." She hugged him, then turned to Phineas."What should we do now?"

"Leave. Nice to meet you, Nate." Phineas grabbed Brynley's arm and escorted her from the room.

"Be careful!" Nate called after them.

"We will, thanks!" Brynley yelled back as Phineas led her across the foyer and out the front door.

She fumbled in her handbag for the car keys. "Shall we drive back to the cabin?"

"We'll drive." But not back to the cabin. If his vampire mind control had failed on Kyle, then Brynley's father would soon know she was in Wyoming. It wouldn't take a genius to figure out she was probably staying at her brother's cabin.

She climbed into the driver's seat and gave him a surprised look as he teleported into the passenger seat. "Why'd you do that?"

"A precaution. This location is now embedded in my psychic memory."

"Oh." Her eyes narrowed. "You look worried."

"Everything will be cool." He smiled at her, but he was worried. Worried that he'd screwed up and left too many loose ends. He should have erased Nate's memory. And John Brighton's, too. "Drive to the nearest town."

"That would be Ten Sleep." She headed down the driveway to the Carson ranch entrance. "Why are we going there?"

"It's close by." Phineas shrugged when she shot him an annoyed look. He had to protect her. And the best way to do that was to get her the hell out of Dodge.

He remained quiet until they arrived in Ten Sleep, where he spotted a grocery store with a parking lot. "Pull in here. Park over there." He pointed to a dark spot close to a tree.

"The store is closed," she objected, but did as she was told. She turned off the engine and looked at him. "What are we doing here?"

"We'll overnight the keys to your friend, and she can pick up the car here tomorrow." Phineas climbed out. "Lock up and bring your purse." He shut the door and strode toward the dark shadow of the tree.

She scrambled out of the car and swung her handbag onto her shoulder. "Tell me the plan."

"Come here."

With a huff, she strode toward him. "We're partners, remember? We should plan together."

He scanned the area. No one in sight. "The plan is to keep you safe." He wrapped his arms around her and teleported.

Chapter Fourteen

*A*s soon as Brynley materialized, she realized she wasn't in Wyoming anymore. Her inner wolf tensed, and she pulled away from Phineas. "Where are we?"

"Romatech Industries." Phineas motioned toward the nearby building.

"In New York?" Her gaze swept over the building, the gazebo and well-manicured garden, then shifted to the woods. She winced. "What happened to that poor tree?"

"Nothing."

She turned to Phineas. "Why did you bring me here? I want to go back to Wyoming." Her inner wolf snarled, demanding to return home.

"It's not safe."

"It should be," she insisted. "Didn't you erase Kyle's memory?"

"I'm not a hundred percent sure that it worked. When I tapped into his brain, it seemed kinda weird to me."

She narrowed her eyes. "Are you saying werewolves have weird brains?"

"I wouldn't dare. Not with you glaring at me like that. What I mean is I think the dude was on something."

"Drugs?"

Phineas tilted his head as he considered. "I would say steroids."

"Oh." Brynley nodded her head slowly. "He did seem a lot more muscular than when I last saw him. Becoming a werewolf wouldn't automatically add all that bulk."

"And he was acting like a prick."

She snorted. "Unfortunately, that's not a new development. He's always had a chip on his shoulder. Racked up some bad gambling debts he couldn't pay off, so Nate offered to buy his half of the ranch for twice what it was worth. Kyle took the money to pay his debts, but he's always resented his brother for coming to the rescue."

"What an ass."

"Yeah. I can't believe he's a werewolf now." Just what the Lycan world needed—another mean, overbearing male like her father. "I still want to go back to Wyoming."

"I'm not sure the cabin is safe for you now." Phineas led her toward the side entrance. "Is it unusual for a mortal to become a werewolf?"

"Yes. Most mortals have no idea we exist. And we don't go around telling people. Or biting people. We keep to ourselves. Usually if a mortal is changed, it's because he was bitten by a werewolf who was forced to defend himself."

Phineas swiped his ID card, then opened the door for her. "It sounds like Nate's new neighbor is a werewolf, and he might be the one who changed Kyle."

"The guy who bought the Haggerty ranch?" She walked down the hall, trying to remain calm even though her inner wolf was growing increasingly agitated. "Can you take me back tonight?"

"And risk your father capturing you? I thought you were terrified of that."

"I am." Unfortunately, the wolf didn't care. It was growling inside her. "Aren't we supposed to be hunting Corky? We can't do that if we stay here. She might be at the Haggerty ranch."

"I'll do it alone. I'm not putting you at risk."

She came to a stop. "You don't want me to guard you anymore?"

"I can teleport back here for my death-sleep. I'll just have to keep track of the sunrise."

She grabbed hold of his arm. "You don't understand. I have to go back. I need to. Especially tomorrow night for the full moon."

"You can shift at the school. Or I'll take you to Howard's cabin in the Adirondacks. You know, the place where you guarded Marielle."

"No!" She squeezed his arm. "One night at home. My wolf needs it. It's growling inside me, Phineas. I feel like it'll claw its way out my throat if I don't do what it says!"

"Okay!" He eyed her warily. "Sheesh. I didn't realize it was so demanding."

"I need to do what it wants. Please."

He nodded slowly. "I'm just worried about your father finding you."

"Believe me, if I roam around the Bighorn National Forest, no one would ever find me. Unless I wanted them to. It's over a million acres."

"Okay. We'll figure something out." He spun toward a door that opened, then relaxed with a smile.

The guy who came out looked like a skinny, younger version of Phineas.

"Hey, bro. I didn't expect you back tonight." He gave Phineas a knuckle pound, then turned to Brynley, his dark brown eyes twinkling. "You must be the wolfie-girl."

"I'm Brynley." She shook his hand. "You must be Freemont."

"You got it! I'm Da Freeze, the Ice Man." He motioned toward the open door. "Welcome to my humble working quarters. It's a busy night at Vampireville. Lots of people stopping by. I use the term *people* loosely, you understand."

Brynley followed him and Phineas into the office and found three more people—two men and a beautiful redheaded woman. They looked familiar, but she'd never socialized much in the Vamp world and couldn't recall their names.

The woman grinned and grabbed her hand. "You must be Phil's sister! I'm Lara di Venezia. And this is my husband, Jack."

"How do you do?" Jack shook her hand.

"I am Zoltan Czakvar." The third man took her hand and bowed over it. He was a striking man with shoulder-length dark hair and almond-shaped amber eyes.

"Hey, dudes." Phineas gave Zoltan and Jack knuckle pounds. "Dudette." He gave Lara a hug. "So did you guys just arrive?"

"A few hours ago," Jack said. "We've been catching up on reports. Angus thinks you're following a strong lead in Wyoming."

"Yes," Zoltan agreed. "We were just about to call you to see if we could join you there."

"Why don't we all go?" Brynley turned to Phineas with a beseeching look.

"The cabin may not be safe for you." Phineas quickly explained the situation. "I don't know if my mind control worked on Kyle."

"We'll never know if we don't go back," Brynley insisted.

"She has a point," Lara said. "We can't tell if her father's been informed if we stay here."

"If my father knows, he'll send some of his goons to Phil's cabin," Brynley added.

"Then I'll go and see if anyone comes looking for you," Jack suggested.

"I shall go, too," Zoltan offered.

"Is there a television there?" Lara asked. "I want to go, but I don't want to miss Maggie and Darcy's new show."

"What new show?" Jack asked.

Lara huffed. "I told you about it a dozen times. It's

the latest celebrity talk show on DVN. *Real House-wives of the Vampire World.* The debut is tonight!"

"I tried to forget that," Jack muttered.

"I know." Lara gave him an exasperated look, then turned to Brynley. "Maggie asked if we would do the next show at our palazzo in Venice."

"Wow," Brynley breathed. "You have a palazzo?"

"Yes!" Lara's eyes sparkled with excitement. "It would look fantastic on television. And I could show off all my favorite places in Venice."

"It's an invasion of privacy," Jack grumbled.

"Heather and Jean-Luc did the show for tonight," Lara said. "If they can do it, why can't we?"

Jack gritted his teeth. "We'll talk about this later. For now, we need discuss who is going to Phil's cabin in Wyoming."

"You, me, and Zoltan," Lara answered. She glanced at Brynley. "There's a television, right?"

"Yes." Brynley nodded. "In the basement." She turned to Phineas. "I want to go, too."

"No." He held up a hand when she started to argue. "Think it through. If your father's minions show up at the cabin and find these three guys watching television, they'll just think they made a mistake and leave. But if you're there, they'll attempt to take you, by force if necessary, and it'll turn into a battle. Do you want to risk any of these guys getting wounded or killed?"

Brynley swallowed hard. She hardly knew Lara, Jack, and Zoltan. She assumed they'd fought in the battles at Mount Rushmore like she had, but she'd been in wolf form at the time and too involved in the battle to pay them any mind. "I don't want anyone to get hurt because of me. Even without me there, my father's men might give you some trouble."

"Don't worry about it," Jack told her.

"We are pleased to be of service," Zoltan added.

Lara touched her arm. "We're all one big family here. We're happy to help—"

"But I'm not . . . one of . . ." Brynley started.

"You're Phil's sister," Jack said. "You *are* one of us. And we look out for our own."

Brynley's heart squeezed in her chest. A family that truly cared and protected one another? Instead of using one another as pawns? It was a beautiful thought. And it struck a deep need inside her that had long been neglected. This was the way a pack should act. Truly caring for one another. Never banishing boys who showed great potential. Never treating women like bargaining chips.

"Hot damn!" Freemont punched a fist in the air. "We're like the Musketeers! All for one, and one for all!"

Everyone chuckled except Brynley, who blinked to keep tears from crowding her eyes. All this time she'd hated the Vamps, but they were willing to endanger themselves to protect her. They considered her family.

"I'll teleport you guys to the cabin so you'll know the way," Phineas offered. He patted Brynley on the shoulder. "I'll be back soon."

She nodded, her face averted so no one would know she was struggling not to cry.

Phineas turned off the alarm system, then teleported away with Zoltan. While the rest of them waited, Brynley explained their theory that Corky might be hiding at a ranch once owned by the Haggertys. And that the new owner might be a werewolf.

"I'll see what I can find out." Freemont sat at the desk and started a search on the computer.

Phineas and Zoltan reappeared in the office, then teleported away, taking Jack and Lara with them.

Less than a minute later, Phineas materialized and turned the alarm system back on. "Everything's set. Zoltan took the first watch on the porch, and Jack and Lara are in the basement watching television."

Brynley nodded. She still ached to return, but she knew this arrangement was for the best. "I can still go back tomorrow night for the full moon, right?"

"I believe so. Like you said, it's a big place. We should be able to find someplace safe for you to shift."

"Thank you." Her inner wolf grew calm, and she smiled with a sudden comforting feeling of peace. The wolf was happy, and she was happy to be surrounded by people who were willing to help her. "By the way, your brother's investigating the Haggerty ranch on the computer."

"Great." Phineas gave his brother a thumbs-up.

"I got it going on," Freemont murmured, his eyes focused on the monitor. "The Ice Man is too cool for school."

"Speaking of ice, would you like some ice cream?" Phineas asked her. "I could take you to the cafeteria."

"Oooh, it's never too late for a red-hot date," Freemont whispered.

Phineas shot an annoyed look at his brother, then turned to Brynley. "The cafeteria is closed, but the soft-serve ice cream machine is always working."

"Oooh, a little chocolate swirl for the wolfie-girl."

"Enough, Freemont," Phineas growled.

Brynley bit her lip to keep from grinning.

Freemont's mouth twitched. "Ooh, look who's pissed, when he'd rather be kissed."

"Let's get out of here." Phineas grabbed Brynley and led her out the door.

"Wishing you luck," Freemont called after him. "So you'll have a good—"

Phineas whirled around to glare at him.

"—time on your date," Freemont finished, his eyes twinkling.

"I'm sure we will." Brynley grinned as she looped her arm through Phineas's. "Our first date, Phin."

His dark chocolate eyes gleamed. "Let's do it, Bryn."

"Look what I found in the kitchen." Phineas set a chocolate brownie on the table next to Brynley's bowl of chocolate swirl ice cream and glass of milk.

She smiled at him. "You're spoiling me."

"I hope so." Anything to keep her mind off going back to Wyoming tonight. He sat beside her and plunked his bottle on the table.

"Where is everybody?" She pinched off a corner of the brownie and popped it into her mouth.

"Most of the night shift are Vamps, so we don't use the cafeteria very much."

She sniffed when he twisted the top off his bottle. "That smells like beer."

"It's Bleer, a mixture of beer and synthetic blood."

Her mouth twitched. "Shouldn't you be drinking Blardonnay?"

He winced. "Don't tell anyone, but I don't really like Blardonnay very much."

She grinned and spooned some ice cream into her mouth. "Well, you do a great job on the commercials. Do you have a lot of fans fawning all over you?"

He shrugged. "A few."

She pointed the spoon at him. "I think it embarrasses you to be a sex symbol."

He made a face. "It's kind of . . . artificial. I want to be liked for the real me."

"I sure understand that." She took another bite of ice cream. "I hate it when people pretend to like me because I'm Caddoc Jones's daughter. I want to be liked for the real me, too."

"I do like you just the way you are," he reminded her, and she looked away, her cheeks growing pink.

He touched a lock of hair that rested on her shoulder. It was silky smooth against his fingertips. "I'm beginning to think we have a lot in common. We can both live for a long time. We have lousy fathers. We lost our mothers."

"We're both survivors," she whispered. "Wounded souls."

That seemed a little dramatic. He swiveled in his chair to face her. "What wounded your soul, Brynley?"

Her face grew pale. "I-it's just an expression." She bit off a chunk of the brownie. "This is so good. Thank you."

"Brynley. I told you my story. Why won't you share yours?"

She swallowed and sipped some milk from her glass. "I don't talk about it. To anyone." She avoided looking at him, and focused on the flat-screen television mounted on a wall.

Someone must have hurt her bad. It made him angry just to think about it. "I'm not just anyone."

"You're . . . you're on TV!" She pointed at the flat screen.

He frowned at the Blardonnay commercial that had just started.

"Quick!" She shoved at his shoulder. "Turn up the volume!"

With a frustrated groan, he zipped over to the TV and punched the volume button.

"Hello, ladies," his voice filled the room.

Brynley grinned at him. "I love it!"

He shook his head and returned to the table with the remote control. She giggled when he said he had the family jewels in his hand.

He grunted and took a long swig of Bleer. He'd come so close to getting past her defenses until he'd been interrupted by himself.

"Oh look." She gestured at the flat screen. "It's the

show Lara was talking about. *Real Housewives of the Vampire World*."

On the television screen, Maggie was standing with Heather Echarpe, who was introducing her husband and children.

"Of course, everyone knows that Jean-Luc is a famous fashion designer," Heather said, glancing at her husband with adoring eyes. "But he's so much more. A wonderfully loving husband and father."

Jean-Luc shifted his weight, looking uncomfortable.

"And these are your children?" Maggie asked.

"Yes." Heather drew a pretty girl close to her. "This is our daughter, Bethany."

"I know her from the academy," Brynley said. "She's a sweetheart. But those twins—my God, they're a handful."

After Heather showed off the toddlers, Jean-Pierre and Jillian, she gave her husband a hug. "Did you know Jean-Luc is a champion swordsman? The best fencer in all of Europe."

"Amazing!" Maggie said.

Jean-Luc smiled, looking much more at ease.

"Would you mind showing us around your home?" Maggie asked.

"I'd love to," Heather replied.

Maggie smiled at the camera. "My associate will be taking the tour with Heather. Darcy?"

The screen shifted to a sunny day outdoors and showed Darcy in front of the camera.

"This is Darcy Erickson, reporting from Schnitzel-berg, Texas. We have a special treat for you. You'll be the first Vamps to see the Echarpe home in daylight!" She turned, and the camera turned with her to show Jean-Luc's house behind her.

"Wow." Brynley sat back. "That's their house?"

"Yeah." Phineas frowned at the screen. "I've been there before."

"It's huge. Is it real fancy inside?"

"Yes." He sipped more Bleer. "You know, I'm not rich like the old Vamps around here. I can't afford a place like that."

"I know."

He gave her a worried look. "That's something we don't have in common. You grew up rich, and—"

"And I was miserable," she interrupted him. "I don't care about wealth, Phineas."

He heaved a sigh of relief. "I make a good salary here, and the commercials pay really well—"

"Phin." She touched his arm. "I like you just the way you are."

His heart swelled. He grabbed her hand and kissed it. "You don't mind anymore that I'm a vampire?"

She winced and withdrew her hand from his grasp. "I was wrong to hate Vamps. I feel bad about it now. I was just . . . so angry."

"Why?"

She picked up her spoon and swirled it around in the ice cream. "I was devastated when my mom died. And then right after that, Phil got into a terrible fight with my dad and was kicked out. I thought he would come back. But he didn't."

Phineas muted the volume on the television. "It must have been hard on you."

She grimaced. "That doesn't even begin to describe it. I was abandoned by the two people I loved the most. The only two people whom I could talk to and trust. I— I've always felt like my mother didn't fight the cancer. She just gave up."

"Why?"

Brynley sighed. "Remember how you were in denial over your father? I did the same thing. I was about twelve years old before I could admit what was happening. You see, as Supreme Pack Master, my father believes he has the right to take any female in the pack he desires."

Phineas gritted his teeth. "He cheated on your mom?"

"Yes. She endured years of humiliation. Not only was it demeaning to her, but to the other women, too. Some of them were married and didn't want to be unfaithful. But their husbands didn't dare say no to the master. Some of the women actually considered it an honor, but the whole thing made my mother so ashamed. She— she didn't want that kind of life for me."

Phineas squeezed her hand. "I think she would be proud of you now."

Brynley smiled with tears in her eyes. "Thank you. I miss her so much. Her death was hard on my younger brother and sister, too. They were just eleven, so I tried to be a mother to them. When they were fourteen, they shifted for the first time, and then Howell thought he was too old to be babied, so he grew more distant. But my sister, Glynis, she's always depended on me. I hated leaving her there alone."

Phineas nodded. "You feel responsible for her."

"Yes." Brynley took a deep breath. "So after my mother died, Phil had his fight with my father and left. It nearly killed me. I kept leaving notes at Phil's cabin, hoping he'd see them and come back. I *begged* him to come back. And then finally, nine years later, he shows up at the cabin with Vanda. A vampire! And I find out he's been living with vampires all those years when I needed him so much."

"You felt betrayed."

"Yes! And angry. And happy, too. I was delighted to have Phil back in my life, but I was so angry that he'd chosen vampires over me, his twin sister. So I guess I channeled all that rage into a hatred of vampires. Vanda, especially. I've been so rude to her."

Phineas rubbed her back. "It's okay. I think Vanda understands."

Brynley sighed. "She's always been kind to me. I don't deserve it."

"Don't say that. You deserve kindness as much as anyone."

She gave him a sad smile and touched his cheek. "You're such a good man, Phineas."

He rested his hand on top of hers. "Brynley, I'm falling in love with you."

With a gasp, she pulled her hand back. "Don't say that. We can't . . . there's no future for us. You know that. You said it yourself."

"I've changed my mind. I used to think we were all wrong for each other, but now I think you're perfect."

She shook her head. "No! I'm not perfect for anyone. My father would try to kill you."

"I'm not afraid of him."

"You should be!" She jumped to her feet with tears in her eyes. "You should stay far away from me. My father will track you down and punish you. You don't know how terrible he can be. He—" She backed away, a tear tumbling down her cheek.

Phineas's breath caught in his throat. She'd already admitted that her father had mistreated her mother. And other women in the pack. What had he done to his daughter?

"Brynley," he whispered. "What did he do to you?"

With a strangled whimper, she pressed her hands to her mouth.

"Oh shit." Phineas felt sick to his stomach. He thought back to the expression she'd used earlier when she'd called them survivors. "He's the one, isn't he? He wounded your soul."

Chapter Fifteen

*B*rynley paced across the cafeteria, but the room wasn't big enough. Her wolf clawed at her insides like a caged animal. Free, it had to get free. Panic swelled in her chest, threatening to explode.

She pulled open a glass door and dashed outside. Tears blurred her vision, and she stumbled to a stop in the middle of a basketball court.

Dammit, she should have never fallen for Phineas. Now she'd have to chase him away, and it was going to hurt like hell. Once again she would be left all alone.

You have me, her inner wolf growled, louder than ever before.

It's not enough! she screamed back. *I want more!* But she couldn't have Phineas. Ever. Her chest seized with a pain that nearly doubled her over.

"Brynley," Phineas called after her. A door clicked shut behind her.

Oh God, no. He would want an explanation, and she couldn't talk about it. The memories hovered over her like a toxic cloud. She couldn't breathe. She swiped at the tears on her face and sprinted toward the woods.

"Brynley, wait!" Phineas ran after her.

She plunged into the woods and weaved through the trees, heedless of the branches that swatted her face and caught at her hair. She couldn't run fast enough.

Flashes of memories bombarded her. Memories she'd tried so hard to forget. The night she was chased. Hunted. The fear. Terrible, escalating fear. Terror. *Panic.*

Her wolf howled with despair. It was supposed to be the hunter, not the hunted. *Run!*

Footsteps pounded behind her. They were coming after her. Hunting her. Getting closer. No escape. *Don't look back! For God's sake, don't look.* She'd made that mistake before.

"Brynley!" Phineas yelled. "Slow down! You'll hurt yourself."

His voice. His beautiful voice that made her melt inside. Her steps faltered.

"Brynley!" he called to her. *Behind her.*

With a start, she whirled around to face him, her hands lifted to defend herself. An animal-like growl escaped from her mouth.

"Whoa!" Phineas raised his hands, palms up. "It's me. I would never hurt you."

She struggled to breathe and looked around her. Oh God, what had she done? She'd freaked out again.

"Breathe slowly." He stepped toward her.

She immediately stepped back, then halted. She wasn't

a cornered animal. And this was Phineas. He would never harm her. She ran a trembling hand through her hair, brushing away the leaves that had tangled in the wild strands.

She took a slow, deep breath. The scent of wood, fern, and spongy earth filled her nostrils and calmed the beast inside her. She'd stopped in a small clearing where the nearly full moon shone brightly.

Phineas was watching her, his expression alarmed and worried. *Great.* She wouldn't have any trouble chasing him off. He probably thought she was crazy and already regretted any feelings he had for her.

He motioned toward the building. "You want to go back? We could talk."

She shook her head. "You can teleport me back to the school. Those other guys at the cabin can help you. You don't have to work with me anymore."

"You don't want to help me now?"

She steeled her nerves. "I . . . don't want to see you."

He frowned at her. "Are you trying to dump me?"

"We both know we can't . . . be together." Her heart ached with every word. "We should just say good-bye and—"

"No! I'm not giving up on you."

"I—I don't want you."

"I don't believe you. You were all over me last night."

"That was nothing. Lust."

"Really? Then jump me again, and we'll see what happens."

With a wince, she stepped back. "You don't want me. I—I freak out. I'm damaged."

"No, you're beautiful. But some asshole has hurt you really bad. Tell me what happened."

Tears filled her eyes. She shook her head.

He took a deep breath. "Fine. I'll just figure it out. Nod your head if I'm right."

"No. Please, don't."

He leaned against a large maple tree and folded his arms across his chest. "Let's see. You were hurt and abandoned when your mother died and Phil was banished. You were eighteen, right?"

She remained silent, but a touch of fear fluttered in her stomach.

"So I guess you went to college then? You teach English at the academy, so that must have been your major."

The flutter skittered up her chest to her throat.

"You felt alone, betrayed, and abandoned. So . . . you reached out to someone." He grimaced. "I hope I'm wrong."

He wasn't. The flutter made her feel light-headed, so she rested a hand against a tree trunk to steady herself.

"Did you fall for someone?" he asked softly.

Her fingers dug into the bark. Her first lover. His arrogant face flitted across her mind. Why had she ever thought he was handsome? "Seth."

"Seth." Phineas said the name as if it left a foul taste in his mouth. "He listened to you. Made you feel special. Warm and fuzzy. And furry. I bet he was a were-wolf, too."

She nodded.

"And you were so damned lonesome," Phineas grumbled. "And hurt."

More like pathetic. A tear rolled down her cheek. "He said he loved me. He asked me to marry him, and I said yes."

"You thought you were in love?"

"Yes." She wiped away the tear. "I wanted to be in love. I wanted to believe love still existed, and someone could love me."

"So you got engaged."

She nodded. "I took him home to meet my family. My dad approved of him, and I thought everything would be perfect."

"What happened?"

"I overheard him talking to my father one night. Dad was congratulating him on a job well done. And Seth asked how many ranches he would get for marrying me."

"Damn," Phineas whispered.

"Yeah." With a groan, she leaned her back against the tree. "My father set the whole thing up."

"Asshole," Phineas growled. "And that Seth was an idiot if he couldn't see how lucky he was to have you."

She waved a hand. "It's typical male werewolf mentality. All they can think about is acquiring territory. Land means power to them. They want power, prestige, big herds of cattle, horses, and sheep. A mate is just the bitch that gives them cubs."

"That's sick." Phineas paced across the small clearing. "Why do the women put up with it?"

"They're all hoping for the prestige of mating with an Alpha. Only a chosen few can do it. The other women—they're not any different than the non-Alpha males. They're all pack members and have to submit to their master."

"It sounds archaic."

She shrugged. "It's how the pack works. There can be only one Alpha, and the others must submit. Or be banished. It's drummed into us from birth that we must be in a pack. We can't survive otherwise."

"You're brainwashed."

"Most werewolves are very happy in the Lycan world. Everyone knows the rules and knows their place. There's a strong sense of community and security."

"Tell that to the Lost Boys."

She winced. "Obviously, it didn't work for them."

"Or for you. You're surviving without the pack. I bet you never wanted to submit."

It was true. Even as a child, she'd never wanted to obey. Her father had deemed it Phil's fault, that he'd influenced his twin sister with his rebellious Alpha tendencies. But it was more than Phil. It was years of watching her mother suffer and seeing how totally oblivious her father was to the pain he caused.

Deep inside her gut, she'd known it was all wrong. She'd read about love in books, seen it portrayed in movies, and knew it had been twisted into something ugly in the Lycan world. There was no love there. Only manipulation and deceit. Users.

"I was alone with my mother when she died. She regretted that she'd always submitted. She said I should have a choice, that I could choose freedom if I was strong enough."

Brynley sighed. "She wanted me to be strong, but after she died and Phil left, I became depressed. I felt lonely and weak. So I fell for the first guy to come along."

"Seth," Phineas muttered. "Please tell me you didn't stay with him."

"No, I broke off the engagement. His family already had a big ranch in Idaho, but he didn't want to give up the ranches that were promised to him, so he pestered me until I managed to chase him away." She tilted her head, remembering. "In hindsight, it was actually a good thing. It pulled me out of my slump. His betrayal made me angry, and the struggle to get rid of him gave me a purpose. It made me a stronger person."

"How did you get rid of him?"

She shrugged. "Male werewolves like to think they're especially gifted in the sack. It just took a few rumors flying around campus that I'd dumped him because he couldn't perform. Then of course he had to prove the rumors wrong with as many girls as possible. He got one of them pregnant, the daughter of a local Pack Master, and he was ordered to marry her."

Brynley smirked. "Over the years, I've gotten really good at chasing guys away."

Phineas gave her a stern look. "It won't work on me."

She matched his look. "That remains to be seen."

He prowled from one end of the clearing to the other.

"So what happened then? Did your dad keep picking out suitors for you?"

"I really don't want to talk about it anymore."

"Why not? Are we getting to the bad part?"

She made a face at him.

"When did you join the rodeo?"

She crossed her arms. "After I graduated. Dad just sent the suitors there. I kept chasing them off. It was really frustrating."

"I guess your father was pissed off."

She swallowed hard and nodded.

"What did he do?"

Brynley turned to rest her brow against the tree. This was the part she didn't want to talk about. She'd never told anyone. Not her sister. Not even Phil. If only her brother had been there. He would have protected her.

"Brynley."

Right behind her. She whirled around. "I told you not to do that."

"I told you I'd never hurt you." He rested a hand against the trunk and leaned toward her. "I'm not leaving till you tell me."

"Why are you so pushy?" She shoved him away and paced across the clearing.

Chicken, her inner wolf chided her. *Tell him. Are you going to live in fear for the rest of our life? Will you keep on jumping in terror whenever someone comes up behind us?*

No, she couldn't talk about it. It was too painful.

A surge of power swept through her suddenly,

taking her by surprise. It was the wolf, pushing at her restraints, urging her to rebel. *Where is your anger? We're a noble wolf! A fierce hunter! And they turned us into prey.*

A shudder skittered through her body as if the wolf was shaking her. *Tell him! Let the world know what your father did to us!*

She took a deep breath and let it out slowly. *Trust the wolf. The wolf knows best.* It was right. Why was she hiding the truth?

She clenched her fists. This wasn't going to be easy. This was five years of nightmares.

"Brynley?" Phineas asked softly. "Are you all right?"

She squared her shoulders. "My father requested I come home for the Hunt. All the local Pack Masters hold hunts the first night of the full moon, but my father's hunt is the most prestigious in three states. It's invitation only, so it's a big honor to attend."

Her skin chilled and she crossed her arms. "It started off like every other monthly hunt. We all shifted and took off into the woods. I caught the scent of a pair of elk and gave chase. I heard wolves behind me. They'd caught the scent, too. That was normal. Wolves usually kill in groups. I didn't think anything of it. Until I realized . . ."

Tears gathered in her eyes, and bile rose in her throat. She swallowed hard and pressed the back of her hand against her mouth. "They were hunting *me*!"

"What?" Phineas stepped toward her. "Why?"

"I didn't know. I was so afraid, and I couldn't understand why I was the prey. I ran and ran. I tried going upstream, swimming in icy cold lakes, anything to lose them. But they kept coming. And then they . . ."

She strode to a tree and rested a trembling hand on it. "They were young males. They surrounded me. Tightened the circle. Snarling and snapping. And then he attacked."

"From behind," Phineas whispered.

She nodded, and tears ran down her cheeks. "He bit me in the neck and used his weight to hold me down and . . . take me."

There was a tense pause.

When Phineas finally spoke, his voice sounded choked. "He raped you."

"No." She shook her head. "A male wolf always takes his mate that way. It's an animal thing."

"Bullshit. Did you want him to? Did you invite him?" Phineas's voice grew louder, and when she didn't reply, he slammed a fist into the tree.

She jumped back, looking at him for the first time.

"It was rape!" He crashed another fist into the tree.

She stepped back, shocked by the rage on his face.

"Did you turn the bastard in?" he demanded.

"I—I tried to. I ran back to the house and stormed into my father's office. I told him what they'd done, and he just looked at me and said I'd defied him for too long, refusing all the men he'd chosen for me. I needed to learn how to submit."

Phineas's eyes grew wide. "He—?"

She nodded as more tears rolled down her face. "He

arranged it. He'd chosen a new mate for me, and he'd told him to—"

"To rape you?" Phineas growled.

"To take me as his mate. It's the normal way for a—"

"Really? Then why did you run? Why were you so terrified? Why do you still freak out if a man comes up behind you?"

She wiped the tears off her face. "I've had trouble dealing with it."

"Of course you have! The bastard terrorized you and forced himself on you. And your father, that bastard—" Phineas punched the tree again. "I'll rip his damned head off!"

"Stop! Your hands are bleeding." And the tree wasn't looking too good, either. Strange, but it looked like the other damaged tree she'd seen earlier.

"You had better hope I never meet your father." Phineas wiped his knuckles on his shirt. "How long has it been since . . ."

"Five years."

He glanced up at her. "And how long have you been doing the underground thing, helping out the Lost Boys?"

"Five years."

His eyes gleamed. "Good for you. You fought back."

She grimaced. "Only in secret. I've never stood up to my father. When he pulled this last stunt, arranging a wedding for me, I just ran away."

"Are you going to let him choose a husband for you?"

"No, of course not."

"Then you plan to choose your own husband?"

She groaned inwardly and pushed her hair behind her shoulders. "I'm not choosing anyone right now. If my father doesn't approve of my mate, he'll kill him. He'll never allow me to defy him."

"Are you going to live your entire life in fear of him?"

She winced. Her inner wolf longed for its native territory, but if she ever returned to the Lycan world, her father would control her. She would be forced into a life of submission. Centuries of submitting to her father and the mate he chose for her.

A crushing pain seized hold of her heart, and she pressed a hand against her chest. Her inner wolf howled in despair.

She could never return to the Lycan world. Not as long as her father lived. And that could be centuries.

She should have known that the moment she'd fled her father's house. Instead, she'd fooled herself into thinking her exile was only temporary. But she was like Phil now. She could never go home. Never spend time with her younger brother and sister. Not for hundreds of years.

She'd end up abandoning her sister just as Phil had abandoned her.

Tears crowded her eyes once again. Why was the cost of freedom so damned high? "I can't go home."

Phineas touched her shoulder. "I'm sorry."

She reached for him, and he pulled her into his arms.

"Bryn, sweetheart." He held her tight and smoothed a hand up and down her back. "It'll be all right.

You're not alone. You have me. And your brother. And all of us."

"Phineas." She drew back and touched his cheek. "I need to go back. One last time. For the full moon tomorrow night. So I can say good-bye."

Rape. He couldn't get past it. That a father would actually subject his daughter to something that heinous, that cruel.

Phineas accompanied Brynley back to Romatech, silent because he couldn't trust himself not to curse her father. Hell, he'd been afraid just to touch her elbow as he escorted her back. Would she object to being touched after all she'd endured? It was no wonder she was prickly and suspicious, afraid to get close to anyone. She'd been betrayed over and over.

But he wasn't a werewolf. He didn't have any ranches or cattle to gain by pursuing her. He simply loved her for herself. Just the thought that she could marry a Lycan someday who would treat her like an inferior broodmare filled him with rage. He wouldn't allow it. Dammit, she shouldn't allow it. She needed to be strong like her mother had said and choose freedom.

She needed to choose him. He'd never mistreat her. A part of him realized that not all werewolf males were bad. Phil certainly wasn't. If he ever mistreated Vanda, she'd take her whip to him.

Still, he didn't want Brynley to end up with a werewolf. He wanted to be the one to give her the love she deserved, and the freedom she needed. As far as he was concerned, he was her best choice, her best chance at happiness. He just had to convince her of that.

She was quiet, and he couldn't help but wonder what she was thinking. At least she wasn't asking to be returned to the academy. She seemed happy to stay by his side.

The cafeteria door she'd escaped through earlier had automatically locked upon closing, so he led her to the side entrance and used his ID to get them inside.

"Let's check with Jack and Zoltan to see if any of your father's minions have shown up at the cabin," he suggested.

She nodded. "Good idea."

He used his ID again to get inside the security office. "Hey, Freemont."

"Hey, bro, Wolfie-Girl." Freemont glanced up from his computer and grinned. "I saw you guys run into the woods. Playing hide-and-seek?" His smile faded. "Is that blood on your shirt?"

"It's nothing." Phineas glanced at the wall of monitors. There were no cameras that deep in the forest, so their talk had been private.

"He punched a tree," Brynley said quietly.

"Again?" Freemont asked.

"Again?" Brynley regarded Phineas suspiciously. "You have a habit of punching trees?"

He ignored that and frowned at his brother. "Have you heard from Jack or Zoltan?"

"Yeah. About ten minutes ago. No one has shown up,

and Lara was very excited because Jack has suddenly agreed to do that TV show."

"Real Housewives of the Vampire World?" Brynley asked. "What changed his mind?"

Freemont chuckled. "Well, apparently Heather claimed her husband was the best fencer in Europe, and Jack thinks he is. So now he wants on television to set the record straight."

The phone rang, and Freemont answered. "Just a minute, Mr. Whelan. Let me put you on the speaker-phone."

Phineas strode toward the desk. "Do you have news, Sean?"

"Phineas, is that you?" Sean Whelan asked. "I thought you were in Wyoming."

"I was. And I'll be going back. What's up?"

"We've been staking out the Russian Coven House in Brooklyn, monitoring Dimitri. As far as we know, his tracking device is still operative. And it's moving. He just jumped to Cleveland, then Omaha. Headed west. Wait. It jumped again. He's in . . . Wyoming."

Phineas exchanged a glance with Brynley. "Then we were right. Corky's there."

"Looks that way," Sean agreed. "We'll get Dimitri's exact location to you soon. But if he discovered the tracking device, he could be taking us on a wild-goose chase."

"We'll let Angus know. Thanks, Sean." Phineas hung up, then turned to his brother. "Angus will be in his death-sleep right now, so can you send him an e-mail?"

"Will do." Freemont swiveled in his chair to face the computer. "Oh, I found out who's the current owner of the Haggerty ranch. Some dude named Rhett Bleddyn."

Brynley gasped.

"You know him?" The shocked look on her face put Phineas on edge. His hands clenched into fists. If this Rhett was the one who'd raped her, then his days were numbered. "Is he the one who—"

"No." She shook her head, her face pale. "That guy died in a drunken brawl three years ago."

"Good riddance," Phineas growled. Though he would have enjoyed beating the crap out of him. "Then who is this Rhett Bleddyn?"

"He's the guy from Alaska I was supposed to marry."

Chapter Sixteen

The next evening, Brynley hurried to the basement of Romatech, a warm bottle of synthetic blood in her hand. Phineas would be waking soon, and no doubt, he would be hungry.

She'd spent a restful day at Romatech, hanging around the security office, cafeteria, or a bedroom she'd been given in the basement. Phineas was in the bedroom next to her, and she'd checked on him earlier in the day. He lay still in his death-sleep, a sheet pulled up to his waist, his gorgeous chest bare.

He looked so peaceful, nothing like the angry Vamp who had punched a tree till his hands bled. She touched his hands, running her fingers over his. They were cold, but healed. Tears came to her eyes as she recalled how upset he'd been when he'd heard her story. He'd shared the pain and outrage with her. He did love her. She didn't doubt it. She just didn't know how their relationship could work.

Phil seemed very happy with his vampire spouse, Vanda, but he'd given up so much. He'd been disowned by their father, his inheritance stripped and given to their younger brother, Howell. And worst of all, Phil had given up the chance to have children.

She'd always hoped that somehow, someday, she'd find a werewolf husband who didn't care that her father was rich and powerful. He'd love her for herself, and they'd have little werewolf babies. They could make their own little Lycan world somewhere in the country.

Phineas did love her for herself. And like the other Vamp men, he could probably father children. Half-Vamp, half-werewolf children? Was that even possible? Could the genes coexist? Could she be happy living in the Vamp world? Phil had lived with the Vamps for nine years before marrying Vanda. He'd had plenty of time to adjust and put the Lycan world behind him.

He'd managed to make a clean break, but Brynley wasn't sure she could. She'd spent too many years at home with their younger siblings, so she was attached to them in a way that Phil wasn't. Especially her younger sister. Glynis had been only eleven years old when Mom had died and so distraught that Brynley had sheltered her from the ugly truth about their father's unfaithfulness and their mother's hopeless despair. Maybe that had been wrong, but Brynley hadn't wanted to burden her younger sister with more pain.

Brynley winced. If she chose to stay with Phineas, her father would probably banish her. She could end up separated from her sister for centuries. Glynis had grown up so trusting and eager to please that it would be akin to leaving an innocent lamb among wolves.

And what about her inner wolf? It was overjoyed about going back to Wyoming tonight for the full moon, but it would object to being banished. Hell, it would tear her up inside if she could never go back. With a groan, she realized she didn't know what to do. But she did know one thing for certain.

She'd fallen in love with Phineas.

That morning, she'd gathered up the pile of clothes he'd left on the floor and washed them in the basement laundry room along with hers. Lara had loaned her a bathrobe to wear, and after putting the clothes in the dryer, she'd gone to her bedroom for a long nap.

After waking up, she'd showered, put on her freshly laundered clothes, and stacked Phineas's clothes in his bedroom. He was still dead.

With a sigh, she headed to the cafeteria. Freemont was there, so she joined him for an early supper.

Now, with the sun due to set in three minutes, she was hurrying to the basement. The full moon was rising, and she could already feel her inner wolf growing impatient to shift.

She wondered briefly if Kyle would be shifting at his brother's ranch and perhaps mutilating more cows. Maybe he drained all the blood to give to Corky. Maybe she was hiding out at the Haggerty ranch with Rhett Bleddyn. Why would her ex-fiancé buy a ranch in Wyoming when he had so much land in Alaska? And why would he ally himself with an evil vampire? So many questions, but she knew Phineas and his friends could be counted on to find the answers.

Meanwhile, she was eager to shift and roam the Bighorn National Forest that backed onto Phil's land.

She let herself into Phineas's bedroom and set the warm bottle of blood on the bedside table. He was still dead, but soon that would change. She paced across the room. Any minute now.

She halted at the foot of his bed when his body jerked. His chest expanded and lifted off the bed, causing his back to arch. She winced. It looked painful.

"Phineas." She rushed to his side. "Are you all right?"

His eyes opened and immediately focused on her.

She smiled. "Welcome back. I brought you a bottle—"

His eyes flashed red, and with vampire speed he grabbed her arms and tossed her over him and onto the bed.

"Phineas!" Her heart thundered in her ears. Good Lord, he'd lifted her like she weighed nothing. Her eyes widened as he leaned over her.

He touched her cheek, then ran his fingers down her neck. The fingertips pressed against her throbbing artery, and his nostrils flared. "So hungry."

She had a strange urge to let him bite her. A part of her was appalled, but a larger, more insistent part found his desire exciting and the act compelling. Intimate. His fangs would be inside her. Her blood inside him.

The wolf inside her stirred, drawn by the thought of blood. It growled softly. Good Lord, if she shifted now, she might lose control and bite Phineas, and that would be disastrous.

She motioned to the bedside table. "I brought you some blood."

He glanced at the bottle, then back at her. His eyes still glowed red.

She gestured at the bottle once again. "It's nice and warm. And fresh."

His mouth curled up. "Not as fresh as you." He traced her collarbone. "Or as warm."

She winced. This was a hitch in her schedule she hadn't counted on. "Phineas, don't vamp out on me. Get a grip. The full moon is rising, and I need to—" She stopped when his finger touched her lips.

He traced the curve of her upper lip, then the lower one. "Do you know how much I want you?"

Her body responded with a surge of lust and desire, but she tried to ignore it. "You're hungry. I understand that." She pointed at the bottle. "Hurry up and drink."

"I wasn't talking about food." He sat up and reached for the bottle.

She started to sit up.

With vampire speed, he pushed her back down. "Stay."

He lifted the bottle to his mouth with one hand, his other hand on her shoulder, keeping her pinned to the bed.

Her inner wolf hissed, annoyed at being restrained and anxious to shift. "Phineas." She attempted to sit up once again.

He didn't let her budge. "Stay."

"I'm not a dog."

"That's for sure." His hand slid down to cover her breast.

Her breath caught. Her nipple hardened beneath his palm, and she fought the urge to arch against him. This was not the time to succumb to desire, but my God, she wanted him.

He lifted the bottle back to his lips and drank. His Adam's apple moved with each swallow. Such a strong, manly neck. His hand gently squeezed her breast in time with each swallow of blood. And with each squeeze, her desire grew stronger.

Was he nude beneath that bedsheet? What she could see of him was beautiful. Smooth velvet skin over rock-hard muscle. She ran a hand up the corded muscles of his arm, over the bulge of his biceps, and up to his broad shoulders. When she stroked his chest, a deep groan rumbled in his throat.

Oh God, she wanted him something fierce. She squeezed her thighs together. If he didn't rip her clothes off soon, she'd do it herself.

No! her inner wolf objected. *Tonight is* my *night.*

She groaned with frustration. Phineas finished the bottle, set it down, and leaned over her once again.

"Your eyes are still red," she whispered.

"I want you." He brushed her hair away from her brow. "I've wanted you for so long."

"Then why did you turn me down the other night?"

"You wanted a short affair based on lust. I want more than that."

She skimmed her fingers over the prickly whiskers along his jaw. "I want more, too. But I don't see how—"

"If we want it bad enough, we'll make it work."

She gazed into his red, glowing eyes and dared to believe that somehow their love would survive.

His gaze lowered to her mouth. She wrapped her arms around his neck as he inched closer.

"Yes," she breathed, letting her eyes drift shut.

His lips touched hers, gently at first, although there was nothing gentle about her reaction. Her fingers dug into his shoulders. Her heart beat wildly.

Her wolf objected, threatening to shift.

Phineas deepened the kiss, molding his lips to hers, and she opened her mouth to let him in. She swirled her tongue with his. He tasted of blood, but she'd tasted blood many times as a wolf, and it only made her hungrier for him.

A surge of wolf power shot through her, and she broke the kiss with a gasp. "Phineas, I have to shift! I can't wait much longer."

He sat back, grimacing. "Damn."

"I can't help it. We have to hurry!"

With vampire speed, he zipped out of bed and into the bathroom, so fast she barely had a glimpse of his naked body. But what she saw was enough to make her collapse on the bed with groan of frustration. A few seconds later, he was back and throwing on the clothes she'd washed.

She scrambled out of bed as he pulled on his cowboy

boots, and noticed a surveillance camera close to the ceiling. It was blinking red. "Is that thing on?"

He glanced at it, his eyes back to their normal dark brown. "Damn."

"That's a yes?"

"Yeah." He set his cowboy hat on his head and tossed her his jacket. "Let's go."

She strode alongside him. "So we showed up on a monitor in the security office?"

"Maybe." He headed down the hall, snapping his plaid shirt together as he went. "I should have thought about it, but I was . . . distracted." He punched the button for the elevator. "I owe you an apology."

"Why?" She watched him stuff his shirttails into his jeans and considered offering some help.

"I manhandled you." He buttoned the top of his jeans and buckled his belt. "I wasn't thinking clearly."

"Phineas, I'm okay. I . . . enjoyed it."

He glanced at her. "Really?" When she nodded, his mouth curled up and his gaze drifted to her chest. "You were right about the B-cup."

She smiled. "It's good to know the Three-Step rule is still in effect. I was worried after you turned me down the other night."

He waited for her to enter the elevator, then punched the button for the ground floor. "What is this Three-Step rule?"

"In my experience, men tend to be rather simple." She paused when he arched a brow at her. "Well, it basically means that at any given moment, a man's brain is only three steps away from thinking about sex."

He frowned, considering, as he took his jacket from her and put it on. "I disagree."

"You don't think about sex that often?" She scoffed. "I find that hard to believe."

He gave her a wry look. "I don't need three steps. Hell, I just look at you and want sex."

Her cheeks warmed with a blush, and she smiled slowly. "You know, after I've been a wolf for a few hours, I could shift back, and we could have a date. I tend to have a lot of excess energy I need to work off."

He moved toward her. "I could help you with that."

"Goodness. You are faster than three steps."

"You bet." He planted a hand on the elevator wall, close to her head. "I've got a fast mind, but slow hands."

She licked her lips. "Sounds perfect."

He tilted his hat back and leaned in for a kiss.

A thrill shot through her, and her toes curled inside her cowboy boots. What a sexy kisser. Making love to him was going to knock her boots off for sure. "Phin?"

"Mmm." He nuzzled her neck.

"The elevator door has opened."

He glanced back. "Damn."

They hurried to the MacKay security office. Zoltan was selecting a sword and pistol from the caged weapons area. Freemont was focusing on a computer screen, but his eyes were twinkling and his mouth twitching.

Brynley glanced at the wall of monitors and spotted Phineas's bedroom on the bottom row. Damn was right.

Phineas put on his shoulder holster and checked his sidearm. "Where are Jack and Lara? We need to go."

"They just left," Freemont replied. "Jack teleported her to the school. The were-panther lady went into labor, and Lara insisted on going there. Jack said he'd catch up with you guys later."

"Caitlyn's having the babies?" Brynley asked. Damn, but she hated to miss that. She couldn't help it, though. She had to shift. "Oh my gosh, what if Caitlyn has to shift?"

Freemont shrugged. "I don't know. Some Vamp doctor from Houston is with her."

"Robby has been teleporting Carlos back," Zoltan added. "Now that it's dark here, they should be arriving soon."

Phineas touched her arm. "I can take you to the school if you want."

She winced. "I have to shift." The wolf didn't care about her new friends. It growled inside her. *Let's go now!* "I need to go back to the cabin. Now." Hopefully, after a few hours, she could return to see how Caitlyn was doing.

"Okay." Phineas slipped knives into his boots, then turned to Zoltan. "Ready to go?"

Zoltan sheathed his sword. "Yes."

Phineas grabbed Brynley, and within a few seconds, they were materializing at the cabin in Wyoming.

Zoltan glanced around quickly. "It looks the same. No one came during the day."

For a second, Brynley's form shimmered as she fought to keep the wolf from breaking free.

"Whoa!" Phineas jumped back.

She regained control. "That was close."

"You're telling me!" Phineas yanked off his hat and ran a hand over his hair. "For a second, I thought I was hugging a wolf!"

"You almost did." She sat and yanked off her cowboy boots. "I hate shifting with clothes on. It rips them all up." She pulled off her socks.

"You're stripping now?" Phineas shot a warning look at Zoltan.

"I think I'll check on the horses in the stable." He strode to the front door, then glanced back at Phineas, his eyes twinkling. "You're not joining me?"

Phineas dropped his hat on the kitchen table. "In a minute."

Zoltan snorted and left, closing the door behind him.

"Does he know how to feed the horses?" Brynley stood to unbuckle her belt and unzip her jeans.

"Sure. He's used to horses. He's a medieval dude." Phineas moved to block the front window. "You need blinds in this place."

"Afraid a deer might see me?" She dropped her jeans to the floor and kicked them aside. Her hands trembled as she unbuttoned her shirt. "I'm so excited. I can hardly control myself."

"I'm getting a little excited, too."

Her cheeks grew warm. "We always strip before shifting. It's no big deal." She'd done it in front of others for years, but she suddenly felt self-conscious with Phineas watching her so closely. She removed her shirt and dropped it on the chair. "You want to come with me? There are a whole bunch of trees out there you could punch."

"Very funny. I have some investigating to do, but I'll come back for you in, what—two hours?"

She reached behind her back to unhook her bra. "I don't know how long I'll be gone. I won't be wearing a watch, you know." She slipped the bra off and dropped it on top of her shirt.

He sucked in a breath of air.

She blushed.

"Hello, ladies."

She laughed, thankful her shyness was short-lived, and strode toward the door. "I'll see you later, big boy."

He glanced down at his jeans. "It is that obvious?"

She grinned as she stepped outside onto the porch. The cool air chilled her skin, but soon she'd be warm in a thick fur coat.

"Didn't you forget something?" Phineas said from the doorway.

She wiggled out of her panties, then tossed them back at him over her shoulder. "Keep those for me, will you?"

He caught them, his eyes gleaming red.

She ran down the steps and into the grassy meadow.

At last! The full moon shone down on her, and she lifted her arms, surrendering to the inner wolf.

The surge of power was orgasmic, so strong and overwhelming she didn't feel the pain of bones shifting or fur sprouting. Within seconds, she was the wolf.

She was free.

Chapter Seventeen

*B*e safe, sweetheart," Phineas whispered as he watched Brynley trot into the woods.

Her father and ex-fiancé didn't know she had returned to Wyoming, so she should be safe roaming about for a few hours. The national forest was over a million acres and filled with animals, so finding her would be like finding the proverbial needle in a haystack. Hopefully, Rhett Bleddyn would remain in the vicinity of his ranch. As for her father and his minions, they would be miles away at his ranch in Montana, busy celebrating their big monthly hunt.

Still, Phineas tensed with worry when Brynley disappeared from view. *You have to trust her*, he chided himself. She'd been shifting since she was a teenager. She knew how to handle herself in the woods. And it was important for her to have this last night at home.

He strode into the stable and found Zoltan whispering to Molly as he filled her manger with hay. "What's up?"

Zoltan glanced at him with the hint of a smile. "It appears you are not the only one here in love."

"What? Who?"

Zoltan tilted his head toward Molly. "The mare. She is smitten with a wild white stallion."

Phineas's eyes widened. "You can communicate with her?"

"Yes. By the way, she approves of you and Brynley. The gelding does as well."

"Oh, that's a relief. I'd hate to leave them off the invitation list."

"Then you plan to marry soon?"

"I was joking." He winced. Not really.

Zoltan gave him a knowing look.

"Well." Phineas headed back out the stable door. "Let's get some work done, okay?" The sooner they completed their mission, the sooner he could get back here for Brynley.

Zoltan accompanied him to the cabin. "You believe Corky is hiding at the ranch owned by Rhett Bleddyn?"

"It's possible. We know for sure he's a werewolf. An Alpha." And the one Brynley's father had wanted her to marry. Phineas gritted his teeth. Bleddyn was probably still hoping to marry her. He might have bought a nearby ranch so he'd have a reason to stay in the area and pursue her if she ever returned.

"He'll be shifting tonight."

"Yeah." Phineas mounted the steps to the front porch. "He and his pack will be off hunting, so we should be able to sneak into his house. Hopefully, we'll find Corky there."

Zoltan smiled as he followed Phineas inside the cabin. "While the wolves are away, the Vamps will play. I like it."

"Bleddyn's ranch is next to Nate Carson's place," Phineas continued. "We'll teleport to Nate's house and ask him to call Bleddyn's ranch. Then we listen in and teleport straight into Bleddyn's house."

"Excellent. Corky will never know we're coming."

"We need the element of surprise." Phineas checked his sidearm. "She may not be alone. Dimitri could be with her."

Zoltan tucked a pistol under his belt, close to his sheathed sword. "We should knock her unconscious to make sure she doesn't escape. Then we can teleport her straight to Romatech and put her in the silver room."

"Got it." Phineas checked the knives concealed in his boots. "I teleported on Nate's driveway before, so that's probably where we'll land."

"Let's do it." Zoltan looped an arm around Phineas's shoulders to hitch a ride.

They arrived and quickly looked about. The full moon gleamed off the smooth white concrete of the circular driveway. It was quiet, except for the howl of a wolf far in the distance. A werewolf most probably. Phineas tensed. He should have stayed by Brynley's side.

But it was the perfect night to hunt for Corky. Her werewolf allies would all be busy.

"Nice house," Zoltan murmured.

"Yeah." Phineas strode to the entrance and rang the doorbell.

Footsteps ran toward them and the door jerked open.

"Thank God!" John Brighton shouted. His hopeful expression quickly crumpled into one of confusion and disappointment. "I thought you were the paramedics." He pushed past them and ran into the driveway. "Where's the blasted ambulance? I called ten minutes ago."

"What's wrong?" Phineas asked.

"It's Nathan! Dear Lord, if they don't hurry, he could die!" John dashed back into the house, headed for Nate's office.

"What happened?" Phineas followed with Zoltan close behind.

"That damned brother of his. He brought a monster into the house." John stopped by the office doorway, where a maid stood, crying into a handkerchief. "Bring more towels. Hurry!"

She scurried away, and John ran into the office.

Phineas paused at the doorway, surprised by the level of destruction. The floor was littered with papers. Chairs overturned and broken. Holes punched in the walls. Nate's mangled wheelchair was resting on its side. And Nate lay in a bloody heap on the floor.

"You have to apply pressure." John grabbed the bloody towel from Nate's limp hand and pressed it against the gaping wounds across his chest and abdomen.

"Too . . . weak," Nate whispered.

"What happened?" Phineas zoomed toward them at vampire speed and knelt beside Nate.

John was too focused on Nate to notice. "Kyle and Mr. Bleddyn came to see him. I heard them shouting and crashing furniture. I rushed inside and . . ."

"What?" Phineas asked.

John grimaced. "Bleddyn had turned into a monster! His head was human and he was shouting, but his arms were like a wolf, and he was clawing at Nathan."

"He's an Alpha werewolf," Phineas explained. "Capable of a partial shift."

John's eyes widened. "Werewolf?"

"Kyle is one, too," Phineas said. "Most probably, Bleddyn is the one who changed him."

"I wouldn't tell them about Brynley," Nate whispered. "Is she all right?"

Phineas swallowed hard. "Yes." He hoped that wasn't a lie. "Your brother remembered seeing her?"

"No," Nate whispered. "But he knew something was wrong, so he checked the security tape. Saw you both at the front door."

"Shit," Phineas muttered. He'd forgotten about that damned camera.

"That's enough, Nathan," John ordered. "Save your strength."

"He is bleeding out," Zoltan said quietly. "We must move quickly."

John glanced up at him. "Who the hell are you?"

"Zoltan," he replied. "A friend."

"We both are," Phineas said. "And we could have Nate at a clinic in two seconds."

John scoffed. "Impossible."

"You will have to change your mind about what is possible," Zoltan told him. "A werewolf just attacked your friend."

"And we can teleport him to the clinic." Phineas leaned over to gather Nate into his arms.

"What?" John scrambled to his feet. "You're not taking him anywhere without me. Who are you?"

"Vampires," Zoltan replied.

John stumbled back. "No."

"I have more towels!" The maid rushed into the room.

Zoltan whipped around to stare at her, and she halted with a jerk. Her face went blank, then she turned and left the room.

"What was that?" John demanded. "What did you do to her?"

"Mind control." Zoltan gave him a stern look. "Do I need to use it on you, or will you come along quietly?"

"I—I—" John gasped when Zoltan latched on to him at vampire speed. "What—?"

They vanished.

Phineas teleported Nate straight into the security office at Romatech. The alarm went off, and Freemont leaped to his feet, grabbing his automatic.

"Holy crap, Phin." He lowered his gun and turned off the alarm. "You scared the shit out of me!"

"I'm taking this man to the clinic. Hurry, get the door!"

Freemont opened the door, and Phineas dashed into the hallway, carrying Nate. Zoltan was coming in the side entrance dragging John.

"Where are we?" John demanded. "This is kidnapping!"

"Get Roman and Laszlo to the clinic now," Phineas told his brother.

Freemont winced. "Roman's not here. He's at the school, helping with Caitlyn's delivery."

"Send Laszlo then!" Phineas zoomed toward the clinic at vampire speed.

He set Nate on a gurney and turned on the overhead lights. Zoltan zoomed in and set John on his feet.

"Get away from me!" John reeled back. "You—you're some kind of monsters!"

Zoltan looked annoyed. "Have we harmed you?"

"You kidnapped me and Nathan!"

"We took you to a clinic to save his life," Zoltan argued.

John looked frantically about. "Where is this place?"

"Romatech Ind—" Phineas stopped when Laszlo rushed in.

"Oh dear." Laszlo's eyes widened at the sight of Nate. He zoomed over to the sink and washed his hands with vampire speed. "He's fading fast. We'll need at least four bags of"—he sniffed—"Type A positive."

"I'm on it." Zoltan rushed toward the refrigerator.

Laszlo snapped on some gloves and zoomed over to the gurney. He inserted a needle into Nate's arm and motioned with his head toward the tray. "Phineas, take the scissors and cut the shirt off him."

"Right." Phineas lifted the blood-soaked shirt away from Nate's torso and began cutting.

Nate moaned.

John approached the gurney. "What can I do?"

"Pray," Laszlo answered. He grimaced as Phineas peeled back the shirt. "He has a lot of internal damage. I'm not a doctor. I can sew up a cut, but this is too much."

"What if we give him vampire blood?" Zoltan suggested as he stacked bags of blood on the work tray. "Won't that heal him internally?"

"Or we could transform him," Phineas said quietly.

Zoltan and Laszlo stopped and exchanged looks.

"What?" John asked. "What are you talking about?"

"If we turn him into a vampire, it will heal his wounds," Phineas explained.

"No." John shook his head. "Then he would be dead. He would be a monster."

Laszlo frowned. "Do we look like monsters?"

John studied the short man with the innocent, round face. "I'm not sure. Do you bite people?"

"I'm a chemist." Laszlo lifted a bag of blood. "And this is synthetic blood we manufacture here at Romatech. We make our food, we don't steal it."

"Nate?" Phineas leaned over him. "Can you hear me? We can heal you if we turn you into a vampire. You'll be dead during the day, but alive at night. And you could live for centuries."

Nate blinked at him. "Legs?"

Phineas glanced at Laszlo. "He has a spinal cord injury. Will it heal?"

Laszlo twisted a button on his lab coat as he considered. "Possibly. He has such severe injuries across his abdomen, the transformation might trigger all sorts of healing."

"Then it's possible?" John asked. "He could walk?"

"Possibly," Laszlo answered. "For certain, it will save his life."

"Do it," Nate whispered.

Phineas exchanged looks with Laszlo and Zoltan. "I'm not sure I know how." His own transformation had been brutal and violent. He didn't want to repeat that.

"I can do it." Zoltan rested a hand on Nate's brow. "When I give you my blood to drink, you must accept it."

Nate licked his cut and swollen lips. "Okay."

Zoltan peeled the shirt collar away from Nate's throat.

Phineas grabbed John's arm and led him across the room. "Did Kyle attack him, too?"

"Yes. That bastard."

"Was he in wolf form?" Phineas asked. "Did he bite Nate?"

"No. He was still human." John's mouth twisted with disgust. "He was punching and kicking his own brother." He glanced back at the gurney where Zoltan had sunk his fangs into Nate. "What is he doing? Is he hurting Nathan?"

"He's transforming him. John, look at me. Nate will

be alive and strong at night, but completely vulnerable during the day. He needs someone who will guard him and protect him from his brother."

"I can do that." John nodded. "And I'll have my son help, too. We won't let anyone harm Nathan. He—" John's eyes filled with tears. "My son was a photo-journalist, traveling with Nathan's unit during the war. When Nathan was injured, he saved my son's life."

Phineas rested a hand on John's shoulder. "He's fortunate to have you now."

John nodded and glanced back at the gurney. "Will he be all right? Will he still be . . . Nathan?"

"Yes. His personality won't change. Will you stay here with him till he wakes tomorrow night?" When John nodded, Phineas continued, "I need to go back to Wyoming and make sure Brynley is all right."

"Is she a vampire, too?"

"No, she's a werewolf, but a good one. She would never hurt anyone."

John gave him a curious look. "You're a vampire with a werewolf girlfriend? How does that work?"

"Good question," Phineas muttered. He just hoped she was all right and he could find her.

As he dashed back to the security office, he spotted Jack coming in the side entrance. *Great.* Jack and Lara could help him look for Brynley. "Is Lara with you?"

Jack shook his head. "She stayed at the school. Caitlyn's been shifting back and forth, scaring the shit out of Dr. Lee, so Carlos is the only one allowed in the delivery room with her now."

"No babies yet?" Phineas asked.

"Yeah!" Freemont opened the security office door and peered outside. "Did she have kittens?"

"Not yet," Jack replied. "I came back to see if you guys had captured Corky."

"We have another problem now," Phineas said. "Brynley could be in danger. Rhett Bleddyn knows she's back, and he's a vicious bastard. Nearly killed a mortal. Zoltan is in the clinic right now transforming the guy. And Brynley—she's alone."

Freemont winced. "Wolfie-Girl's in trouble."

Jack nodded. "Let's go."

Phineas zipped through the trees for another half a mile, then paused to listen. Nothing.

This wasn't working. He and Jack had teleported back to the cabin and split up to cover more ground. So far, no sign of Brynley. No word from Jack. And they'd been searching for almost an hour.

Bleddyn was one nasty character. Attacking a guy in a wheelchair? Sheesh, he'd nearly killed Nate. And Kyle, that creep deserved to die. The thought that those two bastards could have shifted and gone hunting for Brynley, it made his heart clench in his chest.

She'd been hunted down once before. And raped. He couldn't let that happen to her again.

He needed a new strategy. He gazed up a tall pine tree and zeroed in on a strong branch. A second later, he materialized there and grabbed hold of the trunk. This was better. He had a bird's-eye view. And eyes as good as a bird. He scanned the area and listened carefully.

A small herd of elk at twelve o'clock. At one o'clock, a small lake glimmered in the moonlight. Farther off to the right, Jack was searching. He turned to the left. Bushes thrashed far ahead at ten o'clock. Something was being chased.

He focused on a treetop and teleported there. The chase was just ahead of him. He teleported to another tree.

There. A mule deer darted into a small clearing, and a wolf charged from behind. A large wolf, moving at an incredible speed. It had to be a werewolf.

He teleported closer and materialized on a tree branch just as the wolf pounced on the deer. Within seconds the deer was down and its neck broken with a mighty wrenching of the wolf's jaws.

Damn. If that was Brynley, she was amazing. He whistled softly to see if the wolf would look up.

It did. Sky-blue eyes.

He grinned. He'd found her, and she was fine. More than fine. She was freaking powerful.

A loud growl emanated from the forest.

Phineas tensed, his fingers digging into pine bark. Was it Bleddyn?

Brynley froze, her ears flattening, the fur on her back bristling.

Out of the woods lumbered a huge black bear. It reared up on its hind legs and roared.

Brynley stood her ground.

"Back off," Phineas whispered. *Don't argue with a bear. Let it have the deer.*

The bear roared again, and moved toward the deer. Brynley bared her teeth and growled back.

"Damn." What was she thinking? Phineas took out his automatic and fired a warning shot to scare off the bear.

The bear shifted into a large, hairy man. He lifted his hands in surrender and looked frantically about. "Don't shoot!"

Phineas's mouth fell open. *Digger?*

Brynley shifted into human form. "You're a werebear?"

He stared at her. "You're a werewolf?"

Phineas teleported down, and with vampire speed, he whipped off his jacket and covered Brynley.

Digger gasped. "You're one of them damned aliens!" He shifted back into a bear, and with a growl, he charged.

Chapter Eighteen

*P*hineas teleported Brynley across the clearing.

Digger roared when his pounce hit nothing but air. He spun about and spotted them.

"Digger," Phineas began, but quickly levitated with Brynley when the bear charged again.

"Digger, stop!" Brynley yelled at him.

Digger shifted back to human form. "You need to get away from him, little lady, so I can kill him. He's an alien."

"I'm not an alien," Phineas muttered.

"Maybe you can kick him in the balls," Digger told her, then frowned. "But I ain't sure them aliens have balls."

She gave Phineas a wry look. "Shall I verify that you have balls?"

He arched a brow. "This is not how I envisioned our first intimate encounter." He glanced down at Digger. "Can we come down now?"

"Sure. But I'll have to kill you."

"I'm not an alien!"

"You are, too! You appeared out of nowhere. You must have beamed down from the mother ship."

Phineas groaned. "I was in a tree, watching Brynley. And what the hell were you doing, attacking her?"

"I wasn't gonna hurt her," Digger mumbled. "I just wanted the deer."

Jack zoomed into the clearing at vampire speed. His eyes widened at the sight of Phineas and Brynley hovering twelve feet in the air. "I heard a gunshot. Are you all right?"

"Dagnabbit! Another alien!" Digger bellowed.

"Where?" Jack glanced behind him, then gasped when Digger shifted back into a bear and charged. He levitated, too. "*Merda!* Now I see why you're floating."

"Cut it out, Digger!" Brynley yelled at him. "These are my friends."

Digger changed back to human form. "You shouldn't make friends with aliens."

"We're not aliens," Phineas ground out. "And would you please cover yourself? There's a woman present." He adjusted his jacket around Brynley. Luckily, it was long enough to hit her at mid-thigh.

The corner of her mouth curled up. "You seemed a bit concerned about my virtue."

"Damned straight. And what the hell were you doing, growling at a bear?"

She winced. "I know it was crazy. My inner wolf has been acting so weird lately. Like it thinks it can take on the world."

Phineas's attention shifted back to Digger when the old man whistled. His dog, Jake, trotted into the clearing. He still wore the foil-covered football helmet on his head, but now also sported a pack strapped to his back.

"The dog plays football?" Jack asked.

Digger snorted as he pulled a pair of jeans out of the dog's backpack. "Dogs don't play football. You aliens ain't as smart as you think."

Phineas's eyes watered as he caught a whiff of Digger's clothes. "Did you run into a skunk?"

Digger chuckled as he pulled on the jeans. "I spray my clothes down with skunk oil. It covers up my scent."

That was true. Usually Phineas could always tell a shifter by his scent. Digger had caught them by surprise.

"But of course I knew right off that the little lady was a shifter," Digger continued. "I hoped she was a bear like me, but it ain't surprising she's a wolf. Lots of werewolves in these here parts."

"Not all of them good," Phineas said. "There's a dangerous Alpha in the area named Rhett Bleddyn. He attacked Nate Carson tonight and almost killed him."

Brynley gasped. "Nate was attacked? Is he all right?"

Phineas nodded and lowered his voice. "We took him to Romatech. We had to transform him."

Her eyes widened. "Is he going to be okay?"

"Yes. He'll be fine. Zoltan's taking care of him."

"Why would a werewolf attack Nate Carson?" Digger asked. "Nate's a good guy."

"Bleddyn is trying to find Brynley," Phineas explained. "Nate was protecting her, and he nearly died for it."

"Oh no." She shuddered in his arms. "Poor Nate."

Phineas hugged her tight. "Bleddyn knows you're here. That's why we came looking for you. I was afraid he would be hunting you."

"A werewolf hunting another werewolf?" Digger scratched at his beard. "That don't seem right."

"My father tried to force me into marrying him," she grumbled. "I ran away."

Digger frowned. " 'Cause you're in love with an alien?"

"I'm not an alien!" Phineas growled.

"We're vampires," Jack said.

Digger stepped back, his eyes wide. "What in tarnation? Vampires?"

"Yes," Phineas said. "We can teleport and levitate, as you can see—"

"Did you mutilate those cows and drink their blood?" Digger asked.

"No. We drink synthetic blood from bottles," Phineas replied.

"They're the good guys," Brynley insisted. "When I ran away from home, they took me in. And they've taken in all the Lost Boys that my father kicked out of the pack."

"Who's your pa?" Digger asked.

She took a deep breath. "Caddoc Jones."

Digger's eyes widened. "Well, ain't that somethin'? I

know Cad from way back. Well over a hundred years ago." He ran a hand through his shaggy long hair. "Haven't talked to him in a spell. Seemed to me he got too big for his britches. Started acting like a jackass. No offense, ma'am."

"None taken," she answered wryly.

"Can we come down now?" Phineas motioned to the ground.

"I reckon." Digger eyed him suspiciously. "You ain't gonna bite me or my dog, are you?"

"I'd rather starve." Jack waved the air in front of him, his nose wrinkled against the foul odor.

"Vampires." Digger shook his head. "I knew there was something strange going on in these hills. You sure you ain't seen no aliens around here?"

"No. We're looking for a bad female vampire." Phineas lowered himself and Brynley to the ground. "We think she's allied with Bleddyn and staying at the old Haggerty ranch."

"A lady vampire?" Digger asked. "Did she mutilate the cows?"

"I'm not sure," Phineas replied. "Maybe."

Digger tugged at his beard. "This is all very strange. I could have sworn there were aliens around here. Well, I'll be going now. And taking the deer, if you don't mind."

"Go ahead." Brynley waved a hand. "Bye."

Digger heaved the dead deer over his shoulders and lumbered into the woods. "A werewolf in love with a vampire. Don't that beat all?"

Phineas gave Brynley a questioning look as he drew her into his arms. "Could Digger be right?"

"About aliens?"

"No." He kissed her nose. "About a certain werewolf being in love with a vampire."

She wrapped her arms around his neck. "Depends on the vampire. Is he in love with a certain werewolf?"

Phineas's vision darkened to a dusky pink as his eyes turned red. "I've always heard that actions speak louder than words."

She touched his cheek. "What actions do you have in mind?"

"Okay," Jack interrupted. "I'm feeling a little unnecessary at the moment. I'll teleport back to the cabin to see if Bleddyn has shown up."

"Thanks, Jack," Phineas said without looking back.

He chuckled and teleported away.

"Alone at last." Brynley smoothed her hand over Phineas's jaw. "We were talking about action?"

"And words." He pulled her close. "I do love you, Brynley. I know it won't be easy. I'm dead half the time. And—"

"Stop." She placed a finger over his lips. "Don't come up with reasons not to love me. I want you to love me. Now."

His eyes turned red. "I can do that." He teleported away with her.

Brynley landed on cool, soft grass. She quickly looked about and smiled. Phineas had taken her back to the meadow below the Cloud Peak Glacier. One of the most beautiful places she knew.

"Is it all right?" he asked. "I could take you to Romatech or the cabin in the Adirondacks. We could have a bed there—"

"This is perfect." She breathed deeply of the cool, crisp air. "This is home."

"It's not too cold?"

"Cold?" She pulled off his jacket and tossed it on the ground. "Do I look cold?"

His eyes flared a hotter red as his gaze sizzled over her naked body, then settled on her hardening nipples. "Maybe a little chilled."

"Then make me hot." She rushed toward him and ripped open the snaps on his shirt. "The animal in me wants to claw the clothes right off your body."

He pulled her close and nuzzled her neck. "The Vamp in me wants to nibble"—he trailed kisses down her neck —"and bite"—he nipped her shoulder—"and suck the life out of you." He planted his mouth on her nipple.

"Oh." She arched her back as he suckled hard.

He picked her up, his hands on her bare rump, and she wrapped her legs around his waist. He tugged at one breast, then started on the other.

"Phineas." She ran her hands over his short hair.

"Mmm." He tickled the tip of her nipple with his tongue, then pulled her closer so her core was pressed against his bare stomach.

He tugged on her breast in rhythm to rocking her

against him. Moisture seeped from her, and tension built higher and higher.

Oh God, she was going to come before she'd even gotten his clothes off.

"Stop!" She pulled his head back and wiggled out of his arms.

"You don't like it?"

"I love it." She yanked his shirt off his shoulders and kissed his chest, his nipples, his six-pack abs. He was gorgeous, muscular . . . and walking her backward. "What—?"

He shoved her back, and she landed on her rump on his jacket. With a grin, he pounced on top of her.

He kissed her mouth, then moved down her body, kissing and nibbling past her breasts to her stomach. "You're so beautiful."

"You're still dressed." She pushed him back, then pulled his legs up to make him fall onto his back on the grass. With a yank, she had one boot off. She tossed it aside and grabbed the other boot. It proved to be more stubborn, and she tugged so hard she lost her balance.

He took advantage, giving her an extra shove so she tumbled back.

"Umph." She landed on her back with the boot in her hands.

He seized her ankle and nipped at her calf. "Now I have you."

She tossed his boot aside. "Oh yeah?" She planted her other foot against his chest and shoved him back.

As soon as his butt hit the ground, she leaped forward to pin his shoulders to the ground. "Now I have *you*."

"Wolfie-Girl, you are wild."

"You'd better believe it." She leaned forward and rubbed her breasts against his chest.

He kissed the top of her head.

With her heart thundering in her ears, she sat back on his thighs and unbuckled his belt. "All right, Love Doctor." She unbuttoned his jeans. "Let's see what you've been hiding." She struggled, getting the zipper to move over the bulge.

Finally, it unzipped, and she grasped the waistband of his jeans and underwear and pulled. He sprang free.

She gasped.

He took advantage of her momentary shock and pushed her back onto his jacket. She struggled to sit up, but he pinned her shoulders down.

"Stay."

"I'm not a dog." She glanced down his beautiful body to the magnificent erection that pointed at her, wide and blatant, smooth and rock-hard. "Woof," she whispered.

He chuckled. "Now be a good Wolfie-Girl and let me ravish you."

Moisture pooled between her legs, and she ached for him to fill her. "Hurry."

"Patience." He smoothed his hands over her breasts and down her belly. Her skin prickled with gooseflesh, and she shivered.

He clasped her thighs and pushed her legs apart. "I want to look at you."

She whimpered as more moisture seeped out.

He leaned closer till she could feel his breath against her wetness. "So pretty. And juicy."

She jolted when his tongue licked her slowly.

"Tasty." He inserted a finger inside her. "Tight. And wet."

"Oh God, please!" She wiggled against him. "I can't take it anymore. I want you inside."

"I'm not done with the outside." He skimmed his juice-slickened fingers up to her clitoris, and she jolted again. "Look what I found."

Tension built rapidly as he rubbed against her. Pinched and tugged. She shook her head, moaning. When he lifted her hips to clamp his mouth on her, she screamed and shattered.

Spasms shot through her. Her toes curled and her vision blurred. He showed no mercy. With two fingers inside her, he coaxed more spasms from her till black stars twinkled before her eyes.

"Enough," she wheezed, struggling to catch her breath.

"We're just getting started." He smiled smugly.

"You're—you're—"

"Sexy? Incredible?"

"Ridiculous!" She shoved him back. "You still have clothes on." She yanked his jeans and underwear down his legs.

"You recovered quickly."

"You'll have to work harder than that to wear me out." She eyed his erection. "Oh yeah. This is good." She traced a vein along the silken hardness.

He sucked in a hissing breath.

Joy burst inside her. She loved how strongly he reacted to her. "Does it feel good?" She circled the crown.

He gritted his teeth. "I want inside you."

"I'm not done with the outside." She leaned over and licked the bead of moisture from his tip.

"Dammit." He shoved her back and wrapped her legs around him. "We're doing it now."

"About time!" She grabbed on to his shoulders and trembled when his erection nudged into her damp folds.

He stopped. "Brynley."

"*What?*" She gazed into his eyes and forgot her frustration. He was looking at her so tenderly, it made her heart ache.

"I love you."

Tears filled her eyes. "I—ay!" She squealed when he plunged into her. "Oh, Phineas." He was so wonderfully big and hard.

He kissed her brow and started slow. That didn't last long. She was soon begging for more. Harder. Faster.

Her nails dug into his shoulders. Her heels dug into his back.

She screamed, and the spasms seemed to last forever as he pumped into her. With a long groan, he collapsed beside her. The aftershocks continued, and she gasped for air.

He lay still beside her.

"Are you still alive?" she asked.

"Until sunrise." He kissed her neck. "Did you need more?"

She groaned. Was he trying to kill her? "I just want to lie here for a while."

"Good plan." He rolled onto his back and gazed at the stars. "It was better than I ever imagined." He took her hand in his and laced their fingers together.

Her heart swelled with love. "This is perfect."

"Yes."

They lay together holding hands until the cold night air made her shiver.

"You're cold." He sat up and dug into a pocket of his jeans. "You might want these back." He dangled her panties in the air.

"You kept them?" She grabbed them and slipped them on.

"You can wear my shirt." He handed it to her, then pulled on his jeans.

She snapped the shirt together. "What do we do now?"

He pulled on his boots. "We still have to find Corky."

"I mean about us."

He stood and slipped his jacket onto her. "We make it work."

She bit her lip and looked away. It had been perfect, but perfection could never last.

"Bryn." He nudged her chin back so she'd look at him. "We can do this."

"I want to believe that."

"Then do it." He pulled her close. "Let's get the rest of your clothes."

She nestled her cheek against his bare chest. Everything went black, and she materialized in the cabin.

A gun fired, and Phineas stiffened.

She gasped. There was a dart in his arm.

He ripped it out.

Another shot exploded, hitting Phineas again. His body jerked, and she stumbled back, bumping against Jack on the floor. He lay, stiff and motionless, a look of horror in his eyes.

Phineas yanked the dart from his shoulder and grabbed her. "Let's go."

"No!" a blond woman shouted, firing her pistol again and again. *Corky.*

Brynley pulled the darts from him as fast as she could. His body shimmered as he tried to teleport, but then he solidified and collapsed onto the floor.

It had all happened so fast. Shock quickly morphed into full rage. She threw off Phin's jacket and shifted, growling and ready to attack Corky.

"Don't even think about it," a man's voice said.

She whipped around and saw three men standing at the back of the room. Kyle and two others.

"Allow me to introduce myself." The tallest one stepped forward. Dark hair, dark eyes. But not a friendly brown like Phineas's. His eyes were cold and hard like flint. "I'm Rhett Bleddyn. This is Dimitri. And I believe you already know Kyle."

She shifted back to human form. When Rhett's cold

gaze drifted over her ripped shirt, she put Phineas's jacket back on. "What do you want?"

Rhett smirked. "You, of course."

"Not going to happen." She glanced down at Phineas. He seemed to be conscious and watching her.

"The vampires are paralyzed." Rhett motioned to Dimitri. "Thanks to a special potion Dimitri brought us. Kyle, would you care to demonstrate?"

Kyle came forward and kicked Phineas in the ribs. He lay there, helplessly taking the attack.

"Stop!" Brynley shouted.

"Oh, it could get much worse," Rhett said. "You see, Kyle has a stake, and he's ready to plunge it right into the hearts of these vampires."

Kyle whipped a wooden stake from his belt and held it over Phineas's bare chest.

Brynley's heart stuttered.

"So, Miss Jones," Rhett continued with a sly grin. "I believe we were going to get married?"

Chapter Nineteen

*N*ightshade. Phineas struggled to make his body follow orders, but it lay attached to his active mind like a sack of dead meat. Too ironic. The former drug dealer taken down by a drug. And not just any drug, but the same damned drug that had inspired his death and transformation. The Malcontents had murdered him and made him a vampire so he could get them the ingredients to make Nightshade.

Karma was a bitch. It had come back to kick him in the butt. Or the ribs. He winced inwardly as Kyle rammed another pointed cowboy boot into his side. The creep had done the same thing earlier to his brother.

Shit kicker, Phineas wanted to yell at Kyle, but then that made him the shit. And rightly so. He should have called Jack before coming. He should have managed to teleport Brynley away before succumbing to the drug. Now she was in danger. Her eyes met his, and he cringed inwardly at the fear he saw there.

Be strong. You're a survivor. As long as you're alive, you can fight.

A rebellious spark lit in her eyes, as if she'd heard him.

"You haven't answered me, Miss Jones." Rhett Bleddyn strode toward her. "Have you agreed to marry me?"

She narrowed her eyes. "I'll consider it if you leave these men alone."

"You'll agree or the vampires will die." He motioned to Phineas. "That one first. His scent is all over you." He stepped closer, his face twisted in a sneer. "You reek of sex with him. It disgusts me."

She lifted her chin and glared back. "Frankly, Rhett, I don't give a damn."

He slapped her hard enough to make her eyes water.

Rage burst inside Phineas, but with nowhere for it to go, it felt like his head would explode. *Stay strong, sweetheart. Don't give up hope.*

"I have heard of your disobedience to your father," Rhett growled at her. "With me, you will learn to submit."

She avoided looking at him and focused on Phineas, her cheek aflame with a red handprint. "I will marry you a week from today."

Hope flared in Phineas's chest. She was looking at him, making the promise to him.

"Three days," Rhett countered. "On the first night after the three nights of the full moon."

It was a strategic maneuver, Phineas realized. Any werewolf could shift on the three-night period of the full moon, but only an Alpha like Rhett could shift the following night. He wanted the ability to defeat any ordinary werewolf that might object to a forced marriage. Brynley's father was an Alpha, too, but he was obviously for the marriage.

But this was a mistake on Rhett's part. It gave Phineas and his friends three nights to gather their troops and rescue Brynley. Unless, of course, Rhett intended to kill him and Jack tonight.

Brynley inclined her head. "I want the ceremony to be at my father's ranch in Montana."

"Of course. We'll be going there shortly. I suggest you dress appropriately and wash that vampire's stench off you." Rhett motioned to Dimitri. "Make sure that restroom is secure."

Dimitri peered inside. "No windows, no doors. She can't escape here."

She picked up the clothes she'd discarded earlier and with a worried glance at Phineas, she went inside the bathroom and shut the door.

Rhett sneered down at him. "She will do everything I ask. Kyle will remain here with his stakes, and if she gives me any trouble, I'll call him, and he'll turn you to dust."

"He deserves to die," Corky hissed as she moved toward them. "He is the one who betrayed me and tried to capture me."

"There, there, love." Rhett pulled her close and kissed her brow. "I was happy you came to see me again."

She gave him a sly smile. "Our plans are going well." She glanced down at Phineas. "Dimitri found the formula and ingredients to make Nightshade hidden in a safe at the Coven House in Brooklyn. He cooked us up a batch and brought it here."

She nudged Phineas with her foot. "We have plenty more. You and your traitorous companions will not be able to stop us."

Phineas wondered what Corky and Rhett were up to. They appeared to be lovers, even though Rhett was forcing Brynley to marry him. His motivation for marriage was clearly not love, but most probably wealth and power. Just as Brynley had said, she was more of a pawn than a princess.

She emerged from the bathroom, dressed in jeans and a plaid shirt. She ignored Rhett as she walked past him, and aimed a look of love at Phineas. He tried to return it. She sat nearby at the kitchen table and pulled on her socks and boots.

"Your father will be pleased that I've returned you to the pack," Rhett boasted. "And he will be impressed by how well you obey me."

She shot him an annoyed look as she tugged on the last boot.

"You will obey," Rhett reminded her. "Or I'll call Kyle, and he'll stake the vampires."

Her gaze shifted to Phineas and Jack, then to Kyle. "If you hurt them, the entire Vamp world will come after you. Including your brother."

Kyle snorted. "Nate's dead."

"Undead."

Kyle turned pale. "What?" He gave Rhett a frantic

look. "You said he would die, that the ranch would be mine."

"It will be." Rhett glowered at his minion. "You will obey me in all things and be rewarded. You will not question me again."

Kyle inclined his head. "Yes, master."

Rhett shifted his glare to Brynley. "You're back in the Lycan world now. Adjust your loyalties." He motioned to Corky and Dimitri. "Take us to the Jones ranch in Montana."

Corky wrapped her arms around Rhett and cuddled up to him, then they vanished.

Brynley rushed toward Phineas, but before she could reach him, Dimitri zoomed to her and grabbed her. One last look, her eyes filled with a mixture of hope and despair, and then she was gone.

Her emotions transferred straight from her eyes to his heart. Despair that she was gone, that he'd lost her, that she would suffer abuse and humiliation at the hands of Rhett Bleddyn and her father. And hope that he would find her, rescue her, and spend the rest of his life giving her the love she deserved.

"You'd better hope Rhett doesn't call." Kyle tapped him on the chest with the stake. "And I don't care if you made Nate a vampire. I'm not afraid of him. I have plenty of these." He stuffed the stake in his belt.

"Anything to eat around here?" He glanced toward the kitchen, then back down at Phineas. "Don't run off."

He chuckled at his own sorry joke and wandered out

of Phineas's view. If Phineas strained his eyes to the left, he could make out one of Jack's shoes. No doubt Jack was just as frustrated as he was.

Noises came from the kitchen. Kyle was raiding the refrigerator, banging cabinet doors shut, and dropping utensils into the stainless steel sink with a clatter.

Brynley would be at her father's ranch now. A prisoner. She'd run away before, so she would probably be watched and guarded.

Footsteps headed to the sofa, then a creak as Kyle settled down, and gulping noises as he wolfed down his food.

Time crept by. He thought about Brynley, recalled every detail of their lovemaking, and prayed he'd have a chance to love her again. He strained, trying so hard to make his body move that beads of sweat rolled down his temple.

Snores came from the couch. Kyle was sound asleep. He was a lousy guard, but then he knew they weren't going anywhere.

More time passed. Phineas kept trying to budge, but to no avail. A phone buzzed on the kitchen table. One of the sat phones. Freemont, most probably, wanting to know why they hadn't checked in. Luckily, it was set on vibrate, and Kyle was sleeping right through it.

Come on, Freemont. If his brother played it smart, he would report their lack of communication. As a mortal, he couldn't teleport here to check on them, but he could ask Zoltan to drop by.

The minutes dragged by. Kyle kept snoring, and no one teleported in. No call from Rhett, so Brynley must be cooperating to keep Jack and him safe.

The sat phone buzzed again. *Dammit, Freemont, send someone!* Was it already dawn in New York? If the Vamps had all fallen into their death-sleep, there would be no rescue.

A terrible thought crept into his mind. If he and Jack were still on the floor at dawn, the sun would shine through the cabin windows.

And they would be toast.

She'd forgotten what an orgy of blood and guts occurred each month at her father's house. Brynley had avoided the official hunt for five years now, ever since that night she'd become the prey. She'd started going to smaller hunts, hosted by friends she could trust, or she'd hunted with the Lost Boys at Phil's cabin.

Dimitri had materialized with her, arriving next to Rhett and Corky in the woods bordering her father's enormous backyard. It was there, in that grassy clearing, that the werewolves returned from their hunt, naked and bloody from gorging on their kills, many of them dragging dead carcasses behind them.

Each month, steel rods were erected down the length of the backyard, like rows of clothing rods in a closet, but with hooks instead of hangers. There, the elk and deer would be suspended and dressed. A row of fire pits were ready with spits for roasting.

Up on the hill, the giant ranch house sprawled. It had been purposely built on a hill, so her father could look down at anyone approaching.

Her father's pride and joy was the covered back patio, equipped with an enormous outdoor kitchen and bar. Slabs of meat would be barbecued, bottles of beer guzzled down, and the party would continue for three nights. Gorging and hunting. Food and blood. Booze and sex. The Alphas who attended her father's parties were allowed to take any women they wanted. Of course, the Supreme Pack Master's daughters had always been off-limits, until that night five years ago.

She spotted her father on the patio, dressed in jeans and an unbuttoned shirt, talking to a female werewolf, still nude and smeared with blood across her breasts. Caddoc Jones didn't look a day over forty-five, although he had to be four times that age. He fisted his hand in the woman's long hair and pulled her close for a kiss.

Brynley looked away. She'd always suspected his infidelity and cruelty to Mom had incited the fight between him and Phil, resulting in her brother's banishment.

Rhett noticed her discomfort and chuckled. "Wait here." He strode into the clearing.

His stride and posture, clearly that of an arrogant Alpha wolf, made him stand out. Also the fact that he was neatly dressed while most of the returning hunters were nude and covered with blood, guts, and grime.

He marched down the center alley, framed on each side with rows of hanging carcasses. Blood dripped, staining the grass. Female Lycans reacted to his prowess, brushing their long hair over their shoulders to show off their breasts.

Brynley was suddenly immensely grateful that she'd fallen in love with a Vamp.

"Rhett!" Caddoc Jones strode to the edge of the patio and gazed down onto the backyard. "It's about time you showed up. You're late for the Hunt."

Rhett stopped in the middle of the yard. "I've already been hunting tonight. And I've caught the most amazing prey."

Caddoc lifted an eyebrow. "Indeed? Where is this prey of yours?"

Rhett glanced back, motioning to Dimitri. The Malcontent grabbed Brynley and zoomed forward, depositing her next to Rhett. He dashed back to the woods and Corky.

It seemed odd to Brynley that no one looked surprised that Rhett traveled with a few Malcontents. Apparently, they were accustomed to seeing him with vampires. But they were surprised by her appearance. Murmurs spread among the werewolves till everyone in the yard was staring at her.

She took a deep breath and looked up at her father.

He stared at her. At first she thought his face completely expressionless, but then she noticed the clenched jaw and eyes so intense he could probably kill a deer without touching it. He was pissed. Well, she supposed she had caused him some embarrassment by running away from the wedding he'd planned. That had been a rule drummed into her and Phil since infancy. Never,

ever contradict or embarrass their father in front of his minions.

"I've brought her home," Rhett boasted. "And she's agreed to marry me in three days."

Caddoc's eyes narrowed. "Has she?"

He didn't trust her. Well, he was right. She had no intention of marrying Rhett. Ever.

"Brynley!" a female voice squealed. A pretty young woman in a flowery cocktail dress ran across the patio, or attempted to. With a laugh, she kicked off her high-heeled sandals and sprinted barefoot across the yard.

Brynley's heart expanded. "Glynis." She grinned when her sister threw her arms around her with an exuberant hug.

They'd always hugged, especially after Mom had died and Phil had left. As the only females in the family, they'd clung to each other for support. They'd always understood there were no hugs to be had from their father or Glynis's twin brother, Howell.

"Thank you, Rhett! I knew you could do it." Glynis grinned at him, then at Brynley. "I've been begging him to bring you home."

"Mission accomplished." Rhett winked at her.

She giggled and pulled Brynley toward the patio. "Isn't he dreamy?" she whispered.

More like a nightmare. "Glynis, we need to talk."

"I know!" Glynis frowned at her. "I was so devastated when you ran away. If you had just stayed one more day, you would have met Rhett, and you would have seen how perfect he is for you." She glanced toward their father and lowered her voice. "And you wouldn't have upset you know who."

Brynley stopped about six feet from the patio, where her father was still staring at her.

Glynis stepped between them, a wide grin plastered on her pretty face. "Brynley's come home, Dad! Isn't that wonderful?"

Bless her, Brynley thought. Glynis had always wanted to believe they were a happy family. This was the only world she knew, so she clung to the notion that it was a good one. Brynley had never had the heart to purposely burst the pretty bubble her sister lived in. She'd protected her over the years in hopes that her sister would escape by marrying a nice werewolf who would treat her well. Whenever a questionable guy had shown interest in her, Brynley had chased him off.

Caddoc glanced at Glynis, then back at Brynley. "I'm sure you two have a lot of catching up to do. Glynis, she will share your room until the wedding."

Glynis clapped her hands together and grinned at Brynley. "We'll have so much fun! It'll be like summer camp."

Poor Glynis. She didn't realize she'd just been assigned twenty-four-hour guard duty.

Caddoc motioned to three of his minions, who were, thankfully, dressed. "See that my daughters are . . . comfortable."

"Yes, master." They bowed their heads.

Three more bodyguards. Her father was making sure she'd have no chance to escape.

One of the guards strode toward the house and opened the back door. "This way."

Glynis linked her arm with Brynley's. "I can't wait to hear all about your adventures. I'm so glad you're back home. I missed you terribly!"

"I missed you, too," Brynley murmured, glancing back to find the other two guards behind them, steering them like cattle into a pen.

"And we have wedding plans to make!" Glynis pulled her inside. "I'm so excited!"

Brynley winced as the door slammed shut behind her. She was back home.

In prison.

Chapter Twenty

*B*rynley paced around her sister's large bedroom suite. It was no wonder pack members thought they were princesses. Glynis's king-sized bed was covered with Egyptian cotton sheets and a pink satin duvet. The large armoire housed a big flat-screen television and library of DVDs.

The adjoining bathroom sported gold-plated fixtures on the marble sink and giant Jacuzzi tub. The walk-in shower was lined with marble and boasted three spray nozzles. No bathroom window for escape.

She eyed the white marble floor and thought of Phineas and Jack lying helpless on the bare wooden floor of her brother's cabin. Were they still paralyzed? If she escaped, would Rhett call Kyle and order him to stake them? Maybe she should give them more time before she made her move.

She wandered back into the bedroom.

"Come on, Bryn." Glynis patted a spot next to her on the bed. "Tell me where you've been. What have you been doing?"

"Teaching school." She peered out her sister's large upstairs window. It was a big drop to the ground below. But not so bad if she had a rope. Or expensive Egyptian cotton sheets.

The circular drive in front of the house was jammed with SUVs and pickup trucks from the hundred or so guests attending the Hunt. Maybe she could borrow one. It was common for her father's guests to leave the keys in the vehicles in case one needed to be moved. No one worried about robbery here. There were always a few guards on duty.

Besides, anyone who messed with her father or his property would find himself mauled to death by a pack of wolves. Anyone who helped her escape would probably face a similar fate. She was on her own.

"Do you like teaching?" Glynis asked. "The kids aren't mean to you?"

"The kids are grateful they have a home." She glanced back at her sister. "I'm mostly teaching the Lost Boys."

"What Lost Boys?"

Brynley sighed. "I'm afraid I've overprotected you." It had felt necessary when her sister was eleven and mourning the loss of her mother, but unfortunately, it had become a habit that was hard to break. "Glynis, our father banishes young boys from the pack. Just like he did Phil."

She blinked. "Phil chose to leave—"

"No. Our father kicked him out. He does it to boys every year. Some of them as young as twelve years old."

Glynis shifted uneasily on the bed. "I didn't realize

they were so young. We're not supposed to talk about them. Once they're out of the pack, they—"

"They still exist. Imagine being without your home and family—"

"Don't." Glynis shuddered. "They wouldn't have been banished if they hadn't misbehaved."

"How can you say that? These are young boys with nowhere to go."

Glynis gave her an injured look. "I'm not heartless, you know. I'm glad you found a home for them. But you weren't banished like them. Your home is here."

"Doing what?" Brynley muttered as she sprawled into an armchair upholstered with pink roses. "You're twenty-three years old, Glyn. Don't you want to do more than play hostess every month for the Hunt?"

She looked indignant. "I do plenty of things. I get to travel—"

"With an escort."

She waved that aside. "I feel safer with them. And I get to shop—"

"With Dad's money."

Glynis huffed. "Well, someday I hope to marry, but Dad insists that you get married first."

Brynley dropped her head back on the cushion. "No wonder you're eager to marry me off."

"Brynley!" Glynis tossed a pink satin pillow at her. "Don't make me sound so selfish. I want you to be happy. And Rhett really wants to marry you. He promised me he would be a good husband to you."

Brynley groaned.

"He's handsome and charming." Glynis ticked off a list on her fingers. "He's a powerful Alpha. He's almost as rich as Dad. He has a dozen ranches in Alaska and one here so you could always spend time here in your old hunting grounds. And they call him the King of Alaska! That would make you a queen."

"He already has a queen. A vampire named Corky who's probably his mistress."

Glynis rolled her eyes. "He's a very virile man, Bryn. You couldn't expect him to stay celibate while he was waiting for you to return."

Brynley gave her sister a worried look. "Have you fallen for him?"

"No." She blushed. "I'm interested in someone else."

"Really?" Brynley sat forward. "Who?"

Glynis's blush deepened. "He's a werewolf, but not an Alpha. He's not interested in power or land. He's an artist. Dad hired him to paint a mural in the great hall, and when no one was looking, I would bring him water to drink. He's so sweet. Not at all like . . ."

"Our father?"

Glynis winced. "I'm not blind. I can see how Dad and the other Alphas behave."

Brynley sighed. "Our father's not going to allow you to date a guy who's not an Alpha or doesn't own land."

Glynis hung her head. "I know."

"Then why do you stay here?"

Her eyes widened with surprise. "Where else would I go? I live here. I have most everything I could want here." She smiled. "Especially now that you're back. I want you to be happy, too. And I think Rhett is perfect for you. You were always the strong and fearless one, and he's that way, too."

"Me? Strong and fearless?" Brynley shook her head. She'd lived most of her life in fear of her father.

"Yes, you are," Glynis insisted. "You've done all kinds of things I would never have the nerve to do. You went off to college, you joined the rodeo, you're teaching school." Her eyes glimmered with tears. "You're always leaving me. And I need you here."

"Oh, Glynis." Brynley sat beside her on the bed and hugged her. She couldn't blame her sister for taking comfort by clinging to the security of the Lycan world. Unfortunately, the world that made Glynis feel safe made her feel trapped.

"Please give Rhett a chance," Glynis begged with tears in her eyes. "He wants you. And it's not just for power and prestige. He's taken a real interest in you. He's always asking me questions about you. What do you like? What do you dream about? Where do you go when you want to be alone?"

Brynley winced. "You told him about Phil's cabin?"

"Sure. I told him lots of things. I want you to be happy with him."

She felt the prison bars closing in.

"He plans to court you, you know." Glynis beamed with excitement. "So you'll be happy to marry him. Isn't that romantic?"

Brynley started to explain that Rhett's idea of romance was threatening to kill others so she would submit. But as she studied her sister's hopeful smile, she couldn't bring herself to tarnish the gilded cage her sister enjoyed living in.

"And only three days to the wedding!" Glynis clasped her hands together. "It's so exciting! And guess what? Dad had a beautiful gown made for you for the last wedding. It's still hanging in your closet."

A seed of panic stirred in Brynley's chest. She had to get out of here. If only she could teleport like the— She gasped. That was it! All she had to do was call a Vamp, and he'd teleport in and swoosh! She'd be outta here!

"You look shocked." Glynis grinned. "But don't worry. I've seen the gown, and it's really lovely."

Brynley nodded. She needed a phone. Her gaze swept the room. No phone in sight. But close to the door there was a bombé chest with Glynis's bright red designer handbag sitting on top. There had to be a cell phone inside. What wealthy young lady didn't own a cell phone?

"I'll be your maid of honor, right?" Glynis asked.

Brynley nodded, still focused on the red handbag. Her portal to freedom.

"Oh, I bought the cutest dress the other day in Billings. It's teal-green. Is that all right for the wedding?"

"Why don't you try it on?" Brynley suggested. "I'd love to see it."

Glynis jumped to her feet. "That's a great idea! Then you can help me decide which shoes to wear with it." She dashed into her giant walk-in closet. "I'll just be a sec!"

"Take your time." Brynley rushed over to the red handbag and dug through its cavernous interior. No phone? She checked inside pockets, outside pockets. Dammit. She opened the drawers of the bombé chest. Scarves, mittens, hats, berets, gloves.

She ran to the bedside tables and checked the drawers. No phone. There had to be a phone somewhere in this damned house. Her bedroom had a phone. At least it had before she'd run away. It was just down the hall.

She eased open the door, and a guard quickly appeared.

"Can I help you?"

He was a new guard, probably from a pack far away in Idaho. The other two guards stood nearby. Strangers to her, but loyal to her father.

She cleared her throat. "I thought I'd go to my bedroom for a second. My wedding dress is there, and I'd like to see it."

"We'll arrange it," the guard responded. "Anything else?"

Could you arrange to jump off a cliff? "I'm a bit hungry." Actually, after killing that deer and having wild sex with Phineas, she was starving. She needed to keep her strength up.

"We'll have a tray brought up for you."

Before she could say anything else, the guard shut the door in her face.

"What do you think?" Glynis bounced from the closet, wearing a beautiful teal-green dress.

I think I'm screwed. She heaved a big sigh. "It's lovely."

With a laugh, Glynis twirled in a circle. "Only three days till your wedding!"

Three days to escape. She wondered again how Phineas was doing. She should have told him she loved him while she had the chance.

The sat phone buzzed again. Phineas groaned inwardly. Freemont had to know something was wrong. He was going to get chewed out for sure if—

Four forms materialized nearby. Zoltan with Roman hitching a ride. Vanda giving Gregori a ride. Of course. Freemont's choices had been limited to those Vamps who had teleported here before. Zoltan and Vanda. The location of the cabin was embedded in their psychic memory. And they'd brought Roman and Gregori, because most of the MacKay employees were still in Russia and Eastern Europe.

Zoltan and Roman were armed with swords, Gregori with an automatic pistol, and Vanda with a whip.

Roman sheathed his sword. "Jack? Phineas? Are you all right?" He knelt beside Phineas. "Can you talk?"

Phineas blinked.

"We're not alone." Zoltan pointed his sword toward the couch. "Let's get back to Romatech now."

"Just a minute." Roman picked a dart off the floor and looked curiously at it. "I think they were drugged."

"It must be Nightshade," Gregori said. "I don't think they can move."

A groan sounded from the couch, then a sleepy "What the hell?"

"Vanda," Zoltan whispered. "Go. Take Jack with you."

She fell to her knees beside Jack, wrapped her arms around him, and vanished.

"Roman, take Phin—" Zoltan stopped.

A huge growl sounded behind Phineas, and he knew Kyle must have shifted.

"Watch out!" Zoltan shouted.

Roman jumped back just as the werewolf leaped, his vicious jaws snapping.

Gunshots fired, and the wolf jolted in midair, then landed with a thud on top of Phineas. He winced inwardly as the two-hundred-pound weight squirmed in death throes on his torso.

Zoltan shoved the wolf off him, and it shimmered, returning to human form.

"Shit," Gregori said softly, the gun still in his hand. "Is he dead?"

Zoltan felt for a pulse on Kyle's neck. "He's gone."

Gregori grimaced, then muttered another curse.

"You had no choice," Roman told him. "He was attacking us."

Gregori holstered his gun. "I thought he was going to bite you. I just meant to stop him. I didn't mean to . . . Shit!" He paced away.

Phineas blinked slowly. Nate Carson would have a lot to deal with when he woke up. His first night as a vampire. And the news that his brother was dead.

Zoltan straightened and looked around the cabin. "Brynley's gone. The werewolves must have taken her."

Phineas managed to make a sound something like a moan.

Zoltan leaned over him. "We'll get her back."

Roman knelt beside him. "The drug should wear off during your death-sleep. Tomorrow night, you'll be as good as new."

"And tomorrow night, we'll have a small army," Gregori added. "Angus ordered everybody to return to New York. They'll arrive tomorrow."

Zoltan picked him up. "We'll find her, Phineas. Mark my word."

The next night, Phineas awoke in his basement bedroom at Romatech. Alone. It was only last night when he'd kissed Brynley in this bed. Just last night when he'd made love to her by the Cloud Peak Glacier.

Frustration seethed in him that he had spent the rest of the night drugged and entirely helpless, unable to rescue her. He guzzled down two bottles of blood, threw on some clothes, and zoomed upstairs to the MacKay security office.

"Hey, bro!" Freemont grinned at him from behind the desk. "You're looking a lot better. Last night, you looked kinda stiff."

"What took you so long to send someone? We could have fried there on the floor if the sun had risen!"

"Dude, it was only fifteen minutes."

Phineas blinked. "What?"

Freemont snickered.

Damn. "It felt longer than that," Phineas mumbled. "I was paralyzed, you know. I couldn't see any clocks."

Freemont nodded, his eyes twinkling. "You have to admit I did pretty good, huh?"

Phineas shrugged. "Yeah." So there had been several hours of darkness left, hours that he should have spent rescuing Brynley, but he'd been unable to move.

He turned away, and one of the monitors caught his attention. Nate Carson was sitting up in bed, drinking a bottle of blood. His sire, Zoltan, was standing nearby, talking to him. Nate's bare chest looked completely healed.

"We have a new Vamp," Phineas murmured.

"Yeah." Freemont walked over to stand next to Phineas. "I heard your wolfie-girl is missing. I'm sorry."

His heart squeezed painfully. "It was my fault."

"I think it was mine." Jack walked in, a bottle of blood in his hand. "I should have managed to escape. I felt so damned helpless, lying there on the floor, unable to move and worried that you and Brynley might return at any minute."

"Well, we have good news from the school." Freemont gave them an encouraging grin. "Caitlyn had her twins this morning. A boy and a girl. No fur, but healthy lungs."

"That is good news," Phineas agreed.

Jack nodded. "I should go pick up Lara."

"Whoa!" Freemont pointed at a monitor. "Angus and the guys just teleported in."

They stepped into the hall as Angus and ten of his employees entered the side entrance. Angus lifted a hand in greeting. "Phineas, Jack, how are you? I heard ye were drugged last night."

"We're fine, sir," Jack said. "Did you hear the good news? Caitlyn had the twins, both healthy."

Emma clasped her hands together, grinning. "That's fabulous! Oh, I'd love to see the babies."

Angus chuckled. "Go ahead and go. I'll take care of things here."

She kissed his cheek, then teleported away.

Angus motioned toward the conference room. "Let's get started. I want to hear everything that's happened."

Everyone filed into the room and took a seat around the conference table.

Phineas was too anxious to sit, so he paced toward Angus at the head of the table. "We need to rescue Brynley. She's been taken to her father's house, and they'll force her to marry—"

"Lad." Angus stood and rested a hand on his shoulder. "The sun is still up in Wyoming. We have two hours before we can teleport there."

Phineas took a deep breath. "You're right." He should have known that. He wasn't thinking properly.

"Doona fash," Ian told him. "We'll get her back."

"Who took her?" Phil demanded.

"A nasty werewolf named Rhett Bleddyn," Jack said.

Howard Barr stiffened. A low growl vibrated in his chest.

Rajiv, who was sitting next to him, gave him a worried look. "You all right, Pooh Bear? We could go to cafeteria and get you donuts."

"I'm not hungry," Howard gritted out.

Howard not hungry? Phineas turned to look at him and noticed everyone else was staring, too.

"Do you know Rhett Bleddyn?" Austin asked.

Howard shimmered for a second, then resumed his usual large human form.

Rajiv moved back. Phineas could never recall a time when Howard had struggled to control the Kodiak bear within him.

"If we go to battle with him," Howard growled, "then I will be the one to kill him."

Chapter Twenty-one

Would ye care to elaborate, Howard?" Angus asked.

"No."

Everyone exchanged glances. As far as Phineas knew, Howard had grown up in Alaska, and since Bleddyn was also from Alaska, there was obviously something that connected the two shifters. Something bad.

Phineas took a seat at the table. "Bleddyn is allied with Corky. She's the one who drugged Jack and me."

Angus motioned to Jack. "Tell us what happened."

"I was at the cabin when an SUV pulled up," Jack began. "Tinted windows. I could only see the front seat. Bleddyn and Kyle got out and asked to see Brynley. I said she wasn't there and they should leave. That's when I heard shots. I whirled around and spotted Corky and Dimitri just as the darts hit. They must have been in the back of the SUV, and they teleported behind me to attack."

"They shot you with Nightshade?" Mikhail asked.

"Yes. I fell down, and they dragged me into the

cabin." Jack made a face. "I couldn't warn Phineas to stay away."

"At least we now have proof that Corky is there," J. L. Wang said.

"She claims to have a lot more Nightshade," Phineas said. "We'll have to careful capturing her."

Angus nodded. "And you believe she's hiding at Bleddyn's ranch?"

"Yes," Phineas replied. "She and Dimitri. After she shot me, they teleported Brynley and Bleddyn to her father's ranch. Bleddyn left Kyle behind—"

"Who exactly is Kyle?" Angus asked.

"My brother," a voice said from the doorway.

Everyone turned. Nate Carson stood there with John, Zoltan, and Gregori.

Zoltan stepped into the room. "Allow me to introduce the newest members of our community, Nate Carson and his mortal guard, John Brighton."

Phineas rose to his feet. "Dude, you're standing."

Nate smiled sadly as he walked into the room. "I have my legs back. But I've lost my brother."

Phineas glanced at Gregori, who remained in the doorway, a pained expression on his face.

"Welcome." Angus shook hands with Nate and John. Then everyone walked over to the new guys and introduced themselves.

Phil shook Nate's hand. "Thank you for always being there for Brynley. She's my sister."

Nate's eyes widened. "Then you're a werewolf, too?"

"Yes." Phil nodded. "My father banished me from the pack years ago. Best thing that ever happened to me, actually. These are good people here."

"Great to see you walking, dude." Phineas slapped Nate on the shoulder. "How do you like being Undead?"

Nate's mouth quirked. "It's strange. A few days ago, I didn't even know vampires existed, and now I am one." He glanced around the crowded room. "Everyone seems very supportive. I didn't expect that."

"Yeah, it's cool." Phineas winced. "I'm really sorry about your brother. If I had been able to talk—"

"It probably wouldn't have changed anything," Nate interrupted him. "I've known for months that Kyle was hanging around a bad crowd. I tried to warn him, but he wouldn't listen. He—he helped Bleddyn attack me. I don't know what hurts the most. That he's gone, or that he turned on me."

Phineas patted his shoulder. "He was messed up, dude. I think he was on steroids."

Nate sighed. "He was certainly too aggressive. Zoltan told me he was trying to bite you all. You had no choice but to shoot him."

"It was me." Gregori approached them. "I pulled the trigger. I'm sorry."

A pained look crossed Nate's face. "I understand. In war, we have to make tough decisions."

"And live with them," Gregori muttered.

"Let's get back to business," Angus announced, and everyone took a seat. Angus looked at Nate. "My condolences on your brother. Zoltan just explained the situation to me."

Nate nodded.

"As soon as the sun sets in Wyoming," Angus continued, "we can teleport you and John back home with a supply of synthetic blood. We'll do whatever we can to help you with your transition."

"Thank you," Nate said. "I think I'd like to try one of those Bleers."

Everyone smiled. Except Howard. He was frowning with a fierce gleam in his eyes.

"Any ideas what this Rhett Bleddyn and Corky are up to?" Angus asked.

"Power," Howard said quietly. "Bleddyn wants all werewolves in North America to swear allegiance to him."

"Corky could be planning to use vampire mind control on mortals," Ian suggested.

Angus nodded. "So together, they could control both mortals and werewolves?"

"That would make us their enemy," Phil said. "Vamps and shifters they can't control."

Howard fisted his hands. "He's a cruel bastard who kills other shifters and any mortal who gets in his way. Even children."

Silence permeated the room.

Phineas sucked in a breath. "I guess we'll have to kill him."

Howard gave him an intense look. "I thought I had."

Angus sat back. "All right. We'll go after Bleddyn and Corky—"

"And we rescue Brynley," Phineas added.

Phil raised his hand. "I'll take care of her."

A surge of anger shot through Phineas, and he pivoted in his chair to face Phil. "*Now* you're worried about her? What about all those years when she left you letters, begging you to come home?"

Phil gritted his teeth. "I was banished."

"Do you have any idea what she went through?" Phineas yelled. "Abuse. Humiliation." He stopped himself from saying *rape*. "She suffered, and you weren't there to protect her."

Phil's form shimmered for a second as the inner wolf crashed against his restraints. "You think I don't care? I left letters, too, begging her to leave with me. She never responded."

"Enough, ye two." Angus regarded them sternly. "We'll get her. For now, ye need to calm down and keep yer wits about you."

Phineas took a deep breath. "I want to be in charge of her rescue team."

Angus studied him, then shook his head. "Ye're too emotionally involved. Zoltan will be in charge. You and Phil will be on his team."

Phineas cursed silently.

"I want a second team at Phil's cabin," Angus continued. "Jack, ye'll head that team, since ye know how to teleport there. Any werewolves or Malcontents who show up—"

"Won't live long," Jack finished the sentence. "I'll pick up Lara on the way, and I'll take J.L. and Austin."

"Verra well," Angus agreed. "Then we need a third team, the biggest team, to assault Bleddyn's ranch house and hopefully eliminate him and Dimitri and take Corky prisoner. Robby and I will be in charge so we can attack from two fronts. Freemont will remain here to coordinate the three teams."

"Yes, sir!" Freemont sat up.

Angus scanned the room. "On Robby's team, I want Ian, Stan, Rajiv—"

"And me," Howard grumbled.

"I'll go, too," Nate offered. "I was in the army. I know how to fight."

"'Tis no' yer battle, lad," Angus said.

"I think it is," Nate replied. "Bleddyn and his pack turned my brother against me."

"If I may suggest?" John lifted a hand. "Bleddyn's land borders on the Carson ranch. You could use Nate's home as a base to launch your attack." He gave Nate a sheepish look. "If you don't mind, sir."

Nate smiled. "It's a great idea. I should have thought of it myself."

"Verra well." Angus stood. "As soon as the sun sets in Wyoming, we move out."

Brynley answered a knock at the bedroom door.

"These are for you." The guard passed her a crystal vase containing a dozen long-stemmed yellow roses.

The minute she took the vase, he shut the door.

"Gee, thanks," she muttered. Not that she minded being closed up in the bedroom with her sister. It was much preferable to spending time with Rhett Bleddyn or her father. Thankfully, neither one of them had contacted her during the day.

Since the Hunt went on all night for three nights, the werewolves tended to sleep most of the day. Only now, almost suppertime, was the house stirring. A big buffet was usually served at seven to energize all the guests for that night's hunt.

She glanced at the window where the sun was lowering in the sky. What had happened to Phineas and Jack? Were they still in the cabin? Would they wake at sunset no longer paralyzed? If they did, they could probably overpower Kyle. If he hadn't already used his stake . . .

"Oh my!" Glynis rushed forward, her eyes sparkling with excitement. "What beautiful roses! Are they from Rhett?"

"Who knows," Brynley mumbled.

Glynis plucked the card from the clear plastic trident and read out loud. " 'All my devotion, all my life.' And it's signed, 'Your loving Rhett.' Isn't that sweet? And they're your favorite color, too. That's so romantic!"

"Did you tell him yellow was my favorite?"

"Well, yes. But it's still romantic. The nearest florist is miles away."

"And he had one of his minions drive to it." Brynley strode into the bathroom and set the vase into the white porcelain trash can.

"What are you doing?" Glynis pulled the vase out. "It would be insulting not to accept this."

"That's the idea."

Glynis huffed, then returned the vase to the bedroom and set it on the bombé chest. "There, perfect." She smoothed down the long skirt of her rose-colored silk gown and wrinkled her nose at Brynley's jeans and T-shirt. "You know, you really should dress for dinner."

Brynley rolled her eyes. "I never did understand that. Why does everyone dress so fancy for dinner when they're just going to strip it all off when it's time for the Hunt?"

"It's tradition," Glynis insisted. "It's been done this way for centuries. Besides, I like dressing up. It's fun. You can borrow one of my dresses."

"I'm not going."

Glynis set her hands on her hips. "Dad will expect you to be there."

"You can tell him I'm ill."

Glynis's face turned pale. "You want me to lie for you?"

Brynley saw the fear in her sister's eyes. Damn but her father had picked her guard well. He knew she'd never do anything that would endanger her sister. "Don't worry. I-I'll eat dinner. I won't get you in trouble."

Glynis smiled with relief. "Thank you. Maybe, if you're lucky, Rhett will ask you to hunt with him to-night."

"Right. 'Cause nothing says romance like slaughtering a defenseless animal together."

Glynis tilted her head with a confused look. "Don't you want to hunt?"

And risk being the prey? "Not tonight." Not here. What she loved most about hunting was not the kill, but the rush of the wind as she ran through the woods, the power and freedom she felt as a wolf. But here, she could never feel powerful or free. Here she was helpless and trapped. Her inner wolf growled with frustration. "I'll stick close to the house."

With a smile, Glynis hugged her. "I'll keep you company then. Would you like to try on one of my dresses now?"

Thirty minutes later, Brynley was dressed in a midnight-blue gown, and her sister had pulled her thick hair back into a loose French braid. The guards escorted them down the staircase.

A few dozen guests were lingering in the great hall, sipping wine and chatting. They looked so posh and elegant. No one would ever suspect that in a few hours, they would be furry and ripping into dead animals to feast on bloody entrails.

"Do you see the mural?" Glynis whispered. "Isn't it wonderful?"

Brynley spotted the artwork through the crowd. It showed a pack of wolves moving through a forest. "It's beautiful."

Glynis grinned, then stiffened. "He's coming for you."

"Who?" Brynley groaned as Rhett moved to the base of the stairs, where he waited for them. He was dressed in a black tuxedo, his shoulder-length dark hair slicked back, his dark eyes watching her intently.

"Good evening, ladies."

His voice did nothing for her. God, how she missed Phineas.

When she remained silent, Glynis quickly spoke up. "It's lovely to see you again, Rhett. Thank you for the roses."

"My pleasure." He lifted a hand to Brynley. "Would you take a walk with me outside?"

"Oh yes, Brynley, you should." Glynis begged her with her eyes. "The garden is lovely this time of year."

The guards crowded around her, so she had nowhere to flee. The guests stopped their chatting to watch. Rhett grabbed her hand and tucked it into his elbow.

"Come." He led her to the front door.

One of the guards opened it.

"I wish to be alone with her," Rhett murmured to the guard, then escorted her onto the porch.

"You must at least pretend to like me." He squeezed her hand tightly till it hurt. "I will not be embarrassed in front of others."

"Then you should marry someone who is willing."

He led her down the steps to the flagstone path that would take them to the garden on the side of the house. "You are my choice."

"Why?"

He arched an eyebrow at her. "You don't believe you're worthy of me?"

She snorted. "I'm not going to be cooperative."

"Not a problem." He squeezed her hand painfully again. "I'll enjoy forcing you to submit."

Pig. Alpha pig. She pulled her hand from his grip. Her inner wolf growled.

A door slammed in the driveway, and a young male werewolf ran toward them. "Master! I need a word with you." He glanced at Brynley. "In private."

Rhett frowned at him. "It had better be important."

"I'll go back inside," Brynley offered, and hurried back up the steps and into the house before Rhett could object.

She weaved through the guests in the great hall and eased into the parlor. More people mingled there, but she ignored them and rushed across the room, peering out the windows till she could see Rhett and his minion where they'd moved farther down the flagstone path. She raised the window an inch and squatted next to it. Even with her extra-sharp hearing, she had trouble hearing their conversation over the voices in the parlor until Rhett suddenly shouted.

"Kyle is dead?" he bellowed.

"Yes, sir. Three shots to his chest."

"And the vampires?"

"Gone, sir. The cabin was empty."

Brynley's breath caught. *Yes!* Phineas and Jack were all right! They'd escaped. And they would come looking for her.

The minion kept talking. "We took Kyle's body back to your ranch. What do you want us to do with it?"

Rhett scoffed. "Dump it back at his brother's house."

The window suddenly clicked shut. "What are you doing?" Her father's clipped voice sounded annoyed.

Brynley straightened. "Enjoying some fresh air."

"I doubt it." Caddoc Jones glanced out the window. "Come. The buffet has started." He took her elbow and steered her toward the dining room. "You defied me when you ran away. Have you ever known me not to punish a member of my pack for disobedience?"

She swallowed hard.

His grip tightened on her arm. "I will forgo punishment this time under one condition. You will go through with the wedding and marry Rhett Bleddyn."

The prison walls were closing in. "May I join the Hunt tonight?" If she shifted, she could run like hell. The thought of her father's wolves chasing her down was terrifying, but she was getting desperate enough to take the chance.

"You will remain indoors." He handed her a plate. "Enjoy your evening." He turned on his heel and left.

She set the plate back in the stack. She couldn't eat when she was suffocating. She pivoted, feeling entirely hemmed in by her father's well-dressed, happy minions.

She spotted one who looked uncomfortable. He was standing in the corner, quietly eating. Thomas, Trudy's husband. She'd mentioned he would be here.

She eased over in his direction. "Hey, Thomas."

He inclined his head. "Miss Jones. I didn't know you had returned."

"It was . . . unplanned." She lowered her voice. "Corey's doing great at school."

Thomas exhaled with relief, and a brief smile flitted over his face before his guarded expression returned. "You shouldn't say his name here."

"Do you have a cell phone on you?"

He gave her a wary look.

She shrugged. "I can't seem to find a single phone in this entire house. Crazy, isn't it?"

"Miss Jones, I suggest you do whatever your father tells you to. Excuse me." He strode from the dining room.

With a groan, she leaned against the wall. What was she doing? Thomas and Trudy were good people. She shouldn't get them into trouble. She was just so damned frustrated!

"Oh, there you are!" Glynis rushed toward her, grinning. "Guess what? Dad made special plans for us. He ordered all the latest movie releases. We get to have an all-night marathon in the media room!"

With a dozen guards outside the door, no doubt. *Phineas, please hurry.*

The wedding was in two nights.

Chapter Twenty-two

$\mathcal{T}$his is where you and Brynley grew up?" Phineas asked as he scanned the enormous house. He was with Zoltan and Phil, hidden in the woods behind Caddoc Jones's ranch house.

They'd arrived ten minutes earlier, a half hour after sunset. Phil had recalled the number for an old phone in the stable. The elderly werewolf who had answered it had been stunned when they teleported in, but Phineas had quickly erased his memory while Zoltan had communicated with the horses to keep them calm.

"This is the main residence," Phil answered quietly. "There are two more, one in Idaho and one in Wyoming."

"When do they start shifting?" Zoltan asked.

Phil glanced up at the full moon. "Soon." He motioned for them to follow. "They'll shift in the backyard and head straight into these woods. We need to move."

They kept to the forest, circling around the north side of the house.

So far, Phineas had seen only one guard, and he was

relaxing in a lawn chair on the back porch. "They don't seem too concerned about security."

Phil snorted. "Who in their right mind would attack a house full of a hundred werewolves? Most of the guards are inside, making sure the guests don't attack each other. And they're probably watching Brynley's every move."

"If you spot her, even in wolf form, let me know," Phineas said. "I'll teleport straight to her and get her out of here."

Phil shook his head. "I doubt my father will allow her to participate in the Hunt. She'd probably try to run away."

"Or she might get hunted down and assaulted," Phineas muttered.

Phil stopped with a jerk. "What are you saying? Did that happen to her?"

"You wouldn't know, would you? You weren't here for her."

"She never answered my letters," Phil insisted. "Never agreed to escape with me. I thought she must be happy here."

"You thought wrong!"

"Enough," Zoltan growled. "Keep your voices down or the guards will hear us."

Phineas took a deep breath. He was having a hard time dealing with the abuse Brynley had suffered. It was wrong of him, but he was taking it out on her brother.

"Look at it," Phil whispered, pointing at the huge

mansion. "I didn't think she'd be willing to leave that behind. I left here with nothing but the clothes on my back. I nearly starved before I ended up a poor college student, living in the basement of Roman's townhouse and working during the day as a security guard. I asked Brynley to come away with me, but I didn't push it. I didn't think I had much to offer."

Phineas swallowed hard. He knew that feeling. It was hard to believe Brynley would choose him, a poor Undead guy from the Bronx with an outstanding warrant for his arrest, when she could have luxury and security.

He followed Phil and Zoltan toward the front of the house. They came to the edge of an asphalt road that led to the circular driveway.

"We'll teleport across." Zoltan pointed to a wooded area. "Land over there." He grabbed hold of Phil and vanished.

Phineas joined them. They were a far distance in front of the house now, but with their superior vision they could still see. However, much of their view was blocked by the SUVs, pickups, and campers parked in the driveway.

Phineas pointed up. "Let's get a better view."

"Good idea." Phil walked over to a thick pine with sturdy branches. "I used to climb this as a kid." He leaped and caught hold of the lowest branch. With a grunt, he swung a leg over the branch and straddled it. Holding on to the trunk, he stood, then reached for the next branch.

Phineas levitated and hovered close by. "Going up?"

Phil gave him a wry look. "Show-off."

Phineas offered him a hand. "Come on." When Phil looped an arm around his shoulders, he continued levitating to the top branches of the tree.

"Slowpokes," Zoltan murmured from the top of a neighboring tree. He must have teleported.

Phineas landed on a sturdy branch and surveyed the house and grounds. One guard stood by the front door. The house sprawled along the top of long hill. On the south side, a garden had been planted where the land sloped down to a flat meadow. Beyond that, there were some pens and then the stable.

"I was wrong," Phil whispered from a nearby branch. "I should have come here to make sure she was all right. I should have known she couldn't bear it here any more than I could."

"Not your fault," Phineas mumbled. "You didn't know."

Phil leaned against the trunk, gazing at the house. "It's hard to explain what the Lycan world is like to an outsider. On the surface, it all seems perfect. Big ranches, beautiful country, strong families, a really close and supportive community. If one of the men in the pack dies, his widow and children are automatically taken care of. If someone's house or barn burns down, the pack gathers to rebuild it. There's a strong sense of pride and security—"

"But no freedom," Phineas muttered.

Phil sighed. "For me, the cost of staying was too high."

"It's too high for Brynley, too. They'll force her to marry Bleddyn." Phineas's fingers dug into the pine bark. "I saw him slap her in the cabin, and I just lay there, unable to help her."

"Bastard," Phil snarled. "I should kick his ass."

"I'd like a swing at him, too, but it looks like Howard wants the honor." Phineas paused a moment, wondering what the story was there.

"What are your intentions toward my sister?" Phil asked.

That took him by surprise. "I guess it's obvious I have feelings for her." He took a deep breath. "I want to be with her if she'll have me. I'd like to spend my life with her."

Phil turned to him with wry look. "You sure you can handle her?"

Phineas smiled. "It would be one hell of a thrill ride finding that out." He motioned toward the house. "Do you know which window is her bedroom?"

"You're thinking about teleporting in?" Phil asked.

"If I can find her, I'll teleport her straight to Romatech, and you two guys can follow."

"She's probably being guarded," Phil warned him.

"I'll go with you," Zoltan told him. "If you find her, teleport out. I shall return here for Phil."

Phil pointed. "Second window from the right, upstairs. The curtains are shut."

A second later, Phineas materialized in a large, dark bedroom. He pivoted, scanning the room. No one there.

Zoltan appeared beside him. After a quick look around, he opened a door. "Bathroom," he whispered, and went inside.

Phineas zipped over to another door and peered inside. A walk-in closet. Mostly empty, except for a row of pretty dresses and some high-heeled shoes. Brynley had obviously taken her casual clothes with her when she'd run away. Something long and white caught his eye, and he ventured closer. *Shit.* It was a wedding dress in a clear plastic bag. Lots of lace and beads and crap. A lot more expensive than he could ever afford.

He closed the closet door and surveyed the room. The wrought-iron bed was neatly made up with a blue and green quilt. It didn't look like it had been slept in. A white box underneath the bed drew his attention. What would she hide beneath her bed? Old photos of her mom or Phil? Memorabilia from happier days?

He dashed over and pulled out the box. Red letters on top read "Big Boy 1000 EXTREME!" He opened it and winced.

"Damn." Nestled in red velvet was a flesh-colored rubber phallus. He plucked it out.

"Damn." It *was* a big boy. He felt himself shrinking, just looking at the damned thing.

"Nothing in the bathroom." Zoltan exited, closing the door behind him.

Phineas whipped the Big Boy behind his back, but the movement must have hit a button because it suddenly came alive, vibrating and wiggling against his lower back. He arched and shifted his weight, trying to look nonchalant.

Zoltan peered around the room. "Do you hear that?"

"No."

"Sounds like a bee." He gave Phineas a speculative look. "Are your clothes buzzing?"

He shrugged. "Brynley's not here, so we might as well leave."

Zoltan looked him over again, then glanced at the bed. "Okay."

"You first. I'll bring up the"—he winced as the damned thing wiggled against his rear—"uh, rear."

Zoltan's mouth twitched, then he teleported away.

"Damn." Phineas turned the Big Boy off, then noticed he'd left the box on the bed. Damn, had Zoltan seen it? He stuffed the phallus back into the box, but must have jammed too hard, for it started wiggling again.

"Stop it." He punched a button, but it merely increased its speed, the tip spiraling in wild circles.

Damn! He watched in horror. It was like a whirlybird on steroids! How could a man compete with that? He ripped the balls off it and emptied out the batteries. "Die, you freakin' dildo, die!"

"I think I hear something in there," a voice said in the hallway.

"Then check it out," another voice demanded.

Phineas tossed the box back under the bed and teleported away.

He landed back in the tree. "Whew. Safe again."

"I'm not so sure about that," Zoltan muttered from his tree and pointed to the ground.

"It arrived right after you guys left," Phil added.

Phineas glanced down at the big black bear. It reared up on its hind legs and clawed at the tree, shaking it. Phineas held on tight to the trunk.

"I could shift and try to chase it away," Phil offered. "But it's a long way down for me to jump."

"I could try communicating with it mentally," Zoltan suggested.

"Or I could just talk to him," Phineas added dryly. He levitated down a bit. "Digger, what are you doing here?"

The bear shifted into a large, naked man. "How did you know it was me?"

Phineas gestured to the yellow dog sitting under a nearby tree with the foil-covered football helmet. "Your sidekick is one of a kind."

"That's right," Digger said proudly. "My Jake is purty special."

"Your dog could be in danger once the Hunt begins," Phil called down.

Digger narrowed his eyes as he gazed up the tree. "You a shifter?"

"Werewolf. Philupus Jones."

"Caddoc's son? I heard you were dead."

Phil snorted. "Is that what they're saying? I was banished twelve years ago."

Digger motioned to Zoltan. "What about that one? He has funny eyes. Could be an alien."

"He's Zoltan, a vampire like me," Phineas explained.

"Are you sure? Zoltan sounds like an alien planet." Zoltan chuckled.

"What brings you here, Digger?" Phineas asked.

"My truck. I left it about a mile down the road."

Phineas tried again. "Why are you here?"

"Well, I've been thinking about what you said about that bad werewolf, Rhett, that's trying to force the little lady to marry him, and then I thought maybe I should have a word with Cad about it, see if he could stop that bad fella from pestering his daughter. We used to be friends, Cad and me, about a hundred years ago."

"I'm afraid my father knows about Rhett," Phil said. "And he's trying to force the wedding, too."

"Dagnabbit!" Digger slapped his thigh. "That ain't right. I'm telling you, there's some bad things going on around here. I saw two of them aliens beaming down in the backyard about five minutes ago."

"You saw aliens?" Zoltan asked.

"A male and a female. They headed over to the stable. Really fast. They ain't human, that's for sure."

Dimitri and Corky? Phineas glanced up at Zoltan. "Can you see them?"

From the top of his tree, Zoltan surveyed the area. "They must already be inside. A group of people are gathering in the backyard, starting to strip."

"They're getting ready for the Hunt," Phil said.

"Do you see him?" Zoltan pointed. "A man in a tuxedo. He's headed toward the stable in a hurry."

Phineas levitated up to where he could see. "That's Rhett Bleddyn. And that looks like Dimitri at the stable door."

"Let's go hear what they have to say," Zoltan suggested.

"An alien powwow. I'll meet you over there." Digger and Jake trotted through the woods toward the stable.

Phineas, Phil, and Zoltan materialized at the back of the stable, then teleported into the hayloft.

Two voices were speaking below: Corky and Rhett. Corky was screaming so loud the horses were growing agitated.

Zoltan closed his eyes and mouthed some words.

Phineas gave him a questioning look, but when the horses settled down, he realized what Zoltan had been doing. He eased forward on his stomach to peek over the edge.

"It was terrible!" Corky shouted. "Dimitri and I barely escaped!"

"Calm down," Rhett told her. "What happened?"

"It was those wretched MacKay men! They attacked us! The vampires had swords and guns, and there was a huge bear and a tiger!"

"They had shifters with them?"

"Yes! And they were ripping your werewolves into dog food. Dimitri and I barely made it out in time."

Rhett stiffened. "You're saying my men lost?"

Corky waved a dismissive hand. "They were falling like flies. I've never seen such a bunch of useless—"

"My men *lost*?" Rhett shouted.

"Yes! Have you been listening?" Corky screeched. "Those bloody MacKay bastards took over your ranch. Now where on earth am I supposed to do my death-sleep?"

Rhett dragged a hand through his hair. "I'll find a place for you here."

Corky huffed. "Let's just go back to Alaska. You have plenty of land there."

"I need more!" Rhett's eyes gleamed. "I need more wolves. I need more power. And I'm so damned close. I'll get more men down here quick. The wedding is in two nights."

"I don't want you to marry that bitch!" Corky screamed. "You're mine."

"Get a grip, Corky," he hissed. "It's just a damned formality so the land can transfer to me legally. Once I'm married to the Jones girl, we'll kill her and the entire family. Then I'll inherit it all."

Phineas flinched and exchanged a look with Phil.

"Just two more days." Rhett pulled Corky into his arms. "We'll have it all. I'll have thousands of pack members in four states following my every command."

Corky wrapped her arms around his neck. "And I'll have the governors under my control."

Dimitri yelped and ran toward them. "There's a bear charging toward us!"

"Quick!" Rhett ordered. "Take me to the house."

They vanished just as Digger loped into the stable, followed by Jake. The horses went crazy, rearing up and kicking at their stalls.

"Calm yourselves," Zoltan told them. "It will not harm you."

The bear shifted, and the horses returned to normal.

Phineas jumped down to the ground. "Dammit, Digger!"

"What's wrong?" He scratched at his beard. "Am I too late?"

"You scared them off," Phineas muttered. "We missed a chance to capture them."

"Or kill them," Phil added.

"At least now we know exactly what they're planning," Zoltan said.

"What are they planning?" Digger asked.

"A wedding," Phineas muttered. "Followed by mass murder."

The bastards were planning to kill his Brynley.

Chapter Twenty-three

*A*ny sign of Brynley?" Phineas asked.

"Nope." Digger was sitting on the roof of the stable, hidden behind a turret capped with a large weathervane. Wrapped in a dark horse blanket, he surveyed the surrounding area. His dog, Jake, was safe inside with the horses.

"Ain't seen hide nor hair of her." Digger chuckled. "You get it? She could have skin or fur."

Phineas groaned inwardly. "I'll check back with you later. Thanks." He teleported to the front of the house, where Phil was stationed in a tree.

"Haven't seen her," Phil muttered.

Phineas sighed. They'd been watching the house for five hours. "You'd think she'd at least look out a damned window."

There was plenty to look at. Werewolves were shifting back and forth, dragging back carcasses, cutting them up, and roasting them. Some of the guests had opted to remain human tonight so they could party at the house. They were drinking beer on the patio, making out in the garden. He'd spotted a few making love in the woods.

"I'll check on you later," he told Phil, then teleported to his station at the back of the house. He sat on a branch high up in a tree and scanned all the people once again, searching for Brynley.

Zoltan had teleported to the Carson ranch to report on what they'd heard in the stable. Meanwhile, Phineas, Phil, and Digger kept watch. No sign of Corky or Dimitri. They were either inside the house, or they'd teleported elsewhere. Rhett had taken off with a group of his minions in an SUV.

No sign of Brynley. What the hell was she doing in there? She didn't seem to be using her bedroom. Did her father have her locked up in a prison cell? Was she miserable? Or did she have her Big Boy 1000 EXTREME to keep her company?

He snorted.

She probably never used it. After all, she'd left it behind when she ran away from home. And why should he worry if she did use it? It was better than jumping any of these werewolves who strutted around naked, covered with blood and grime.

He shifted on the branch. The sun would rise in less than an hour. He'd have to leave to do his death-sleep. His cell phone vibrated, not nearly as good as the Big Boy 1000 EXTREME, and he checked his text message. Zoltan was back, and he'd landed by the stable.

Phineas teleported over to Phil, picked him up, then

materialized by the stable. They all sat out of view of the house, on the back side of the roof, close to Digger.

"The cabin has been quiet," Zoltan told them. "No action there. Angus and his team defeated all the were-wolves at Bleddyn's ranch. Robby's got a team there, keeping it secure. I told Angus that we saw Corky and Dimitri here, along with Bleddyn."

"What does Angus want us to do?" Phineas asked.

"He'll send us more men tomorrow night," Zoltan said, "but he doesn't want us to attack. We would end up killing Caddoc Jones's pack members, and we don't want to weaken his forces in case Bleddyn attacks him and his family."

Phil shook his head. "This could escalate into a were-wolf war, pack against pack. I need to get my brother and sisters out of here."

How? Phineas wondered. He was tempted to walk up to the house, ring the front doorbell, and tell Caddoc Jones that he and his family were about to be slaughtered.

"If we see Corky or Dimitri, we're supposed to grab them and teleport them straight to the Carson ranch. Angus has some silver chains and handcuffs there." Zoltan took a deep breath. "And of course, if you see Brynley, you can grab her."

"*If* we see her," Phineas grumbled.

"We have thirty minutes left here," Zoltan continued. "Then we'll go to the Carson ranch for our death-sleep."

Phineas groaned. He'd have to wait another night to rescue Brynley.

The next evening, Brynley forced herself to eat some of the buffet. It tasted like dry chalk in her mouth, but she needed to keep her strength up. She'd been awake for only two hours, but she was already stressed out.

First, her guards had escorted her to her bedroom so she could try on the wedding dress. After all, the wedding was tomorrow. She nearly choked on the deer meat she was chewing and drank half a glass of wine to fortify her nerves.

A female werewolf/seamstress had marked a few areas she wanted to alter, then Brynley had been escorted to a small office being used by her wedding planner. She hadn't even known she had a wedding planner. But it wasn't that surprising, really. Her father was not the sort to fool with mundane details. He commanded others to do it.

Since the wedding was happening so quickly, the invitations were merely passed out among the guests who were already there. Tonight was the third night of the full moon, and normally the last night of the monthly party, but the guests would simply stay one more night to witness the wedding.

She swallowed another bite of deer meat. It was all a farce, really. The wedding planner had acted like she wanted Brynley's approval of the dinner menu and flower arrangements, but it was all going to happen whether she liked it or not.

Much to her sister's dismay, she'd managed one small act of rebellion. She'd gone downstairs to eat dinner in her jeans, plaid shirt, and cowboy boots.

She glanced at the window. The sun was going down. The guards made sure now that she didn't get close to a window. Her father's orders, no doubt, after he'd caught her eavesdropping on Rhett.

She scanned the dining room and counted three guards. There was no escaping them. At least she hadn't been forced to endure Rhett's company today.

She groaned. Speak of the devil. He strode into the room, dressed in his tuxedo, wearing a white silk scarf around his shoulders and an obnoxious smirk on his face.

He stopped in front of her. "I have a surprise for you."

Her eyes widened. "You have dog mange?"

Nearby guests chuckled, and his smirk twisted with anger.

He seized her arm. "Come with me."

As he dragged her from the dining room, she glanced back and saw the guards following. Would they defend her if she was attacked, or stand by and applaud?

Rhett pushed her out the back door, making her stumble forward onto the empty patio. He grabbed her once again and pulled her close.

"You will show me respect in public," he growled softly.

"Then I can be rude in private?"

His hands tightened painfully on her arms, and she winced. There would be bruises tomorrow. How fortunate her wedding dress had long sleeves.

"You don't want to know what we'll do in private," he hissed. He whipped the white silk scarf off his shoulders and spun her around.

She lunged forward to escape, but the three guards blocked her. Suddenly, the silk scarf covered her eyes. She gasped and felt a tug at the back of her head. The scarf had been knotted.

She reached up to pull the scarf down but her hands were grabbed by a pair of tight fists.

"Come with me." Rhett pulled her forward.

Her heart raced. She heard the guards following behind, but she doubted they would help her. "What are you doing? If you harm me, my father will kill you."

Rhett chuckled. "Harm you? I plan to marry you, you nitwit. Now two steps down." He held on to her hands and guided her into the backyard.

"Where are you taking me?" she demanded.

"I told you. I have a surprise for you." Rhett wrapped an arm around her shoulder and steered her to the left. "It took all night and all day for me and my men to pull off this feat. You'll be very impressed."

"Only if you all managed to castrate yourselves," she muttered.

He chuckled. "I like the way you resist. It will make your final submission so much sweeter."

The air was chilly against her cheeks. The temperature was dropping, a sure sign that the sun had set. Would Phineas come looking for her?

She strained her ears and could hear the soft thud of footsteps behind her. The guards were still following.

Up ahead, she heard voices. Something about ropes? Tying something down? She swallowed hard.

Images of her last assault flitted through her mind, and her heart thundered in her ears. *No!* She pushed the memories aside. She wouldn't panic. She would be brave.

Rhett stopped her and placed her hands on a horizontal wooden beam. It was the horse pen. She dug her fingers into the wood.

Rhett whispered, his mouth close to the white silk covering her ear. "Your sister told me what you admired the most in the world. I'm giving it to you as a sign of my devotion."

He whipped the scarf off her head, and she gasped.

Her heart lurched, and tears instantly sprang to her eyes.

The wild white stallion was imprisoned inside the pen. It pawed the ground furiously. Its eyes rolled about in fear and rage. Three ropes had been tied around its neck and secured to the fenced enclosure. The horse strained to move, its neck already red with welts as the ropes cut into its white coat.

"You're hurting him," she whispered. *You're killing him. You're killing me.* She could almost feel the ropes around her own neck, squeezing tighter and tighter.

"It's the only way to contain him," Rhett said. "Damned horse put up quite a fight."

She noted the dried blood on the horse's flank. "Let him go."

Rhett scoffed. "Are you kidding? Do you know

how much trouble we—" He looked at her. "Are you crying?"

She wiped the tears off her face, and jutted out her chin. "Let him go."

He leaned on the fence, studying her. "I'll let him go if you'll be my willing bride."

Her heart skipped a beat as it plummeted into her stomach. A feeling of doom sucked her down. Submission, the way of the Lycan world.

She gazed at the wild white stallion, and more tears stung her eyes. If she agreed, at least one of them would be free.

Chapter Twenty-four

*P*hineas nearly fell out of the tree when he teleported there. Was that Brynley? Blindfolded? Rhett Bleddyn was leading her across the backyard. Three guards followed close behind. They appeared to be headed toward the stable.

Maybe he could teleport to her and grab her before Rhett or the three guards reacted. Might be difficult since Rhett had an arm around her. He needed backup.

After waking in Nate Carson's basement, he'd been so anxious to return here and watch for Brynley that he'd guzzled down a bottle and teleported straight here with Phil. He'd left the werewolf in his favorite tree in the front. Zoltan and Jack were supposed to follow.

He texted a message to Zoltan. *Go to stable roof now!*

He pocketed the cell phone and glanced at Brynley. Rhett had taken her to the horse pen.

His breath caught. Gleaming white under the full moon, the wild white stallion strained at its ropes.

Shock quickly gave way to anger. The bastards. They'd found the perfect way to hurt Brynley. This was no slap on the face. It was a wound inflicted upon her soul.

He teleported to Phil, and before Phil could ask a question, he'd landed the two of them on the stable roof.

Zoltan materialized with Jack.

Phineas pointed toward the horse pen and whispered, "Brynley." As he stretched out on his stomach to peer over the ridge of the roof, the others did the same.

Phil hissed in a breath. "Bastards."

"Go get her." Zoltan nudged Phineas with his elbow. "Jack and I will keep the guards busy."

"No," he whispered back. "I want you and Jack to teleport into the pen. You'll use your mojo to calm down the stallion while Jack cuts the ropes. Then you teleport the horse out. While you're—"

"The horse is too heavy," Zoltan interrupted.

"You can do it together."

Jack shook his head. "We could end up ripping it in two."

"Then connect your minds so you'll land together at the cabin. You can do it. And while they're freaking out over the horse, I'll swoop in and grab Brynley. We'll all meet at the cabin."

"Except me," Phil muttered. "But you guys go ahead. Have all the fun."

"Sorry, dude," Phineas said.

Phil snorted. "I was kidding. I want you to get Bryn

out. I'll stay here. I'm worried about the rest of my family, too."

Phineas removed the knife from his boot and handed it to Jack. "Can you do it?"

He accepted the knife. "It's a crazy idea, but I like it."

"Ready?" Zoltan asked. "On the count of three. One, two, *three*."

Jack and Zoltan teleported. Jack zoomed around the horse at vampire speed, cutting the three ropes, while Zoltan faced the horse. The stallion grew still.

Rhett's men hollered and jumped into the pen. Rhett let go of Brynley and shouted orders to his men, and her guards moved aside to watch.

Phineas teleported beside her and grabbed her. She gasped, looking at him in shock. He had a glimpse of Zoltan and Jack vanishing with the horse, then he teleported, taking Brynley with him.

They landed inside the cabin.

"Phineas!" She threw her arms around him and laughed.

He grinned. "I got you. You're safe."

She leaned back, beaming at him, then her expression morphed into panic. "The wild white stallion! We have to rescue him!"

"Brynley—"

"They're torturing him!" Her eyes glinted with tears. "We have to save him."

"I know. You can't bear to be free if he's not free."

"Exactly."

"Come with me." He led her onto the front porch.

She gasped.

The stallion reared up on its hind legs. Jack and Zoltan jumped back.

"You saved him," she whispered. She pressed a hand against her chest, then turned to Phineas. A tear rolled down her cheek. "You saved him."

With a smile, he brushed the tear away. "I know how you feel about him."

"Whoa," Zoltan murmured to the horse. "Calm down. Let us get the ropes off you."

The stallion pawed at the ground, then went still.

Jack approached slowly, then slid his knife under the ropes and cut through.

The ropes fell to the ground, and the stallion tossed its head.

Brynley's gaze shifted back to Phineas, and more tears glimmered in her eyes. "You saved me. You saved the stallion. You beautiful, beautiful man."

Zoltan exchanged a look with Jack. "I thought we did all the work."

Phineas kissed her brow. "As long as I live, I'll fight anyone who tries to capture the wild horse. And I'll never let anyone destroy your beautiful wild spirit."

With a choked sob, she threw her arms around him. "I love you. I was so afraid I'd never get the chance to tell you." She placed her hands on his cheeks. "I really do love you."

He laughed and swung her around in a circle.

"I'm starting to feel a bit unnecessary again," Jack muttered.

"Come on, Casanova." Zoltan motioned for him to follow. "We have another job to do."

They walked into the stable.

"Alone at last." Phineas kissed Brynley, and she laughed against his mouth.

"Not entirely." She motioned with her head toward the wild white stallion. It was regarding them curiously.

"Peeping Tom." Phineas pulled Brynley close. "Get your own girl."

"That can be arranged." Zoltan led Molly from the stable. "Go on, girl. Get your man."

Jack chuckled. "Nothing like *amore*."

Molly shook her head and snorted. The wild stallion reared up, then trotted toward her.

"They're necking," Brynley whispered.

"Good idea." Phineas nuzzled her neck.

"I want you." She kissed his cheek and rubbed a hand over his chest. "I want to kiss you all over. Now."

His vision turned pink.

"What do you think, Zoltan?" Jack said in a loud voice. "It's a nice evening. Shall we stand guard for a little while? About five minutes?"

Zoltan snorted. "Ten at least. He is the Love Doctor, after all."

Phineas teleported Brynley down into the basement.

Brynley ripped his shirt open. "Hurry."

It felt as if all the frustration and anger and fear she'd endured over the last few days had been poured into a hot cauldron, and it was now bubbling over to make her frantic. She attacked his belt with trembling fingers.

"I was so worried about you." He unbuttoned her shirt.

"I don't want to think about it." She unzipped his jeans and pulled them down. She'd come so close to being forced into a marriage with a man she despised, forced into a life of submission that would have killed her slowly and painfully, choking her, humiliating her, diminishing her until there was nothing left of her.

She had to live. She had to be free. Inside, her wolf howled with joy.

She shoved Phineas back onto the bed and yanked his boots off.

He sat up. "Are you all right?"

"Yes." She pulled off his jeans and underwear.

He frowned. "They didn't hurt you?"

She didn't want to talk about how desperate and helpless she'd felt. She wanted to feel strong. In control. Empowered. She shoved him back and straddled him. "Let me do this. I need to do this."

"Do what?"

"Whatever the hell I feel like." Her heart swelled when his eyes turned red. No wonder she loved him. He loved her when she was strong.

She leaned forward to kiss him, to explore him with her tongue. His hands slipped inside her open shirt, and he kneaded her breasts, then unclasped her bra.

She sat up, flung her shirt and bra aside, then leaned down again to rub herself against him.

He tossed her onto her back and with vampire speed, he removed her boots, jeans, and underwear. When he climbed on top of her, she laughed and pushed him onto his back.

"I'm in charge," she told him, and smoothed a hand down his chest.

He attempted to sit up. "You think—"

"Stay." She pushed him back down.

His mouth twitched. "You think I'm a dog?"

"I think you're mine." She curled a hand around his erection. "All mine."

His eyes glowed a rich bloodred.

She leaned over to tease him with her tongue. *Yes.* She was in charge. Full of power. Bursting with freedom. She took him into her mouth and delighted at the moans she wrenched from him. Moisture pooled between her legs.

She glanced up at him and smiled. "Shall I take you now? Ride you like a cowboy?"

He smiled back. "Will you be gentle with me?"

"Hell no."

"That's my girl."

With a laugh, she straddled him and eased him inside her. His thick shaft slid into her wetness. *Sweet.* She started off slow, reveling in the slow, sweet slide when she lifted up, the grounding of their bodies when she slipped down.

"You're so beautiful." He caressed her breasts and tweaked her hardened nipples.

With a moan, she increased her speed. His hands

smoothed down to grasp her hips, and soon he was pulling her harder. She rode him faster and faster.

With a shout, he arched and pumped into her. Stars shattered before her eyes. With a keening cry, she climaxed, then fell forward onto his chest, her body shuddering with spasms.

He held her tight. "Brynley, I love you so much."

Tears stung her eyes. "I was so afraid I'd never see you again."

"I was scared, too." He rubbed her back. "I sat outside for hours last night, hoping to catch a glimpse of you so I could rescue you. Your brother Phil was there, too. And Digger and Zoltan."

"Digger?"

"Yeah. He doesn't want you forced into a marriage against your will."

She shuddered. "It was awful. Tonight I had to try on my wedding dress."

"I saw that wedding dress," he muttered. "I was tempted to rip it to shreds."

She sat up. "You saw it?"

"Yeah. Phil pointed out which window was your bedroom, and Zoltan and I teleported in, hoping to find you."

"That was sweet of you."

He gave her a wry look. "I have my uses."

Smiling, she caressed his chest. "I love your uses."

"I can go all night long."

Her hand slipped down to his penis and tugged gently. "Can you now?"

"And I don't even need batteries."

She paused. "Batteries?"

"Yes. For a night of *extreme* sex."

She let go of him. "You were in my bedroom."

"Yes."

"Snooping under my bed."

"I thought the box might contain photos of your dear mother or maybe a dried corsage from your high school prom, but no. It was the Big Boy 1000 EXTREME."

She winced. "It was a gag gift from college. When I broke up with Seth, my girlfriends claimed they had found a new boyfriend for me. It was just a silly joke."

"And yet, ten years later, it's still close to your bed."

"I didn't say I never used it. I've always been wary of getting involved when the guys are more interested in gaining my father's favor than mine." She gave him a wry look. "Why does it bother you so much?"

"Because the end of my dick doesn't whirl around at warp speed."

She grinned and kissed his cheek. "You have nothing to worry about. You're the Big Man 10,000 Mega-Extreme." She kissed his brow. "You're the Love Doctor, the Blardonnay Guy, and the love of my life."

He patted her rump. "That's right, woman. Don't you forget it."

"I won't." She nipped at his ear.

"I'm gonna rewrite your vows. You'll have to promise to be faithful, forsaking all others, including the Big Boy 1000 EXTREME."

She sat back with a gasp.

He winced. "You like it that much?"

"Did you just ask me to marry you?"

His eyes widened. "You . . . don't want to? I realize I'm not much of a catch."

"It's not that. It just seems kind of fast. I mean, we could live together for—"

"I know it's fast, but I don't think your father is going to give up on trying to marry you off. If we make it legal, then it should give you some protection."

She bit her lip. "Is that why you want to marry?"

"No, that's just me trying to convince you. What I really want is to spend the rest of my life giving you the love you deserve."

She smiled and touched his cheek.

There was a knock on the trapdoor.

"Sorry to interrupt," Jack called down. "But Angus wants everyone at the Carson ranch for a meeting. I'm going to collect Phil and take him there. Meeting starts in five minutes."

"Phineas—"

"We'll talk later. We'd better get cleaned up." He nudged her toward the bathroom.

"Nate! Look at you." Brynley left Phineas at the door and ran into the foyer to give Nate Carson a hug. "You're walking! And you're . . ." She stopped herself from saying *dead*. "You're a vampire."

"Yes. I was changed the same night you were kidnapped." He sighed. "And Kyle died."

"I'm so sorry about that."

He patted her on the back. "At least we have you back safe and sound."

"Hey, dude." Phineas gave Nate a knuckle pound. "Heard you were kicking ass over at the Bleddyn ranch."

Nate smiled. "Never thought I'd fight alongside a bear and a tiger."

Brynley looked around the foyer of Nate's home. Swords were stacked against one wall, and a table was loaded down with ammunition. MacKay employees teleported in with cases of synthetic blood. Jack's wife, Lara, was checking things off a clipboard. Apparently, she'd been given the job of supply manager for their new base of operations. "Wow, your place has become Vampire Central."

Nate nodded. "My life has gotten a whole lot more interesting."

Jack teleported in with Phil.

"Bryn!" Phil jogged over and gave her a hug. "Thank God you're all right."

She grinned. "They rescued the wild white stallion, too."

"Excellent." He pulled her aside. "I need to talk to you."

"Okay."

He looked around the foyer, then dragged a hand through his shaggy hair. "Well, the thing is, I . . . owe you an apology. I should have come back to the house years ago to see if you were all right. I just assumed you weren't interested in leaving when you didn't answer my letters and—"

"*What?*" Her heart froze for a second. "Letters?"

"Yes. I saw the letters you left at the cabin, so I wrote some back, telling you—"

"You wrote me?" Her blood chilled.

"Yeah, several times. I asked if you wanted to come—" He stopped when a strangled noise escaped her mouth. "Oh, shit. You never got them, did you?"

She shook her head. Tears came to her eyes. "I—I thought you'd abandoned me."

"Oh God, no, Brynley." He pulled her into his arms. "Shit! No wonder you were so mad at me."

She wrapped her arms around his neck. "You wrote to me."

"Yes."

She leaned back. "Father must have been watching the cabin. He took your letters away."

"I doubt he did it personally. He probably had one of his minions doing it."

She made a face. "He must have been afraid I would run away."

"You did, eventually."

She gasped. "Oh my God, if he was having the cabin watched, he must have known about the Lost Boys."

Phil winced. "It's possible. Nothing much happens in his territory that he doesn't know about."

"But he didn't stop me." She bit her lip. "Doesn't that seem odd?"

"Hey, guys." Phineas joined them. "The meeting is starting."

They filed into Nate's large parlor that had been filled

with extra chairs from the dining room. Everyone sat as Angus took a position in front of the stone fireplace.

"We're doing well," Angus began. "Last night, we defeated a pack of werewolves and took over the Bleddyn ranch. And tonight, we have successfully rescued Brynley Jones."

Everyone gave her a cheer, and she grinned at Phineas.

Angus clasped his hands behind his back. "We still have some unfinished business. Corky and Dimitri remain free. We believe they are hiding at the Jones ranch. Rhett Bleddyn is there, too. Even though it appears his wedding tomorrow will be canceled, he is still a potential threat since he had planned to murder Brynley and her—"

"*What?*" Brynley squealed.

Phineas patted her knee. "I was going to tell you about that."

"He was going to kill us?" she asked.

Phineas nodded. "Yeah. So he could inherit all your father's land and wealth."

"And take over the wolf packs," Phil added.

"We canna assume he'll give up on the plan," Angus said. "As long as he's anywhere near yer father's house, I believe yer family is in danger."

Brynley jumped to her feet. "He might force Glynis to marry him. We have to go back."

"I'll go." Phil stood. "I'll tell my father."

"It could get ugly," Angus warned him. "We'll go with you. Do ye want to leave now?"

Phil shook his head. "We should wait till tomorrow. This is the third night of the full moon. All the were-wolves will be capable of shifting. If we go tomorrow night, they can't shift to attack us. They'll lose their advantage."

Angus nodded. "Tomorrow night, then."

Brynley took a deep breath. "I'm going, too."

"No!" Phineas jumped to his feet. "We just got you out of there. You're not going back."

"I'll be fine as long as everyone else is there." She turned to him and whispered, "You've helped me see how strong I can be. I can do this." She squared her shoulders. "I'm not running away from my father anymore. It's time I stood up to him."

Chapter Twenty-five

*A*re you sure you want to do this?" Phil asked her the following night.

Brynley was in the kitchen at Nate's house, enjoying a bowl of ice cream with her brother before the night's big event.

She swallowed her last bite. "I've always run away. To college, to the rodeo, to the academy. I can't do it anymore. My inner wolf is rebelling and insists I stand up for myself. I'll never be completely free until I get over my fear of our father."

Phil nodded. "I'm proud of you. But be careful. Stick close to me or Phineas." He put their empty bowls in the sink. "All right. Let's hitch a ride to the ranch."

She accompanied her brother into the foyer, where Angus and his men were arming themselves with swords and pistols.

"Are you sure you don't want a weapon?" Phineas asked.

Phil shook his head. "It would just be confiscated. The guards won't let us near our father if we're armed."

Phineas gave Brynley a worried look. "You're sure?"

"Yes. I want to stand up to him, not kill him."

Phineas pulled her close. "I hate to let you out of my sight."

"I'll be fine. Remember how strong I am?" She smiled as she wrapped her arms around his neck. Nate had assigned her a bedroom upstairs, and she'd managed to pin Phineas down on the mattress a few times. Their wrestling match had gone on until the rising sun had forced him to go to the basement with the other Vamps for their death-sleep.

After a long day's sleep, she was ready to face the dragon tonight. Caddoc Jones. Angus and his employees were hoping to capture Corky and Dimitri. And if Rhett Bleddyn died in battle, no one was going to mourn his passing.

Jack teleported first to position himself in the woods behind the house. Then he called, and Lara put him on the speakerphone. She waved and wished everyone good luck as they vanished.

As soon as they materialized, Angus led the small group to the edge of the backyard. The guard, who'd been relaxing in a patio chair, jumped to his feet and pounded on the back door, shouting.

Within seconds, more guards appeared. Then a group of young male werewolves. Brynley spotted her brother Howell. Then Caddoc Jones strode to the edge of the patio and regarded them with a haughty glare.

"A motley group of bloodsuckers and shifters," he muttered, then raised his voice. "Is there a reason for this invasion of my property? Or shall I consider this a declaration of war?"

Angus stepped forward. "You can consider us a peacekeeping force."

Caddoc snorted. "Do you see a war around here?"

"Give it some time," Angus answered dryly. "Your son and daughter have come to speak to you."

Caddoc's mouth thinned. "I have but one son, and he's here." He motioned to Howell, and whispered something to him.

Howell nodded, then stepped off the patio and walked toward them with two guards.

"Can you do your talk here in the yard?" Phineas asked. "Where I can keep an eye on you?"

Brynley shook her head. "If our father talks to us, it will have to be in private. He can't be seen in public talking to Phil. He banished him, so he can't acknowledge his existence."

Phil snorted. "That's why he sent our brother out to talk to us." He took hold of her elbow. "Ready?"

"Be careful," Phineas whispered.

"I will." She squeezed his hand, then walked with Phil across the yard. They stopped halfway to the patio.

Howell halted about ten feet away, the guards behind him. He ignored Phil and focused on Brynley. "I see you've returned in time for the wedding."

"No—"

"Call Rhett and tell him his bride is here!" Howell yelled back at the guards on the patio.

Brynley gritted her teeth. "I am not marrying him."

"You will." Howell glared at her. "The Supreme Pack Master commands it."

"Bullshit," Phil said calmly.

Howell glanced at him. "Do I know you?"

"Cut the crap. I'm here to talk to our father."

Howell snorted. "The prodigal son returns. Don't think you can weasel your way back into the inheritance. It's mine now."

"Congratulations, Howie. Does that mean you've gone Alpha?" Phil flicked some dust off his shoulder, and his hand flashed into a wolf's paw, then back to human.

Murmurs of amazement rushed over the crowd standing on the patio. Phil had performed a difficult partial shift with incredible ease. Only an extremely powerful Alpha could manage such a feat.

Howell stepped back, his eyes wide.

"I will speak to my daughter," Caddoc Jones announced. "She may bring her escort." He turned on his heel and walked back into the house.

Phil gave Brynley an amused look. "That got his attention."

"Yeah," she agreed, "but you still don't have a name."

Howell jutted his chin forward, his mouth thin with anger. "This way." He strode back to the patio with the guards.

"Thanks," Phil said dryly. "I'd forgotten where the back door is."

"Behave," Brynley warned him as they walked. "We're going into the lion's den."

"Or wolf's den," he murmured back. "I hear they sometimes eat their young."

She gave him an annoyed look. "That's not boosting my confidence."

Howell led them into the house and straight into her father's office.

Caddoc Jones was waiting for them, leaning against his desk. He waved a dismissive hand. "You may go, Howell."

Howell's jaw dropped. "But—" He stopped when his father glared at him.

"Better learn to submit," Phil whispered to him. "It's the price of the inheritance."

Howell's eyes flashed with anger, then he strode from the room and slammed the door behind him.

Caddoc glanced at Brynley, expressionless, then focused on Phil. "Then it's true. You achieved Alpha status on your own without instruction from the Council of Elders."

"Of course I was on my own. You banished me."

Caddoc snorted. "You fool. You were supposed to come back."

"With my tail between my legs?"

"I would have taken you back. You're worth ten of your brother."

Phil shrugged. "Your loss then."

Caddoc lunged forward, his hand fisted. "If you weren't so damned impressive, I would kill you."

Brynley winced. So much for the welcome home. She glanced at her brother. He was standing stiffly, his chin lifted, his face calm, but she knew he had to be hurting inside.

"What is it with you two?" Caddoc paced across the floor. "No creature on this earth is more gloriously alive than a werewolf. But you insist on betraying your own kind to hang out with a bunch of bloodsuckers. They're fucking dead half the time. It's an abomination to consort with them!"

"You." He pointed at Phil. "You married one. And you"—he sneered at Brynley —"you're screwing one of them. Oh, don't look surprised. I know everything you do. I just hope you got it out of your system. We'll do your wedding as soon as Rhett arrives. He's staying in one of the guesthouses down the road."

She swallowed hard. This was it. Time to stand up for herself. Her inner wolf bristled. "I refuse to marry Rhett."

Caddoc scoffed.

"You have to call the wedding off," Phil said.

"And you've come back here to give me orders?" Caddoc asked dryly.

"Rhett intends to kill Brynley and the entire family as soon as the wedding is over," Phil explained. "He wants all your land, wealth, and pack members."

Caddoc gave him a bland look, then shook his head. "You have never truly appreciated me. It's so annoying." He walked over to the desk and perched on the corner.

Brynley exchanged a questioning look with her brother.

Phil's eyes narrowed. "He knows."

Caddoc shrugged. "Of course I know. But two can play at this game. Once the wedding is over, we kill Rhett. He has no heirs, so all his land and wolf packs in Alaska go to his new bride. Well, me, actually, since only an Alpha can be the master of a pack."

A queasy feeling stirred in Brynley's stomach. "You were using me. I've never been more than a pawn to you."

"Don't try that indignant crap on me," her father snarled. "You would come out ahead. You'd have a dozen houses in Alaska and more money than you could ever spend."

"And I would only have to kill someone to get it. Gee, thanks."

"Don't be ridiculous. I wouldn't expect *you* to do the killing."

She scoffed. "Oh, I feel so much better now."

"Are you smart-mouthing me?" Her father stepped toward her, his fists clenched.

She lifted her chin. Phil moved closer.

A knock sounded on the door.

Caddoc took a deep breath and flexed his hands. "What is it?" he shouted.

Howell cracked the door and gave them a nervous look. "Rhett has arrived for the wedding. He's waiting in the backyard."

"Good." Caddoc grabbed Brynley's arm and dragged her forward.

"I'm not marrying him." She pulled her arm away.

"I don't think you have any choice," Howell said. "He's brought fifty men with him. And they're all armed."

Phil whistled. "Looks like Angus was right about that war."

Chapter Twenty-six

*H*ere they come." Phineas watched as Rhett Bleddyn and his small army approached the south side of the backyard.

"Looks like he brought in more men from Alaska," Jack observed.

Phineas scanned the group of fifty young males, noting their weapon of choice—hunting knives. Apparently, werewolves liked their battles bloody. Corky and Dimitri were keeping close to Rhett, and the three were heavily surrounded. No room to teleport in and snatch the vampires. Although if things got out of hand, Rhett was probably keeping them close by as an easy escape route.

On the north side of the backyard, Caddoc Jones's pack members were gathering. The nearly full moon glinted off their knife blades.

A low growl in the woods behind them made Phineas whip around. It was Howard, hidden behind a tree, glaring at Rhett. Angus had asked the shifters, Howard and Rajiv, to patrol the woods in case the werewolves attempted an attack from behind. Carlos Panterra had been given paternity leave, so he was still at the academy with his wife and their newborn twins.

Howard's nostrils flared, and he walked away, pulling a knife from his sheath.

When the scent of skunk wafted toward him, Phineas knew what had alarmed Howard. He hurried into the woods and found Howard pointing his knife at Digger.

"Whoa there, pardner." Digger lifted his hands. "I just came to meet you. Caught a whiff of your scent."

"Who are you?" Howard growled.

"This is Digger," Phineas introduced him. "And his dog, Jake, should be around somewhere." He spotted Jake half hidden behind some bushes.

Digger nodded at Phineas. "Some bad stuff going down around here. How's your little lady?"

"She's good." He hoped. She was still inside the house with her father.

Digger looked at Howard. "You can put away your knife, son. I'm a were-bear, too. Where do you hail from?"

"Alaska." Howard sheathed his knife. "Kodiak."

"Wee doggies." Digger's eyes widened. "You're a big one. Me, I'm a black bear."

"Digger, if you want to help, just stay back here in the woods and make sure no one sneaks up on us from behind," Phineas said. "There's a were-tiger back here, too."

"That's me." Rajiv waved from behind a tree. "I came to check out bad smell."

Digger scratched his beard. "You're a tiger? Well, don't that beat all."

"I'll see you guys later." Phineas hurried back to the Vamps.

The big yard reminded him of a football field with two teams gathered on each side. He and the Vamps were in one end zone. The Jones's ranch house was at the other end.

Caddoc Jones emerged from the back door, followed by his two sons and Brynley. He paused at the edge of the patio and glared at Rhett. "You come to your wedding armed with knives?"

Rhett stepped forward. "We want to make sure the wedding happens." His eyes narrowed on Brynley. "The bride has a nasty habit of running away."

"She's here now." Caddoc seized her arm and dragged her into the yard.

"I'm not marrying him!" Brynley pulled loose and put some distance between herself and her father. Phil ran over to stand next to her.

Howell took a position next to Caddoc, who was glowering at his daughter.

"You will do as you are told," Caddoc growled. "Or you will be banished from this world forever. You will be dead to us."

She lifted her chin. "You can't fire me, I quit. I'm going to marry a vampire."

Phineas sucked in a deep breath. *Yes!* He ran onto the field.

Caddoc lifted an eyebrow. "This is your choice?"

Rhett cursed. "You foul yourself with that damned bloodsucker."

Phineas stopped next to Brynley. "You called?"

She smiled and took his hand.

He turned to her father. "I'm requesting your daughter's hand in marriage."

Caddoc scoffed. "Who the hell are you to think you deserve my daughter?"

"I don't have a lot to offer in terms of wealth, but I can give her all my love—"

"*Love?*" Caddoc motioned to the house behind him. "You think she would give all this up for love?"

"In a second," Brynley said. "You can have all the land and riches in the world, but if you don't have love, you have nothing."

"And will *love* pay the bills? Will it put food on the table?" Caddoc sneered at Phineas. "You wouldn't know, would you? You don't even eat food. But if you dare to feed off my daughter, I'll—"

"I would never harm her!" Phineas interrupted. "I want her happiness more than anything."

Caddoc studied him a moment, then arched a brow. "You would do anything for her?"

"I will not give her up."

Caddoc stepped toward him. "Prove it. Make yourself worthy of her."

Phineas narrowed his eyes. What did the old man want? A duel?

Caddoc glanced at Brynley. "I will only accept a

werewolf as your husband." He motioned to Phineas. "So if you want him, you'll have to bite him."

She flinched.

Phineas sucked in a breath of air. Damn. He hadn't expected this. He didn't even know if it was possible for a vampire to become a werewolf. That might be what her father was counting on, that the transformation would kill him.

Caddoc's eyes glinted with humor as he regarded his daughter. "You're the one who thinks love is so powerful. Do you love this man enough to make him acceptable?"

Brynley gave Phineas a worried look.

"This is ridiculous!" Rhett stepped forward. "She's marrying me! I'm the best choice."

Caddoc crossed his arms over his chest. "It's her choice. If she wants the bloodsucker badly enough, she'll agree. Of course, she can't shift tonight since she's not an Alpha, but I can do the biting." He gave Phineas a wolfish grin. "How much do you really want her?"

He swallowed hard. Somehow he'd always feared it would come down to this. He wouldn't be good enough for Brynley as he was. "I'll do it. Bring it on, old man."

Brynley gasped. "No. Phineas—"

"I'll do anything for you."

Her eyes glimmered with tears. "Phineas, you are worthy just the way you are."

His breath caught. Worthy the way he was. His heart swelled in his chest.

She turned to her father and lifted her chin. "I'm marrying Phineas, and I don't care if you ever approve—"

"You have defied me for the last time!" With a growl, Caddoc lunged toward her, his head shifting into a snarling wolf.

Brynley lifted her arms to defend herself, and they shimmered. "I'm not taking it anymore!" she screamed, and her arms and head shifted.

Caddoc jumped back.

A shock wave rolled over the entire yard. Jaws dropped. Gasps echoed in the stunned silence.

"My God!" Caddoc was back in human form, his face frozen in disbelief.

Brynley shifted back. "What—what have I done?" She stumbled, and Phineas caught her.

Phil grabbed her other arm. "You went Alpha, Bryn!"

"But only males—"

"Not anymore." Phil's eyes lit up. "You're the first female Alpha!"

"Hot damn, girl." Phineas grinned at her. "You released the Kraken."

"Get your hands off her!" Rhett stalked toward them and drew his knife. "She's the most valuable female werewolf in the world. She has to be mine."

Brynley snorted. "Buzz off, Rhett. Why would I marry you when everyone knows you plan to kill me after the wedding?"

"No." He shook his head. "Everything's changed now. You're too valuable to kill. With you, I could rule the entire Lycan world. I would have the strongest children—"

"*What?*" Corky screamed and zoomed over to him. "You can't keep her! You're supposed to stay with me! We're going to rule the world! We're—"

"Forget it!" Rhett sneered at her. "Why would I want you when I can have the one and only Alpha female—"

"You're dumping me?" Corky screeched. "You—you stupid animal. I was mistress to kings before you were ever born."

"And you've outlived your usefulness."

"You think so?" Corky pulled a knife and pointed it at Rhett. "I could slit your throat so fast you'd never see it coming." She glanced at Brynley. "Or I could take out your bitch." She vanished, then reappeared behind Brynley.

"No!" Rhett dashed toward them.

With vampire speed, Phineas pulled Brynley away from Corky's slashing knife.

Phil grabbed Corky's arm and strained against her vampire strength.

"I'll kill you," Corky hissed, aiming her knife at Phil's face. "I'll kill all of you stinking wolves."

Phil's arm shimmered and shifted, and then with the power of his wolf, he shoved Corky back.

She stumbled into Rhett's arms and reached for his face. "Darling, let me take you away from here. We'll rule the—" She gasped as Rhett's knife plunged into her stomach. "What? You can't—*no!*"

Rhett rammed his knife into her heart.

Her scream died as her body disintegrated into a pile of dust.

Silence fell over the field. Phineas glanced at Angus and the others. They didn't seem too upset over the failure to capture Corky. He suspected that even though she would have been found guilty at Coven Court, Roman would have had a hard time determining her punishment.

He looked back at Rhett, who was calmly brushing some Corky dust off his sleeve. "Didn't you just kill your escape route?"

He returned to the side of the yard where his small army was gathered. "I have no need to escape. I'm not leaving until Brynley and I are married."

"You're an idiot," Phil said. "My father and his men plan to kill you after the wedding. You should leave while you have the chance."

Rhett stiffened and glanced at Caddoc. "You think you can kill me?"

Caddoc shrugged. "You think you can kill me?"

Both sides drew their weapons and started hurling insults at each other.

"And the shit hits the fan," Phineas muttered, then held up his hands and shouted, "Are you guys really going to kill each other over Brynley when she doesn't want either of you?"

"He's right!" Brynley yelled. "I'm leaving with Phineas." She glared at Rhett. "Go back to Alaska and leave my family alone." She switched her glare to her father. "Good-bye."

His eyes narrowed, but he said nothing.

A muffled sob came from the patio.

Brynley winced. "Glynis, I'll stay in touch with you. I promise." She turned her back and closed her eyes.

"Are you all right?" Phineas took her hand.

"I'm always leaving her behind." Brynley gazed at him with tears in her eyes.

"We'll find a way for you to see her." Phineas led her toward the Vamps.

Phil walked with them, holding Brynley's other hand.

"Did it work?" Brynley whispered. "Did we stop a battle?"

"Don't know," Phil murmured. "Just keep walking."

They were halfway to the Vamps when Angus shouted a warning.

Phineas spun around. Rhett was running toward them, his knife raised. He gave a war cry, and his men charged after him.

"Go!" Phineas shoved Brynley toward the Vamps.

Caddoc responded with his own war cry, and his men ran onto the field, their knives raised. They clashed with Rhett's men, knives stabbing.

Rhett lunged toward Phineas, but with vampire speed, he wrenched the knife from the werewolf's hand and punched him hard enough he heard the jaw crack. Rhett hit the ground, then jumped up, instantly shifting and repairing his broken jaw. He pounced on Phineas, who grabbed the wolf by the neck as it attempted to rip his throat out. He threw the wolf to the side, but Rhett twisted and snapped his jaw onto Phineas's arm.

He gasped. Hot, searing pain shot up his arm. He tried to stand up, but tumbled back onto his rear.

Phil lunged onto Rhett, both in wolf form, and they rolled, clawing and snapping. Phil pinned him down and bared his teeth, growling.

Howard sprinted toward them, his knife raised. "Let me fight him!"

Phil moved aside with a snarl aimed at Rhett.

Rhett rolled to his feet and shifted to human form, his clothes in tatters, his face shocked as Howard ran toward him. "You." He turned and hollered. "Dimitri!"

The Malcontent teleported beside him.

"No!" Howard lunged at Rhett, his knife plunging just as the werewolf vanished with Dimitri. "No!"

"Phineas!" Brynley ran toward him and fell to her knees beside him.

He looked at her and stars danced around her head.

She ripped her shirt off and wrapped it around his arm. "He bit you."

· Phil knelt beside them, back in human form. "How do you feel, bro?"

Phineas blinked at him. "Do you have two heads?"

"What will happen?" Brynley asked.

"I don't know." Phil shook his head. Or both his heads. Phineas wasn't sure.

"Hi, guys." Phineas waved faintly at the Vamps who were crowding around him with worried faces. He looked over at the field. "They're running away."

"Aye," Angus agreed. "After Rhett disappeared, his army took off running."

Phineas watched Howell and his cohorts giving

chase. "They might chase them all the way back to Alaska." He blinked as their forms wavered.

Brynley touched his forehead. "He's burning up. He has a fever."

Phineas smiled at her. "I'm hot for you, sweetness."

"He was bitten?" a voice asked.

Phineas squinted up at Brynley's father. "You again. I thought we said good-bye."

Caddoc looked at his daughter. "Keep me informed. I want to know what happens to him."

"You care all of a sudden?" she asked.

"I'm curious." He paused, then added. "If he survives the transformation, I might accept him as your husband."

"We don't care what—"

He lifted a hand to interrupt her. "If he survives, he may have powers no other werewolf has. That alone makes him of interest to me. You will be welcomed in my house." He glanced at Phil. "All of you." He turned and strode away.

"Don't you just love family reunions?" Phineas asked, then slumped over as everything went black.

Fire. He was on fire.

Phineas moaned and kicked off the sheets.

Sheets? Was he in bed? He squinted, but couldn't see. Everything was glowing red. On fire.

"Why are his eyes red?" a woman asked. *Brynley.*

He tried to say her name, opening his mouth, but nothing came out.

"I think he's hungry," Brynley said.

"Here," a male voice said. Roman? What was he doing here? "Let's give him a cold bottle. It might help with the fever."

Someone lifted his shoulders.

Careful, Phineas thought. *I'm on fire.*

"Damn, he's hot," the person said.

Told you so. A cold bottle was pressed to his mouth, and blood trickled down his throat. It was cool. It helped with the fire. He drank it all down.

His stomach clenched in pain. He groaned, pushing away the hands that reached out to help him.

He rolled halfway off the bed and threw up.

"Oh no!" Brynley cried.

Hands pushed him back onto the bed. Everything went black.

He woke again. Still on fire. And so damned hungry.

"He's awake!" Brynley exclaimed.

"Let's see if he can eat," Roman said.

Someone lifted his shoulders. He squinted, peering around the room. It looked like the basement at Phil's cabin. Why hadn't they taken him back to Romatech?

"He's not as hot tonight," said the guy holding his shoulders. Phil?

A bottle was placed against his lips. He drank and drank. So good.

It hit his stomach and instantly curdled. He rolled over and vomited.

"I'm not sure what to think," Roman said. "He's had two days of death-sleep. I thought that would heal whatever

Lycan virus is in his system. But if he's rejecting blood—"

"Then he's becoming a werewolf," Phil said. "We should try giving him real food."

"I'll bring him something," Brynley said, then climbed up the ladder.

A werewolf? Phineas lay back, trying to wrap his fuddled mind around it. That was why he was at Phil's cabin. In case he shifted into an animal.

A while later, Brynley was back and spooning something hot down his throat.

"It's soup," she said. "I thought we should start with something simple."

He ate it. Then threw it up.

"What do we do?" Brynley cried. "He's rejecting both vampire and human food."

"The two parts are fighting each other," Roman said. "I'll put an IV in him. We have to keep him alive until the battle inside him gets sorted out."

A battle? No wonder he was on fire. Everything went black.

He woke again. The fire was out. He felt good, as if his body was at peace. Good God, was he dead? The spurt of panic quickly faded away as he smoothed his hands over his bare chest. His body was solid. His heart was beating. His vision clear. He was alive.

Power surged through him, and he took a deep breath. Damn. He felt more than good. His vision cut through the dark room, sharper than ever. His muscles flexed with increased strength.

He sat up. Phil was on the floor, sound asleep on a sleeping bag. A bottle of blood sat on the bedside table. He picked it up and drank it down.

No reaction. Apparently, the battle was over, and the Vamp side had won. He looked around, but couldn't spot Brynley. She must be upstairs.

He pulled the IV from his arm and stood. No dizziness. He smiled to himself. He actually felt stronger than ever. He teleported to the floor above to give Brynley a surprise.

The surprise was on him. He materialized in the bathroom with one foot in the toilet.

"What the hell?" He lifted his bare foot out and shook it off. This wasn't where he'd intended to go.

He opened the bathroom door and froze.

Daylight.

His heart lurched, and he shut the door. What the hell? He couldn't be awake in daylight.

"Who's there?" Brynley demanded.

He cracked open the door and peered out.

She gasped.

He opened the door wider. The room was full of sunshine. He sank back into the shadow, afraid he would burst into flames if the sunlight touched him.

Go into the light, a voice inside him urged. *It can't hurt us. Trust the wolf.*

Wolf? He stiffened. There was a wolf inside him?

The wolf knows best. The light cannot harm us.

"Phineas?" Brynley approached him, watching him carefully.

He slowly reached out a hand, then extended his index finger so the tip barely touched the light.

Nothing happened.

He opened his hand, turning it palm up in the sunlight. A gentle warmth caressed his skin.

Enjoy the light, the wolf whispered to him. *It is my gift to you.*

"Phineas." Brynley took his hands and led him slowly into the sun-filled cabin.

Our mate. He smiled at her, then looked out the window. Blue sky. "I see blue."

"You must be a werewolf now," she whispered.

"But I drank blood and teleported." He glanced down at his wet foot. "Not very well though. Maybe I'm a little of both."

"That would be . . . interesting."

He winced at a sudden thought. "What if I'm lousy at both?"

She shook her head. "You won't be. Look at you. You're awake during the day. Do you know any other Vamp who can manage that?"

"I don't know what will happen to me."

She touched his cheek. "Whatever happens, I'll be with you."

"I love you, Snout-Face."

She smiled. "I may be calling you that on the next full moon."

"Mr. and Mrs. Snout-Face." He pulled her into his arms. "I like it."

Epilogue

Three months later . . .

_G_ood evening, dear viewers! This is Maggie O'Brian
O'Callahan reporting for _Real Housewives of the Vampire World_. Tonight we have a very special guest, the
newest wife of a Vamp, Brynley McKinney!"

"Hi!" Brynley smiled at the camera. "Thank you for
coming."

"Oh, it's quite an honor," Maggie assured her. "I understand you're the only female Alpha werewolf in the
world?"

She shrugged. "We believe so."

"And your husband is that famous celebrity that all
the women swoon over, the Blardonnay Guy!"

Brynley laughed. "I love his commercials, too. And
I love his voice." She motioned for Phineas to join her.
"Come on, say it," she whispered.

He nodded at the camera. "Hello, ladies."

Brynley squeezed his arm. "I love it!"

He winked at her.

Maggie grinned at them. "It's obvious you two are newlyweds. I've never seen a couple so in love. Now tell me, are the rumors true? Has our beloved Dr. Phang become part werewolf?"

Brynley nodded. "He's been shifting every month on the full moon."

"Amazing!" Maggie looked at Phineas. "And yet you're still a vampire, too?"

"A little of both," he answered. "We're still figuring it all out."

"And how do you like being a werewolf?" Maggie asked.

He grinned. "I like chasing my wife through the woods."

Brynley shook her head, blushing.

"Even more, I like catching her."

She swatted at his shoulder. "Hush."

He assumed an injured look. "But of course, she's the Alpha, so she thinks she can boss me around."

"I do not." Brynley nudged him with her elbow.

Maggie laughed. "And you're living here in Wyoming?"

"We go back and forth from here to New York," Phineas said. "I still work for MacKay S and I."

"But he's learning how to be a rancher," Brynley added.

"I can see that." Maggie pointed behind them. "That must be one of your horses?"

Brynley glanced back and smiled. "That's the wild white stallion. He doesn't belong to anyone. But he comes by to see us often."

Phineas strolled over to the horse and patted it. The horse nudged him in the shoulder.

"He doesn't look very wild to me," Maggie observed.

"He likes Phineas," Brynley said, still smiling.

Phineas swung onto the horse's bare back. "Hello, ladies. Now I'm on a horse."

Brynley snorted.

"And this is your home?" Maggie gestured to the side, and the camera shifted.

"Yes," Brynley answered. "It was the old Haggerty ranch. My father bought it for us as a wedding present."

"Really? That was very generous of him."

"Yes." Brynley nodded. At first, she hadn't been sure they should accept her father's gift. She suspected he was keeping them close, hoping he could use them someday. After all, she was the only female Alpha, and Phineas was also unique, possessing powers that no other werewolf had.

She smiled for the camera. "I love being here. This area is home to me, and my sister is close by, so I can see her often. And we have a really good friend just down the road, Nate Carson. He's great guy and a vampire. And single."

"Oh, did you hear that, viewers?" Maggie looked at the camera. "Now, what can you tell me about your house?"

Brynley grinned when Phineas rode by the house on the wild white stallion. "Well, frankly, it was a bit of a mess when we moved in. But we've been working hard to make it our own."

"It was a fixer-upper?" Maggie asked.

"Yes. But once we moved all the dead werewolves out, and cleaned up the bloodstains, we slapped on few coats of paint, and it was as good as new."

Maggie's eyes widened. "I see."

"And we're remodeling the bathrooms and kitchen," Brynley added. "Putting in our own furniture."

Maggie smiled. "I hear you've been working on one room in particular?"

Brynley blushed. "Yes. It appears the Lycan virus re-activated parts of my vampire husband. It caught us by surprise, but we're very excited about it. I'm expecting twins."

"We're delighted for you!" Maggie hugged her, then turned to the camera. "Be sure to keep watching *Real Housewives of the Vampire World*. We'll keep you updated on the McKinney family and all the Vamps you love to visit."

"That's a wrap!" Darcy lowered her video camera and turned it off.

"You're done?" Phineas walked toward them.

"Congratulations, you two." Darcy hugged them both.

"I'll see you at DVN tomorrow night to shoot another Blardonnay commercial," Maggie told Phineas.

She teleported away with Darcy.

"Another Blardonnay commercial?" Brynley asked.

Phineas smiled and gathered her in his arms. "We gotta pay for all this remodeling."

She gave him a wry look. "So many names. The

Blardonnay Guy, Dr. Phang, the Love Doctor. But do you know my favorite name for you?"

"Snout-Face?"

She laughed. "No. Husband."

He kissed her nose. "That's my favorite, too. For now."

"You're going to change your mind?"

"Maybe. I'm going to really like being Daddy."

She hugged him tight. "I'm going to like that, too."

SIZZLING PARANORMAL ROMANCE FROM *NEW YORK TIMES* BESTSELLING AUTHOR

KERRELYN SPARKS

WANTED: UNDEAD OR ALIVE

978-0-06-195806-9

Bryn Jones believes vampires are seductive and charming, and that makes them dangerous. So the werewolf princess is wary when she has to team up with the recently undead Phineas McKinney to stop a group of evil vampires, even though he makes her inner wolf purr.

SEXIEST VAMPIRE ALIVE

978-0-06-195805-2

Abby Tucker has dedicated her life to finding a cure that will save her dying mother and needs only two more ingredients. To find them, she'll have to venture into the most dangerous region in the world—with a vampire named Gregori who makes her heart race.

VAMPIRE MINE

978-0-06-195804-5

After 499 years of existence, nothing can make Connor Buchanan fall in love again. Cast down from heaven, Marielle is an angel trapped in human form who hopes to heal Connor's broken heart and earn her way back home. But suddenly she has these *feelings*—for a vampire!

EAT PREY LOVE

978-0-06-195803-8

Carlos Panterra is looking for a mate, and when the shape shifter spies beautiful Caitlyn Whelan, it's like sunshine amidst the darkness. At last he's found the perfect woman, except…she's a mortal. But Caitlyn knows that their attraction is more than just animal magnetism.

*G*ive in to your Impulses!

These unforgettable stories only take a second to buy and give you hours of reading pleasure!

Go to *www.AvonImpulse.com* and see what we have to offer.

Available wherever e-books are sold.

AVONIMPULSE

IMP 0811